Revolution—U.S.A. 2000

Revolution—U.S.A. 2000

Ray Aman

VANTAGE PRESS
New York

All characters and places depicted herein are fictious. Any similarity to persons living or dead is purely coincidental.

To my mother,
Martha Job Aman

Prologue

The United States of America, the land of the free, the land of plenty, the superpower of the world, will have to go through one of its most difficult periods of transformation since the day of its birth. This country grew from the seeds of democracy and soon must be reborn in order to survive as a democracy. The revolution will be an overdue catharsis this nation will have to endure. Liberalism is necessary in a free society; however, too much of it can lead to destruction. There were some, a few, who foresaw the demise of this country years ago, back in the sixties through the seventies; and certainly it was obvious to many in the eighties that this country, with a national debit around $4 trillion, had better make some fast adjustments or else time would run out for the reduction of such a large national debit.

A government cannot be everything to everybody all the time. Americans will soon learn this after decades of affluent times, and both the takers and givers will wake up with a headache. When a superpower goes down, so goes the world; and who will be there to provide a safety net? Russia and America both will have destroyed themselves fighting the Cold War. There will be chaos in the world without those adversaries, who no longer will be feeding the hands of dictators or restraining their behavior. America is dying from within while showing a strong face to the rest of the world. The outside world sees a mighty military force as a power to behold; however, that very burden of a large defense budget is only one of many burdens that this country no longer can bear. America is about to declare bankruptcy. Who cares? That is an attitude problem this country has had for too many years. The day of reckoning has arrived.

Revolution—U.S.A. 2000

I

Jim Clark was aware of the enormous national debit that the country would have to deal with sooner or later; he also was acutely aware of the moral decay that had been taking place in this country since the sixties. He thought to himself, *When a city calls upon the National Guard to put down youth violence, we have a problem that does not lend itself to a quick fix. This problem will take time and effort to solve.*

Jim Clark had set out purchasing property within the inner city of Denver, an area known as Capitol Hill, back in the early 1960s, and he had kept on buying and mortgaging through the real estate boom days of the 1970s. Over the years he had seen many changes take place, some of a physical nature and some of social behavior. He saw government pass more rules and regulations, taking away rights he once had as a property owner. He witnessed those rights slipping away as government kept granting additional rights to individuals, keeping him from maintaining control over the property he managed for his tenants and himself. A good property owner manages his property for the benefit of all tenants; he cannot single out individuals at the expense of the tenants who make up the majority.

Jim fought prostitution, drug dealers, pimps, graffiti artists; he tolerated street people defecating and urinating around his apartment buildings. He saw the neighborhood changing with every rent-subsidized family that moved into the area. His tenants were great. He could control who he rented to, but the neighborhood was more or less controlled by the liberal do-gooders who used the Capitol Hill area as their social experiment. He and his tenants were paying taxes to the very same government that was destroying their lifestyle.

Jim hated social engineering as much as he hated spending thousands of dollars removing the graffiti artists' creative work from the walls of his buildings. Jim was nearing the end of his rope. He called his female friend, Jan Bailey. "Hi, I bet this is Jim calling."

1

"Yes, it is. We have known each other for too long."

"What's cooking with you today?"

"I am thinking about selling my apartment buildings. I have had it. I am tired of fighting the evil system. I am sick of derelicts, misfits, idiots, and all the misdirected poor souls of our society. I am going to sell out over the next six months."

"Well, Jim, have you really thought this through, or is this a spur-of-the-moment decision?"

"I have made my decision. By the way, you are beginning to sound more like my ex-wife every time I bring up a heavy subject. I want to move to McCook, Nebraska, and spend some time on the farm with your brother."

"That is a dumb idea and you know it. You would miss the big city and get bored to death in McCook."

"Jan, you sure don't know me after ten years of our illicit relationship."

"Come over for a homecooked meal tonight and a little social time. I want to refresh *your* mind as to what you will be missing in Nebraska."

"Okay. Aside from my brief previous marriage, I spent a lot of years by myself and I managed quite well. After all, I am sixty years old. Bye."

It was midafternoon and Jim was looking for something to keep him occupied until dinnertime. He had a property manager and a very capable crew of workmen who maintained the apartments. There was little for him to do. He decided to get a haircut. A haircut was necessary occasionally and sometimes could be entertaining. As he was driving to the Cherry Creek shopping center he was thinking of Jan, a woman who had two degrees in education, made around $50,000 a year with benefits, and the previous week had, with her fellow teachers, threatened to go on strike. She belonged to a damn union. His mind drifted back to selling the apartment buildings and buying gold bullion. He longed to go up to Deerpoint in the mountains and see his old buddy, Judge J. J. Crocker. He had not seen him in a long time. He wanted to run his ideas by J. J. Lately he had been talking to himself. He was concerned about that. He looked into the mirror and wondered if he was flipping out. He had spent most of his life putting property together as an investment. He had done well and now he was confused, talking to himself, and wondering if he was going crazy.

He walked into the men's barbershop and started to feel better. "Hi, Jim. Need a haircut today?"

"What the hell do you think I am here for, to have my mind intellectualized?"

"Ahem, those queers on Capitol Hill are getting to you."

"That is not it. I get along with my tenants. Sure, eighty percent of them are gay, or so my manager tells me. That is not what is bothering me. It is that damn graffiti that ticks me off to no end."

"Well, Jim, they tell me that it is the gangs who spray graffiti to mark their territories."

"I doubt that. I think kids have reverted to a primitive state of mind, marking their territory like wild animals. Sure would like to catch those kids and find out who they are and why they leave those markings on buildings."

"Well, Jim, you should call the police."

"The police have better things to do than watch every alley for delinquent kids from dusk to dawn. I am going to give it up, sell my apartments, and leave the big city. Enough is enough."

"You are not married, are you?"

"No. I am single and footloose. My ex-wife and I never had children, so I have no family responsibilities. I pretty much answer only to myself."

"Ahem, what do you think of the haircut?"

"Clem, it looks good. Either you are getting better or my eyesight is failing me. Thanks, see you in about three weeks."

Around six o'clock Jim got into his brand-new shiny BMW and drove from his house through the park to Jan's townhouse. Whenever Jim got behind the wheel of a vehicle, his mind drifted off to matters in the future. He was thinking of the fate of this great nation and where it was headed in years to come. What would happen when the country declared bankruptcy? How would citizens handle themselves through a revolution? Would the politically correct politicians who reside in Washington, D.C., rise to the occasion of saving their country? He was thinking too much; he needed some diversion. Jim had started his dreaming and scheming while driving around his sales territory as a factory representative for a big corporation years ago; old habits are hard to break.

He walked up to the townhouse and knocked. Jan was there to greet him with open arms. What a neat gal. With apron on, sweet aroma floating from the kitchen, she gave him a nice big hug. "Honey, how I do miss you at times."

"Well, well, what came over you this afternoon? I just talked to you this morning, remember? Let's sit down and have a little sour mash on the rocks and wait for the boys to arrive. My two darling offspring are on their way over for dinner this evening."

"How old are those two fellows?"

"Twenty and twenty-two. Your mind has been yonder lately."

"Yes, I know. I apologize for that."

Bill and Mark arrived shortly after and dinner was served as discussions of everyone's failures and successes of the past week were reviewed. Jim brought up the matter of graffiti on his apartment buildings and the boys suggested he hire a strong-armed night watchman to catch the midnight paint sprayers. Jim said that he would be willing to pay $1,000 per culprit caught in the act of defacing his buildings. Bill and Mark decided that it would be a challenge to catch the guys, $1,000 per head caught in the act sounded pretty good to them.

"What should we do with them after we catch 'em?" asked Bill.

"Work them over a bit, spray them with their own paint, call the police, or, better yet, call the TV guys and let the media spread the word that we no longer tolerate graffiti artists in our neighborhood."

Jan became incensed. "I did not raise my boys to become thugs paid and bought by you."

"Whatever you say, Jan. It was an idea, probably a bad one at that. I'd better go home before I come up with some more bizarre ideas."

Jan was put out. She wanted to remind him of what he would be missing in Nebraska, but Jim was gone for the night.

Jim shuffled his feet along as he made his way to the pride and joy of his life, a new white BMW that he had bought only three weeks ago. Lo and behold, the window on the driver's side was smashed to smithereens. He opened the car door and saw that the radio had been pulled out, the dashboard was torn apart, and there was glass all over the front of the car. He uncorked. "Goddamn kids! Dammit anyway!"

He leaned his head against the car and pounded his fists on the roof. A patrol car pulled up and the officer asked, 'What is the problem?"

"Kids smashed the window on my brand-new car and ripped out the radio; that is what is wrong."

The officer responded, "There has been a lot of this type of activity in the area recently."

"You're telling me, as if I didn't know."

"Where do you live?"

"None of your damn business where I live."

Jim got into his car, sat on the broken glass, started the car, spun the wheels, and headed home. After parking the car in the garage, he walked to the front door of the house and from the corner of his eye saw that the fuzz had tailed him to his home. He thought, *Those jerks driving around with nothing to do but wait for a call on their radio.* He went to bed, didn't sleep well, he kept tossing and turning all night long. The next morning he was dead tired.

After a meek breakfast, he drove the BMW to the dealership, laid the keys to the car on the salesman's desk, and told him to sell the car for whatever price he could get.

"Mr. Clark, you just bought the car three weeks ago. Why are you getting rid of it?"

"Damn kids smashed a window and pulled out the radio. The car has become a liability. Sell it! Deduct the repair bill from the proceeds of the sale."

"Whatever you say, Mr. Clark."

The car salesman was puzzled. Three weeks earlier Jim Clark had walked into the dealership, picked out a car, and wrote a check for it without haggling over the price. He just walked in and bought a car, just like that, and now he was selling it just like that.

Jim called a cab and returned to his house, backed out his favorite vehicle, the black, dirty old four-wheel-drive pickup truck, and drove over to Jan's townhouse. He parked in the driveway. Jan arrived and parked by the curb. Jim was sitting in the truck with his head resting on his hands on the steering wheel. Jan opened the door to the truck. Jim jerked up. "What is the matter? I thought you had had a heart attack."

"I give up. They won."

"Who won what?"

"The predators won and I lost. I give up. Years ago I saved up $10,000 of hard-earned money and bought my first duplex, then another one. That led to a set of row houses, and then I bought my first apartment building. I got married about that time. The struggle to hang on to my property was immense. I destroyed my marriage. I was left alone, facing a huge debit after the divorce, knowing that I could lose it all in bankruptcy; but I hung in there and made it. The government has always been my predator. They heap property taxes on me at the local and state level; and if anything is left at the end of the year, the federal and state income tax people take half of that. Society has legislated ninety percent of my ownership rights to people claiming more individual rights. Where does that leave me? Now I have new predators, the graffiti artists, drug dealers, and street people.

"All these years I have been trying diligently to maintain the integrity of my apartment buildings and protect and care for the well-being of my tenants. I have gotten out of bed at two A.M. to fix a water leak, crank up a furnace, clean out sewer lines on holidays and on Sunday mornings, and now the do-gooders passed an ordinance that demands I clean off graffiti within twenty-four hours or be fined. I get fined. What about the graffiti artists and their delinquent parents? What is their responsibility?"

"Jim, I have been teaching for more years than I like to remember. I too have become exasperated with the task of raising other people's neglected children. Come inside and have a drink of Jim Beam on the rocks."

"Jan, I am at the end of my wits. I feel like I have been the lone protector, and now I have new predators who have more protection under the law than I do; yet I carry the responsibilities for them, their parents, and everybody else in the neighborhood. I think I am cracking under the stress of fighting society. Let society have all the individual rights, let them take over my property without me; in the end I will survive and they surely will perish by their own ignorance,

6

indifference, and selfishness. God help America! I have things to do. I will be back for supper."

Jim drove to a gun shop on Broadway. Within two hours he'd bought a .222 Swift with scope, a .270 Savage with scope, a .38-caliber long-barrel pistol, a 12-gauge pump shotgun, and, of course, he had to buy that 12-gauge over-and-under-barrel Browning. He had always wanted one when he was younger. The shotguns brought back memories of his days growing up on a wheat farm and cattle ranch in eastern Colorado, where bird hunting was a way of life. He thought those were the good old days and what in the hell had happened to the country since then? He ordered a case of ammunition and a carrying case for each weapon. This was hardly the normal preparations for a hunting trip. His mind drifted back to the time he'd spent in the army. He decided to buy a .3006 rifle with open sights, no carrying case. The clerk totaled the bill. Jim wrote a check for the purchases. The clerk pointed out that there was a waiting period for the guns; however, he could take the ammunition with him. They loaded the ammunition into the truck. Jim drove to one of his apartments and stored the ammunition in a locker in the basement. On his way home he reflected upon his purchases. The scope on the .222 Swift was as long as the barrel itself. His mind moved to his new project, the tokens.

He went upstairs to a room he kept as an office and proceeded to sketch out the details of tokens he would have Fred Goldsmith make up for him. Fred owned the Fine Jewelry located on East Colfax Avenue. He placed a nickel on a sheet of paper and traced the coin, then drew an X in the circle and described the token to be the size and thickness of a nickel, with the X having a spread of 40 degrees and inlaid with gold, the width equal to the thickness of a nickel. The face of the token would be ruby red baked enamel. On the gold-plated back side of the token the word "Terminator" would be stamped or engraved. The second token he drew was the same size as the first one, with a cross on the face with four equal parts of 90 degrees each. The cross was tapered from the center, a width of the nickel, and progressed outward to the edges to a double width of the nickel. The face of the token would be baked ivory enamel. On the back of the token the word "Director" was to be inscribed. Like the first token, the back side was to be gold plated. He took the drawings to the Fine Jewelry on Colfax Avenue.

Jim waited around for all the customers to leave the store and then approached Fred. "How is business today?"

"Hello, Jim. Oh, I am surviving."

"You definitely are a survivor. I have drawings of two tokens I would like to have made up, custom work initially."

Fred looked at the drawings and said, "These I can make in the back room. I have the tools on a bench that have not been used since my father died years ago."

"Good. Could you make up twenty-five of each, a total of fifty tokens?"

"I would love to give it a try. I haven't done work like this in ages. My father taught me the trade. Nowadays I just sell costume jewelry. Rather sad, isn't it? When did you want the tokens?"

"Whenever you finish them."

"Are you starting a new fraternal order?"

"Something like that." Jim Clark had had quite a day.

He went home to take a shower, put on a quick supper, scan the newspaper, watch the news on TV, and pack it in for the night. At six o'clock he flipped on the TV to watch the evening news while his supper was cooking. The news was a repetition of the previous day; Americans held hostage in the Middle East, a bombing in New York by suspected terrorists, religious fanatics raising hell all over the world, a hung jury in California (they feared a guilty verdict would cause another riot by the blacks). The local news had the usual drive-by shootings, supposedly gang or drug related. One six-year-old had been killed by her mother or father. The parents were on drugs, so it was alleged. A white teenage slime ball robbed a convenience store by sticking the barrel of a handgun into the mouth of a seventeen-year-old girl and demanding all the cash in the register. The poor girl probably would never be the same after her traumatic experience with the slime ball. The only good news was that the liberal governor had called a special session of the legislature to pass another gun-control bill. He said that he wanted to send a strong message to the criminals. The governor should have endorsed capital punishment, but he could not do that; he was a reborn liberal.

Jim was thinking of the message he hoped soon to deliver to law

8

breakers, a silent message. He ate his supper and prepared for bed. He forgot all about Jan. As he lay down on his bed, the past kept creeping into his mind. It was difficult for him to accept the present in contrast to the past. Jim knew that if this kind of violence had taken place forty years ago the public would have been appalled. By the standards of the past, we should be hanging, frying, or shooting criminals on a daily basis, but these were the 1990s and times had changed. Social engineers had had forty years to screw up our laws, morals, and the nuclear family.

The forties had produced World War II heroes who insisted on fighting the Cold War, which ultimately destroyed the country financially. The fifties had produced the silent generation. They said nothing and did nothing. They were content to walk in the shadows of the World War II veterans. The silent generation fought in a Korean police action. The country refused to call it a war; the double standard was alive and well. The generation of the sixties had been raised during the affluent times that took root in the fifties and lasted through the seventies. Social revolutionists of the sixties had started out on the right foot. They'd resented the double standard and distrusted politicians, but between the birth control pill, which led to free sex, and marijuana purchased on their mothers' credit cards, they lost their way. They changed an established lifestyle by growing their hair long, screwing indiscriminately, and listening to hard rock music. The creed of that generation was to say "no" to every problem that confronted them. Inflation of the seventies had driven people to spend like there was no tomorrow. That had set the stage for the final fling in the eighties, the decade of greed. After a series of different cycles, society had stretched the elasticity of a free democracy in every area, economics, politics, and social behavior.

The nineties has become the decade of reality and no one seems to care what will or will not happen. "Who cares?" is the general attitude? The "me generation" of the sixties is complacent that the government will guarantee society's safety, welfare will always be available to dropouts, children can raise themselves with the help of government, insurance companies will pay for mistakes in life, and if you need easy money, sue a corporation.

The generation of the nineties is the last product of all the superpower years the citizens of this country have lived through.

Liberal politicians are having their last shot at convincing people that good times will last forever and we will never have to redeem our mounting national debt. There is a general attitude that the federal government will never go broke, and if it does who really cares? Besides, the rest of the world cannot afford to let the world's super-power, world policeman, world moral director, sink because it would take the rest of the industrial world down the tubes with it. This is all wishful thinking by an innocent and naive people, the Americans. Jim lost control of his thoughts; he fell asleep.

The next day started out with a beautiful morning. He tended to his bathroom duties as he glanced out of the window overlooking the park; this was open space at its best in the big city. The park couldn't compare with the open space on the prairies in eastern Colorado, where he'd been born and raised on a wheat farm and ranch. His great-grandfather homesteaded the place and turned it into a ranch; his grandfather expanded the operation and planted wheat on some of the land. His father raised every conceivable animal to pull the farm through the dust bowl days, the Great Depression. Jim remembered the Depression vividly as a boy. His vicarious experience of the dust bowl years were through his parents but very real to him. Times did get better, the rains came, WWII created a market for their products, there was plenty of food on the table for all to eat, they had money in the bank again, and he and his sister had new clothes to wear when school started in the fall. In reflection, those days were not so bad after all. Nature had a hand in the Depression of the thirties. The ensuing bankruptcy Jim antici-pated would be done by the hand of Americans as they debarked from an era of affluence and muddled through the decade of reality, the nineties.

He finished his short breakfast of a roll, orange juice, and coffee. He poured a second cup of coffee and took it to the patio overlooking the park, which he enjoyed with his pipe. It had rained the day before and the park stank of dog urine and dog manure. The park was so overused by dog owners and street people that the general public shunned the place. It was embarrassing for a mother with children walking through the park to find couples getting it on in broad daylight, whether that be heterosexual, bisexual, homosexual or some other deprived form of behavior. The smell of urine from the park reminded him of the farm manure odor he grew up with, but that was different. It was a way of life, it was necessary, the family endured undesirable aspects of life by choice. Misuse of the park was a good example of individual rights versus the rights of a majority; liberals always pushed for individual rights. Jim's only choice in Capitol Hill was to sell his property and move out of the stink hole; he would list his property with a real estate agent after a short session with Max, his property manager. The stench from the park always set off a chain of thoughts in his mind and so did the sight of graffiti. He remembered how he told Judge Crocker back in the early seventies that excessive individual rights will leave the majority with few or no rights; society had finally reached that point and there was no turning back, short of a revolution.

The judge saw individual rights as a means to an end; more laws would make for a better social order, he said. The opposite took place, the law-abiding citizen found life restricted by too many laws and the habitual law breakers couldn't care less about laws. The judge was into law and order; Jim was hung up with his idea of freedom coupled with individual responsibility. Jim knew that the property taxes he forwarded to the city were working directly against the wishes of his tenants; it was they who were paying the taxes. If the tenants thought their liberal agenda would be paid for out of Jim's pocket, they were wrong. Likewise, the general public assumed that the national debit in Washington, D.C., belonged to someone else. Many people didn't even know that a national debit existed.

Jim drove to his and Max's office, a small room located in the basement of an apartment building. "Good morning, Max. How are you this morning?"

Max was not a morning person; he commenced to function on all four cylinders near lunchtime. "Max, what do we need to discuss this morning?"

"We need a new refrigerator and a new gas stove for one of the apartments."

"What else?"

"Ahem, I, ah, let's see."

"Max, are you awake? Let me wake you up."

11

"Oh! Yes. The salesman at the BMW dealership called and said that he had a buyer for your car."

"Good, I will pay a visit to my bean counter and get the title for the car."

"Why are you selling that beautiful car when you just bought it only a month ago?"

"Because those damn kids out on the streets like to break windows and jerk out radios, that is why. I have had a love affair with the best-built driving machine in the world and those kids out there decide for me whether I am allowed to own and drive it. Criminals in our neighborhood dictate my lifestyle for me. Parents pass laws to protect their children from existing laws. Can you believe that? That ticks me off to no end.

"Max, today I will list all of my property with our local real estate agent, the guy who works for Capitol Hill Real Estate, I think you know him. Assist him with the showings of the apartments and help him with the routine paper work." Max leaned back in his chair, tilted his head upward, then rolled his eyes and scanned the ceiling. He usually showed this peculiar mannerism when he was in deep thought, today he was in deep shock.

Max snapped forward, leaned on his desk and asked, "How about your beautiful house on the park?"

"I hope it will be the first to go. Are you awake?" Max didn't answer, his mind was reeling; the walls of his little office were closing in on him. "Don't alarm the crew unnecessarily, give it to them gently. We have thirteen buildings to sell, it will take time to see them all. Promise the men one year of salary as severance pay when the time comes to make a reduction in the work force. By the way, Max, I have a plan to solve the graffiti problem. Didn't you tell me that you saw some skinhead types hanging around who were harassing drug dealers, male prostitutes, and just sort of looking for trouble?"

"Well, ah, yes."

"Why don't you make contact with them and offer five hundred for every graffiti artist they work over or discourage from our neighborhood, but do it discreetly. We will pay them in cash. You leave no traces that lead back to me or you. You call them, they don't call us. They never learn your name, phone number, or the location of your office. We will pay them after we see their results in the newspaper or on TV. Give them a general outline of the alleys and streets where our apartments are located; do not be specific. We do not want to go to court and maybe serve jail time for exercising our basic right to protect our tenants and property. The only alternative is to call the police and then we will get involved with the others of these culprits. The police have their hands tied, so we lose."

"I understand, sir." Now Max was wide awake; he was hitting on all four cylinders and shifting gears fast.

"What do you think of my plan; and don't patronize me? Tell me if you can pull off this caper."

"Yes, I can, I would like to get even with those damn kids. There is no respect for life or property anymore, no pride of ownership. Yes, let's give 'em hell. I will show those creeps who is boss of the streets."

"How often do our men clean off graffiti these days?"

"Just about every day."

"Go for it, Max.

Jim went to lunch with his bean counter and then sold the BMW. It hurt to let go of his pride and joy, but reality won out over his passion for the car. He had told the bean counter how the criminals determined where he lived, how he lived, how he behaved, what he owned, and how he managed and maintained his property. He resented such a lifestyle imposed upon him. The bean counter concurred with him but had no solution to his problem.

Jim called Jan. She was not at home, so he left a message. "Hi, Jan, I will be by with steaks and a bottle of Jim Beam. Maybe this evening you can refresh my memory as to what I will be missing if I moved to McCook, Nebraska. Bye."

Jim called the real estate agent. "This is Jim Clark. How would you like to sell thirteen apartment buildings and a house on the park?" The agent did not respond. Jim figured he'd probably wet his pants. "Call Max, my property manager, for the details on the apartment buildings and the house. Give me a selling price for each property. I prefer cash on all sales or terms of twenty percent down in cash and the balance over ten years with a balloon payment in five years, with interest at two percent over Colorado prime. I will give a ten-percent discount for cash prepayment of the financed balance."

"Do I understand correctly that a buyer of a five-hundred-thou-

13

sand dollar apartment building can pay off his loan within thirty days after closing and receive a ten-percent discount for prepayment of the deed of trust?"

"You got it. I want to sell and I prefer cash; that is the basic message. Bye."

Jim whistled as he drove to his house. He checked the answering machine for messages. He had finally succumbed to the electronic age and bought a modest answering machine. Max was proud of Jim; the purchase of an answering machine put him into the twentieth century, according to Max. Jim had a disdain for electronic gadgets, he liked a hands-on approach to management and insisted on meeting people face to face in his business dealings. There was a message on the machine from Mark and Bill. 'We roughed up some kids who were spraying paint on one of your buildings. You owe us one thousand dollars." Jim took a deep breath and wondered if he had made a mistake in suggesting that Jan's boys partake in violence on his payroll. If Jan finds out about this he will be a cooked goose. He didn't want to jeopardize his relationship with Jan nor get the boys into trouble.

As he went through his junk mail he realized that he had not seen Jan in days, or was it a week, he could not remember. He showered and then glanced through the morning paper and the *Wall Street Journal* when the phone rang.

"Hello!"

"I am waiting for steaks and the Jim Beam. Don't be late." She was short, sweet, and to the point. Jim liked that. He loved that gal. She is a beauty indeed, all five feet and six inches of her: the golden hair, hazel eyes, the freckles, a slender trim body, great smile, beautiful set of teeth and a nice, firm fanny. Nothing wrong with her head lights. How he loved that gal. Very bright, and such a gentle way about her. She was born to be an outstanding school teacher. She was dreading her fiftieth birthday, which was coming up soon.

He knocked on the door and there she was, apron on, arms outstretched, and a nice hug. She gave him a kiss and he gently stroked her firm fanny. "Let's have some sour mash on the rocks while the char-broiler heats up. You must have been busy this week. I haven't seen you in days; no phone messages; what have you been doing?"

"I have set into motion some earth-shaking things."

"Like what?"

"I listed all of my property and hope it sells in a matter of weeks."

"You're kidding. Selling the house?"

"That should be the first to go."

"I used to fantasize over playing house with you in that two-and-half-story Tudor home on the park. So much for idle dreams. Now you can move in with me. We could get married."

"I don't know about that. I am in middle of a divorce from my apartment buildings."

"I am happy for you. I am happy for us." She leaned towards him and kissed him on the forehead. He didn't like that. It felt like Mother patting Sonny on the head for being a good little boy, without bare breasts swinging behind a thin blouse. God he hated that.

"I will never marry again, you know that, Jan; we have been over that before. Why did you get a divorce from your husband? He impressed me as a decent capable fellow. Your two sons are living proof that somebody did something right."

"Coach Bailey is a great husband for the right person. Life became boring with him, he lacked ambition."

"My wife thought life was a giant bore with me because I was over-ambitious, greedy in other words. I don't understand you women. I once had two marriages, one to my property and the other to a delightful person. She got tired of sharing her marriage with the apartments, so she took her half and went down the road by herself."

"Did she ever remarry?"

"I have no idea."

"You and your wife worked hard for the property and then you almost lost it after the divorce. Facing bankruptcy must have been dreadful."

"That is all history now. I lived through it. Now I want to quit, hang it up, cash in, buy gold, and retire with you."

"Very touching. Will we feast on gold, King Midas? I will be able to retire comfortably in a couple of years but I have nothing to leave to my boys. My dear former husband had little interest in investments, he was willing to live from paycheck to paycheck for the rest of his life."

"I will take care of that tomorrow; you shall be in my will with my sister."

Jan sat on his lap and said, "You do love me." She gave him a gentle kiss.

"And you love me and my pocketbook, so what is wrong with that? I don't want money to become a barrier between us, money should never enter into our relationship."

"Are you serious about buying gold? Why not some other kind of investment?"

"Soon this country will declare bankruptcy and I am going to hedge my bets. What if I am wrong? Gold is still gold."

"Whatever you say." They stood up, she gave him a hug and a kiss. "Let's cook the steaks and then watch a movie I picked up on the way home."

Jim stayed for the night. Life was rewarding for him on this day; he was living for the moment, something he seldom did. He was forever preparing for the unknown in the future. Morning came much too soon for both of them. Jan had to hustle off to a classroom of teenagers. Jim had his second cup of coffee with his pipe on the deck. The morning paper had a story about some kids attacking another group, skinheads versus the bloods or crips, nobody seemed to know for sure, so the media labeled the incident as a gang war.

He called Max. "Max, do I need to come down to the office today?"

"Yes, you do. The real estate agent wants to see you about the listings on the apartment buildings and the skinheads are probably ready for their payoff."

"You take care of the skinheads and I will stop by the real estate office and see the bean counter this morning."

As he drove downtown he reminisced back to the fifties when everything was so clean, free of smog, light traffic; it was such a free and easy way of life. During those days everyone was gainfully employed, the streets were friendly, the city of Denver was about to move from a cow town to a major hub of the West. People back then were busy; they had a purpose in life. The old western spirit of openness made for a simply easy and enjoyable life. Those were days of deeds and not politically correct messages. The term "politically correct" had not been invented and people didn't wear that stupid button that read, "Have a Nice Day." Rockwell's paintings were not corny; they depicted the true spirit of the times. Thanks to the generation of the sixties that part of America was destroyed forever.

Jim parked his dirty old truck in the parking lot of the Bank of Colorado where the bean counter and Jim's legal counsel had offices above the bank. The four-wheel-drive pickup truck looked out of place among the shiny new Mercedes, BMWs, and other nameless vehicles in the immaculate parking lot.

Jim walked into the bean counter's office. He was in, he was always in his office. Jim discussed the sale of his properties with the C.P.A. and received the usual comments from him, ways to delay the income tax burden, but Jim would have none of that. "I am going to sell my properties as soon as possible, all at once, if I should be so lucky. I will pay my income taxes to the state and federal government and buy gold with what is left over."

"Gold. You are going to buy nothing but gold?"

"The United States will declare bankruptcy within a few years and gold will be worth its weight in gold, or something like that."

"Good. Nothing but gold."

"I appreciate your advice on taxes but don't advise me on investments. I have done pretty well in Denver over a short period of time." The bean counter started to shuffle papers on his desk. Jim left.

He drove back to the house to check on his new electronic device, the answering machine. His house had become a secret office away from his office, or Max's office. He switched his calls to the house and used the answering machine to avoid Max monitoring his calls. The boys left a message on the machine, "We roughed up some graffiti artists, this time we ran into some blacks with guns, no one was killed. We want to drop the graffiti patrol duty. You owe us $1,000."

Jim sat down in the overstuffed chair and sighed with relief; he was glad to see the end of that chapter in his life. There was a call from Max. He needed to see him today; it was important.

He returned the call to Max. "Max. What is it?"

"The skinheads are claiming five thousand dollars for last night's patrol duty. They exchanged gunfire with some teenagers. They detained two of them, tied them up, sprayed them with paint.

The skinheads called the media and we should see their nifty work on TV this evening."

"How do we recognize their nifty work?"

"They tied up two kids, pulled down their pants, sprayed their penises with red paint and their little black asses with white paint."

"Good God, what next."

"Well, Jim, they got the job done and did it well."

"Pay the guys and let's not get involved in gang wars."

"Yes, sir. I do have another approach to the graffiti problem."

"Max, spare me, I don't want to hear it. Things have gotten out of hand, abandon the graffiti war. Let's wash our hands of this and forget it ever happened."

Jim picked up his weaponry downtown and moved it into the storage locker with the ammunition. Jim was beginning to question himself about the graffiti war and the purchase of a small arsenal. Doubts crossed his mind about what he may have started and lost heart to finish.

In the meantime, Max, the creative property manager, was leaning back in his chair, staring at the ceiling, rolling his eyes back and forth incubating ideas.

"Ah, yes," he said to himself, "I see a way to set fire to the graffiti war." Slowly his ideas were hatching into a wonderful scheme. He would call his favorite radio talk show host; he had done this before many times. The talk show host was not timid about tackling difficult social issues and took a great deal of pride in provoking everyone except the radicals.

"Hello, this is your talk show host. Go ahead, caller."

"Well, yes, I am calling to shed some light on the recent attacks on graffiti artists. I am the one who hired skinheads to subdue the little misbehaved boys who spray paint on buildings along the alleys in my neighborhood."

"What neighborhood?"

"I am a property manager in the Capitol Hill area."

"You must know that what you are doing is illegal."

"Yes, I do."

"Why don't you call the police for help?"

"I did, but to no avail, so I decided to solve the problem for the police and the property owners in my neighborhood."

"Have you noticed a decline in graffiti activity since you started to do your own policing?"

"Yes, I have."

"Are you in anyway responsible for the recent attacks on graffiti sprayers?"

"Yes, I directed the entire operation." Then Max decided he'd better get off the air. "I must hang up now." Click.

The host piped up, "Well, folks, you heard it live on this show. We have a vigilante making his response to graffiti sprayers. He succeeded where our law-enforcement people failed." What a story, thought Max. He was pleased with himself.

That evening Jim saw pictures on TV of what Max had described to him the day before. Jim was hoping that Max was not involved with the radio talk show host, but he knew Max called into radio talk shows. He would have to have a chat with Max tomorrow morning. Jim walked into the small cubicle which he and Max called an office. "Good morning, Max."

"Yeah, Mr. Clark."

"Do you need a jolt to wake up this morning?"

"Nope. Tomorrow you have a closing on two apartment buildings."

"I will call my legal counsel and arrange to sign the documents today."

"You are not going to attend a two-million-dollar closing?"

"No. I don't like real estate closings, I have attended a few in my time; besides, it is not all cash. I will be taking back a one-point-five-million-dollar deed of trust at twelve percent interest. Interest rates have gone up along with the inflation rate, which is at about six percent. It is time for me to get out of this business and buy gold."

"What is the price of gold on the market today?"

"Five hundred dollars per ounce. It went up this week, that tells me the country is on shaky ground. Americans are not aware of their country's financial instability, but foreigners know America is floundering."

"Are you sure of your facts?"

"Max, the fact is that this country is five trillion dollars in debt and spending money faster than it is collecting it. Who needs more facts? I can see the handwriting on the wall; it is there for all to see.

19

A person does not need a degree in economics to figure out that with unemployment around ten percent, interest at ten percent, inflation on the rise, and the country importing more than it is exporting, the affluent ride is near its end. It is a question of when this country will declare bankruptcy and not if. I assume that you never took Economics 101."

"I never finished college. Had to drop out to help the family."

"I am sorry, Max. Sometimes I am too hard on you. We should make the rounds of our apartment buildings, let's go for a ride around Capitol Hill."

Max and Jim got into the old truck and drove from building to building, discussing the usual problems of plumbing, lighting, garbage removal, graffiti, and the well-being of the tenants as they had done many times before.

"Max, follow up with a note to each tenant giving them the name and address of their new landlord after the closing."

"Yes, Mr. Clark."

"Did we fix the leak in the basement of this building?"

"No."

"Call the plumber and have it fixed."

"I thought since you are selling out we did not want to fix the leak."

"Max, have it fixed tomorrow. I believe in preventive maintenance; it will cost far less to have it fixed now rather than wait until the basement is flooded and all hell breaks loose; besides we have tenants to take care of. We have collected rent from these people in good faith and it is our obligation to provide them with proper services. I am going to fulfill my part of the rental agreement."

They kept driving on past the remaining buildings. "Look at those two guys walking past our building. See how that fellow wadded up his gum wrapper and put it into his pocket? He is a typical Capitol Hill resident. See that slop over there who just tossed a taco box onto the lawn by our building. He probably moved here under the federal-subsidized rent program and bought his taco with food stamps. We have to thank our congresswoman, the welfare queen, for this piece of social engineering. Max, do you realize we are paying for the well-being of that slop and then we get to clean up after him? See that trash over there by our garbage bin?"

"Yes."

"Have my men clean it up."

"Yes, sir."

"Max, stop calling me 'sir.' Just do your job. You are a super salesman, but not a manager. How do you think I became successful? By wishing it or doing it? I just don't understand your generation. Didn't your parents teach you how to work, how to perform on the job, how to function in society?" Max remained silent, he had heard this lecture before. "I am closing on my house next week. Do you have an apartment for me?"

"I have to check the files."

"Max, I need a place by the first of the month, preferable sooner."

"How much are you getting for the house?"

"One point two million. Don't ask. I will buy my first bar of gold with the proceeds from the sale. We have covered a lot of ground today; let's call it a day."

"Yes, sir."

"Damn it, stop calling me 'sir.' " Jim let Max off at the office and went home to check his answering machine.

Fred Goldsmith left a message. He had fifty tokens for Jim. He had a couple of Jim Beams on the rocks, showered, went out for some sea food, and then hit the sack. The next morning's newspaper had stories about graffiti wars, drive-by shootings. Too many arrests clogged the court system. Men on death row have become an unbearable expense to the state; prisons are full to the brim with criminals; jails are over capacity with lawbreakers. There was a feature story on how the graffiti war started, all speculation, of course. The media was probing but way off base. Jim couldn't care less at this point, he was selling out. He said to himself. "To hell with them all, I am going fishing in the mountains."

Jim entered Fine Jewelry to find Fred alone on this dreary day. "Hello, Jim. I have them over here. They came out beautifully, if I say so myself."

Jim picked up the ruby red token with a gold X embossed on the front. On the back was the inscription, "Terminator," with a number and the current date. The other token was baked enamel of ivory color with the strange cross on the face of it. On the back there was the inscription, "Director," with a number and date.

21

"You did a nice job, how much do I owe you?"

"About fifty dollars each. That will come to $2,500 plus tax." Jim wrote a check in that amount and handed it to Fred.

"Thank you, Fred. You did a beautiful job on the tokens."

"It would be cheaper to have them made overseas in larger quantities."

"No problem. This is a test run."

Jim drove back to his house and packed up his gear: a small suitcase of clothes, fly rod, his homemade flies, waders, fishing vest, and his favorite fishing hat with flies hooked to the hat band. He was ready to go. He left a message for Jan on her answering machine. "Going fishing in Deerpoint for a few days, need to do some male bonding with J. J."

He was off to the mountains. As he made his way through Capitol Hill, a muscle car barreled through the alley, crossed the street in front of the truck. He barely avoided a collision.

This ticked him off. He mumbled to himself, "Goddamn Mexicans—temporary license plates, probably no insurance, no driver's license—no wonder my insurance costs a thousand dollars every year. I am paying their premium for them." Jim profiled the two Mexicans as illegal aliens who had just splashed across the border days before.

Jim continued heading west towards the four-lane highway that led up to Deerpoint. Traffic was heavy, his mind went back to the good old days, thirty years ago, when traffic on the two-lane road was about one-tenth of what it was today. He was gaining altitude as he made his way up into the foothills of the Rocky Mountains. He took one last glance into the side mirror to see the brown cloud shrouding Denver, which slowly disappeared. He lived right in the middle of that oppressive ominous sign of the times, smog, with over a million people moving through that mess twenty-four hours a day. His mind shifted to better things, J. J. Crocker in Deerpoint, fly-fishing, and his private time to think and reminisce. His father used to call that daydreaming. Whatever. He settled into a steady pace, rolling along with the traffic. It was a real haul getting up the Continental Divide in the three-quarter-ton, four-wheel-drive truck, which sucked up gasoline.

The radio had cut out because of the mountains so he let his mind wander into the past. He was thinking back to when he met J. J. It was at the student union over a cup of coffee and a cigarette break between classes. J. J. was a freshman, a linebacker for the Colorado Buffalos, the university football team. J. J. had a scholarship right out of high school to play for the University of Colorado. He was an affable eighteen-year-old jock who was courted by the fraternities. He had a job at the dormitory cafeteria that consisted of showing up for a free meal on a regular basis. Jim was in another world from freshman who had just recently enrolled at the university. He was twenty-two years old, signed up as a Korean veteran for the educational benefits awarded to him. He was lucky he was alive; many of his comrades came back in a pine box. The war was still boiling over the thirty-eighth parallel in Korea. He had just left the front lines weeks before. He was in culture shock, to put it mildly. The university allowed him to register on a ninety-day probation basis. He was walking on thin ice and he knew it.

His father wanted him to take over the farm, but he declined the offer; so there he was in a do-or-die situation. His cold sweats and the nightmares from the war didn't make it any easier, but he was determined to hang in and someday graduate with degree in business. What a contrast between Jim, at the age of twenty-two, who had aged quickly to thirty-two as a sergeant in the infantry on the front lines, sitting alongside eighteen-year-old kids who had just been weaned from their parents. Over coffee and a cigarette, J. J. and Jim had become friends. J. J. asked the obvious question about Jim's dress. "Looks like you just came back from overseas." Jim laughed and told J. J. how he took the brass off his uniform, cut the patches off his shirts, and made a quick adjustment to the classroom. They shared their Colorado heritage, J.J., a miner's son, and Jim, the son of a farmer.

The two fellows were miles apart on campus. J. J. moved into a fraternity house and Jim lived off-campus with two medical students and two law students. It was in their junior year at the university when Jim, for the first time, shared his experience in Korea with another person, and it was with J. J.

Word of his father's sudden death brought back the past that he had kept to himself. J. J. couldn't understand why Jim was reluctant to attend his father's funeral. Jim explained to him that he and his father never communicated with each other. His father had turned over the family farm to his sister and her husband without a single cent going to him. He had not received any help from his family while in school. Jim told J. J. that he would attend the funeral for his mother's sake. He felt sorry for himself for never having had a relationship with his father. He only had pity for his father. This astounded J. J. because he could not imagine Jim in a dysfunctional family.

Jim then told him how he was called up for court-martial on insubordination charges, but the charges were dropped. The following week he was recommended for the Congressional Medal of Honor but declined to accept it. He was so battle-fatigued that he was bordering on insanity and only wished to go home. J. J. left the coffee break dumbfounded. He learned more about Jim Clark in forty-five minutes than he had learned of him over a period of three school years.

J. J. and Jim saw a lot of each other during that spring semester, and that changed dramatically in their senior year. J. J. entered law school and Jim was marking time until graduation. He was ready for the real world outside the university walls. Jim graduated and J. J. returned for two more years in law school. They did not meet again for five years.

J. J. met Betsy while stationed in Washington, D.C. They married and relocated to Deerpoint after J. J. finished his two years in the army.

Jim had crossed the Continental Divide and was coasting into the turnoff that would take him to Deerpoint in about twenty minutes. He shifted the stiff old truck through its gears and rolled along the two-lane highway, driving at nearly the speed limit, when a muscle car with California license plates shot past him. A couple of young Mexicans in one hell of a hurry to go some place. Jim profiled them as drug couriers, supplying the ski towns in the Rocky Mountain region. It was beyond Jim why America tolerated the bastards; they had invaded the United States. He decided that he didn't care either; he was on his way to do some fly-fishing.

He slowed down as he approached the outskirts of Deerpoint, the former mining town, now a prosperous ski town. Jim had become intimate friends with J. J. and Betsy through his weekend fly-fishing and skiing trips to Deerpoint; he usually stayed at their house. His former wife didn't fly-fish; she sort-of skied. She never liked J. J. and tolerated Betsy. There were many things in Jim Clark's personal program she disapproved of and eventually she opted out of it completely with a divorce. The Crockers held his hand, so to speak, throughout his divorce , as they sympathized with him.

J. J. thought Jim's wife was an eastern snob with a big mouth, a know-it-all smart ass. The Crockers endured her for the sake of Jim's relationship. J. J. marveled over how Jim had changed after his five-year stint with the big corporation. He was not the same fellow he once knew at the university.

Five years of traveling the states of Washington, Montana, Idaho, Wyoming, and Colorado had made Jim hate the inside of a car and loath motels, but on the flip side were money saved and free time for newfound pleasures. He took ski and tennis lessons, hunted elk, deer, ducks, geese, and pheasants. He developed his personal life and saved enough money for a down payment on two duplexes. His wife helped him acquire numerous properties and then got bored with that and divorced him. After his brief marriage he reverted to his single ways of life like a duck takes to water.

Jim had his own agenda, he would never get married again except to his beloved apartments. He had come full circle, now he was divorcing himself from the material world he had created. The old truck bounced over the bridge that spanned the small stream flowing through Deerpoint. Off to the right he saw smoke curling out of the metal chimney from old man Crocker's cabin. He was burning wood; on real cold days he added coal to the fire in order to heat the cabin.

The old cabin sat on a mining claim established by his father, supposedly an Indian-fighter, miner, and hero of many legends, as told by Mr. Crocker. The old man told stories of his own legends. True or false, they made for good local folklore. He symbolized the legends of Deerpoint. J. J. and Betsy wanted the old man to sell the cabin on the mining claim and move into the heart of town, but the old man and his companion, the little sheep dog, wouldn't move from the homestead. Old man Crocker's cabin on the edge of town and his life style was Deerpoint's past, personified.

Crocker chewed plug tobacco and rolled his own cigarettes. The plug tobacco was an old habit he retained through the years but the cigarette rolling was an act to show off a lost art of the past. He hardly ever left the town of Deerpoint. There was no need to. Since the town became a ski resort they established a clinic with two doctors, and a dentist opened an office. He seldom visited doctors; he maintained that if you stay away from doctors you have a better chance of living longer. He often told his younger friends that a plug of tobacco and a couple of draft beers kept the greedy doctors away from him.

Jim parked in front of the courthouse and hiked up the stairs looking for the judge. "Hello, Jim, what brings you to Deerpoint?" They shook hands for they had not seen each other in a while.

"A little fly fishing up the stream. Should be good this time of the year."

"Let's go for lunch. I can't go fishing with you today, court is in session and I am on the bench." They went to the local gathering place, the Last Chance Bar. "How is the rental market in Capitol Hill?"

"Very good at this time. I am selling out. Just sold two apartment buildings and next week my house is scheduled to close."

"Are you retiring from the business world?"

"I guess so; according to my property manager I am already retired."

"I saw on the news a story about the uprising against graffiti in your neighborhood."

"My manager and I started the uprising but we pulled back. It became too dangerous for us." The judge gave him that I-don't-believe-you look. Jim didn't blink an eyelash. The graffiti war was something out of the past; it was history in his mind. "I am going to buy gold with the proceeds from my real estate sales. I plan to bury the gold in a secret place until the revolution ends or plays itself out."

"What revolution? What have you been smoking in that pipe of yours lately?" The waitress took their lunch order and asked J. J. if he wanted the usual, a bourbon on the rocks. "What are you having, Jim?"

"Ah, coffee. Oh well, give me a draw, a glass of beer." Jim seldom ever had a drink during the middle of the day. His routine was a Jim Beam on the rocks at sunset. "I am surprised that you are having a

26

drink before lunch. Didn't you say that you will be on the bench this afternoon?"

The judge gave him a smirking smile and said, "I am the judge."

"Yes. You are the judge."

"Have you flipped out, talking about investing in gold bullion, burying it, making preparations for a revolution? You started a graffiti war in Denver; are you going to start another revolution by yourself?"

"In a few years this country will go broke and all hell will break loose. I see signs of the revolution in different parts of the country. Take California, for example. The jury let those Blacks go free because they feared a rebellion from the Black community. In Colorado I see killers turned loose because the prisons need space for incoming criminals. The punishment no longer fits the crime. We need to bring back capital punishment."

"I agree with you on capital punishment, but the law is the law. My hands are tied."

"I remember when we were students at the university. I was confronted with capital punishment in a speech debate class. I lost that one. The assignment was on capital punishment versus rehabilitation. I chose capital punishment and my friend chose rehabilitation. My presentation was better than his; yet he received a B grade and I got a C minus. The professor graded me down because I didn't properly defend my position. I stood up at the podium and presented my views on capital punishment as a proven method to deter violent crime. My friend pointed out at the podium that we still have crime despite the existence of capital punishment. He proposed to rehabilitate criminals and return them to society as productive citizens. I was dead in the water. We had had capital punishment and still had crime and his theory on rehabilitation had not been tested at that time. The seeds of liberalism were sown back in the midfifties. My friend believed in capital punishment as much as I did, but he compromised himself for a higher grade on that assignment. He was politically correct and I was politically incorrect. I know, the phrase 'politically correct' was not in use back then."

"I must say that rehabilitation makes sense, but we never did it in an effective way," the judge said. "We have psychologists, psychotherapists, psychiatrists, sociologists, and an array of specialists visit with prisoners at a great expense to the state, and it is all for naught. Prisoners play head games with our people."

"That is my point," said Jim.

"I have the same criminals come through my court time after time and it frustrates me."

"We should be teaching people in prison a trade. Instill some pride and self-respect in them."

"Hell, Jim, most of them learn to be better criminals. When the parole board grants their release, those fellows are less prepared to live in a structured society than before they went into prison."

"It is a losing battle. Capitol Hill once was a peaceful community; now I consider it a war zone. There are so many misdirected souls bouncing from welfare checks to shelters and back again to the streets. Liberals insist on calling the bums homeless people."

"Jim, how do you propose to bring about changes in the judicial system without having it come from the voting citizens through a democratic process?"

"A tough question. Probably by provoking the silent majority into realizing that they can effect a change. I had great apprehensions when we legislated individual rights in abundance back in the sixties and early seventies. An individual has more rights than a majority. We have reached legal anarchy, too many laws that contradict each other and the lack of public support to enforce laws on the books."

"You should have become an attorney, you would have made a great lawyer."

"J. J., I didn't have the reading abilities and comprehension necessary to make it through law school. I knew it then and am still aware of that shortcoming. I wanted very much to become an electrical engineer, but didn't have enough science courses in high school. Original thinking, new concepts, inventions fascinate me. On the other hand, I loathe legal beagles, shrinks, and social engineers."

"My job is to provide law and order in my community."

"I would not trade places with you, J. J., your work is too structured. Besides, I would lose my cool sitting on the bench."

"Are you staying for a few days?"

"Yes, I have a room at the motel."

"Come up to the house at about six-thirty for supper. Betsy will be expecting you."

"How can I possibly refuse Betsy's cooking? I will be there on time."

"I have to get back to the courthouse."

Jim drove slowly upstream from Deerpoint, parked his truck, and started to make some practice casts. He had not been fly-fishing in some time and needed to practice a little. Fly-fishing is an art. Reading and studying fly-fishing helps but the real skills are acquired in the field. In this case, a particular stream, a certain time of the year. The local fly fishermen know their streams like they know the back of their hand. They can read the water. They know what excites trout in different seasons. They are pros because they know the trout's environment and mood. Jim skipped the deep pools and moved up towards the beaver ponds near the head waters of the stream. Brook trout were very active and this gave Jim an opportunity to practice his casts. The entire stream above Deerpoint was barbless-hook fly fishing. He worked his way down to the deep pools where his truck was parked. He found a spot by a large fir tree to take a rest and smoke his pipe. Jim pulled out his tobacco pouch and packed his pipe with natural burley, lit it and had a slow smoke. The only sounds about were from the gurgling steam and some birds who were chirping. His mind was on this evening with J. J., the real reason he came to Deerpoint. He marveled over how Betsy, a lady of five feet and four inches, who majored in music, humanities, art, and probably attended finishing school, came to link up with roughneck miner's son in the Colorado Rockies.

He remembered his last hunting trip with J. J. and some local cronies. They'd made camp and dispersed in different directions in search of elk and deer. Jim had taken his 30/30 lever-action deer rifle, slung it over his shoulder by its strap, and wandered towards a stream below camp. J. J. had made his way to a large meadow where he'd invariably encountered elk year after year. After he'd made his kill, the butchering started and J. J. commenced to gut the animal. The height of his primitive act was when he'd cut the heart of the animal and licked the blood off the knife and let out a savage war cry. Whoever heard the cry knew that the judge was ready to move an elk carcass to camp.

Jim had been ambivalent about big-game hunting, but he'd tagged along for the camaraderie in the wilderness by an open

29

campfire. He'd come face to face with himself when he passed on a buck by the pond near a stream. He couldn't pull the trigger. He had lost his desire to kill for the sake of killing. Breaking camp was a welcome experience for Jim. He would never go big-game hunting again.

They'd packed their gear into the four-wheel-drive vehicles and the little two-wheel trailers. J. J. had grabbed a cold beer with his left hand and shifted with his right as he careened down the dirt road, leaving behind a trail of dust for a quarter of a mile. They'd made straight for the local watering hole, the Last Chance Bar, where exaggerated stories would be rehashed, expanded upon , and properly seasoned for local consumption. The judge loved to tell tall tales; he'd learned that from his father, old man Crocker.

Approaching footsteps startled Jim. It was a fellow fly fisherman.

"Are the trout hitting flies today?"

"I had fun with brookies upstream in the beaver ponds."

"This turned out to be a beautiful day."

"It sure did."

The man walked upstream. Jim had a hot flash hit his brain. He grabbed his fishing gear, tossed it into the truck, took off his fishing hat, and wasted no time in driving back to Deerpoint, whereupon he immediately bought a fishing license. He had forgotten that detail. His mind had been preoccupied with something else the entire trip.

It was getting late in the afternoon, so he decided not to go back upstream but instead went to his motel room. There was a message for him from Max. He had not told Max where he was staying on this trip, but Max had ways of seeking out details.

"Hello, Max, what's up?"

"I need to talk to you. Can you come back to Denver today?"

"No, Max. I am on a fishing trip. Can't it wait until tomorrow?"

"Well, yes."

"What is the problem?"

"Cops have been around checking out the graffiti confrontation, and our painter got us into deep trouble."

"How?"

"He tried to make out with one of our tenants, and it turns out she is a lesbian. According to his story, he made a pass at her."

"What amounts to a pass?"

"He hugged her, she spun around, he grabbed her from the back and cupped his hands over her breasts. She twisted loose and jammed her knee into his crotch, then drove a fist into his jaw. This caused him to stumble backwards. He fell onto the couch and rolled to the floor. He bled from his nose. The commotion stirred the tenant in the apartment below."

"Good God, what got into him?"

"I don't know, Mr. Clark."

"Does he have problems with his wife?"

"I don't think he did, but he does now."

"Stop talking in riddles. What is 'now' supposed to mean to me?"

"He told his wife about his failed encounter."

"Max, you are around the guys all the time. Tell me, what got into him?"

"Mr. Clark, ever since he started to wear that rug on his head, he thinks of himself as a Romeo."

"My God, the guy puts on a toupee and he becomes an instant irresistible lover. Max, talk to her, smooth it over; you excel in public relations."

"Sir, she is going to sue us."

"Max, I am pleading with you. I need your help. Bail me out of this one. That gal has been one of my best tenants for over ten years."

"I will do what I can, sir."

Jim showered and prepared himself for an evening with Betsy and Judge J. J. Crocker. He could smell the roast cooking as he knocked on the front door of the house. He was greeted by Betsy, like a long lost friend. "Jim Clark, in the living flesh. Do come in. J. J. will be home shortly."

"How have you been, Betsy?"

"Fine, just fine. How is Jan?"

"Still teaching, cooking, running, exercising at the spa, and staying beautiful."

"I like her, she is a great gal for you."

"Thank you."

J. J. arrived by the back door and made his presence known. He poured bourbon on the rocks for Jim and himself. Betsy had a glass of light red wine. The two moved into J. J.'s den to watch the evening news on TV while Betsy continued with her cooking. They watched a report on how the police were investigating anti-graffiti efforts of Denver property managers in the Capitol Hill area. Police feared that vigilante-ism might spread throughout the metro area if not thwarted at this point. The police chief forewarned citizens from taking the law into their own hands. "This is a matter for the police to resolve," he said. The mayor threw in his two cents' worth by telling people of Denver that his police force would protect life and property. This was a job for the police. They were professionals in law enforcement.

"Did you start the graffiti war?"

"I guess I did. It was a property manager who called in to a radical radio talk show host that fostered the idea for other property managers to join in the battle. Police have not been effective in slowing down graffiti artists. I had immediate results. They are staying away from my buildings."

"According to this report, neighbors are cheering the property managers and booing the police department."

"The police are overloaded with work in Denver and cannot take on the burden of policing graffiti artists. Our mayor is a political leader; he put pressure on the police department. If we enforced all the laws that our politicians enacted, we would have to triple our police force, double our court system, and double our prison and jail capacity. That could bankrupt us."

"You got that right."

The rest of the news was routine; weather, domestic violence, gang/drug-related shootings, convenience store robbery, a cardinal was accused of child molestation, a pedophile was exposed in the Boys Scouts of America, and so the announcer rambled on.

"J. J., our country is morally bankrupt."

"You are telling me . . . I hear and see it every day from the bench."

"Soon the country will be financially bankrupt and then there will be hell to pay. We are on the tip of the iceberg."

"Let's try some of Betsy's roast." J. J. and Betsy never had children so she doted over J. J. like an only child. Jim absorbed the attention Betsy extended to him and partook of good food with the best company he had had in months. It was relaxing for him to be removed from the big city turmoil.

After their meal J. J. and Jim settled down in the den with coffee, cognac, cigars, and some long overdue conversation. "J. J., I envy you. You have a devoted wife, live in a small town that is free of crime; no smog and no graffiti. You have it made."

"I always thought you had it made with those millions of dollars in real estate working for you instead of you working for an employer."

"The grass is always greener across the street, so they say. I enjoyed building my real estate investment, but now I want to sell. I am sick of the city. The market is ripe to sell, and the revolution is around the corner. I contracted to buy my first two bars of gold next week after I close the deal on my house. Five hundred dollars an ounce. What do you think?"

"I think you are crazy."

"A lot of people have been telling me that recently, including Jan."

"Jan is a wonderful person. You two should get married."

"Not on your life."

"After you sell out you can move up here and enjoy the good life. No need for you to stay in Denver."

"I don't think Jan is ready to leave the big city. When the revolution hits I intend to move to Jan's home town, McCook, Nebraska."

"Do you seriously think a revolution is necessary to bring this country back on track?"

"I don't see any other way. If we could make responsible citizens aware of the dangers that lie ahead, there might be a slim chance of averting disaster."

"You are alone in fearing a highly improbable scenario."

"No, I am not. There are others out there who are trying to warn people of the consequences that will follow a national bankruptcy but folks only listen to what they want to hear. Some people think it is impossible for the federal government to go broke, others feel that a large national debit is something we owe to ourselves, so who should care. I have an idea."

"You never lack for an opinion or an idea; let me hear it."

"Sure, I have an opinion because I think, ponder, search, review, analyze the world around me. I believe about twenty percent of what I read and discount ninety percent of what the TV media pundits put out." He reached into his sports jacket pocket and pulled out ten ivory-colored tokens and ten ruby red tokens. He laid them on the coffee table face up.

"Are you starting a new fraternal order?"

"No. This is my idea how we can restore law and order in this country." He turned over the tokens to show the back side. The ivory tokens had the term "Director" inscribed and the red tokens had the term "Terminator" inscribed on the back side. "I had Fred Goldsmith at the Fine Jewelry on East Colfax make these up for me. I see he put a date and number on the tokens. Fred outdid himself. He made them in the back of his jewelry store. A director is the person who knows which accused criminal is guilty and is about to walk away a free man. A terminator receives word from a director to terminate a criminal. These tokens in the right hands can bring swift justice, law and order, as you like to put it."

The judge was stone faced. He couldn't believe his ears; this was not happening. *It must be a joke or Jim Clark had really flipped out,* he thought, perplexed.

"Graffiti artists have not touched my apartment buildings in over a month. The victim of crime strikes back and wins. I think the time is right for this idea and, eventually, it will be practiced by the silent majority. I am not asking for your approval or disapproval. I will leave these tokens with you."

"I don't know whether to take you seriously or write you off as a lunatic."

"Give it some thought."

"Let me tell my story as a victim. The graffiti artists spray paint on my apartment buildings in the Capitol Hill area, repeatedly. My crew cleans it up again, again and again, it costs me thousands of dollars. My manager calls the police time after time, all of no avail. Finally, bingo, the police arrest two boys; we go to court. The fat broad has two delinquent boys she is raising on welfare. She was moved into the area and is housed by a federal-subsidized housing program. Undoubtedly she is on food stamps and draws money from Aid to Dependent Children. She is represented by a public defender; the liberal judge buys her story; he rules in her favor. I am the victim who is paying for all of this and I leave the courtroom a villain. A few months later the city council passes an ordinance requiring property owners to clean off graffiti within twenty-four hours or face a fine. By law the victim becomes a criminal. I took it upon myself to do something about it and my efforts paid off, to a point. Do you understand where I am coming from? I have reason to be paranoid, don't you think?"

"Buying gold bullion is crazy. The tokens border on insanity."

"I will hit the hay. Have to return to Denver in the morning. My painter made a pass at a lesbian and she is going to sue me. You see, Judge, I am a victim without recourse. Society punishes me like a criminal and I have no recourse." After saying his goodbyes to Betsy and J. J., he returned to his motel room. He fell asleep thinking about his first gold purchase.

He awoke the next morning refreshed; he had slept well. After breakfast he stopped by the liquor store to pick up a bottle of cognac and a bottle of sour mash for Mr. Crocker. He drove his truck down the road to the edge of Deerpoint and made a left turn that led to a little bridge spanning the stream and parked in front of Mr. Crocker's cabin. A crude homemade sign that read "Mine Shaft" was nailed to the left of the entrance door. As he approached the cabin, he could hear the dog bark. Mr. Crocker's companion. Man and dog, the two were inseparable. Jim knocked on the door and the old man yelled, "Come in."

"Hello, Mr. Crocker."

"Well, well, look at what the east wind done blowed in."

"I brought some spirits for you but nothing for Patsy."

"She has plenty to eat but I run short of liquor from time to time. Betsy only lets me buy groceries, but once in a while I walk downtown and get me a bottle."

Jim sat down by the potbelly stove and looked around the cabin. "I came up to do a little fly-fishing and visit with J. J. and Betsy."

"When are you heading back?"

"Within the hour." Jim saw the gun rack holding a rifle, a single shotgun, and a pistol that appeared to weigh a ton. The rifle had flat sides on the barrel. Mr. Crocker, Patsy, and the inside of the cabin were a page torn out of a western history book. "Mr. Crocker, this is truly rustic."

"Ah, it's old, that's for sure."

"What do you do, way out here?"

"Oh, I read the paper; they deliver it to my cabin. I walk downtown and visit here and there. Then there are my daily chores of cooking, washing dishes, washing clothes, buying groceries, and just generally, looking after the place." Every once in a while Mr. Crocker would lean forward and spit chewing tobacco into a bucket. He was chewing Red Man.

"Did your dad fight Indians with that old rifle?"

"Oh, I reckon so. He was an Indian-fighter, you know. He filed for a patent on this twenty-two-acre mining claim and called it 'the mine shaft.' There still is gold up there in that shaft." He pointed up the mountain behind the cabin.

"Have you ever tried to dig for gold in the mine shaft?"

"No. Was too busy making a living for the missus and little J. J."

"I must be getting along; have business to attend to in Denver."

"Yeah, do you still own apartments in the queer part of town?"

"Yes, but I am in the process of selling out. Sold a couple of buildings last week and will close on my house next week."

"Ah, it seems like yesterday when you and J. J. were in school at Boulder."

"It was a long time ago. I was a young fellow then and now I am getting old like you. Times have changed so much since those great years."

"Them good old days ain't ever gonna come back. Hell, they don't let you smoke in stores no more; it's the state law, they say. I remember when a fella could eat, drink, and fart all at the same time and nobody minded."

"I see you have electricity, propane gas, and city running water; you have the convenience of living uptown. Is the cabin hooked to the city sewer?"

"Naw, I use the outhouse; it suits me fine. I still got my gas-power electric plant with a set of batteries in case there is a power outage, and there is my wood stove for cooking and heating the cabin. The stream never runs out of fresh water."

"Mr. Crocker, you are the complete opposite of people living in the big city; you are self-sufficient. People in the metro area are in a constant dependency mode."

"Betsy and J. J. want me to move into town, but I like my place out here. Ain't nobody around to bother me none."

"I must run along, Mr .Crocker, see you next time I am up this way."

"Thanks for stopping by, you're always welcome at my cabin. Bye now, Jim, and take care."

Jim rolled the dirty old truck along the state highway, known as Main Street of Deerpoint, and took one last look at his sanctuary through the rearview mirror. He didn't want to leave. He dreaded having to return to smog and crime. Residents in Deerpoint lived like human beings. They looked out for each other; they didn't steal from each other. The big city was a zoo without cages. Social engineers and shrink-a-dinks were in charge of social behavior in Denver Metro's zoo without cages.

Like Betsy said, "I can find Mr. Crocker anywhere in town by calling Patsy. She waits outside wherever he is keeping company." Patsy was unofficially exempt from the town's leash law. She ate scraps from Crocker's dinner table and then curled up on her favorite blanket by the stove. At night she slept at the foot of his bed. Patsy was a good little watch dog; she kept track of Mr. Crocker.

Deerpoint residents looked after Patsy and Mr. Crocker like family. Two truant boys teased Patsy while Mr. Crocker was in the pool hall passing the time of the day. A young man in his twenties saw this and reprimanded the boys. The boys in defiance kept taunting Patsy. The young construction worker grabbed the two rascals and marched them to the truck. One of the kids wiggled loose and started to run away. The young man let go of the second boy and took three giant steps behind the get-away and gave him a boot with his right foot, vaulting the kid ass-over-tea-kettle into a cloud of dust. He then took the two back to school where the teachers were waiting for them. That evening dad's western leather belt was felt on the butt, a direct means of communications. Discipline, kindness, love, and respect go a long way to prevent the leather strap from being used frequently.

Jim's mind had not shifted to Capitol Hill; he was wondering how the Crockers handled the bomb shell he had laid at their doorstep last evening.

The Crockers hadn't slept too well. They'd discussed Jim's outlandish ideas about a coming revolution. Lying in bed J. J. told Betsy that Jim was paranoid and in due time would find his rational mind again. Betsy intuitively sensed that Jim might be on to something; she believed in him. She understood Jim like J. J. never would. J. J. devoted most of his life sitting on the bench and the rest of his time was spent in the confines of Deerpoint, much of it in the Last Chance Bar.

Jim was approaching Denver; he could see smog hanging over the city. His mind started to scan next week's agenda. He would buy his first bar of gold. He remembered that he sold the house. He would have to move out of the house. He kicked up the speed a bit. His mind was back in Capitol Hill and, soon, so was his body. He parked his truck in the garage driveway. He checked the answering machine. He had the usual calls; Max had a question, the real estate agent had a contract on five more apartment buildings, a co-op deal. Jan wanted to know if he was still with the living or was he dead.

He called the real estate agent and left his instructions, "Take the paper work to the bean counter and he will leave them with my legal counsel." He left a message on Jan's machine, "See you tonight for supper."

"Damn answering machines." He didn't like talking to machines; he wanted to talk with living people. He called Jan's boys, Bill and Mark. He had furniture for them from the house. He was moving into a small apartment. The next call was to his wishy-washy manager. 'Max, I need to move into an apartment by this weekend. What do we have available?"

"We have a unit coming up in the Grande building. How was your fishing trip?"

"Pretty good until you found me. The Grande apartment building will be under contract after I sign the papers tomorrow. What else do we have?"

"We are selling them so fast, I have to take a look at the records.

Mr. Clark, why don't you take the direct route and move in with your girlfriend?"

"Max, you are not my social advisor. I need an apartment right now. You are supposed to be my property manager; now get with it. What do you need me for today?"

"The lesbian is raising hell. You need to quiet her down or she will sue us."

"Sue *us?* You mean sue Jim Clark. I thought I told you to take care of that matter."

"Well, I did and didn't."

"Grab your briefcase and all your electronic gadgets; we are going to pay a visit to one of our tenants."

They drove the same route to her apartment that they had taken a thousand times before.

"Do you have her current rent check?"

"I have it right here, sir."

Jim drove the dirty old black truck slowly past two buildings under contract; then they passed one that he no longer owned. He could feel the weight coming off his back. He sat up straight and took a deep breath and wheeled the truck into the residents' parking lot. Out of the corner of his eye he thought he saw his painter.

"Max, don't tell me I am seeing what I don't want to see. What in the hell is he still doing around here, particularly at this building?"

"His wife will divorce him if she finds out that he has been fired."

"You were supposed to have taken care of him as I outlined layoffs to you. That paint-brush Romeo better be out of my sight by five o'clock today or you will be leaving with him at five tomorrow afternoon."

Max tilted back his head and rolled his eyes as he looked at the ceiling of the truck. He knew the inside of Jim's truck better than the inside of his little office. Max had spent many an exasperating hour in this torture chamber on wheels. Jim hiked up the stairs to the second floor and knocked on the lady's door.

She greeted him sternly, "Mr. Clark, what are you going to do about your painter?"

"Max fired him."

"He is down there in the parking lot talking to Max." Jim walked over to the window overlooking the parking lot to see for himself. The two were engaged in an intimate conversation; Max was talking on his cellular phone while chatting with the painter. The cellular phone made Max feel like an upper-echelon executive.

"Max assured me that the painter was history. I see he lied to me. Ms., what we have here is a wishy-washy manager and a spineless painter. The painter will, in fact, be gone by sunset today or the two of them will be leaving together by sunset tomorrow; you can quote me on that." The sight of his manager and the fired painter made Jim's stomach ache. He walked to the center of the apartment, away from the window. "Ms., I have sold two apartment buildings and five more are under contract. This apartment building will no longer be mine thirty days from now. You will have a new landlord."

"Oh no, Jim, I have been your tenant for ten years. You can't do this to me."

"I am sorry, but I am going to retire. I have been in this business over thirty years. I need to get away from apartment buildings, tenants, managers, painters, and all the other problems involved with the rental business. I will be moving along; too many irons in the fire; selling apartment buildings, firing painters, and probably a manager. I almost forgot, this is your current rent check." He tore it in half and handed it to her with a sigh. "You may stay in this apartment for free until I transfer the property to the buyer." She held the torn check in her right hand and looked Jim straight in the face. She pecked him on the cheek and gave him a heavy bear hug. Jim was nonplused.

"Mr. Clark, you have been the most wonderful man in my life."

Jim said, "Thank you," and promptly left the apartment. Jim remembered her as a twenty-year-old, giggling, curly redhead, and she turned into a thirty-year-old bomb shell. She stood about five-foot-eight-inches tall with a terrific build, beautiful legs, walked like an athlete on her toes, and her chest was something else. She even had muscles in her grapefruits. The embrace rattled Jim's brain. She had a perfect set of teeth, full lips, and a great smile. God must have made her with his right hand. Hell, she is a lesbian. Jim couldn't help but think that God had played a cruel trick on mankind

Jim exited the building and made a bee-line for the truck. The painter dashed around the building and was out of sight. Max got into the truck and rearranged all his electronic paraphernalia. He was wearing a beeper; had a headset dangling from his neck; the cellular phone was clipped to the belt holding up his pants; and then he stuffed the electronic organizer into his briefcase. "What do you use that thing for?"

"I organize my schedule, list my phone numbers, etc."

"You keep track of all the women in your life by a system, a kind of Max File."

The ride back to the office was like a ten-hour nightmare for Max. "After I close on the next five apartment buildings, I want you to explain to the men what is coming down the pike; they probably already know. Again, I will pay one year's wages as severance pay to each employee as he makes his departure. Start by giving notice to the leasing gal and one maintenance man."

"Should I fire them?"

"You don't fire anyone. Do it in a prudent way. I want you to be very direct and up front with all our tenants and employees. If you don't do it, I will."

Max knew what Jim meant by that remark. Max's job was fading before his eyes and his personal life was about to take a nose dive. Jim let Max off at the office and then returned to his house. Mark was waiting for him in the driveway.

"Hello, Jim."

"Mark, tomorrow we have to move my furniture out of the house."

"Where to?"

"Wherever you want to store it. This is my early wedding gift to you and your bride."

"Holy smoke, wait until I tell the girls about this."

"I will take a few pieces and move them into the Grizzly apartment building. Bill may want a few things for his apartment."

"Will Bill be here tomorrow?"

"I think so; he is supposed to be here today."

"Why don't you move in with Mother?"

"Thank you, but I cannot do that. I am afraid we would destroy, rather than nurture, our relationship."

"I understand."

41

"If I were your age I would approach the situation quite differently, but I am an eccentric old fellow."

Mark helped Jim move a few things to his apartment in the Grizzly building. "Who came up with the idea of giving all the apartment buildings names?"

"I have no idea." Jim later moved his arsenal into a storage locker in the Grizzly building; that was something he had to do by himself. A few days later he closed the sale on his house and bought his first two bars of gold at the contracted price of $450 per ounce. He had the sale of five more apartments coming up and the pay off on the first two he had sold. The price of gold rose to $500 per ounce; he contracted for five more bars. It was time to celebrate his success of the past few weeks. He made a date with Jan to dine at the Brown Palace on Friday evening.

The Brown Palace had the grace and elegance of a hundred years ago. Many a mining king, cattle baron, railroad tycoon, famous cowboy and many a president of this country had dined, danced, drunk and smoked cigars in this historic hotel. They finished off the evening with cognac, coffee, and a slow waltz. Jan was still in a festive mood when they arrived at the town house. "Thank you for a delightful, fabulous, outrageously decadent evening; I loved every minute of it." Jim lit his pipe, took off his tie, slipped out of his jacket, and removed his shoes. He turned on the TV for some evening news. Jan emerged from the bathroom in a sheer negligee. Leaning against the doorway, she nodded towards the bedroom. Jim didn't waste any time getting to the bedroom. Jim Clark's world was back in sync again.

They had a leisurely breakfast the next morning and piddled around the rest of the day. Jan loved playing house; it was very natural for her. "It is great to see you so relaxed for a change. Why didn't you move in with me instead of moving into that dingy old Grizzly?"

"Next time I have to move I will move in with you." She sat on his lap and kissed him on his forehead. God, he hated for her to do that. Jim stayed the weekend.

On Monday morning Jan darted off to her teaching job and Jim returned to his apartment with nothing in particular to do except gather up his newspapers and do his laundry. Jim read the newspaper from back to the front, reading the comic section first, his horoscope next, then he did the word jumble and moved on to the business section and finished off with the editorial section. An article discussed the national debit, which was over $6 trillion and the interest rate was at 13 percent. Inflation was around 8 percent. The alarming part of the article was the distribution of federal spending; 35 percent of the budget was used to pay interest on the $6 trillion debit. The federal government was in a pyramid scheme, defrauding its investors and fooling the taxpayers. Jim went downstairs to the furnace room, which also served as a makeshift office for the time being. He needed to occupy himself with something.

He decided to play tennis at the Gates Tennis Center. He got lucky. His old tennis friend of many years was seated on a bench overlooking the courts, waiting for a pickup game.

"Doc, how long have you been waiting for me?"

Doc laughed and said, "Jim, you are right on time."

They played their best two out of three sets and enjoyed a soda pop. They enjoyed playing each other because neither was hell bent on beating the other. They played for fun. As Jim used to say, 'I don't get paid to beat people in this game; that is why it is fun." The only people who got paid for hitting a tennis ball at the club were the teaching pros. Jim decided to stop at the barber shop on his way home and get a hair cut.

"Hello, Clem!"

"Well, well, the landlord from queer town." Jim ignored the remark, he was accustomed to disparaging comments from the barbers. "Who is winning the graffiti war on Capitol Hill?"

"I don't know and I don't care. I am busy selling my apartment buildings. Within few weeks I should be closing on five more buildings."

"How many do you have left to sell?"

"A few more."

A fellow two chairs down spoke up and said, "I hear the mayor stepped in to prevent citizens from taking the law into their own hands."

The customer in the third chair said, "It's about time somebody took the bull by the horns and showed those damn liberals who is really in charge."

The guy in the second chair pointed out how his neighbor shot a smart-ass kid who was trying to break into his garage and now the poor fellow is sweating out a possible prison sentence. Apparently a few weeks prior to the shooting there was a slight verbal altercation between the two and the punk threatened the man. The kid said, "I know who you are. I will come back and get you."

Slim added his thoughts to the discussion. "The criminals are holding law-biding citizens hostage in their homes. What in the hell has happened to law and order? Is there no punishment for the criminals?" The customer in the sixth chair suggested that people should call the police. Slim jumped right down his throat, "How about the guy who did call the police when he caught two kids spraying paint on his garage door at midnight? The next day the mother defended her boys on TV."

Jim had heard all this before; he also had firsthand experience with the problem. His mind was on getting out of the apartment business and getting away from the city turmoil. Jim paid Slim and left quietly. He went back to his apartment and called the bean counter.

After a brief conversation with his C.P.A. he learned that $250,000 was due in January to the Internal Revenue Service and his gold contract was due in February. A closing was scheduled during the month of February on five apartment buildings. He had his shower, took two bottles of red wine from the cupboard, and left to have dinner with Jan at the town house. Max was parked in front of the Grizzly talking on his cellular phone. He motioned Jim to join him in the car.

"Max, have you found a job for yourself?"

"No."

"You better start looking. I will have the head maintenance man look after the operation by himself, after I sell five more buildings." Max sat motionless behind the steering wheel, staring through the windshield. "Max, I didn't come to see you; you came to see me, speak up."

"I have this problem?"

"So you have a problem. I am supposed to read your mind?"

"I have to tell you the truth."

"Max, get to the point and don't beat around the bush with me. We have been through this scene many times before."

"I have been servicing some chicks on the side and two of them are pregnant. I am afraid my wife will find out."

"I don't see how I am involved." Jim pushed open the car door with his right hand, holding on to the wine bottles with his left.

"They are our tenants."

"Max, you have a problem that only a neurosurgeon can solve. Every time you see a cutie in a tight skirt your brain malfunctions. Your brain short circuits through your testicles. Have a surgeon rewire your system. I can't help you. God knows I have tried. What about the children you are randomly siring? Who is going to take care of them?"

"The gals are going to become single parents."

"No father, no support from a nuclear family, what a precarious way for a kid to come into the world. Max, tell me, how would you like to come into the world under those circumstances?"

"That never crossed my mind."

"Get a vasectomy; shut down your sperm delivery system if you can't control your emotions."

Jim slammed the car door and left for Jan's place. Max knew this was the end of his comfortable ride with Jim Clark; he now would be on his very own.

Jim knocked on the door. It swung open, and there she was with apron on and opened arms to welcome him. She gave him a nice hug, a little kiss on the lips. He tapped her firm left fanny as he held onto the wine with his other hand. "Did you have a nice day?"

"Just another day, just one more day." He put the wine into the refrigerator and went to the living room to catch some of the evening news on TV.

The news was a repeat of the previous day's news except for a report on an old man killed in Deerpoint. The old man was a former miner, living in his cabin on the edge of Deerpoint. He was gunned down in his cabin by unknown assailants earlier in the day. "Oh, my God! Jan, I think somebody killed Mr. Crocker."

"Are you sure? Couldn't it have been someone else?"

"I can't call the Crockers now. We will have to wait for the late news and hope for more details about the shooting."

45

They managed small talk and little else, neither wanted to speculate on the death of an old friend. Jan had met Mr. Crocker several times but was not intimate with the man. Jim had a relationship with Mr. Crocker that went back to his days at the University of Colorado; that was a lifetime in the past. The late news was confusing and vague. It was reported that Mr. Crocker and a Mexican were dead. The matter was under investigation.

"I'm going back to my apartment tonight, must do some soul searching."

"No. You are staying here. I am here for you. It is the holiday season. We can sleep late tomorrow morning."

The season of joy, the season of giving, turned into a time of mourning. Bill, Mark, and his bride-to-be spent Christmas Eve at Jan's townhouse. It was a gloomy time for everyone, especially for Jim. The news media was hot and heavy on the story that involved the father of a local judge in Deerpoint. One reporter made reference to three Mexicans, probably aliens, who hung around the Last Chance Bar having a beer on the day of the murder. Mr. Crocker liked telling stories to strangers about the mine shaft. Locals had heard the stories many times and discounted them as Mr. Crocker's personal folklore. The news reporter repeated that Judge J. J. Crocker was the son of the dead miner, who lived in a cabin on a legendary mining claim. Mr. Crocker never was a miner, but so goes the press in the realm of sensationalism. Jim hardly slept; he was a light sleeper anyway. He tossed all night and kept Jan awake most of the night. Max called him after breakfast at the townhouse. This was something he was never to do; Jan's townhouse was Jim's sanctuary. "This better be important, Max."

"It is. We have a problem at one of our apartment buildings with a paraplegic. He wants us to adapt the building to accommodate him."

"What for? He does not live there. The building is under contract. We are supposed to close the deal in a month. Max, you are good at public relations; smooth it over and quiet him down."

"It is too late for that; he is protesting in front of the apartment building with his buddies. The news media is sponging up the story with their cameras."

"Let the guy have his day in the sun with the media; hopefully that will satisfy him."

"The real estate agent called and said that the buyer feels uneasy about what is happening at the apartment building."

"Oh, shit! What next?"

"I may have ticked him off last week when I told him to wheel his ass out of the area. I think he is selling drugs to the tenants in this two-block area. I threatened to call the police and that may have pissed him off."

"Is he still over there?"

"Yes."

"I will be right there."

This particular apartment building was only five blocks from the townhouse, and he walked the distance in five minutes. The media had left but the derelict was still there, rolling back and forth in front of the apartment building in his two-wheeler. Max was following the guy around and talking to him. Jim walked up to the fellow in the wheelchair and asked him why he was picking on his building.

"I want to live in this building and I demand that you accommodate me."

"This building was constructed in 1925. The builders never planned on renting to cripples and neither do I. I can't afford to accommodate you. I would have to build ramps, put in an elevator, and spend money I cannot afford on this old building."

"That is your problem. I have my rights."

"You have your rights. Where in the hell are my rights? You guys are dressed like a bunch of war veterans. Are you a veteran?" asked Jim.

"I am."

"How did you come by your injuries?"

"A motorcycle accident."

"I bet you were stoned to the hilt when it happened."

"You can't talk to me like that, I will get you for this."

"Look, you wheel your ass right out of here or I'll get you for selling drugs."

"I'll see you in court."

"And I will see you in jail."

The self-anointed crusader of human rights was determined to exercise his rights at the cost of everyone else's. "Damn pseudo-do-gooder. Max, I think you have the correct profile on this derelict. Let's video the guy selling drugs."

"I need to buy a state-of-the-art camera."

"How much?"

"About two grand."

"Max," Jim looked him over.

"Mr. Clark, you are still living in the nineteenth century."

"Okay, fine, buy it. But I am putting you in charge of this project, so don't screw it up. You have a chance to redeem yourself." Jim immediately returned to his apartment and called the real estate agent and assured him that the wheelchair episode would be resolved in short order. He told him, "Watch for our results on TV." His apartment became his office; Max never used the office in the furnace room.

He leaned back in his recliner and stared at the ceiling like Max used to do and cogitated over recent events. On his mind was the funeral and whatever else might go wrong between now and when the last building would be sold. Funerals and weddings depressed him. One marked the end of a struggle on earth and the other was the beginning of a new struggle in life. He inadvertently took a nap. Jim was a loner in his own world. He struggled within an imperfect society according to his standards of morals and ethics. He lectured Max on why he never apologized to anyone and never accepted an apology from another person. His reasoning was that if you followed a strict code of ethics there would never be a reason to apologize to anyone. Max couldn't comprehend that piece of advice nor many other adages that he was subjected to over the years by Jim Clark.

The phone rang. He awoke. It was Jan. She was wondering what had happened to him. He apologized to her for disappearing like a phantom. "What time is it?"

"Four-thirty in the afternoon, two days after Christmas."

"Thank you, dear. I will take a shower and be over shortly."

As he was taking his shower he reflected upon the day, or was it days? He wasn't sure, he had lost track of time. *When was the funeral?* he thought, confused. He dried off, dressed, and went to the townhouse.

He walked in and was welcomed by that so familiar hug, a gentle kiss, and that second, soft, comforting hug. He responded with a pat on her firm fanny. She liked that, it was Jim's signal that all was well with him. "Where were you today?"

"That damn property. I just can't divorce myself from those apartments. They hound me like a demon."

"Honey, what was the problem today?"

"You don't want to know."

"I'll crush some ice for a couple of Jim Beams and we will relax. You are going to stay for the night."

"I will, thank you. Tomorrow I have to drive to Deerpoint."

"The funeral isn't until the day after."

"I forgot. God knows I dread making this trip, but I have to go for the sake of J. J. and Betsy."

"Why do you have such a disdain for funerals?"

"Funerals are for the grief-stricken survivors, and sometimes funerals become a public orgy for the benefit of a community."

"What a strange perception."

"The people of Deerpoint will attend a mass confession, a needed catharsis, and I don't relish mass-organized exercises."

"We will have a light supper, watch a little TV, and go to bed early. You need me tonight, admit it."

"I need you all the time." She was a beautiful woman, nearly fifty years old, showing strands of gray in her golden hair, a few more wrinkles on her face, but the most beautiful part about her was the warmth that came from within. Jim needed an extension beyond himself. He needed Jan's unconditional love but wouldn't admit it to himself; he was too independent. He disliked such a flaw in his character. The next morning he returned to his apartment, packed his overnight bag, and headed for the mountains in hopes of beating the incoming winter storm.

Snow fell all the way to Deerpoint and it appeared that the day would be cold and dreary, but it wasn't. The sun broke through clouds while Jim was having his late breakfast. It turned out to be a delightful morning. People gathered in midtown and the procession started with the media swarming all over the place. The visiting tourists to the ski area had no idea what was taking place. Jim marched along with the crowd; he was one of many and it felt

49

comfortable. Folks turned out to witness the burial of an old friend. They would be burying part of themselves on this day.

Betsy asked the judge to bury Patsy with Mr. Crocker, but, at first, he refused. All grave-site services are pretty much the same, ashes to ashes, placing the body by green pastures, and then a line of words that deal with a time to be born and a time to die. A choir sang "Rock of Ages" as they prepared to lower the casket into the freshly dug hole. Ace, the backhoe operator, was leaning against his machine waiting for the services to end so he could finish his job, to cover up Mr. Crocker. The county sheriff, according to Betsy's request, put Patsy's blanket at the foot of the casket, and a big fellow in a state highway patrolman's uniform placed the curled up little dog on the blanket. Patsy, in her reddish fur with that yellowish tail and a splash of white on her throat, looked like she was asleep, very life-like. The Deerpoint chief of police unfolded one of Patsy's blankets and draped it over her. This jolted the judge. Tears started to stream down his face. They lowered Mr. Crocker and his dog into the grave. The judge fell apart, lost his composure, and sobbed deeply.

The service ended.

Betsy guided the judge and a small group up the hill to their home nearby. Jim gave Betsy a wave of the hand from a distance. She acknowledged him with a slight nod. Jim walked over to the grave after the crowd dispersed. He looked down into the hole with the casket and dog at the bottom. He was thinking of the grave-site services, ashes to ashes. Mr. Crocker had not been cremated. This rocky hill, known locally as Boot Hill, was miles from a green pasture. Mr. Crocker had been born, lived a full life, but his death was premature at the hand of evil in society. Ace waved to Jim as he scooped dirt into the hole with his backhoe.

Jim strolled back to his truck and started his long journey back to Denver. The radio in the old truck did not pull in a station until he reached the foothills of the Rockies so he amused himself by daydreaming. He had never met Betsy's family. Her father was a retired judge, one brother retired as a colonel from the army and now was with the CIA, another brother was an attorney who worked for the federal government. J. J. graduated from law school as a second lieutenant in the Judge Advocate Corps, the legal branch of the U.S.

Army. He was assigned to the duty of shuffling papers in Washington, D.C., for two years, and there he met Betsy. They married and moved to Deerpoint after J. J. was released from the service. He practiced law for a while then became a district judge.

Jim crested the Continental Divide and soon would be coasting into the foothills near Denver. He was in range to pick up Denver radio signals, so he dialed to Max's favorite station, a radio talk show. Jim often wondered what Max found so fascinating about talk shows. Max fancied himself as an expert on many things, especially local political action, and sometimes he even attempted to solve problems at a national and international level, which were beyond his scope of comprehension.

The radio talk show host said, "This is Charlie, your talk show host. Come in, caller."

"Yes, Charlie, I just wrote a rap song called 'The Welfare Rap.' "

"Let's hear your rap."

" 'Gonna make me a welfare family, Gonna see the Welfare Queen, Gonna go to Washington, D.C.' "

"Thank you, caller. We just heard a local rapper."

"Hello, caller, this is Charlie. Go ahead, caller."

"I wrote a song."

"Can you sing it?"

"Yes."

"Let's hear it."

" 'This land is my land, this land is not your land, so get your ass out of here, this country is too small for you and me.' "

Charlie cut off the guy for fear of where he was going with the song. "It appears we have some xenophobic guys out there."

Jim moved the radio dial slowly to his favorite music station. He was getting close to Denver. He could smell the smog. The traffic became heavier. He soon would be right in the middle of the city, on Capitol Hill. He stopped by the townhouse. Jan was not there, so he went on to his apartment, where he still stored his belongings.

Jan had left a message on his answering machine. "See you tonight, honey." There was a message from Max. "I got the bastard. Watch it on TV tonight." Things were looking up instead of down for him. He liked that for change. He took a short nap, showered, and went to Jan's place.

"Hi, honey." A hug, a kiss, and a tap on the fanny. "Did you get Mr. Crocker buried?"

"Yes, and his dog." He gave her the entire unabridged story from start to finish with all the details. "Should we go out tonight?"

"I would like that since I didn't prepare anything for supper. Didn't know if you would be back today."

They had their customary refreshment while watching the evening news.

"Max left a message for me to watch the news this evening."

"Is he going to be in the news?"

"Knowing Max, my guess is that he will be in the news. He likes to face cameras; he should have become a news man or a movie screen actor."

There it was, video pictures taken from a rooftop, showing two squad cars pulling up in front of the apartment building. The guy in the wheelchair saw what was coming down. He waved his pistol in the air, the police sprayed lead. Two officers came from the alley with guns drawn; one officer out of haste nailed the guy again even though he was slumped over in the wheelchair. The press did a close up of Max as he explained his role in the raid on this lone drug dealer in a wheelchair.

Jan gasped and held her hand over her mouth, "Oh, my God! How awful!"

The reporter switched over to the police sergeant, who pointed out that they had tried in vain to nab the drug dealer but he was too elusive for them. The reporter wrapped up his story by commending Max for demonstrating how citizens can help police solve neighborhood crime.

"That Max of yours is a show man. Did you see how he carried his video camera around? He acted as if he was in charge, the main character of the show."

"He is a character, no doubt about that. I damn near fired him on the spot about a week ago. After I close on the five apartment buildings, Max and I will go our separate ways."

"How long has he been working for you?"

"Ten years."

"That was about the time I met you at the Gates Tennis Center."

"Let's go to dinner; I want to celebrate."

"'How can you possibly celebrate after what happened today?"

"I will tell you the whole story. . . . There is always more to a story."

Jan was a lady of leisure; she was still on her holiday vacation. After they returned from dinner they watched the late news. There was a short clip of the funeral in Deerpoint. He pointed to the TV screen and said, "Look, that is me on the left."

"You sure have had an active day."

There was nothing new in the Crocker story, just a rehash of previous reports. Locals were interviewed by the media and gave their opinions on the subject.

They went to bed. Jan squeezed Jim's hand and said, "You had more happen in your life today than I experience in an entire school year."

"I don't look for excitement; it seems to follow me around. You are all the excitement I want in my life." She kissed him, rolled to her side, and promptly fell asleep. "Good night, Jan," he said as he stared at the ceiling.

The following day the temperature was a warm sixty-five degrees. They walked around most of the afternoon. They passed the house Jim had recently sold and they walked by a number of apartment buildings he used to own. "You know, Jim, I have learned a lot about business from you in the past year."

"Business is business. Learning about people is important, you learn about people in the real world. Most schoolteachers live in a vacuum, in a world unto themselves. I am retiring, I have done my thing, now I am positioning myself to survive the revolution that will follow bankruptcy."

"Why must you always be worried about the future? Can't you ever enjoy the present?"

"I am enjoying the present with you. Tomorrow will come and it will pass, but I will never be poor again."

"So that's it. You have this fear of becoming impoverished. You are obsessed with money because you once were poor."

"Maybe. I shall never be poor again. What does money mean to you?"

"Oh, a lifestyle it can buy for me, security for myself and something for my boys. If I had your money, I wouldn't drive that dirty old black truck. I would buy something nice and new." Jim put his arm around her shoulder. They walked back to the townhouse. Jim was a practical man, the truck did the job, he couldn't care less if someone scratched it or dented it, and no one in their right mind would steal it. He never locked the truck; it was so practical to keep the truck.

Jan returned to her teaching and Jim kept busy writing checks to the I.R.S., the State Department of Revenue, and closing deals on his apartment buildings.

Betsy called for the second time, "J. J. is in a trance. He eats little, talks to no one, sleeps in the den. What should I do?" Jim spoke with her but was of no help, he had no experience in these matters.

Max stopped by to see Jim. "Well, Mr. Clark, I am ready for my severance pay."

"Good, phone in your figures to my bean counter and I will sign your check. Have you found a job?"

"Yes, I am going to sell real estate."

"Do you have your license?"

"I should have it in a few days. I am anxious to get started."

"I will give you the listing on the duplexes and row houses, your very first listing."

"Gee, thanks, Mr. Clark. I appreciate that very much. There is one last problem we have to resolve."

"Oh no, not at the very end of our trail."

"I think you might enjoy this one."

"How so?"

"The painter filed for unemployment insurance."

"That bastard almost had me in a sexual harassment suit. We gave him his severance pay and now he wants to rip off the state of Colorado."

"He knows you are quitting business and figures that you will not contest his request."

"Well, he figured wrong. I will not stand by idle and let hm screw the working people of this state. When does his case come up?"

"Two days from now."

"I will have the bean counter and my legal counsel show up with our records and you line up the gal he harassed. See if she will go on live TV and tell her side of the story to the public, on the doorsteps of the state Capitol Building."

"That's vicious."

"Why?"

"His wife will divorce him."

"What is right is right and what is wrong is wrong. I am going to teach him a lesson he will remember the rest of his life. Max, line up the gal and the press, I will take care of my end of the deal."

Max did well. The gal showed up dressed like a female executive and brought along her own cheering section. Max oversold the media on the sexual harassment bit, but what the hell, it was a job well done. Jim, the bean counter, and the legal counsel stood off to the side with briefcases in hand prepared to do battle. The redhead charmed the cameras; she became an instant star on TV.

She told her story about the painter's lewd sexual advances made at her in her apartment. The TV reporter asked her if she had filed a sexual harassment suit against the painter. She answered, "No." She pointed at the painter, who was standing below with his wife. "That man wearing a black toupee is the man who sexually attacked me; he tried to rape me in my apartment."

The TV cameraman focused on the painter. The painter smiled for the cameras. He thought this was great; to be accused of making a pass at a beautiful redhead on local TV was neat stuff. His wife scowled at the cameras. She had not planned on this kind of event. She looked like a jar of sour grapes.

The attorney said, "Jim, this could backfire."

"It won't, trust me."

The reporter asked, "Why haven't you filed a suit against the man?"

"Because he works for my landlord, who is the nicest man I have ever known. He resolved this matter for me."

"How did he do that?"

"He promptly fired the painter and paid him one year's salary as severance pay. My landlord, Jim Clark, is a very fair man."

They all cheered her and the interview was over. Max was standing behind the redhead's cheering section in hopes of receiving some TV coverage. The painter's wife gave her husband the elbow in the ribs and then they left. The bean counter expressed his empathy for the painter.

"Don't feel sorry for him. His wife will drag him home, kick him in the groin, and it won't hurt a bit because he doesn't have any balls," Jim snickered.

The victim, as she was portrayed by the media, walked over to Jim and asked him, "How did I do?"

"You were marvelous and you look gorgeous!"

"Thank you, Jim." Her red hair glistened in the bright morning sun, her blue eyes sparkled, she looked scrumptious. She reached around Jim's head with her hands and gently gave him a kiss on the lips and then hugged him.

This excited the bean counter. "Hey, Jim, do you have something going on the side with her?"

"Hardly. She is a lesbian, a wonderful person."

The attorney laughed and said, "You may know your tax code, but you don't know flesh too well." They all laughed together and rejoiced in their victory. Jim thanked Max for his stage directing. He didn't thank the attorney or the bean counter because they were charging him by the hour for having fun. Jim was happy, he had just won another battle, but the war was not over.

Jim returned to his apartment and called Betsy. "How is J. J . doing?"

"He is coming around. He is searching the cabin for clues that might lead to the killers."

"I am glad to hear that, he had to work out the death of his father just like I once had to struggle through an emotional problem."

"You are referring to Korea?"

"Yes."

"J. J. is coming to Denver tomorrow. He wants to see you about some more tokens. He will call you."

"I will check my machine for messages."

"Bye, Jim."

"Bye, Betsy."

Jim met with J. J. at a short-order restaurant that was something out of the fifties. The owner, an old Greek, usually sat on a chair by the cash register smoking a cigar while reading the newspaper or he would shuffle back and forth to the kitchen area. Ashes would fall from his cigar butt that dangled from his mouth and curls of smoke swirled around his head as he moved around behind the counter talking to customers. Patrons could smoke anywhere in the restaurant. How the old fellow managed to escape the wrath of the city of Denver was a mystery. The place was located in the middle of Capitol Hill, a sister community of the People's Republic of Boulder.

"Jim, I have been checking the pawn shops and I think I located the place where the killers sold my dad's old rifle."

"Things are beginning to look more positive for you."

"They sure are. We will deal with the killers accordingly." J. J. was talking up a blue streak; he was effervescent. "Did you bring the tokens?"

"Yes." Jim handed him the tokens. J. J. now had all the tokens except the two Jim had tucked away in his billfold. Jim didn't ask J. J. why he suddenly needed more tokens; he could only guess.

"Criminals may get away with murder in Denver but not in Deerpoint. Law and order are going to become part of the American way of life again, wait and see. Thanks for lunch. It's a great restaurant."

"My pleasure. When are you going to hold court again?"

"Next week." They parted under strange circumstances. Jim was puzzled over the new character J. J. displayed.

Max sold the last of Jim's property; Jim was out of the rental business. He bought his last bar of gold at $1,500 per ounce. Interest rates had risen to 18 percent, inflation was at 15 percent and the national debit was mounting by the month. Jim was waiting for a payoff on two deeds of trust. He had plans to invest $1.5 million in Canadian stock through a bank in Vancouver and deposit $500,000 in a bank in Guaymas, Mexico.

II

Spring passed very slowly for Jim. The country was euphoric as business was booming, a last spiral of inflation before the roof would cave in on innocent people of America. Jan had her dreaded fiftieth birthday. Jim felt isolated and alone; Jan had distanced herself from him and became involved with herself and her personal well-being. She was either preparing for a marathon or running in one; she visited the spa daily and wore shiny black and pink athletic clothes around the townhouse. "Jan, why are you so adamant in becoming a world-class running jock at your age?"

"I want to keep my body and mind active."

"Why don't you jog by yourself occasionally instead of running in a pack with the likes of Thelma?"

"She is a fellow teacher and my friend."

"What does she teach?"

"Physical education."

"That figures. She is built square, five by five, without a brain. I peeked down her bra and she has hair on her chest, and I suspect she shaves the stubble under her nose. Is she married?"

"Divorced, just like the rest of us."

"What do you find so addictive at the spa?"

"Nice people. We work out together and do our thing."

"To me a spa is a modern-day high-tech torture chamber."

"To each his own."

Jim was bewildered by her abrupt transformation; he saw less and less of her. She even had her hair cut short without asking him about it first.

Mr. Crocker's alleged killers were apprehended. They made the connection through Grandpa Crocker's rifle that the fellows had pawned after the murder. According to their story, as told through an interpreter, they stopped by Mr. Crocker's cabin and he shot one of them dead. They fired back, killing the dog and Mr. Crocker, all in self-defense. The public defender did an excellent job; the prosecutor on the other hand was hampered by Judge J. J. Crocker's meddling in the case. The liberal judge hearing the case had no choice but to let the two Mexicans off on lesser charges. Judge J. J. Crocker experienced a revelation; he saw law and order from the same perspective as victims of crime perceive it, where the criminal has more rights than the victim. Two weeks later the two Mexican aliens were found shot to death in their muscle car, no suspects. The police were investigating.

Summer was close by, Bill was going to graduate with a degree in pharmacy and Mark had a June wedding planned. Jim felt he had probably lost Jan. He'd screwed up again. He had done it before in his life, many times. Jim made a lunch date with Jan at the Cherry Creek Shopping Center, her favorite place. He knew she liked this particular restaurant because it was the place where everyone who wanted to be somebody wanted to be seen in the company of somebody. Jan was seated at an outdoor table dressed in her pink head band, white and pink shoes, and black skin-tight pants. She looked like an aging model, beautiful and gorgeous.

"Hi, Jim, thanks for the lunch invitation."

"I was hoping we could play tennis, but I see you are running today."

"We are running in an AIDS prevention marathon."

"Why do you people always run under a banner for some so-called worthy cause? Don't you people ever run just for yourselves?"

"Sure, we have our races. We always run to win. Sorry, but I have to run now." She grabbed a croissant, nibbled on it as she hopped and skipped towards the starting line of the race. Jim lit his pipe and blew smoke into the air, causing much consternation among the customers. He left the yuppy café and decided to look for Doc at the Gates Tennis Center.

He was in luck. Doc had just finished a match and wanted some more tennis before he called it a day. They had the usual soda pop after their set of tennis. Seated on a bench overlooking the tennis courts, Doc and Jim would discuss the fate of the country and its citizens. They had these discussions after tennis for many years.

Today's subject was Jan. What ailed her? Why was she so strange? asked Jim.

"Jim, has it ever occurred to you that she might be going through a change of life? How old is she?"

"She just had her fiftieth birthday."

"You never married her. She feels insecure. Her youngest is graduating from college, and her oldest son is getting married in a few weeks. You refuse to move in with her and have been doing your own thing lately, not involving her in your life. When was the last time you took her out to dinner? When was the last time you bought her jewelry or flowers?"

"Doc, you make me feel like a heel. I am not a flower and jewelry type of guy. I have not taken her out to dinner recently and I am not going to marry her."

"You are one stubborn SOB, in my opinion. You are not deserving of that charming woman."

"I needed that. You are right, I am a first-class asshole."

"I didn't say that. I said you need to think beyond yourself and your bars of gold."

"I noticed that you haven't made any derogatory remarks recently about my gold purchases."

"I used to think you were crazy, obsessed, and certainly much too pragmatic for your own good, but now I see things in the news that make me realize that not all is well with this country."

"I appreciate you setting me straight about Jan. I confess that my independent life has caused me problems. I don't want to spend the rest of my life by myself. There must be more."

"By George, I think you are finally catching on. When shall we play again?"

"You set the time and date. I'm retired and available at any time."

"I will call you."

"Thanks, Doc."

Jim went back to his apartment and found an eviction notice posted on his door. He had forgotten to pay his rent. He wrote a check for the rent and called the manager of the building. He left a message on Jan's answering machine, "Honey, I have to see you tonight. It is important." He showered and took a long look in the mirror at himself.

When he arrived she was dressed in her skin-tight exercise suit. He presented her daisies and two bottles of wine. She gasped in surprise. After her shower she returned to the kitchen. Jim knew that they both were selfish, strong-willed, and determined individuals who had to find a better way of reaching out to each other. He had not earned her unconditional love that he desired. Jan desperately wanted the relationship to work. She had just turned fifty and was about to lose the richest man in her life. Jan made two drinks without comment. Jim was seated at the kitchen table, watching her every move. She joined him while the TV dinner was heating in the microwave oven. "A toast to my proposition."

"OK."

"I would like to move in with you."

"You know you are welcome to do so at anytime."

"Tomorrow I will change my will." Jan leaned back in her chair. "I want for you, the boys and I to be a family."

"That is easy. They already consider you their second father."

"I was hoping you might consider taking early retirement. I don't relish walking around Capitol Hill by myself with nothing to do. I want to travel, enjoy life, and I want you to join me. I am tired of living alone." Jan choked up, tears came to her eyes, she sat on his lap and cried. "Jan, did I screw up again? I have been rehearsing this all afternoon."

She broke out laughing. "You knuckle-head. I have been waiting for you to ask me to be your . . . well, woman, for years. What took you so long? When are you moving in?"

"After the wedding. I don't have much to move."

Jan couldn't contain herself when she arrived at school the next morning; she just blurted it out for all to hear, "I am retiring and will travel the world."

Her fellow teachers gathered around her to get the announcement firsthand. "When are you getting married?" was the question they all had.

"My man is moving in with me and we will be as married as you guys are." Thelma didn't take the news too well. Jealousy raised its ugly head. "Thelma, you are supposed to be happy for me."

"You are selling yourself to the highest bidder. Clark bought himself a whore."

"How can you say something like that; we are friends?"

Bill graduated; Jan finished her school term and resigned. She was all hyped up for Mark's wedding. Jim detested weddings; he'd once faked a furnace problem with his first wife only to read a book in a dingy furnace room while she attended the wedding by herself. He was looking forward to this wedding. He had a stake in it. Mark Bailey. He didn't concern himself with a gift since he had given Mark a truckload of furniture from his house a few months before.

The wedding was an event of happy relatives and friends. Jan was the star of the show. She was decked out in a yellow dress, wearing daisies Jim had bought for her. Frank Bailey, Mark's father, walked up to Jim and thanked him for giving Mark the truckload of furniture. "My pleasure, Frank. I needed to get rid of it when I sold the house and moved into a small apartment."

"My boys think the world of you," Frank said as he shook Jim's hand.

"Thank you, Frank. I never had children so I play uncle to the boys."

"The boys would like to see you marry Jan."

"That is a nice compliment coming from the boys but I had my chance at marriage and screwed it up."

Frank was celebrating his son's wedding with more booze than he could handle. He was not a drinker and it showed. Jan swirled across the ballroom floor to Jim, embraced him, and kissed him. This embarrassed Jim in the presence of Frank, her former husband. She looked youthful with her tan. Except for the gray in her golden hair, she could have been mistaken for the bride.

Frank returned with a fresh drink, holding the glass slightly tilted, spilling most of it. "Jim, watch out for her. I was married to her and she divorced me. Did she tell you why she divorced me?"

"Not that I can recall."

"You know I love teaching and coaching. It is my life, and she wanted me to give it up and go into business and make big bucks, like you. She is greedy, a pushy woman. Never underestimate her. She wants you for your money." Jim became uneasy listening to Frank's confessions of a failed marriage. "She said that I was not

aggressive enough for her." Jim looked for ways to disengage himself from this conversation. He saw Bill at the bar. "Yeah, she wants
your money and will get it; watch out for her."

"There is nothing evil in wanting to enjoy the fruits of one's
labors."

"She wants money but didn't want to risk her teaching job for
it. You know, I love teaching and coaching."

"Frank, you have the best of all worlds. You love your work. You
and Jan raised two fine boys. You have a good marriage. God, how
I envy you."

"She thinks money can buy happiness. Yes, she wanted me to
go into business, but I love teaching and coaching."

Jim felt very uncomfortable in this no-win situation. Bill saved
the day by waving him over to the bar. "Sorry about Dad. He's not
a drinker. Can't hold his booze."

"I noticed that. Thanks for rescuing me. Have you found a job?"

"Not yet, but I have some more interviews lined up; I am
hopeful."

"How do you feel about euthanasia?"

"What a question to ask at my brother's wedding."

"Here is a check for ten thousand dollars, your graduation gift
with a catch. I would like for you to come up with a farewell pill. Get
a patent, copyright a name, later obtain FDA approval and license
the pill to manufacturers. Times are changing and a farewell pill
eventually will be accepted by the public. Give it some thought. I
will keep funding the project as you make progress with the pill."

Bill took the check, smiled, and thanked Jim. He looked just like
his dad, black wavy hair, dark brown eyes, husky build, but he was
neither like his father nor his mother. Mark on the other hand looked
like his mother and had her temperament. Mark married a gal that
must have reminded him of his mom. Mary looked like a doll,
blue-eyed, blond hair, slender build, square shoulders, narrow waist,
and shapely legs. Mary, too, was a schoolteacher and had just finished her first year at the profession.

Jim and Jan returned to the townhouse acting like a couple of
newlyweds. Jan was happy; she had her man. After moving his
belongings into the townhouse he prepared for his trip to Deerpoint
to see Judge J. J. Crocker and do a little fly fishing. Jan needed time

to unwind from her recent highs and wanted to spend time with her female friends.

Jim found J. J. at the Last Chance Bar having lunch. "Jim, how is fly-fishing?"

"Not too good this morning but I will go back up this afternoon."

"I am selling the mine shaft."

"You are selling the Deerpoint history book?"

"Yes, too many memories. You are right about capital punishment. You are on target about the revolution. And I no longer consider you a loony. I apologize for calling you a crazy man. My father's untimely death woke me up. I see this country coming apart at the seams. The judicial system has broken down under the strains of liberalism. Our jails are full, the courts are jammed, violent prisoners are being released to make room for criminals of lesser offenses. We cannot house thirty percent of our population behind bars, it will bankrupt us."

"I want to buy the mine shaft."

"I won't sell it to you."

"Like many locals I have eyed the setting at the mine shaft for a chalet with steep roof lines, floor-to-ceiling smoked glass windows, a couple of fireplaces, steam room, garage beneath the chalet dug into the ground. I would set the chalet right up against the mountain."

"What would you do with the cabin and the outhouse?"

"I would move the cabin to the city square for community use and tear down the outhouse."

"Sounds like a creative idea."

"You and I will set dynamite to the mine-shaft entrance and blow the damn thing shut."

"Jim, you got yourself a deal."

"Do you have the property listed with a real estate agent?"

"Yes, our local auctioneer and real estate man has an office in his house but is probably socializing somewhere around town."

"Good, I will find him and sign a contract to purchase the mine shaft. We should toast our deal with a short drink. How is Betsy?"

"She went back to Maryland to visit her brothers. She needed to get away from Deerpoint and me for a while. I took the funeral badly, and the town folks keep reminding her of my dad. Come by the house for a drink this evening before we go out for a steak dinner. You can sleep in the den. There will be just the two of us."

Jim nodded in agreement. "I will be by this evening."

Jim went to the mine-shaft property and walked the entire twenty-two acres. He could see that the bridge needed replacing, a sewer line had to be extended to the property, the water line was inadequate. He looked at the outhouse and the idea struck him that he had found a place to bury the gold bars. What a day, he had not planned on any of this; it had just happened. He wanted to move out of Denver and was looking for a safe place to bury his gold.

That evening J. J. discussed the local architect, general contractor, local attorney, and the various procedures involving annexation, zoning, and the building permit with Jim. Jim was prepared to pay the $220,000 in cash to the judge, but he would only accept $200,000. "You are paying me in cash; that is worth twenty-thousand to me." They shook hands on the deal despite the contract Jim had signed that afternoon. Jim liked hand-shake deals. It reminded him of how westerners used to do business. Colorado no longer was like the Old West and neither was America.

The two men were on the same wavelength again. They both knew that the United States of America had risen to a superpower of the world, become the economic engine of the world, and soon would have to face destruction in order to rise again as a reborn nation. The former university students enjoyed the evening as something out of the past, with one exception. They were both about forty years older. Jim never stopped dreaming and scheming, he believed in the future much like he did back in the fifties. J. J. was back in step with him. Jim had lost many friends in his journey through life because they stopped to dream. They became frozen in time, the past. Jim, on the other hand, planned too much into the future. He often missed enjoying the present. Jan constantly reminded him of that shortcoming in his character. After breakfast, the judge went to the courthouse and Jim hustled back to Denver. He had news, a new plan for Jan. He was anxious to see her. But first he had to stop in Denver to see the bean counter. He had to budget funds for the IRS, his new project, and maintain a steady cash flow. He no longer had rent money pouring into his bank account on a regular basis.

"Honey, I have a surprise for you," Jim told Jan.

"What is it?" she asked.

"How would you like to build a chalet on the mine-shaft property in Deerpoint?"

"Oh my, are you going to buy it?"

"I signed a contract for it. We will buy it and build a chalet on the twenty-two acres, and move away from the city. Do you want to be my partner?"

"I think it is a divine idea, but I want to keep the townhouse."

"Sure, we need a base in Denver. This will be our project. I arranged for an architect to draw up a rendition of the chalet and you are to lay out the interior, decorate it, and select the furniture. Shall we shake on it?" Jan hugged him. "So, is it a deal?"

"Thanks, honey, for making me part of your life. Yes, I am excited about our new love nest in the mountains." Both of them needed this project to give their lives a purposeful meaning and a new direction. "Oh, Jim, my youngest son called. He needs to see you about a secret project."

"Nothing secret about the farewell pill."

"What is 'the farewell pill?' "

"A peaceful method for people to make that final choice in life, through euthanasia. Bill is supposed to develop a pill and I offered to fund him."

"How horrible. Has he agreed to your plan?"

"Not yet. He will let me know today."

"I don't want my son involved in developing an instrument of death."

"Think of it as a method for civilized people to make their final choice, to make the trip to the promised land on their own terms, and not by those of society or by fate."

"I believe people should have the right to choose, but I disapprove of man interfering with God's work."

"I think you Lutherans are frustrated Catholics."

"I wish you would discuss these matters with me before you approach my boys with your off-the-cuff ideas. He told me that you gave him ten thousand dollars as a graduation gift. I didn't know you had strings attached to the gift."

"Hereafter, I will keep you informed of my dealings with your boys."

"Thank you."

Bill was late for lunch. Jim had already ordered. According to Jim, you ate lunch at noon; after a hard day's work, you ate supper, took a shower, and went to bed. His habits went back to the farm in eastern Colorado. He had not changed all that much from his past.

"Hi, Jim, I'm sorry I'm late."

"Sit down and order. What is your verdict?"

"You will not appreciate how I feel about the farewell pill."

"You are beginning to sound like my former property manager. Let's have it."

"Well, I don't think society is ready for your pill. The doctors are afraid of it, the lawyers see it as new business, the religious and governmental leaders will balk at the idea of euthanasia."

"So what else is new? I agree with your conclusions. However, today's thinking will change with the revolution that is sure to come upon us sooner than you can imagine. Bill, if you want to become successful, you have to come up with a good idea and support it with money. I gave you the idea and am supplying the funds; all you need to do is to do it."

"Why do you always come to this Greek restaurant?"

"I have been coming to this restaurant for thirty years. I like the burgers and the place is conveniently located for me. Do you see the old Greek sitting on his high chair reading a newspaper and smoking his cigar? That is the real reason for my coming in here."

"It is against the law for him to allow smoking in this place."

"If it is against the law to give the finger to social engineers, I am all for breaking the law." Bill twisted his head in disbelief. Jim reached into his billfold and handed Bill a check. "Here is forty thousand to go with my idea; go do something with it."

"Wow, thanks."

"Bill, I have a philosophy about making money that you should know about." Jim took a puff on his pipe. "Do something worthwhile for mankind and you shall profit thereby."

"Does Mother know about the pill?"

"This is between you and me. I have given you the idea and

money to become rich and maybe even famous. Let me see what you can do with your talents."

"I will give it a lot of thought."

"You do that."

The bean counter wanted to see Jim about the taxes that were coming due.

"Hi, Jim. Thanks for coming in. I came up with a plan to circumvent your tax bill."

"Is it legal? Will I have to go to jail for the circumvention?"

"Since you have most of your money in gold bullion or invested in foreign countries, with no assets in this country, we could fake a bankruptcy."

"Forget it. I will pay my taxes like all other citizens pay them."

Jim returned to the townhouse. Jan was home. She embraced him and he patted her firm left fanny. "Jim Clark, you are a dirty old man."

"And you entice me to be dirty." Jan was dressed in loose garments that reminded Jim of long underwear he wore on the prairies in eastern Colorado and again when he was in the infantry in Korea. "Why do you women wear long underwear in public?"

"Jim, you are old-fashioned. You are still living in the nineteenth century."

"Max accused me of that many times. Your son Bill thinks I am ahead of times, you think I am old-fashioned, Max thinks I am living in the past. My criticism of all you people is that you have forgotten where you came from and none of you have the faintest idea where you are going. What lies beyond today? Today's society lives for the present without regard for the future."

"Have it your way. To each his own."

"How about a trip to Guaymas, Mexico, for the holidays?"

"That sounds great, away from family, a trip tailor-made for the two of us. Hmm, sounds like our first honeymoon." She sat on his lap and smooched him.

"You make the arrangements and put the charges on this credit card that I had issued in both of our names."

"I love this togetherness."

"Tomorrow I have to drive up to Deerpoint. Our property is being presented to the city council for annexation."

"Should I come along?"

"No need to. It will be just another routine, boring trip. The day after I close the deal with J. J. I will put the property in both of our names."

"I will be a co-owner. I like that. Do you want co-ownership in my townhouse?"

"You and you alone are enough for my happiness."

"How romantic. Just like my Jim Clark." She liked to tease him when he was tenderly clumsy.

He drove his dirty old truck to Deerpoint and parked in front of the architect's office. He signed some papers and left a $75,000 deposit with the architect who was in charge of the project. The property survey of the twenty-two acres known as "the mine shaft" showed the existing structures and utility lines, with an overlay showing the proposed structure and utility lines. The mine shaft itself was at a high elevation on the property. "See you at the meeting tonight."

"J. J. and I will be there on time."

He went over to the Crocker house and visited with Betsy as they both waited for J. J. to come home. Betsy was her old self again and that was a pleasure for Jim. He liked Betsy. He waited for J. J. in the den, reading the newspaper and enjoying a sour mash on the rocks. Betsy's cooking always smelled better than anyone else's. That was a mystery to him. It was the ambiance; it was Betsy herself. J. J. arrived busting through the back door like a burglar. "Hello, Jim. Tonight is the night. You and Jan will officially become part of Deerpoint."

"I hope so. The architect tells me that the annexation will be a routine matter for the city council."

"They will approve it but not without a hassle. There is a gal in town who shows up at every town meeting and injects her unsolicited comments. She will belch out her bile. Be prepared." J. J. briefed Jim for the meeting in detail. "The town mayor is also the subcontractor who will be digging the footings, installing the utility lines, and doing the road and bridge work. The council has no grounds to reject your annexation plan. And if they do, there is always Mr. Silverman, our local attorney, who can scare the pants off the whole bunch." J. J. tossed out his two tokens and turned them over, showing the number two inscribed on the back. Jim laid his tokens on the coffee table, showing the number one on the back. Jim always carried his tokens with him and so did the judge. They had supper and went to their scheduled meeting.

The Deerpoint town council went through its normal process of paying bills and other general discussions and then moved to the matter of annexing the mine-shaft property. The architect made a very detailed presentation of the property and its planned use, then sat down. The mayor entertained comments from the attending residents and the gal, formerly from Boulder, now residing in Deerpoint, took the floor to provide her input.

Ms. Environmentalist cleared her throat and began her canned speech. "I like the way the property looks at the entrance of this quaint town. I like driving by the place and seeing smoke curl from the fireplace of the cabin. That neat little outhouse by the cabin represents the true image of our old mining town; it is the West and should be preserved. The entire landscape with the log cabin is like a Chamber of Commerce billboard for the town. I oppose Mr. Clark coming to this town as an outsider and throwing around his money and changing the landscape of the mine-shaft property forever. Deerpoint lost some of its true image when a ski area was forced down the throats of locals by outside money people. When out-of-state money comes to Deerpoint, the local real estate agents, contractors, developers, and greedy land owners suck up to these people and help them destroy this town." She sat down and the few attending this meeting sighed in relief. The mayor asked for further comments and nobody responded. He then looked at Jim and asked him if he had anything he wanted to present. Jim rose, walked over to the display holding the rendition of the chalet as it was to be located on the twenty-two acres, and then addressed the council.

"Ladies and gentlemen, I am buying twenty-two acres known as 'the mine shaft' property from Judge J. J. Crocker, and I intend to move the cabin and outhouse off the land and build a small chalet on the property. The sewer district wants the property hooked up to the sewer system, the county wants the hazardous mine-shaft opening closed off permanently, the city wants the property annexed for tax and zoning reasons." He pointed to the drawings. "Once upon a time there were trees along this stream, but the miners cut them

70

down. As this sketch shows, I will plant a grove of aspen trees along the stream and place a few spruce trees among the aspen and around the chalet and on both sides of the bridge, which I will have to rebuild to city specifications. The small chalet will be tucked against the mountain and, hopefully, blend in nicely." He turned around to face Ms. Liberal and addressed her.

"I am not from out of state. I grew up on the eastern plains of Colorado. I attended the university and graduated in four years; I did this on the Korean G.I. Bill. You, Miss, spent eight years at the university earning degrees in many things including social engineering. Do you realize how many Colorado tax dollars you wasted fiddling round in the People's Republic of Boulder smoking grass and cogitating your bewildered destiny? Then you moved to Deerpoint and have been harassing the locals and natives like myself, while you are sucking off your family fortune that generations of your family toiled to amass. You are a lost flower child, who grew up with wealth back East, and now you are here and we are stuck with you. Why don't you go back East or move back to the People's Republic of Boulder?" He sat down and waited for the council's next move.

The mayor called for a vote but was sidetracked by a mousy little council woman at the end of the table. She wanted the matter tabled.

Jim rose and addressed the mayor. "If you people do not vote on my petition this evening I will turn the matter over to Mr. Silverman. Judge Crocker and I will be at the Last Chance Bar." Jim and J. J. departed.

"Ms. Liberal was on the warpath because she failed to purchase the property from me," explained J. J.

"I didn't know she made a bid."

"She offered two hundred thousand dollars with terms of ten years. She was trying to fit the payments in with her annual allowance from the family trust. I rejected the offer."

"So she was ticked off about the sale rather than what I was going to do with the property?"

"Yes."

"I could have built twenty to thirty condominiums on the land."

"She has made a real pest out of herself in this town. No one has summoned the courage to address her because we are an intimate people here. Did you talk to Silverman?"

"No. I never met the man. You recommended him."

"He puts the fear of God into the people around here. He never loses a case. He was one of the best criminal attorneys in Denver."

"What is he doing up here?"

"He is here for the same reason you are moving to Deerpoint. He got fed up with the rat race in Denver. He practices law for the sheer joy of it. He doesn't need the money."

They seated themselves in the Last Chance Bar and ordered their usual round of drinks. "Who was the cowboy and the good-looking buxom lady seated behind the gal who opposed my annexation?"

"Oh, that is my old friend and his wife, Joe and Shirley Parker."

"He was smiling as I dressed down the feminist, environmentalist, or whatever she pretends to be."

"He loved every minute of it. Joe and I go way back, we both grew up in Deerpoint. Joe never liked ranching but his father kept him on the land with personal favors. First, he put in a gravel air strip for Joe. He loves to fly. Then he sent Joe to Fort Collins, Colorado State College. Two years later the Korean War broke out and Joe joined the air force. He finished his tour of duty and returned to Deerpoint."

"Sounds like my past."

"Very much like your past. He married a local woman. His father died and Joe stuck with the ranch, for better or worse. Joe was like his father and therein lies the rub. They could never agree on anything."

"My father and I didn't get along for the same reasons; we both wanted to be boss. He was and I wasn't. My sister and her husband took over the firm and that made him happy. Joe's wife looks much younger than he."

"His first wife passed away and he met Shirley. Shirley came up from Denver to sell real estate. She and Joe met in this very bar and it was love at first sight."

"Joe finally found happiness. Good for him."

"He and Shirley fly to Las Vegas every month, he loves to roll the dice. You probably noticed that big Cadillac around town. That belongs to Joe. He is Mr. Republican in this country. Joe is a colorful character."

"I would like to meet him sometime."

J. J. nodded and said, "Speak of the devil and he shall arrive in the flesh." As Joe and Shirley walked in, he took off his cowboy hat and gave them a salute. He marched up to Jim and extended his hand.

"I wanted to meet you and congratulate you for telling that broad to move her ass back to the People's Republic of Boulder." They sat down with J. J. and Jim. "The council approved your petition for annexation of the mine-shaft property."

"Great. I am relieved. Now we can celebrate." Jim became an instant hero. If only for one day or maybe only for one night, nevertheless it felt good to win with honor. Shirley was a down-to-earth gal with a great sense of humor. She complemented Joe in many ways.

"J. J., I was happy to hear that your dad's killers got nailed. I considered going after them myself."

"Someone else beat you to that task."

J. J. and Jim returned to the house and made up a bed in the den for Jim. "I used to help Joe drive cattle from the ranch up through town to the mountains for summer grazing. Joe never made money with cattle, he came into big bucks when the ski area was built. His ranch stretches two miles along the river and it is all gravel. I put up some cash and signed loans with him at the bank and we have been in the sand and gravel business ever since."

"I didn't know you were a local investor."

"I have a thirty percent interest in the Last Chance Bar."

"You probably drink up most of the profits."

"That's what Betsy thinks. Have a good night's sleep. We will wake you for breakfast." Jim fell asleep easily.

Jim had a place to bury his gold. He had had visions of moving to the mountains for years, but it had always remained a dream, but tomorrow he and Jan would become the owners of the mine shaft. The following day, before going back to Denver, he walked the twenty-two acres again to satisfy himself.

As he approached Denver he turned on his radio in the truck for music but instead located the news. The mayor was pleading for

73

peace in the streets of Denver. He wanted to increase the police force to deter violence. The news commentator thought that the mayor's intentions were admirable but in vain. He pointed out that the criminal forces had an edge on the police and society. He reviewed an incident of the past week about the guy who shot it up on a bus. Five were dead and five wounded; the police paralyzed the killer. The commentator enumerated how the lives of ten families have been affected by this mayhem. The five wounded would require medical help, the five dead would leave vacuums in the lives of their families. They all were innocent people, victims of crime. The crippled killer would be an expense to society for the rest of his life. What a waste. He suggested that one bullet from the police officer's gun during the criminal's first encounter with the law years ago would have saved the community in many ways. He summarized the report with his opinion on the cost of too much liberalism. Jim shut off the radio and tried to block out what he had heard. He turned his mind to Jan's Christmas gift. He parked the truck near the Fine Jewelry store.

Fred was cheerful this time of the year. He was selling merchandise. "Fred, I want a big diamond mounted on a solid band for Jan and a wedding band."

"You are getting married?"

"Not exactly."

"How much money do you want to spend?"

"Two hundred and fifty thousand for the diamond and about one hundred thousand dollars for the wedding band."

"Holy smoke! I would have to order them; I don't carry anything like that in my inventory."

"I want them for Christmas."

"No problem with that."

Jim was full of excitement, he could hardly wait to see Jan.

He knocked on her door and there she was to greet him with open arms. She hugged him as always and then gave him a little kiss and he patted her firm left fanny. "Honey, how did it go?"

"We are the owners of the mine shaft."

"I made the arrangements for our trip to Guaymas, Mexico. We leave in three weeks. Let's go out for dinner. I didn't know if you would be back today."

74

"I'm sorry, I forgot to call."

"I understand; these are exciting times for us."

"They sure are. Everything seems to happen so fast."

The following day was one of those gorgeous, mild December days; they went to the Gates Tennis Center to hit some tennis balls. Doc showed up, he was looking for a game. Jan opted out for the Cherry Creek Shopping Center to do some Christmas shopping. Jim and Doc did their thing on the court and resigned themselves to a soda pop on the bench facing the southwesterly December sun.

"Are you prepared for the holidays?" asked Doc, making conversation.

"Sure am. Jan and I are flying down to Guaymas, Mexico for a few weeks. I have a surprise for her, a two-hundred-and-fifty-thousand-dollar diamond and a one-hundred-thousand-dollar wedding ring."

"I see you have taken my advice to marry the woman."

"Not exactly; the next thing to marriage."

"You might as well enjoy your money now; you are not getting any younger. How has your health been?"

"Good. Don't worry about my condition, we all have to die sometime."

"You should come in for your annual physical before you go to Mexico."

"I will. I moved some money into Mexico but am a bit apprehensive about their government and economy; they seem to move from one catastrophe to another and fail to reach any stability in their country."

"Are you still buying gold?"

"No, I am finished with that part of my defense plan. Now I am moving money out of the country, I just placed some money in Canada."

"Are you really serious about the coming revolution?"

"I know the country will have to declare bankruptcy sooner or later. The revolution itself is a mystery to me."

"Last weekend I worked with some young doctors in the emergency room. I felt like I was back in Korea in a M.A.S.H. unit. The casualties were coming in faster than we could cope with. I think the violent part of the revolution is happening right now and has been taking place for sometime. We don't recognize it as such because we have accepted violence as part of our daily lives. The large cities throughout our country are the battlefields."

"Now you are beginning to sound like me. My friends think I am paranoid. I sometimes think of you as a liberal."

"If I am a liberal you are an ultra conservative."

"I am not a conservative, I am a realist; and you, Doc, are a person in science who is constantly exposed to liberal thinking."

"Don't you think we all have liberal tendencies?"

"Sure, after three or four decades of liberal thinking in an affluent society we all have become victims of the liberal movement."

"When did it start in this country?"

"Probably when we were in college. I remember the debate between capital punishment and rehabilitation. I lost out on capital punishment in the classroom. Professors in political science departments preached federalism, to push changes down from a national level upon local governments to equalize every town and county in the country. It all sounded so idealistic, even I believed the professors at first."

"Most of my friends in the medical circles are liberal thinkers."

"So are my friends. They are wonderful people. Liberals are mostly well-educated professional people who mean to improve the welfare of mankind but fail to see the probability of dependency. When I was in school we labeled people as socialist if they invited government into their lives."

"I think I finally understand what you have been trying to tell me all these years. The easy way out of a situation is not necessarily the prudent solution to a social problem in the long run."

"Doc, you are catching on. Finally you are seeing the light at the end of the tunnel. People have been passing the buck for years. Let someone else do the dirty work; it is not my fault, I am not responsible for my actions; it is my parents fault; the government is responsible for me. And some criminals profess that the devil made them do evil things, that they are not accountable for their acts."

"Jim, who is the real enemy out in the street?"

"We are the enemy, we have done it to ourselves."

"How can we prevent the big revolution?"

"We can't, it is too late. The president of the United States with the backing of our Congress could avoid the giant vortex that will swallow up this country and flush it out to sea. Somehow we need to go through a massive catharsis and start all over again as a new nation."

"What advice do you have for me? Should I buy gold?"

"I have my opinions, as my friends remind me occasionally, but I don't give out advice as a rule. However, in your case, I would suggest that you invest some money in Canada. Plant a garden in your back yard and make friends with a farmer who raises grain, cattle, hogs, and chickens. You still eat meat don't you?"

"I will deposit some money in a Canadian bank but the garden and the farmer with grain and fresh meat is a bit far out for me."

Jan returned from her shopping trip.

"Jan, Jim tells me you two are going to spend the holidays in Mexico."

"That's right, our little honeymoon. I think I earned one, don't you agree?"

"You should receive a medal for living with a crazy man."

"Doc, why do you have to confirm what my friends think of me? Judge J. J. Crocker in Deerpoint used to think I was wacky and now he is a believer and follower of mine," Jim pointed out.

"Do you know Judge Schultz?"

"Never met him."

"He and Judge Crocker were in the same law class at Colorado University. I saw him last week. He talked about a revolution, and I didn't put much credence into his comments at the time."

"Did Jim tell you that we are going to build a chalet in Deerpoint?"

"No. He didn't tell me that you two were moving away."

"We are going to keep the townhouse; it will be our Denver base."

"Thanks you for the match, Jim; I will go home and see if I still have a wife."

Jan smiled at Doc and said, "You do. She will be waiting for you."'

"Bye now." Jim put his arm around Jan's shoulders and walked her to the car.

"I am glad you have Doc as your friend. He seems like a very interesting person."

"He is a great man; he understands people."

"I like J. J. and Betsy, but J. J. can be so insensitive at times."

"He has been sitting on the bench for too many years. I think it has callused him."

"Doc has seen the seamy side of life and he is a gracious, gentle person."

"Individuals react differently to the same experiences, one of man's phenomenal characteristics. You are an ex-school teacher; explain it to me."

"It will be a cold day in hell should I ever win an argument with you."

"Try me."

They returned home and as they walked into the kitchen Jim cleared his throat and said, "Jan, I bought a couple of rings for you as a Christmas present."

"Oh my, you have become a romantic."

"Fred Goldsmith at the Fine Jewelry wants your ring size. Would you stop by tomorrow and have yourself sized up? . . . Well, you know what I mean." She hugged him and planted many kisses on him. He patted her firm spot.

The evening news was about to come on so he slouched down in the living room chair. Jan took her shower and he followed her while she was preparing supper. They had established a routine after many years of living together on a part-time basis. The news didn't vary much from day to day. On this day the police killed two innocent bystanders while chasing down a drug dealer. Schoolteachers threatened to go on strike and a storm was going to hit the city later in the evening.

There was a short report on Wall Street. The boys in New York are concerned over the increase in the supply of money, interest rates moved up to 20 percent, inflation remained at 15 percent and the national debit was a $8 trillion. The pundits on Wall Street fear that the national debit will eventually topple the federal government. They see instability in the market place. The report was typically vague and glossy in content and difficult for the public to relate to. The viewer had to guess between statements to find the real message.

Jim took a deep breath and picked up the newspaper. He was working from the comic section toward the business report when the phone rang. It was the manager of the apartment building he used to live in.

"Mr. Clark?"

"Speaking."

"I need that locker space you are using. Could you move out your belongings?"

"When?"

"Before the first of January."

"OK. I will clean out the locker and leave it unlocked for you."

"Thank you."

Jim finished the paper and took a shower. Jan fixed a light meal, small portions of meat, fresh bread, noodles, and vegetables. Jim loved his fresh bread and butter.

"I like your style of cooking."

"How is that?"

"You seldom cook in grease. I am lost in a kitchen without a greasy frying pan. I need to clean out my locker in the apartment building I used to live in and move my things to J. J.'s garage. Do you want to come along for the ride tomorrow?"

"I would love to walk around the mine-shaft property and see the architect's drawings of the chalet."

The next morning Jim loaded his weaponry and ammunition onto the truck bed and wrapped a green tarp around it. They called Betsy and briefed her on the trip and then motored off to the mountains. Trips to Deerpoint had become repetitious for Jim, but he didn't mind this trip since he had the company of Jan with him. They had many things to discuss, the chalet, moving to Deerpoint and their honeymoon trip to Guaymas, Mexico.

After arranging for a motel room they went to the Last Chance Bar. The judge was having lunch with someone so they sat at a table for two and continued their conversation about the chalet, Mexico, and moving to Deerpoint.

"Hi, guys. What brings you to Deerpoint today?"

"I have a few boxes I need to store in your basement until our place is built."

"We have plenty of storage space."

"We have a room at the motel for the night, but we would like to have dinner at the steak house with you and Betsy this evening."

"Fine with me. Let Betsy know of our plans."

Jim unloaded his cargo at the Crocker house. Jan and he spent the afternoon at the architect's office. This was a first time experience for each of them, they had never planned or built a house of their own before. Jan was in her glory; she dug into the interior of the chalet. Jim cared only about the outside of the building and the grounds. They walked the mine-shaft property and returned to their motel for some rest and prepared for dinner.

"Jan, thanks for taking over the interior of the chalet."

"Honey, for me this is a dream come true, I am loving every minute of it."

"Good, I will stay out of your way."

"I have color schemes, a floor plan . . . I have so many ideas to review, I don't know where to start."

"Do your floor plan and then stick with it and the rest will fall into place."

During dinner Jim told J. J. what he had in the boxes. J. J. winked at him and said, "I know the revolution is on its way, and you are smart to be well-equipped for it. The tokens are in place. Watch for their effects in news reports. You will be able to recognize token activity from time to time." J. J. was discreet in the way he conveyed his clandestine message to Jim.

The next day, on their way back to Denver, they walked the entire twenty-two acres of the mine-shaft property again and studied the site where the chalet was to be located. They walked up to the chalet site. It had a commanding view of the valley to the north, the town and ski area to the south, and the stream with a bridge across it to the east. Architectural drawings showed the foundation of the chalet dug into the mountain below the mine shaft with a garage below the chalet. They were thoroughly satisfied. They returned to Denver.

Jan rambled on about the floor plan of the chalet as Jim bounced the old truck towards home. Jim's mind was already in Mexico, he had not told her about the connection he was planning in Vancouver, Canada. The trip seemed short in distance because he had his companion with him to pass the time.

Jim picked up the rings from Goldsmith. Jan distributed her Christmas presents and gave everyone a seasonal hug. Jim finished his tennis game with Doc and said, "Happy Santa Day, I will see you when I get back in a couple of weeks or months."

"Merry Christmas, Jim. See you when you get back."

On the flight down to Guaymas they held hands like a newly-wed couple, napping most of the way. When the plane landed in Guaymas Jan sprang to life. So did Jim. Neither had ever been to Mexico before. Jim had plans that would bring them back many times. They went through the normal tourist's exercise, running around and trying to see everything on the first day; they soon slowed down to a moderate Mexican pace. They rented a little convertible sports car and toured the area by maps on brochures of newly built complexes. They found a large development built on a mesa overlooking the town and the bay where a boat dock was located. Jan was spinning in a circle by the pool and said, "Let's buy today."

"Not so fast. I want to check out who built it, who runs the operation, and what we can get for our money in this foreign country." The complex was blockaded for maximum privacy and probably protection. The Mexicans always build a wall around their dwellings and for a good reason. There was a guard on duty at the gate twenty-four hours a day. That impressed Jim. Jan was taken in by the large swimming pool in the center of the complex and a dozen or more tennis courts at the end of the horseshoe-shaped complex. The manager turned out to be an American in his midthirties, who had worked with the developer for a number of years. They had built and sold complexes like this in California with Mexican investors and the same group had put together this complex. He showed them a one-bedroom unit completely furnished down to the dishes in the kitchen and the linens on the beds. One hour later they signed the papers to purchase the villa. The very next day they moved into their unit for the remainder of their vacation.

On Christmas Eve Jim presented his gift of rings to Jan. She put on the rings, sat down, and cried like she always did when she was extremely happy. Jim got on his knees before her, placed his hands on her thighs, and asked her if she would be his woman forever. She kissed him on the forehead and he didn't mind.

"My God, this stone is so big. How much did it cost?"

"Two hundred thousand. The wedding band with the small diamonds cost a mere one hundred thousand dollars."

"Oh, they are so beautiful. Why so much?"

"Consider it an investment, an ace in the hole, should you ever be in a predicament that may require quick cash."

"You are thinking about the revolution?"

"Yes, but let's not talk about that now. We are two people on vacation, having the time of our lives, and nothing should distract us."

"Thanks, honey. Why a wedding band?"

"You and I are married in our own way, an unwritten contract between the two of us. Don't cry again. We have a Christmas dinner reservation, I want you to look your best." She dressed in a light tan suit. With a trace of lipstick, her new flashy rings, and a set of gold earrings, she looked like a million bucks. They enjoyed their dinner and more.

They needed a car to go with the villa. Jan picked out a yellow convertible sports car. It was easy for them to fall into the lifestyle of a tourist with nothing to do but swim, play tennis, go sailing and deep-sea fishing. They ate their evening meal on the patio at sunset and had breakfast on the patio with two newspapers from the states every morning. They took many little tours in their convertible and drove the two miles into town for lunch every day.

"Jan, do you realize it is the middle of March? We probably should be thinking about Deerpoint soon."

"I want to go home but I don't want to leave our Mexican love nest."

"This is the year we are to build our haven in the mountains, remember."

"We better go back to reality." Upon their arrival in Denver, Jan immediately had her boys and Mary over for dinner. She had so much to share with them. Jan showed Jim love of family that he had never known.

Jim called a meeting with his bean counter and legal counsel. He walked into their meeting room to find them all ears in waiting. "The first thing I must do is to change my will and split the estate between Jan and my sister. Secondly, I will run everything through your offices since I will be living in Deerpoint, sometimes in Guayma. And this fall I intend to buy a place in Vancouver."

"Did you get married in Mexico?"

"Not legally. Emotionally yes, and that is all that matters to me." The bean counter and the attorney both clapped. "Thanks, guys. I intend to survive the revolution in one place or another with most of my funds invested in Canada." The two fellows grew numb, this no longer was just rhetoric. Jim Clark was into his defense strategy. He signed the revised will and slipped a folded piece of paper into the envelope with the will and sealed it.

"Since my sister is the administrator of my estate, only she shall have access to this envelope in the event of my death."

"I understand, Jim." They shook hands and he departed. The bean counter looked at the attorney and said, "Mr. Clark has done some bizarre things in the past but nothing so deliberate and with such conviction."

Jim made a three-day trip to Deerpoint to oversee the blasting of the mine shaft and the removal of the cabin. He had the cabin moved to the town square. He suggested to the architect that the environmentalist from Boulder pay for a foundation for the cabin. He said, "Let her get involved with the community she so much wants to protect from me."

It was time to blast the mine shaft. J. J. was like a little kid playing with fire crackers. He couldn't wait to push the handle that set off the blast. The moment finally arrived and J. J. pushed the handle. The entire town shook. The mine shaft closed in a cloud of dust, with boulders tumbling down the mountainside. No one was hurt, thanks to the quick feet of the foreman and Ace. Two huge boulders rolled down and blocked the bridge. The foreman was quick to point out that the boulders could easily be pushed aside and could serve as monuments at the bridge entrance. Jim agreed. Ace cranked up the bulldozer and moved the boulders. They demolished the outhouse and hauled it off with other junk Mr. Crocker had accumulated. Jim asked Ace to scoop out the pit of the former outhouse with the backhoe so he could search for artifacts. Jim was not interested in artifacts; he had something else in mind. Jim jumped into the hole and leveled off the bottom. He discovered a few whiskey bottles and some coins.

Jim stopped at the architect's office before leaving Deerpoint. He then rolled his dirty old pickup towards the superhighway and shifted into high gear; he was on his way home. Jan saw the old truck rumble into the garage driveway. She went down to greet him.

"Welcome home, honey. How did it go up there?"

"Well, J. J. fulfilled one of his childhood dreams. He set off the dynamite. The whole town shook for a few seconds."

"Sounds like you guys had fun."

"He did. He was like a little kid today." They went upstairs to rehash the day's events in detail. After lunch Jim paced the living room floor.

"What is bothering you?"

"I don't have anything to do."

"You can accompany me to the furniture store. And then, I have an appointment with a lady who designs kitchens."

"I would only get in your way. This is your project. Besides, shopping is a real killer for me." She gave him a light kiss and was gone. Her golden hair blended in with her recent tan. A few more freckles showed; what a beautiful woman. He was alone with nothing to do. It was time for a hair cut. He stashed his tennis racket behind the truck seat in case the urge hit him to pick up a game at the tennis center.

Clem's barber shop was the same as he had left it months ago, the same chairs, same cutters and clippers, the same Clem.

"Hello, Clem."

"Why, our long lost landlord from queer hill. Have a chair and I will trim you up." They were happy to see him, they needed someone to needle. The fellows were like a pack of wolves; they would pick a subject, sniff around it and then choose up sides and attack the prey. "Where have you been? We haven't seen you since the holidays."

"I am retired. Jan and I spent the winter in Guaymas, Mexico."

The barber in the third chair threw the first knife, "Must be nice to have money."

Jim turned and gave him a shot from the hip, "Sure as hell is. I enjoyed myself." Jim knew that the top dog, Clem, would come to his rescue if he needed help. Clem switched to the old subjects of graffiti wars, street people, and welfare. Sooner or later he managed to irritate a liberal and the hunt was on. This was better than radio talk shows, this was live, you could see the expressions on the victims' faces. Clem referred to hospitals and doctors as the medical industry without ethics. They are no better than sleazy lawyers. This started the ball rolling. The cutter at the third chair had his theories on AIDS. He suggested that it was a disease that punishes people who practice immoral behavior.

"God does not condone abnormal sexual practices nor will he tolerate the drug addicts."

Clem had his own theory on AIDS. He thought that it is a self-eradicating disease and some day would run its course and cleanse society of sex deviates.

The fellow working chair number five was hung up on capital punishment, which he felt tended to clean out scum from society on a selective basis.

The guy cutting at the fourth chair suggested that Mexican aliens would drag California into bankruptcy and a federal bail-out would most certainly kill this country.

Jim took his turn and spoke up, "I predict that this country will sink under its own largess, political neglect, and social misbehavior by the year 2000." Jim's statement silenced the shop.

The customer in chair six spoke. "We must help people raise themselves up to the middle class and become productive citizens."

A customer in chair three retorted, "We have made cripples out of a lot of people. They are as dependent on welfare as a caged animal is dependent on hand-outs. We have to force them into self-sufficiency."

"Jim, when do you think the shooting will start?"

"It already has. Watch the evening news and you can see it every day. The eruption will take place when the federal government declares bankruptcy."

"When is that?"

"On the day when the middle class and the silent majority take up arms and decide to free themselves from the shackles the liberals placed on them over the years." The room fell silent again. Jim paid Clem and drove to the tennis center.

It was a quiet day at the center. Doc was not around. Jim sat on the bench overlooking the tennis courts and contemplated his plight as a retired person. He had visualized a rotary engine for years but never attempted to build a model because it was obvious to him that it would never perform in the market place. On second thought, he decided to work on the idea; he would make some drawings of his idea. He returned to the townhouse which he now called home.

He was seated at Jan's desk when she arrived. "Honey, who are you writing to?"

"Nobody. I am making some drawings of a rotary engine, a project I never had time for in the past."

"I think I missed my true calling, I should have been an interior decorator."

"And I too missed my calling, I wanted to become an electrical engineer but didn't have the necessary courses in high school to make it into engineering school. Like you, I had to concern myself with making a living before I could fulfill my fantasy."

"Mark has a degree in electrical engineering. Have you asked him to help you?"

"He is not interested in my wild ideas. Besides, he has a job and wife to look after."

"Well, I can't help you. I only know how to teach, raise children, and play housewife."

"The contractors should have the utilities in place for the chalet. They've poured the foundation and probably are working on the bridge. I think I will go to Deerpoint for a few days."

"Do you want me to come along?"

"No need for you to go up there at this time."

The next morning he backed his truck up to the loading dock at the Bank of Colorado. They moved the thirty-two bars of gold bullion to the truck bed. He wrapped a green tarpaulin around the stack and fastened it with a rope.

The president of the bank watched the loading process and said, "You should keep the gold in our vault where it will be safe."

"Like hell. When the country declares bankruptcy, the federal authorities will grab everything in sight and you will let them have my gold. I will not leave my gold behind so that you can take it and satisfy the debits of your ill-fated bank. This gold is mine and I will do what I want to with it."

"Where are you going to store it? At one of your apartments?"

"Maybe I will and maybe I won't." Jim got into his truck and lit his pipe and turned the truck west towards the mountains; he was headed to Deerpoint. He never liked Fish Face very much. The president of the bank was such a pompous ass, a know-it-all. Smoking in the truck became a ritual since it was his last sanctuary to smoke in peace. Everybody bugged him about his pipe smoking, even motorists who passed him on the highway would make lewd gestures. As he motored along the four-lane highway he felt gratification. The bastards had taken away many things that he enjoyed, but they would not get the gold. Chugging across the Continental Divide in his old, four-wheel-drive truck, he looked like any other contractor heading to a construction site, except he didn't have crushed beer cans or other trash bouncing around in the truck. He crossed the little bridge and parked by the construction site of the chalet. The place was busy. About ten men were bustling around, digging trenches, laying water lines, a gas line, the sewer line, and making the electrical hookup. The landscaping boys were digging holes for the trees that had been spotted throughout the property. His timing was perfect. The crew was getting ready to knock off for the day. The foreman invited him to have a beer with the boys at the Last Chance Bar. He accepted but would take time to walk the property again and check the spotting of the trees. He backed up to the outhouse pit, took the loose bricks out of the truck, and laid a base in the hole. He then unloaded the gold and stacked it in the hole, placed the tarpaulin around it and shoveled dirt on top of it. He placed three small rocks in a triangle as markers and gleefully drove to the Last Chance Bar.

He walked in and saw the crew lined up at the bar. Ace commanded the view of the entire place from the far end of the bar. That was his official position in the pecking order among the patrons of the Last Chance Bar. He stood out among the crowd with his white hair. He had the demeanor of Mr. Stud personified. Jim bellied up to the bar with Ace and the foreman. His first words were, "A round for the boys."

"Ace, when will you be qualified to fly commercial planes?"

"In about six months."

J. J. and the subcontractor walked in and took their place with Jim at the end of the bar.

"I didn't know you were coming up today."

"Last-minute decision." He ordered drinks for J. J. and the subcontractor. The subcontractor, also the mayor, told Jim that he need not fear seeing the bitch from Boulder in here; this place would contaminate her soul. They all laughed.

Ace said, "Yeah, she probably is at home lying on the floor stroking her beaver and French inhaling grass." The crew related to that wise crack.

Jim knew it was time for him to leave but he waited around in hopes that J. J. would invite him for supper. "Judge, I will go to the motel and shower up."

"Come up to the house at about six-thirty. I think Betsy is cooking a ham for supper."

"I don't care what she is cooking; I will be there with bells on." Jim would remember the supper at the Crockers for the rest of his life.

J. J. started the conversation on liberalism during the middle of the meal. "Jim, the legal people are running this country."

"Don't I know it."

"Judges are getting involved in running prisons, bussing school children, and making business decisions. They legislate from the bench in every area of a citizen's life. They overrule laws that a majority of the citizens vote for. They are literally using their trusted positions to promote their own liberal agenda."

"People elect them after they have been appointed."

"Yes, I know that. A judge is suppose to weigh justice and not make laws or nullify a law of the people if it does not measure up to his liberal way of thinking. The liberals are everywhere. We have only one conservative on our state supreme court. The others are all liberals. Our governor has converted to the liberal cause. He calls himself a reborn thinker. It is against the unwritten law of the liberals to think politically incorrect. This is short of thought control. Your mayor in Denver and his wife are in the main stream of the welfare state."

"I remember while in school at Boulder our professors used to shock us with progressive ideas and now we are living the reality of those liberal thoughts."

Betsy spoke up, "We are suffering the consequences of the New

Deal, the War on Poverty, and social reforms of the Great Society. I believe that liberals are nice people who never envisioned the aftermath of give-away programs. People I talk to don't realize how we created a dependency in our society, they just don't know how we got to where we are today. If one does not know how they got into a mess they most likely will not be able to figure a way out of a mess. Oh, how I long for the days when I was a little girl in Maryland; life was so rich, so rewarding. I do miss those times."

Jim was back on his same old theory, "I think that America drifted into its final chapter as a super power like European nations have done through the centuries. It will take a massive economic down turn before America will reshape itself."

"Law and order will bring people back to basic values. A liberal judge let two Mexican killers off the hook and I freed Colorado of them. I believe in justice where justice is due." The statement hit Jim like a ton of bricks. He suspected the judge's involvement but did not know that he had taken the law into his own hands. Jim blocked out what should have been quite apparent to him. His stomach twisted, he swallowed hard, took a drink of water from his glass and regained his composure. Betsy watched him intently.

"The tokens work, Jim. You had a good idea and I implemented it."

Betsy looked directly at Jim and said, 'The tokens are in high places: the FBI, CIA, the Senate, the Defense Department, and the Supreme Court of the United States. We have to save this country while we still have a chance to do so." Jim was speechless. They moved to the den for coffee, an after-dinner drink, and a smoke of green-wrapped cigars. The judge liked his green-wrapped cigars. Betsy seated herself with the men to continue their dinner conversation. Jim was seeing a side of Betsy he had never noticed before. He wished to change the subject from the dinner discussion.

"Jan is working on a floor plan for the chalet."

"When is she going to present her floor plan to the architect?"

"Soon, I suspect."

"I am looking forward to having her in Deerpoint."

"We both are anxious to leave the big city. Hopefully, we will be living in the chalet by Christmas."

The judge took another puff on his cigar and said, "You can't imagine how pleased I am to see the twenty-two acres cleared of that cabin, outhouse, and all the other junk my dad kept around the place. I am adjusting to the sight of the cabin in our city square."

"I'd better turn in for the night."

"Are you staying over for another day?"

"No. I will go back to Denver tomorrow. I have someone special waiting for me in Denver."

"Ah, times have changed. I remember when you dreaded going back to a place called home. Matter as a fact, you refused to call your house a home. You said it was a place where you occasionally slept." Betsy gave Jim a smile. She was happy for him. She had seen him go through difficult times in the past.

"Why don't you retire, J. J.?"

"Not yet, I have too many irons in the fire."

Jim said good night to his host and went back to his motel room confused and perplexed. He didn't sleep well.

He had breakfast at the local cafe and then walked to the architect's office to check in; he had forgotten to do that the day before. He left the office and returned to the motel to call Jan and rent the motel room for a few more days.

"Jan Bailey speaking."

"Jan , you need to bring your floor plan to the architect."

"Do you want me to come today?"

"Yes. Take a flight with Eagle Airways and I will pick you up at the airport."

"I will be on the afternoon flight. Bye."

Jim checked the stones on his gold burial site, everything was intact. He had delegated all of the construction responsibilities to the architect; therefore he was not needed at the site. He meandered around downtown having coffee and smoking his pipe as he walked along the store fronts. He drove back down to the building site.

The subcontractor was building an intake box for the .125-cubic-feet-per-second water right. Mr. Crocker had maintained the water right but never made good use of it. Jim intended to pump water up from the stream to irrigate grass along with the aspen trees.

"Do you have a recorded water right?"

"I don't know. I assumed the water right came with the land."

"You'd better go and see Mr. Silverman. Have Mr. Crocker's water right transferred into your name."

"Thank you. I will do that."

Mr. Silverman and the judge would take care of the water conveyance. He sought to kill more time at the building site. He enjoyed that. He saw Eagle Airways land at the county airport from the upper part of the mine-shaft property; he hustled down to the airport shack. Jan got off the airplane carrying a briefcase and a carry-on bag. "I am glad you are here. I had no idea that we both were needed by the architect."

"Honey, I am here and ready to plan ahead."

"I always knew I could count on you." He gave her a little kiss on the cheek, then put his arm around her shoulders and walked her to the truck. He drove Jan to the architect's office and then returned to the building site. He took a balled-up juniper and planted it over the gold burial site.

Ace saw what he was doing and said, "The juniper should do well in that fertile ground?"

Another workman said, "There is rich soil beneath that scrub."

Jim replied to the wise guys, "It will grow and grow, I am sure of that." It was the end of the day for the crew. They went to the Last Chance Bar for a beer. Jim parked the pickup in front of the architect's office and left a note under the windshield wiper for Jan that read, "Last Chance Bar."

The scene at the bar was identical to his last visit to the bar. Ace was standing with the foreman at the end of the bar and the subcontractor stood behind them. Jim fulfilled the builder's duties, he ordered a round for the boys. Ace pointed to the corner of the seating area, "There is Ms. Activist of Deerpoint."

She was seated by herself at a table in the corner smoking a cigarette, drinking coffee, and reading a paperback book. "Hey, Ace, I bet she is not sexually active."

Ace was prepared for this piece of horseplay, "Here is twenty bucks that says I can lay her within one week."

No one challenged Ace on the wager. Jim shook his head, knowing that some things never change. Young guys still lie and brag to boost their egos. He left before the crew got raunchy. He saw the judge parking his little truck as he was leaving the bar. "Hi, Jim. I thought you went back to Denver."

"Had to stay over. Little details keep coming up."

"Why don't you stay at the house tonight?"

"Jan flew in this afternoon to meet with the architect; we will be staying at the motel."

"Do you care to join us for dinner at the steakhouse?"

"I will call Betsy. She probably would like to go out tonight."

Jan finished her day at the architect's office. Jim waited for her in the truck. "Honey, I made a new friend today, the gal who works with the architect. She and I are going to lay out the floor plan and she will help me with the interior throughout."

"Great, I will leave those details to you and your new-found friend." Jim was relieved; interior decorating can be a strain on a relationship. "I was thinking that it would be convenient to leave the truck at the airport; then we could fly back and forth and have transportation from the airport to our chalet."

"Great idea."

"I could also bring up my old roadster, the Fiat Spider," said Jim.

"I forgot you had that little car."

"My divorce car. I bought it the day after my divorce was final. Later, when I met you, we had a few rides in it."

"Oh, I remember you and I driving around Cherry Creek with the top down. Those were fun days, so romantic," Jan reminisced.

"We can leave the truck at the airport, fly back, and bring up the irrigation pump in the sports car."

"It would be neat to have the little car up here for the summer."

"That car is a worthless piece of junk, and a pain in the you-know-what."

"How can you say that? You courted me in that pretty little car."

"I never told you how many times it broke down on me, I have learned to hate that Italian bitch."

They prepared themselves for dinner with the Crockers at the Olde Steak House.

They were welcomed at the restaurant like locals; the Crockers commanded respect among the locals in Deerpoint. Betsy and Jan immersed themselves in conversation as J. J. and Jim got into their discussion. "Have you read about those assassinations of released prisoners who served time for killing citizens?"

"No. Were Mr. Crocker's killers victims of the tokens, a Director and terminator?"

"Yes. I planted a Terminator token with a state highway patrolman and placed a director token in the state supreme court, and Judge Schultz is working with the police chiefs in the Denver metro area. The Mexicans who killed my father had a record of running drugs from California to Colorado. On that particular day they made a delivery to Deerpoint and then shot my father because of his loose talk about gold in the mine shaft. The Denver police department executed the bastards and then planted drugs in the trunk of their car. They placed a call to the police department and the rest of it is a matter of record. Case closed, drug-related killing. Very swift, neat, and clean. The directors call the shots and cover for the terminators. They called it instant capital punishment."

"Who planted the tokens in Washington, D.C.?"

"Betsy's brothers. One works for the FBI and the other has connections all over Washington, D.C. Her father was a judge and her uncles are still active in law enforcement. It is my new approach in bringing back law and order to the citizens of this country. I took your idea and put it into action."

"J. J., you are going to start a shooting revolution."

"What about those guns you are storing in my basement?"

"They are for protection when the revolution kicks into gear after the country declares bankruptcy. The country could conceivably go broke and not have a shoot-out. I never intended to start a revolution."

"What about the graffiti wars you started in Denver?"

"I solved a problem in the short run, but, probably, it was a bad idea. I lost my appetite for vengeance and gave up the fight."

"So you lost and threw in the towel?"

"I decided to adapt and circumvent the entire ordeal that will face the country."

"You can't run away from yourself."

"No, but I can leave the country. Live some place where they shoot the bad guys and protect the good guys."

"I know of a few countries run by dictators where you would be very happy."

"Sometimes I think the world is not ready for democracy, not even the United States. We wasted trillions of dollars fighting the cold war, supporting the United Nations, and now the world hates our guts."

"The United Nations is nothing without American muscle. In theory the idea of a United Nations sounds great but in practice it is a failure. You said so yourself when we both were freshmen at the University of Colorado. I still remember how you expressed your feelings about the Korean police action fought under the United Nations banner. 'What a joke,' you said, and you were right."

"Law and order alone will not turn this country around. It would take a dictator with police powers to save America from itself."

"We can turn it around. We have to take the country back from the liberals."

Jan interrupted the two, "My, but you two are in a deep debate."

"Not really. Jan and I bought a villa in Guaymas, Mexico, as a vacation spot and a hide-out when the revolution gets rolling in America."

Jan gave Jim a stare, "Are we back on that subject again?"

"Jan and I decided to let the liberals and their counterparts face the music by themselves. After all, they wrote the music for this country years ago, let them face it."

"Law and order is only as good as people want it to be and the same applies to democracy."

"I couldn't agree more." They finished their meal with a quick cup of coffee. They had to go outside to enjoy a smoke.

Jim flipped on the TV at the motel room to catch the late news. Congress was concerned about the national debit, the Federal Reserve raised interest rates to put inflation into check. Business was booming, foreign money was still pouring into the country, and the stock market became more volatile. Gold prices rose again. Current values on the market were relative to the purchasing power of the dollar. Jim's initial investment in gold rose to $36 million, but what would it buy? He felt comfortable having buried the gold for the duration. A good night's sleep was needed by both of them.

"I see a tremendous change in you since you sold the apartments and retired."

"I live every day as if it were my last and I start every day the same way."

"How do you start your last day?"

"By sleeping late."

They slept late and had their leisurely breakfast. Jim put the bags into the truck. They drove to the building site. Every visit to the site of their dream home was reassuring. They had made the right decision to relocate in Deerpoint. They were killing time until Eagle Airways was due to take them back to Denver. Jim gave his dirty old black truck a sad look as they boarded their flight to Denver.

In Denver it was easy for them to pass time. Jan kept busy buying furniture, appliances, and wallpaper for the chalet. Jim darted around Denver looking for various parts for his rotary engine. "Jan, I think we should buy a condo in Vancouver after our next trip to Deerpoint.'

"Oh, I have never been up that way before."

"Neither have I."

"Is this another hide-a-way for us?"

"Exactly. I question Mexico's ability to remain economically viable during a downturn in this country and that is why I have already invested heavily in Canada."

"Whatever you say. It's your money."

"It is our money, our future. It is our salvation and I want you to be part of the decision."

"I have faith in you, Jim. I respect your business decisions; however, I don't share your thoughts on the demise of this country. You are pragmatic and I am, well, just me."

"Remain that way, I love you for what you are. Never mind my absurd reasoning. I did notice that my friends no longer are accusing me of being crazy for buying gold. Are they catching on or have they written me off as a lost cause?"

"Your friends respect you as I do. You have stimulated their brains; they are questioning themselves. Why would it make any difference to you what your friends think of you; you march to your own drum beat regardless."

"It is important to me what you think of me and my ideas."

95

"I am happy with our villa in Mexico, why not give Canada a try?" He put the irrigation pump into the trunk and tied the trunk lid down with a rope, holding everything in place. Jan helped him fold back the canvas car top and they were off to the mountains once more.

"Jim, where are our bags?"

"I put them behind the seats." They hit the four-lane highway like a couple of tourists.

"Honey, I love cruising through the mountains with the top down. It makes me feel like a young chick." The Italian Fiat Spider purred and hummed as Jim shifted and accelerated along the passing lane. There wasn't any point in turning on the radio, playing tapes, or attempting a conversation while driving at high speeds with the top down; the thundering noise of the wind killed those thoughts. A rain cloud was cresting the mountain peaks. "Do you think we should put the top up?"

"No. It won't rain on us. We are about ten miles from Deerpoint." The car suddenly died. The engine cut out completely. "Damn it, I was afraid of this, giving out at the worst possible time."

Jim coasted a bit and then threw the car into gear and tried to start it, but it failed and came to a dead stop in the downpour. They put the top up and waited for the rain to subside. The small hail dropping on the canvas top gave the sound effect of being inside of a snare drum. Jim grew more apprehensive with every passing moment. His love-hate relationship with the sports car was about to hit a climax. The car had been an agony from the day he purchased it on an ill-fated notion, his divorce car. His wife divorced him and he took up with an Italian bitch, the sports car. Mountain showers come and go; this one gave way to bright sunshine within seconds.

Jim raised the hood of the car and peered inside, just like all men do under these circumstances. He didn't have the faintest idea what he was looking for. "I will take out a spark plug, lay it on the block, and you crank the engine. I want to see if there is a spark." Jan turned the ignition key, the car lurched forward, the hood came down on his head, he stumbled backwards almost into fast-moving traffic.

"God damn . . . car."

"I'm sorry, honey. The car was in gear."

"Get the bags out of the car; I am going to torch the bitch." He took the irrigation pump out of the trunk and unscrewed the gas cap on the car.

"Jim, you are crazy."

"That's what people keep telling me."

Jan took the two canvas luggage bags and started to walk down the road towards Deerpoint. He turned around and held his arms above his head in despair, then he slapped his hips. A patrol car pulled up, and a huge officer emerged from the car. He stood all of six feet and more in height, had a cigar jutting from the left side of his mouth, his right hand resting on a .44 magnum. The pistol looked like a toy on the hip of this man. "Having car problems?"

"Yeah, the bitch died on me."

"Is that your wife up there?"

"Yes."

"It is against the law to hitch a ride."

"Spare me. The last thing I need right now is a lecture on the law."

"Lock up the car and I will give you and the missus a ride into Deerpoint."

"Thanks, that is our destination." Jim lifted the irrigation pump with both hands out of the trunk for a second time. He then slammed the car doors shut and left the car unlocked, he never locked it or the truck; that was his way of avoiding break-ins.

"Do you need to take this along?"

"Yes. It is an irrigation pump, our reason for making this trip to Deerpoint."

The patrolman picked up the pump with one hand and dropped it into the backseat. He asked Jim if he had the keys to his car. He reached into his left pocket and removed some coins and the two tokens; he put them back into his pocket and reached for the keys in his right pocket, where he usually kept keys to vehicles. He looked up at the patrolman and said, "I have them. I think I will leave them in the car. Maybe someone will steal the damn thing."

The officer stared at Jim; he looked like a statue. Jim instantly knew that the officer had seen tokens before. He didn't know how to handle the situation. Fred Goldsmith and J. J. were the only people privileged to know about the tokens, or were they? The officer, wearing a pair of WWII pilot's sunglasses, left hand on his hip, his right resting on the pistol and that ever-present cigar in his mouth, asked, "Do you know Judge Crocker?"

"Yes, we have known each other since our days at the University of Colorado many years ago."

The officer stuck out his hand and introduced himself. They picked up Jan and motored towards Deerpoint. Jim packed his pipe with some golden burley, lit it, and started to puff on it. "It is against regulations to smoke in a state cruiser."

Jim looked at him and smirkingly said, "I noticed that." Jim turned his head around and said to Jan, "Don't fall asleep. You will miss the mountain scenery." She mockingly stuck out her tongue at him. The officer was smiling as he watched Jan sass Jim through the rearview mirror.

Jim was teasing her because she could nap, snore, sleep, drop dead in any position, under any circumstances, during any time of the day or night. Jim envied her. He was a light sleeper. The tensions of the inadvertent token flash had faded. Jim was relaxed riding in the cruiser.

"Could you drop us off at the airport; I have a truck parked near the terminal."

"Sure, no problem." The officer goosed the cruiser to get away from the cars following them; he hit seventy-five miles per hour at the press of the pedal. "What are you going to use the irrigation pump for?"

"We bought the mine-shaft property from J. J. I intend to pump stream water up to the aspen trees and the grass area. I want to utilize my water right."

"I saw the framing go up yesterday. You and the missus are going to have a nice place. Many a time I planned an A-frame house on that property, in my mind. What did the property sell for?"

"About two hundred."

"Thousand?"

"Two hundred thousand."

The patrolman pulled up to the lonely dirty old truck. "I have seen this truck around town before."

"You will see it a lot more often after Thanksgiving." The officer grabbed the pump with one hand and chucked it into the truck. "We are truly indebted to you. Thank you very much."

"Any time, partner." The officer extended his hand, Jim's fingers tingled from the vise-grip handshake.

Jim and Jan drove up to the building site. He immediately checked the burial site, it was unmolested. The framing of the chalet was up, the men were working on the roof, the chalet was taking shape. Ski instructors, ski patrolman, lift operators and sundry other seasonal employees made up the work force for contractors during the off season. The contractor already had built a little house for the irrigation pump which Jan referred to as the dog house.

"Jan, the men have started to put the electrical and plumbing in place, no more changes."

"I won't make any major changes. What are you going to do about the car?"

"I will have it towed back here. I think I will give it to Ace."

"You are going to give away that car?"

"I wouldn't call it a give-away, more like getting rid of a problem." They went to the architect's office where Jan met with her friend and Jim deposited another check into the construction account.

"I'd better leave an advance with you to meet future needs. Jan and I are going to Canada for a few weeks."

"Fifty thousand should cover us until you get back." The secretary said to Jim, "Your wife is well organized; she even has furniture on hold and ready to ship."

"She organizes me all the time."

Jan snapped back, "That will be the day."

The trip to Vancouver was another honeymoon. They fell in love with the surrounding water and lush green countryside. Buying the condo was quick and easy. The condo had a view overlooking the bay. Breakfast at sidewalk cafes gave them a European experience neither had ever had before.

"Our major investments aside from the gold in Denver will be in Canada until the revolution comes to an end," Jim said.

"I am so excited over this place, I love it."

"The people we met this morning at the bank will provide a cash flow for us while we reside in the States or wherever we will be during the revolution."

"I wish that the terms, bankruptcy, inflation, and all the other talk about a revolution were not part of our happiness equation."

"I must confess that those terms are the very reason we are doing what we are doing right now. I want to invest in some mining operations and probably will transfer most of our cash in Denver to this bank." Two weeks passed quickly and the chalet in Deerpoint beckoned them to return.

Thanksgiving soon would be upon them. They had work to do. They changed their mode of travel to and from Deerpoint by flying instead of bouncing around in the truck for nearly two hours each way. Jim played a lot of tennis to kill time. First he would hit balls with Jan and then play his daily match with Doc. After their match, as if by ritual, they had a soda pop. Seated on the bench they would discuss whatever came to mind.

"Well, Jim, we still have a country with business booming." Doc looked to Jim for a rebuttal.

"There usually is a boom before the bust."

"Where did you learn that, at the University School of Business?"

"I spent four short years at the University and forty years in the school of hard-knocks. Now where do you suppose I received my real education?" Doc took another sip from his soda bottle. Jim looked at Doc and asked the question, "You spent half of your life in one school or another; does that make you an expert in all fields?"

"I am a specialist with years and years of schooling. Young fellows fresh out of school have passed me up, I can't keep up with their pace."

A good looking gal with reddish hair and a handsome African-American guy came walking towards the club house. She spoke to Jim, "Hi, Jim, how are you?"

"I am fine. I didn't know you played tennis."

"I play at it. Bye."

"I always suspected you had something on the side and she confirms it."

"Doc, she was a tenant of mine for ten years and I swear to God she is a lesbian. She really puzzles me."

"She is probably researching her desire for procreation."

"You mean crossbreeding?"

100

"I advise patients to do just what she is about to do or has already done."

"What are you saying? She and her partner decided on a child so she gets bred across racial lines. Crossbreeding on a selective basis."

"You got it. One hell of a lot cheaper than the sperm bank; besides, natural selection probably is the best method, to my way of thinking."

"That reminds me of a scrawny, freckled-face redhead with a very heavy English accent that I saw in the supermarket a few years ago. She had with her two of the most beautiful brown children I had ever seen. At first I was dumbfounded and then I deduced that their father probably was a good-looking black sergeant who met this woman while he was stationed overseas. The children spoke excellent English, they were well groomed, they were gorgeous children."

"A classic case of selective breeding of a black man and too much inbreeding of a white woman."

"Crossbreeding can produce some phenomenal results."

"You should have become a scientist."

"I was fortunate to make it through a school of business. You are teasing me."

"The brown-and-black gene will survive the white gene. Eventually all people will be brown with very few whites or blacks in society."

"So the social engineers did get something right. Why is America hell bent to melt down into a brown pot?"

"Who knows? An all-brown pot of people will not guarantee peace within the borders of this country. Mankind will find a reason to kill each other. Either it will be about ideology or over material possessions."

"I fear the religious fanatics the most. They have no rationality about them."

"When I see religious fanatics attack an abortion clinic I am reminded of how Hitler came to power."

"Doc, I share those very same thoughts with you. Judge J. J. Crocker in Deerpoint keeps telling me how law and order will turn this country around, I don't see it that way."

"Judge Schultz sounds a lot like your friend Crocker, he talks of law and order as if it will be the panacea for all our social and economic problems."

"Doc, it will take a major crisis for America to reform itself into a civil nation. I see kids on TV shoot each other over a pair of tennis shoes or a sport jacket. Gang leaders protest city hall because of police brutality. They don't like getting caught and being arrested. Liberal judges and politically correct juries refuse to invoke capital punishment. Victims of crime plead for the death penalty, but are refused. Sad, isn't it?"

Doc finished his soda pop and said, "The middle class has been brainwashed into turning the other cheek. They are told to keep taking it on the chin and some day the criminals of our society will reform. They are supposed to learn from society by example."

"A bad piece of Christianity in my opinion. The criminal knows he can get away with murder in a liberal society."

"Jim, according to my friend Judge Schultz, there are forces working to counter the liberal movement."

"Law and order is only one problem we face in our failing country and it will not correct decades of wealth redistribution and wholesale political neglect by our citizens."

"Do you think your revolution will take place in our lifetime?"

"Doc, it is not my revolution. I am part of this nightmare like everyone else. Just because I am preparing for it does not mean that it will happen."

"I am teasing you."

"I know, but you have no idea how people shun me because of how I think. They want to control my thought process. There are times when I feel completely out of step with my countrymen."

"You are paying the price for planning into the future. Thanks for the match. I have to be on my way; rounds to make at the hospital. I will have to skip tomorrow's match. Attending a seminar."

Jim went home with nothing planned for the rest of the day. "Hi, honey, who won?"

"We play for the joy of the game and the conversation afterwards. Who wins or loses is not important." She gave him a hug; he responded with a half-hearted tap on her fanny.

"What are you going to do this afternoon?"

"I don't know? Read the paper, watch TV; retirement has its

drawbacks." He clicked the TV from station to station until he saw a special report on the execution of a local judge. He'd been shot leaving a gay party early in the morning. He was in drag. "Good, God! Jan, you should see this for yourself."

"That is gross. Terrible."

"Real life, Jan. He had a reputation of being against capital punishment and now he dies at the hands of instant capital punishment."

"You sound confusing to me. I don't understand."

"If you watched the news, you would understand what is happening in the streets and alleys of Denver."

"Look at this," he turned up the volume on the TV. The report indicated that a criminal who had committed four separate murders had been assassinated by a sniper from a building across the street from the city jail. They were transporting the prisoner from city jail to the state prison.

"Jim, I don't feel safe in Denver any more. Thank God we are moving to Deerpoint within a month."

"There might be hope for this country after all. Crime has become a dangerous occupation."

He came up with an idea that would occupy him for part of the afternoon. He would visit the Fine Jewelry Store. "Jan, I want to borrow your car this afternoon."

"Sure, I am not going anywhere. Why don't you buy yourself a new car?"

"Tomorrow we will buy you a new car and I will take your old car."

"What kind?"

"Whatever your heart desires?" He drove over to see Mr. Goldsmith.

"How are you, Jim?"

"I am getting along in retirement like most people. Bored to death. I want to look at watches today."

"How does Jan like her wedding rings?"

"She looks great in diamonds." While glancing at watches, which he had no intention of buying, he asked the question, "Are you still selling tokens?"

"Yes."

"To whom?"

"I don't know the people personally."

"Where do you ship them to?"

"Mostly to the Washington, D.C., area and some throughout the south."

"How about Colorado?"

"Judge Crocker asked me to keep that confidential." Jim selected an inexpensive watch and paid for it. "Thank you, Jim."

"Not a very big sale for you."

"I should have given you the watch."

"Fred, business is business." He left the store and had a cup of coffee.

Now he had a better understanding of what Crocker and his friend Schultz were up to. He concluded that the two judges had started their own revolution. It began with the execution of Mr. Crocker's two killers and now the two were terminating liberal judges and life-term convicts. He had planted the idea and they put it into action. As he drove back to the townhouse he was wondering where it would all end. Soon the police will be killing more bad guys than they arrest.

He tuned into Charlie, the radio talk show host, the obnoxious one. Charlie had helped Max reach his height and glory during the graffiti wars. He was hinting that he knew something no one else knew, how bad guys were getting snuffed out in the streets. News came to Charlie, but he never stopped searching for his own stories. He operated in his own sphere and avoided the usual news media sources. Charlie picked up on a young man who'd threatened to avenge his sister's death. A slime ball had cut a sixteen-year-old girl's throat after raping her. Her body had been found in a garbage container behind a convenience store. The brother made a statement to the press that he would kill the slime ball who'd done this to his sister. Two days later he retracted his statement. He apologized for his emotional outburst and promised to leave the matter for the police to solve. About two weeks later, as the slime ball was being transferred from one facility to another, a sniper picked him off. The police were investigating the execution of their prisoner.

Charlie's suspicious mind was at work. He tried to get the young man live on radio, but the man refused. Charlie persisted and learned that the young man had been instructed to retract his threatening statement to his sister's killer. He was told to avoid the press; they'd assured him that the slime ball would be terminated in due time. The young man never became a suspect in the death of his sister's murderer. He was playing softball with his team at the time of the termination. Jim was mulling over Charlie's verbiage and what he had read in the newspaper about the slime ball. He inadvertently by-passed the townhouse and drove to the west end of town in search of parts he wanted to incorporate into his rotary engine. He located a turbo-supercharger.

Since he did not have access to a workshop, he lost interest in his project from time to time. His ambition was to build a model and prove that he could make his idea work, knowing well in advance that the engine would never become a power machine in the marketplace. Jim had this strange trait of occasionally doing something for the sake of doing it. This did not fit in with his normal pragmatic approach to life. As he was driving back home, he passed the gun shop on Broadway where he had made his purchases two years previously. The store appeared busy with twenty or more customers. That seemed strange to him. He noticed more people hanging around the city square, more people in food and clothing lines, and for a moment he could feel a revolution in the air. He shrugged it all off and drove uphill to the townhouse. Retirement had changed his life. He was no longer in the mainstream of the Denver business community, and he lacked the street knowledge he'd once possessed.

"Hi, honey. Did you have a nice drive?"

"I picked up some parts for my rotary engine. Tomorrow we will buy a car for you."

"What kind of a car?"

"One that you like to be seen in and I like to ride in as a passenger."

"You are so cute when you come on to me." She stuck out her tongue at him in retaliation. "Honey, I am excited about the new car."

Jim reviewed his drawings of the rotary engine. On paper it looked exciting, but in the real world he knew it would never cut muster. He began dreaming of a concept that would aid a tennis instructor in teaching the serve. Jim saw many odd gyrations tennis players performed in vain, all in an attempt to have a great serve.

Few players ever developed a simply smooth motion that produced a strong consistent serve in a game of tennis. He had three basic concepts on this project and attempted to explore all of them to a conclusion. Jan was preparing supper. He clicked on the TV for the early news.

Washington, D.C., was discussing ideas on how to cut the budget. Revenues fell short of their expectations for the fiscal year. Congress suggested cutting the defense budget to offset the shortages in revenues, but the president adamantly refused to do that. The national debit had reached $10 trillion. The annual interest on $10 trillion consumed 50 percent of the annual budget. They could not stop the accruing interest; it would mount and be added to the national debit. Entitlement programs had been cut severely. The president insisted on monies for defense and foreign aid in order to maintain foreign policy, his first priority. The man is a foreign policy president or, as one reporter labeled him, a wannabe king of the world at the expense of the American taxpayer.

Congress in Washington, D.C., was out of sync with the times. They had visions of borrowing and spending the country back to prosperity and they had lost touch with their constituency years ago. Too many politicians were attempting to relive the post–WWII days and those days were gone forever. After WWII, America exported its labor, raw materials, and technology to the entire world without competition; it was a one-way street for America. The country was living a lie. It was no longer a superpower and soon will have to face bankruptcy. The politicians in Washington, D.C., failed to recognize the unrest on the home front and therein lay the fuse that soon would ignite the bomb, the revolution. The United States had been drifting in a downward direction for decades at an invisible pace and that decline was about to accelerate.

Jan had a list of car dealers she wanted to shop. Jim had one place in mind, the BMW dealer who also sold Mercedes. They visited the BMW dealership, where Jim picked out a Mercedes sports car and Jan selected the color of white. The car salesman. Jim's old friend, started on the paper work and Jan interrupted. "We have to look at some other cars before we make a major decision like this."

"OK, but we will be back."

The salesman smiled. He too knew that they would be back to

buy the car. Jim lay back for the rest of the day, mostly puffing on his pipe. Jan drove from dealership to dealership, looking and talking. By day's end she was utterly confused. They returned to the BMW–Mercedes dealership and brought Jan's dream car.

"Honey, would you mind driving home? I am too excited."

"How many cars did we look at today?"

"I don't know. I have what I want, a gorgeous convertible. I never imagined I'd own a car like this. Stop at the store for a couple of steaks; I want to celebrate at home this evening."

"OK, I will stop at the Queens Sooper."

"It is the King Soopers Market."

"We live in a queer neighborhood."

"A gay community."

They picked out two thick rib steaks and waited in line to check out behind a construction worker. He was dirty, dusty, and looked fatigued. In front of him was an obese woman and a gray-bearded fat man, probably in his fifties, with their chubby children. The construction worker's patience was running thin as the checker loaded two shopping carts full with groceries. The fat little kids screamed and messed around, as their parents shouted at them indiscriminately. The youngest one, about three years old, waddled back and forth between his brothers and sister.

Jim said to Jan, "Look at that kid. He reminds me of an oversized butter-ball turkey."

"Jim, for God's sake, not in public." The fat, bearded father pulled out a wad of food stamps and peeled them off to the cashier.

The construction worker became unglued. "How in the hell do you come by funny money like that? I could use some of that myself." The cashier was quick to hold off the construction worker, and the welfare family made their departure. Jan and Jim moved quickly through the check-out line and went home.

"Jan, what you saw at the store is a prelude to what will happen when the top blows off the economy."

"The construction worker was out of line."

"That construction laborer works hard every day to pay for his groceries and at the end of a long day he sees an obese family freeloading on him and he resents it."

"They have a right to live just like he does."

"Without the construction worker, that fat family would starve. I saw what he saw, an obese father and mother, who obviously cannot earn a living, receiving support from our government in the form of food stamps and other welfare, like housing, health care, and pocket money, and we are paying for it. We are rewarding that couple to raise obese children, who undoubtedly will carry on in the welfare tradition."

"I don't see it that way. I don't even want to think about it."

"The construction worker looked like the type of fellow who had a few guns in a rack at home and knows how to use them."

"What a warped mind."

"Liberals planted the seeds of welfare years ago; now their perennial flowers are in full bloom. Wait for the fallout, it won't be pretty."

Jan bounced around in the kitchen as Jim made a couple of drinks of Jim Beam on cracked ice. He sipped his drink as he watched the evening news. "Jan, come in and listen to this guy. Interestingly enough, the liberal media considers him an ultraconservative." She sat on the arm of the chair holding her drink with a napkin. The fellow in steel-rimmed glasses proceeded to make his commentary: "Politicians in Washington should heed the message Wall Street is sending to them, the country is on the verge of going broke. Foreigners are withdrawing their investments from the United States at an alarming rate. How will we finance our ten-trillion-dollar debit without foreign investments? Economists on Wall Street see our economy as weakening rapidly. We are a consumer society, importing more than we export. We are at the point of no return."

"He sounds just like you, Jim."

"I am not alone. There are others who see the handwriting on the wall."

"Honey, you invested money in Canada, bought lots of gold, and have it tucked away at the Bank of Colorado. We are safe and secure."

"I did all that and who thought I was crazy, mad, screwy?"

"I hope for the sake of our people that you are wrong."

"I, too, hope I am wrong. Our people chose to live a lie, but economic forces are trying to tell us the truth." Jim switched to his favored newsman, a fellow who'd been born in Montana, raised in

South Dakota, and graduated from the University of South Dakota. He liked him because he was a straightforward, trustworthy newsman. His kind were rare in the media business. He, like Jim Clark, had become an endangered species.

Jim took off his clothes and stuck his foot into the shower to check the water temperature when a thought crossed his mind. He walked into the kitchen with a drink in his hand and said, "Jan, I want to remind you that I told you so."

"My, my, my, look at you in your birthday suit, sipping a drink. Are you celebrating the coming of the New Year?"

"Now, now, who is being the smart ass?"

"Guess who I had for a teacher? How am I doing?"

Jim rolled his eyes and returned to the shower. Afterward he cooked the steaks on the char-broiler as he sipped on his drink. "We need to fly up to Deerpoint and check on the progress of our chalet."

"I have to finalize on carpeting and the window coverings tomorrow. When will they deliver my car?"

"In a couple of days."

The following day Jim walked downtown to buy some smoking pipes. He had bought pipes from Jerry over the past forty years. It was always nice to see Jerry. Seeing Jerry brought back the past, the good old days, as Jim cared to remember them. After he made his purchase of a dozen pipes, he sauntered over to the building that housed a stock exchange. He had done some business with this firm over the years. He was tempted to walk in and buy stock in a few small oil companies who were exploring for oil in foreign countries, but instead he sat down on a bench overlooking the city and county building of Denver on his right and the state Capitol Building on his left. There was a park and other open space between the two governmental structures. The park area was full of people, lying down, hanging around, people without any real purpose or direction. Jim's mind went into a daze. For a moment he thought the scene before him was in the future. He shook his head and walked over to the Bank of Colorado and there he transferred money he had in certificates of deposit to a bank in Vancouver. He had time to kill so he trudged up the hill to a café that he and Max used to frequent. He no sooner ordered a cup of coffee when he felt a slap on his shoulder from the back.

"Hello, Mr. Clark."

"Well, as I live and breathe, it's Max. Sit down and have a cup of java."

"Boy, you missed out on making some real big bucks."

"How is that? Let me guess. I sold out too soon."

"Yes, you did. You could have bought up most of the apartment buildings on Capitol Hill with a real estate man like me."

"Max, you are forgetting something. I have been around for a while. I have seen some good times and lived through a few bad times."

"Real estate is phenomenal right now. I put deals together and take a percentage of the action. Right now I have my hands on a couple of mil' throughout Metro Denver."

"How much on the down stroke?"

"Ten percent. I get the property appraised higher than the selling price and then come up with fresh cash to do another deal. One property appreciated ten percent in thirty days. There is lots of fast money to be made out there."

"Max, be careful and put some money away for a rainy day. You know the old saying, Easy come easy go."

"Mr. Clark."

Jim held up his hand and said, "Max, you don't work for me anymore; call me Jim."

"Mr., ah!, Jim, force of habit. Jim, you could be making big bucks with that money you put into gold."

"We shall see. We shall see."

According to Max, Max was the real estate man on the hill. They shook hands and parted. Max had not changed a bit and probably never would.

Jim walked to the townhouse. Jan was still out making purchases for the chalet. He called about the car. It was ready; he could pick it up anytime. He perked up. He had an opportunity to surprise Jan. He took a cab to the dealership and immediately drove Jan's new car to the Colorado License Bureau. Jim didn't like having a temporary license; he proudly installed the permanent plates and drove leisurely back to the townhouse. He parked the car in the driveway of the townhouse so Jan could see it from the kitchen window. He went upstairs. She was home. "Honey, I finished my buying spree today. How did you do?"

"I did real well, today. Look down there."

She leaned over the kitchen sink to peek and saw the car. "My car! It's my car! Isn't she beautiful?"

"Take off your apron and I will give you a demonstration ride." They did not celebrate that evening, both were too tired.

Jan got Jim out of bed early the next morning. She was anxious to drive her new car to the mountains, to her dream home. Getting up before eight in the morning was early for Jim. Jan took to the car like a duck takes to water. Besides, she was a good driver; she'd learned to drive tractors, trucks, and old cars on the farm back at McCook, Nebraska. Jan coasted into Deerpoint and turned to cross the little bridge, then parked the car away from the construction activity of the chalet.

Without failure, Jim checked the juniper tree that guarded his cache of gold. It was not a tree yet, more like a bush. It was undisturbed. He gave a sigh of relief. Part of the crew was cleaning up the construction derby. Others were inside putting the finishing touches on the walls, window, and door trimming. Ace and a couple of guys were spreading gravel on the newly graded driveway. The general contractor took Jim and Jan through the chalet, explaining unfinished details as they moved from room to room. Jan left for the architect's office to wrap up details on the interior of the chalet. Jim asked the general contractor to build a small work bench next to the utility room in the garage and frame it in. He agreed to do that for him.

"I will make my final payment to the architect, and he will pay you off in full."

"Thank you, Jim. I appreciate your prompt payments. Your architect has issued checks to me on this job without my requesting them; that has been a first-time experience for me. I like that. The boys are gathering for a beer at the Last Chance Bar, will you come?"

"Thank you for the invitation, I wouldn't miss it."

Jim walked down the slope for a chat with Ace. Ace was leaning on the tire of the road grader. "Hey, Mr. Clark, the sports car runs like a dream."

"It ought to. I had the engine rebuilt only a few months ago. What was wrong with the ignition?"

"The module went out. I replaced it. I will have the body refinished, inside and out."

"Don't kill yourself in that damn car. I took out the seat belts, as you may have noticed."

"Yeah, I noticed that. I only use seat belts when I fly. Are you coming to the Last Chance Bar for a beer?"

"I sure am."

Jan returned in her new Mercedes. All of the crew waved to her and eyeballed the car. The general contractor walked over to Jan and said, "These belong to you, I am told." Jan took the keys to the chalet and grabbed the contractor in a bear hug. He was taken by surprise. Jan hugged and kissed everybody in her delight. She had an effervescent, outgoing demeanor. "Jim, these keys are to our chalet."

"I know, dear. Don't lose them."

They rented a motel room for the last time in Deerpoint.

Jan drove up the road to visit with Betsy, and Jim went to the Last Chance Bar for the finale with the entire crew. The scene at the bar was a festive one. Thanksgiving was only a few weeks away and the week marked the end of the construction season for many of the guys who worked on the ski mountain during the winter. It was a change of seasons, like shifting gears for the entire town. Jim had forgotten to stop at the architect's office. He would do that the following day. J. J. strolled into the bar looking for Jim.

"How did you know I was in town?"

"Betsy called and told me that Jan was bouncing off the ceiling, she has the keys to the chalet with her. The girls made reservations at the Olde Steak House for us at seven."

"Let me set up a couple rounds of drinks for the boys and then you and I can sit at a table and discuss world affairs."

"I prefer to stand, I have been sitting on the bench all day."

"I think I am seeing effects of the tokens in Denver."

"Yes, you are. Judge Schultz has directed the termination of fifteen criminals, two liberal judges, and this is just the tip of the iceberg."

"I think Charlie, the radio talk show big-mouth, is about to figure out the puzzle surrounding the tokens."

"If he does, he will contribute to our cause."

"J. J., you should put some of your savings into a Canadian bank. I suspect the president will freeze all assets in the country. Too much money is being withdrawn by foreigners. American investors in government securities have probably already started to move money out of the country. When the stock market collapses, the president will have no choice but to devalue the dollar and ultimately declare bankruptcy."

"You have all your money in gold at the Bank of Colorado?"

"Not all of it. I just transferred another half million to my bank in Vancouver."

"How do you think real estate investments, business interests, and stocks will hold up if all hell breaks loose?"

"In the long haul, those investments will survive but may be difficult to hang onto through a long revolution. Cash, bonds, certificates of deposit, and other similar investments will become worthless. Inflation will devastate those kinds of investments and bankruptcy will annihilate them."

Joe Parker walked over to the judge and Jim. He was the epitome of the West. Cowboy hat, cowboy boots and that leathery face made him "the local" of Deerpoint. He was a Rocky Mountain rancher, now a sand and gravel man. "Looks like you, and the missus built quite a house on the edge of town."

"Thank you. We had hoped to be moved in by Thanksgiving, but we won't quite make it. Jan and I will throw a party for the construction crew after we get moved in."

"Am I invited? I supplied the cement, concrete, and gravel."

"You are the first to be formally invited and J. J. is the second."

"Has J. J. told you about our sand and gravel partnership?"

"Yes, he did."

"Someday I am going to develop the land to the east of the airport with a golf course, houses, condos, tennis courts, and a club house with a swimming pool. In the gravel pit area I have plans for an industrial park. Would you be interested in becoming a partner?"

"I like the idea. Besides, I am bored being retired. I prefer to be a silent partner."

"You are gun shy because of your previous experience with the town council?"

"Yes. I am still considered an outsider in this town and that could cause problems for you and J. J."

"The judge and I know which levers to pull in this county."

Jim and J. J. left to join the girls at the Olde Steak House. They had a great time. Jan finally started to feel like a local.

The next morning Jim made his last payment to the architect and they returned to Denver in Jan's new white Mercedes. "I don't mind leaving that old truck at the airport, this rides like a dream."

Jan was humming as the car floated along the four-lane highway. Jim couldn't pull in a radio station so he tried one of Jan's discs she had bought for the car. His appreciation for classical music was shallow so he set the radio to pick up his favorite music station as they reached the foothills outside of Denver.

"I don't crave your classical music, Jan."

"I never play my music when you are around."

"Sometimes I forget that I am an uncultured slop."

"I didn't say that."

"Are we going to have Thanksgiving dinner at the townhouse?"

"Yes. I invited the boys. Does that suit you?"

"Oh, I am looking forward to seeing the boys! I have matters to discuss with Bill."

"So have I. He has a live-in girlfriend."

"Your son is living in sin?"

"Yes."

"What about you and me?"

"That is different."

"How?" Jan kept on humming and ignoring Jim. He located a radio talk show. This was not radical Charlie but a different fellow on the air waves. A caller to the show claimed that he was fighting crime and sin in the name of his Lord Jesus Christ.

"Did you hear that, Jan? We don't need the religious fanatics jumping into the fray. America is so fragmented. Our illegal drug distribution system is run by gangs, mostly black. The skinheads openly demonstrate against blacks, Jews, and liberals. The religious zealots are on their own wavelength, depending on who their leader is at the time. I have been reading about the paramilitary units organized in Montana, Idaho, Wyoming, and Colorado. Some of them call themselves Freedom Fighters, Save America for Ameri-

114

cans, the Aryan Nation of America, and they all wave the American flag in the name of their chosen cause. I feel for the American people when all hell breaks loose, particularly those innocent people caught in the middle of the fracas. I sure would hate to be a marked person like a Black or Jew. I lack sympathy for the stalwart liberals who have led innocent people down fantasy lane."

Jan's buttons were pushed, "What about the war-hawks that I protested against when I was a student? They helped destroy America with their huge defense programs, their fight against communism which in many cases supported dictators who suppressed their own people. Liberal dissenters lost out to powerful WWII hawks."

"We all had a hand in the shape of things, including people who remained passive on national issues."

"As a former school teacher I believe that meaningful changes in society have to come at an early age. It is difficult to redirect a high school dropout. We, as teachers and parents, failed the children."

"Amen."

Jan drove up to the garage, clicked the door opener, and parked the car inside. "We are home again, James."

"Nobody calls me James except you, my dear. My late mother, God bless her soul, always called me by my full name."

Jim scanned the newspaper while Jan put together a quick supper. During the building of the chalet and Jim's retirement the two became a compatible couple; they developed routines that flowed in harmony. They were in perfect sync with each other. Jan and Jim would hit tennis balls until Doc arrived, then Jan joined her friends for coffee at the Cherry Creek Shopping Center.

On this day Jim and Doc repeated their ritual. Seated on the park bench, Doc said, "You were right about the president."

"How so?"

"Someone leaked information from the White House. The president is going to freeze all assets in the United States the day before Thanksgiving."

"We are seeing the first official move by our government in the direction of defaulting on Treasury notes. The rest is a matter of time. It is finally happening."

"So you are moving to Deerpoint?"

"Yip."

"Guess I will have to find another tennis partner."

"We are keeping the townhouse in Capitol Hill. We will be spending time in Denver. Her boys live here."

"When are you leaving for Guaymas?"

"Right after Christmas. We will have our first family gathering at the chalet. I am looking forward to Christmas. In my lifetime I spent more holidays by myself than with family."

"You were married once."

"Only for a few years. During my marriage I worked seven days a week."

"I am glad to see you retired. You have changed for the better."

"I'll bet you spent many an occasion away from your family during your career as a surgeon."

"Yes, I have. That is the price we pay for success."

"You, Doc, still enjoy your work. I began to hate the apartment business."

"The graffiti artists got to you."

"That was the straw that broke my back. I remember watching a mother of a graffiti artist defend her delinquent son on TV. She pleaded with the judge that her son was expressing himself as a budding artist. She said, the city should accommodate her son's talents. The judge let the damn kid off with a lecture. My manager and I set out to deal with the problem on our own terms."

"You and Max started the graffiti battle?"

"I guess you could say that. We got out of that situation about as fast as we got into it. I realized that the criminal had more rights than the victim, so we gave up the battle."

"I am going to miss our bull sessions."

"So will I. You are the only doctor I have ever been able to communicate with. The others seem to eat, sleep, and breathe their profession."

"I have always kept my personal life and my practice separate."

"Where did you go to school?

"I graduated from Harvard Medical School."

"I would have never guessed that. Tell me, is it true that God himself comes down to address the graduating law class?" Doc cracked up. "Did Jesus Christ show up for your graduation?"

"Hardly. The American Medical Association would have

frowned on a faith healer, a miracle worker interfering with medical minds."

"Doc, did you take my advice and move your savings to Canada?"

"What happens if the United States take down the rest of the industrial world with it?"

"Good point. Their downfall should be temporary, whereas our trip back to productivity will be a long, arduous one."

"I used to hope that you were wrong about the future of this country. I guess it was wishful thinking. I have accepted the possibility of a downfall and hope it will be short lived."

Jan arrived, "It is time to break up your verbal exercise and go home."

The evening news was revealing. The Attorney General's Office was sending agents into the Deep South to investigate jails and prisons. The Black delegation in Washington, D.C., was aroused over the unexplained deaths of criminals in the South.

There was no mention of any unusual activities in New York. New York was New York, an entity unto itself. Most of the country didn't care what happened in New York as long as it didn't become a national problem, like insolvency. The federal government had to bail out New York once before and it could happen again; the liberals were still around. New York considers itself the capital of the world. Boston had the persona of being the navel of all human knowledge. In reality, New York was the East Coast vortex and Los Angeles the West Coast vortex of the liberal movement that emanated from America's original thinkers in Boston. New York, a mass of humanity, had learned to live with organized crime for centuries and now was adapting to unorganized street crime.

The New York Police Department was ripe for instant capital punishment, but the liberal judges and liberal politicians impeded the new movement of law and order that was silently taking hold in different parts of the country. New York City policemen became utterly frustrated with the liberals who coddled street people, forgave criminals, and tolerated derelicts who called New York City home. They gave up hope and joined in the lucrative illegal drug-distribution system.

Americans could have learned from New York's experience

with crime, drugs, public indebtedness, corrupt judges, crooked politicians, policemen on the take, organized crime, parasitic attorneys crawling all over the place, and Wall Street, the national academy of swindlers, but America did not learn from New York's experience nor from the lush liberal garden called California. In many ways New York and California were in a contest with each other on the path to destruction. California was running in second place. California became a victim of too much prosperity, too much growth, too many illegal immigrants, a large defense payroll, too much milk and honey for too long a period of time. New York, on the other hand, suffered from too many on the take, from generations of welfare abusers, to corruption in government. The burden of welfare eventually would bring down the giant city of capitalism. New York City was considered unique by the liberals. Thank God there was only one New York City in the United States of America. People with means moved out of New York City and people in California deserted their land of milk and honey.

In the past, Oriental and white shopkeepers in Los Angeles restrained themselves when attacked by rioting blacks. In the coming revolution those same people would be well armed and emotionally prepared to meet their aggressors.

In Colorado there were winds of change moving about, the crime rate was decreasing, prisons had vacancy signs hanging at the front gate, local jails were no longer overcrowded and court dockets had openings. The mayor of Denver saw an opportunity and seized upon it. He flaunted his success in reducing crime in the mile-high city. He and his social engineering wife had designs on Washington, D.C. The governor of Colorado also had aspirations of presiding in the nation's Capitol.

The president of the United States shifted his attention from foreign policy to domestic affairs because he didn't have money to give to foreign countries and Congress was about to cut his defense budget. The country was sinking fast. Gold jumped to $2,000 per ounce, inflation rose to 30 percent, interest had risen to 26 percent, unemployment shot up to 30 percent, and the national debit was at $12 trillion. In order to meet budgetary needs Congress added the accrued interest to the national debit and raised taxes. Some business analyses called that a double whammy. Less business activity led to less revenue and interest on the national debit was devouring the budget, leaving only revenues for very basic functions of government. The day before Thanksgiving, when the president froze all assets in the United States, stock markets around the world convulsed as the New York stock market plunged into a deep black hole.

Jan prepared a nice family dinner for Thanksgiving. Mark and Mary arrived early. Bill and his live-in friend were late as expected. Mark had been laid off from his job and was doing interviews. He struggled with rejections and didn't relish living off his wife's wages. Mark was on a slight high. Research, Inc., had asked him to come to Boulder for an interview. He knew the company was small and was deeply involved in cold fusion. He had spoken with Dr. Klein on the phone and learned that Dr. Klein was the owner and manager of this small research company.

They were sitting in the living room having refreshments. Jan and the girls drank white wine; Jim and the boys had their Jim Beam on the rocks. "Bill, how are you doing with the farewell pill?"

"I need some start-up money."

Jan turned to her son and said, "You need what? What happened to the fifty thousand dollars?'

"Mom, I bought a car, put money down on a two-bedroom Tudor house, and we went to Europe for our honeymoon."

"Honeymoon? You aren't even married."

"Judy and I got married last week." Jan was exasperated. "Mom, we got married to please you. I know how conventional you are, so we got married by a judge and now everybody should be happy."

Jan gave Judy a condescending look and asked her, "How do you figure into the scheme of things?"

"We have been living together for the past year and decided to get married for the sake of children, which we intend to have when the time is right."

Jim stood up and announced that he would fix some more drinks. He returned from the kitchen with his drink to see five mute people staring at chairs, walls, and the ceiling. They had ceased to communicate. Jim raised his glass and said, "Here is to Judy, the newest member of our family. Welcome aboard, Judy."

The tension faded, they all raised their glasses to the toast. Judy walked over to Jim, shook his hand, and thanked him. Jim knew immediately that he had met a gal with spunk. He took a shine to her and she responded. "Judy, how much start-up money does Bill need?"

She looked at Bill and replied, "About twenty thousand now and more later."

Jim gave her a fatherly smile and assured her, "Consider it done."

Jan was pouting, she felt left out. "Bill, this time I expect results."

Bill clicked his glass with Jim and answered, "You will have it in spades."

Jim went over to Jan, placed his hand on her shoulder, and spoke to the others, "Your mother has prepared a wonderful turkey dinner for us. Let's sit down, eat, and have a joyous time."

The family sat down to the dinner table. Jan gave her Lutheran prayer and they carried on in a typical adult fashion. The boys preferred to visit their mother during the holidays. Their father's second wife, who had children of her own, was indifferent about the boys. To her they were Frank's boys. The boys considered Jim their mentor, a second father, and their mother's best friend.

Jim looked to Judy and asked the question point blank, "How do you feel about euthanasia?"

"It should be part of our culture like birth control."

"Where do you work?"

"I work as a nurse for the Colorado State Health Department. I make visits to senior citizens' homes and nursing homes. I submit reports to the state on the quality of care the various centers provide."

"So you see a need for the farewell pill in these centers?"

"Yes, I do. Everyday I see someone in poor health who has lost their desire to live. These people do not want to become a burden to their family or the government; they wish to die in dignity. This is particularly true of the terminally ill patients. It is painful to see these people in emotional and physical pain, without a choice. Such a cruelty in our society."

Jim confirmed her beliefs, "I believe in individual freedom. No faction of religious extremists should have the right to dictate another person's destiny."

Judy finished off the discussion on euthanasia. "American culture, if we have one, is a strange one. We want everything to live

120

forever. Few people discuss death as a fact of life and yet it is as real as birth itself."

Mark spoke up, "Mary has an announcement to make." Mary was the beautiful, quiet, forgotten girl. Her personality was so pleasing that it was easy to overlook her physical beauty.

"I am pregnant."

Jan dropped her fork and exclaimed, "How wonderful. I am going to become a grandmother. When is the baby due?"

Mark said, "We don't know for sure."

"Will I have a granddaughter or a grandson?"

Mark answered his mother. "We want a healthy child."

Jim's thoughts flowed along economic avenues. He was acutely aware that Mark didn't have a job and Mary was the pregnant bread winner of the family.

Jim became lethargic the following week. Jan was busy buying linens, glassware, dishes, and all the other household items for her chalet like a new bride. Jan never spent a dull moment in her entire life. She was either doing chores around the home, shopping for something, or visiting with her girlfriends over a cup of coffee. Jim was lost. He didn't have a workshop, and the weather was too inclement for tennis with Doc. He drove around town in Jan's old car, now his Denver car. He would read the *Wall Street Journal* more extensively, and he watched a lot of TV. He did take to Charlie, the crazy radio talk show host. He tuned into Charlie one afternoon.

Charlie had a fellow caller in who claimed that he was going to take out a slime ball who was accused of killing two people and wounding two others in a pizza parlor. Charlie hung in with this fellow until the very end. "What is the name of the slime ball you are going to take out?" The fellow named him and said that the termination would take place in about two weeks. "Are you acting on your own or do you belong to an organization or a gang?"

"I belong to an organization that delivers instant capital punishment. We finish off what liberal judges and juries fail to do for our citizens and we do this at no expense to the citizen. I have to hang up." A click followed and the caller was off the air.

Charlie made the most of his bits and pieces of information he collected. In his weekly column in the local paper he told the whole world that he knew about the organization that reduced crime in

121

Colorado. The governor of the state vigorously denied that anything like instant capital punishment even existed and pointed out positively how his programs of rehabilitation and increased law enforcement reduced crime. Charlie made the national press, was on national talk shows, and revealed little because he didn't have the facts. He was guessing. Charlie drew national attention to instant capital punishment and unintentionally spread the word to directors and terminators that they were succeeding and remaining anonymous. Charlie fell out of the national spotlight as quickly as he rose to fame with unsubstantiated stories. Three weeks after Charlie had received the call from a terminator, the slime ball was executed. Charlie knew he was on the right track but couldn't prove his theory. He became frustrated.

The governor of Colorado realized his greatest dream. The president of the United States appointed the ambitious buffoon to become head of a new cabinet post, the Department of Crime and Violence. The president thought the new post would help solve local crime. All crime is local to the victim. The creation of a new cabinet post was a politically correct idea to send out politically correct messages to the American public. The mayor's wife in Denver also wanted to become part of the power and glory in Washington, D.C., but the president didn't have a position for her husband. Since the president no longer had the tools to play a lead role on the international scene, he concentrated on domestic issues. The man was not a leader. He reacted to obvious existing problems. He suggested cutting defense spending. The Senate was in the process of cutting defense spending in half, recognizing that a reduction of military personnel and the scuttling of defense contracts would exacerbate the terrible unemployment situation.

Americans still believed in their president because they wanted to believe in somebody or something. Besides, he was a charming person, a decent man, a great speech maker, but not a leader for these times. The man was a dreamer who told people what they wanted to hear. The president emphasized positive thinking; he had read all the books on the subject. He never had a negative thought in his life; everything was positive or malleable enough for a twist into a positive idea. He called a meeting of his cabinet and unveiled a scheme to put inflation into check, a wage and price freeze. He saw

122

no downside to this plan. Bankruptcy was the move to make, but he could not entertain negative thoughts. Some of the politicians in Washington, D.C., were in a dream, playing out the last days of a superpower. American citizens who had been asleep for forty years awoke to the crisis their country was facing and could only speculate on the impact of events to follow. Americans had rejoiced in winning the Cold War and now had to admit they'd lost the War on Poverty, the War on Crime, the War on Drugs, and still looming over their heads was high unemployment, underemployment, poorly educated workers at the entry level, and high medical costs. The War of Financial Disaster was patiently waiting on their doorstep.

The Black delegation wore out the carpet to the Oval Office in search of financial aid and more individual rights for their nonworking brothers. The group was made up of mostly ministers who preached fear of God and racism. Without the word *racism* they had no ammunition. The slow-evolving revolution that had its roots in social reform reached a financial pinnacle that crossed all racial lines, vaulted over all barriers in society. The upheaval would touch everyone before its finale and again in the aftermath, the rebuilding of America.

Mr. Reverend, leader of the Black delegation, was called "the Big Black Mouth" by nonliberals and realists in the country. Liberal media reporters considered the remark as racist; they held him in high esteem.

Mr. Reverend capitalized on the misfortune of his own people to feather his political nest and the media covered him like a mother hen protects her chick. A news maker for the media, he never failed to make the national news. During the good old days the House of Representatives had a welcome mat out for Mr. Reverend that read, "Ask not what you can do for yourself but what we can do for you."

One of Mr. Reverend's most interesting social-engineering projects dealt with the imbalance of Black people versus white people in prison. He pointed out that 16 percent of America's population was Black and the Black prison population was 60 percent. He considered that unconstitutional. He suggested a reverse affirmation program to release Blacks from prison and create a level playing field for everyone across the country.

The average American could not afford to confront him for fear of legal reprisals. He had more rights than the people who were supporting Black institutions of higher learning and physical fitness, namely, prisons throughout the country. The man had audacity and it was rubbing people like an irritable rash. Liberals advocated spending more money on potential criminals to stave off a need for more jails and prisons. But since Americans had been down that road before many times since the sixties, they were demanding results for their tax dollars. They wanted revenge. They were ready for instant capital punishment.

Tough times had fallen on America and Mr. Reverend saw an opportunity to improve his political stature. He scheduled a big rally in Los Angeles. He briefed his forum in Los Angeles for a blockbuster rally. He got up to address fifty thousand starving, hungry, thirsty people who had lost their way and the federal government hadn't come to their rescue. The timing was perfect for Mr. Reverend and he knew it. Mr. Reverend commenced his speech by fumbling and stumbling through his repetitive dialogue which he carried on with himself and his alter ego. In the sixties he'd been an unknown figure in the civil rights movement, fighting for a just cause. Now he was king of the Black culture. Overweight, obnoxious, and unafraid to wave the Black banner for himself, he pushed words through his puffed-up checks and occasionally spit venom. He had nothing new or enlightening to present so he turned to his forum, his cohorts seated on stage behind him. He presented a brother, an actor who had amassed a fortune of about $500 million.

Mr. Hollywood spewed out the same rhetoric: society has done it to us, they owe us, they must pay or we will show force. The crowd was getting psyched up for bigger things, like action out on the streets. The actor sat down and turned over the podium to a lady who was the representative to Congress for that area of Los Angeles.

The representative made no bones about whom to blame. She said, "It is the white man who has brought this curse upon the Black man." She encouraged the crowd to revolt by rioting and fighting for what was owed to them rightfully. She was a product of the sixties but never paid the price that Mr. Reverend and others like him paid in those trying days. She was too young to know what separate drinking fountains looked like and had never learned firsthand how humiliating it was to ride in the back of a bus as an American. The representative had climbed aboard what she presumed was an express train to fame. She was riding with lily-white liberals on a train destined into deep darkness of America's unknown future. She rallied the crowd into action. Mr. Reverend and his entourage returned to their plush hotel for refreshments and a lavish dinner.

Drug dealers and gang members attending the rally called their disenchanted brethren on their cellular phones and gave the order to burn, loot, destroy, and rape the city. The city soon was ablaze in twelve different locations. Mexicans followed the Blacks and looted the stores. They loved to steal. It was so easy. Los Angeles was in chaos. The revolt lasted twenty-four hours. Rioters did a lot of damage in the Hollywood area because merchants in that ritzy part of the city relied solely on police for protection. In less affluent areas, Oriental, Black, and white merchants assembled their families to defend their property with guns; other merchants hired gunmen for a line of defense, with anticipation of a riot after Mr. Reverend's rally. Three hundred people were dead, hundreds wounded from a one-day scrimmage between rioters and defenders of personal property.

Media folks flocked to Los Angeles like locusts, reporting the riots as, "America under Siege." California, the land of milk and honey, appeared on TV like any other state in the world where national harmony, a social order, local authority, and individual property rights were being tested on a battlefield. The message from Los Angeles to Americans was encouraging. Victims fought back. Rioting became dangerous. Hope was restored in law-abiding citizens.

Across the country residents and business owners organized themselves into crime protection groups. Citizens had recognized a need for self-protection but lacked initiative to take the law into their own hands until the riots in California rocked them into motion.

Gradually cities and counties gave law-enforcement agencies sufficient authority to do the job they were hired to do. Americans welcomed the change in their communities with open arms. Victims of crime were taking back rights they had lost during the reign of liberals. In years to come the events in Los Angeles would be cited as the beginning of the revolution because American law-abiding citizens took a stand. They stood up to violence. They fought back.

The FBI forewarned Mr. Reverend against holding his scheduled rally on January 15, in Denver, to celebrate the national black holiday. He did not heed their advice and went to Denver as planned. The Denver chief of police, a director, pleaded with Mr. Reverend against holding the rally for fear of his safety. The chief could not assure Mr. Reverend and his speakers unconditional protection.

A Denver newspaper quoted Mr. Reverend as saying, "The police chief is a racist." This pissed off the chief. Mr. Reverend enjoyed going against the law of the land and white law enforcers. He had learned to do that during the sixties while protesting in the south. Blacks created a living hell for southern folks in the early civil rights protest marches. Mr. Reverend, like many Americans, was living in that past. It would catch up with him in the nineties. Mr. Reverend gathered on a stage that had been erected for this event with other local dignitaries, the city mayor, the new governor, one lady known as the welfare queen, and other members of the grand liberal movement.

A sniper had drifted in from Montana days before to set up for his flawless assassination of Mr. Reverend. The shot would have to come in from a great distance because the rally was being held in a large open park, City Park. Mr. Reverend was trying to churn the crowd into a frenzy. He raised his arms, gesturing after an applause, when a shot came out of nowhere and put him down. Big Black Mouth was silenced forever.

The sniper dropped his rifle, removed his plastic gloves, and put them into his pockets. He mingled in the crowd, wearing a common sweatshirt of the day bearing the message, "People-Power." He made his way back to his car, shed his sweatshirt, and dropped it by a tree. He drove nonstop back to Montana. No one would ever know who the assassin was except the leader of the Aryan nation of America. It took the large crowd a few moments to comprehend what had happened, and then, in dismay, they quietly dispersed except for a few trouble-makers who wanted to test their rioting skills. The police were prepared for them.

Different groups throughout the United States who had been preparing for an all-out revolution applauded what they saw on television. This incident prompted an investigation by the Attorney General's Office and numerous law-enforcement agencies based in Washington, D.C. Denver's police chief was prepared for the investigators. He turned over the sniper's rifle and that concluded his participation in the case. The chief was into instant capital punishment and had no interest in random political assassinations.

Jan and Jim moved into their chalet before the holidays. They celebrated their first family Christmas in Deerpoint and then flew to Guaymas, Mexico, for the New Year. By mid-January they had settled into their new environment with the grace and ease of a retired couple. Disturbing news from the north reached them despite their efforts to shun it. Americans vacationing in Mexico constantly discussed the fate of their country during these trying times while shopping for a sanctuary of their own south of the border.

"Jan, do you want to go deep sea fishing?"

"No. You go, I will call Mary and Mark, I think Mary is struggling with her pregnancy. Later I will go downtown to visit with my American friends and do a little shopping."

"I would like a ride down to the docks."

"When?"

"In about thirty minutes."

"With the top down or the top up?"

"I will go either way, baby." Jan dropped him off at the docks and went to her favorite browsing places.

Today she was in for a surprise. She met up with a person whom she'd befriended during peace marches and political campaigns. The last time she'd seen her was in a marathon foot race, an AIDS fund raiser. Jan was enjoying herself so much she lost track of time and missed Jim at the docks. She drove up to the villa, parked in the garage, and found him sitting by the pool smoking his pipe and reading a newspaper.

"Honey, I missed you at the docks."

"I know. We came in early. I caught a one-hundred-and-ninety-six-pound blue marlin within the hour. Got lucky."

"You sure did. Where is it?"

"The Mexicans are cutting it up for supper, catch of the day."

"I wish I could have seen it."

"You will. I had my picture taken with the fish."

"Guess who I met today in the village square from Denver?"

"How in the world do you expect me to guess that? OK. Who did you unexpectedly meet today from Denver?"

Jan went into great detail explaining her afternoon and how she'd met her friend from Denver at the village square.

"What is the welfare queen doing down here?"

"Jim, she is my friend."

"I bet she was all shook up. She was sitting only a few feet from Mr. Reverend when he was shot."

"She is a remarkable woman. She and her husband are looking for a place to buy in Guaymas. They moved money down to Mexico like we did."

"Yeah, I bet she moved money the day before our president froze all assets in the States; inside information. That money probably came from her campaign chest."

"Why are you so damn cynical? She is a good person and you are a pessimistic man."

Jim cooled the conversation; he was treading on sensitive nerves. "How about some tennis before supper?"

"That's about the best idea you have had all day."

Jim could always make up with Jan by playing tennis with her. It was like a private lesson for her. He set up balls to her forehand so she could really whack them; she liked that. They took a swim after their tennis game and had a light supper on the outer patio, facing the setting sun over the docks.

The next morning they had a lazy breakfast on the inner patio, poolside. Jim had his coffee after breakfast, smoked his pipe, and was reading a newspaper when the phone rang. Jan usually answered the phone. Invariably it was from one of her sons. After thirty minutes on the phone she returned and sat down with hands cupping her chin and elbows on the table. Jim had to prompt her, "What is it?"

"It looks bad. Mark was turned down by Research, Inc. They can no longer continue their work in cold fusion. Mary is doing fine, but her salary is barely enough to make ends meet. I told them to move into the townhouse."

"You did the right thing."

"I know what they are going through. My retirement check buys about thirty percent of what it used to."

"You are experiencing a loss of purchasing power due to excessive inflation."

"Whatever, I don't like it and something should be done about it."

"How are Bill and Judy doing?"

"They both have jobs and are keeping their heads above water. It is Mark and Mary I worry about."

"I like the idea of cold fusion as a future source of energy for America. We should invest in Research, Inc. Now would be a good time to do it."

"Really? Do we have the money?"

"No. We could sell the villa and move our funds from Mexico to our bank in Denver and take it from there. Business and family come first in my book. Think about it."

"Oh, I don't know. I just don't know."

"We should get twice what we paid for the villa. Mexico scares me. One season they go like gang busters and the next season they rest on their butts. I don't think we will live long enough to ever see the Mexicans get their act together."

"How does Mark figure into your plan?"

"A job and a piece of the action, stock in Research, Inc."

"I can't ask that of you."

"You didn't ask me. I suggested it as my idea to solve a problem and further our investments."

"I agree."

"Offer the villa at a high price to your friend, the welfare queen."

"Jim, be nice for a change."

"Hell, it is money that belong to citizens of the United States. I am just returning it for a good cause."

"You are a great person, but for the life of me, I will never understand you. You are nothing like Frank."

"I hope not." She laughed off that comment as another Jim Clark remark.

"We will move our money to Switzerland."

"What about Denver or Vancouver?"

"The only money we want to bring back into the United States will be for consumption purposes. I am also skeptical of Canada."

"You don't trust anybody."

"Jan, you and Frank would demand a raise from the school district, and if they refused, you'd threaten them with a strike. You were making around fifty thousand dollars a year for nine months' work with all holidays off and vacation time. I, on the other hand, worked seven days a week and at times felt like the whole world was out to destroy me. We come from different backgrounds."

"Now I can understand why Frank was afraid to go into business. He would have been eaten up by sharks, and he knew it."

"You are becoming a realist. You are short a few semester hours, but you will get there."

Jan sat on Jim's lap and gave him a kiss. This mannerism by Jan confirmed the deal with her man, Jim Clark. They sold their villa and moved funds into a Swiss bank account. The trip home was a sad one for Jan; she had surrendered part of a dream for the welfare of her family. To Jim it was just another business transaction.

Mark was on the phone talking to prospective employers when they arrived at the townhouse. "Welcome back from the land of sand, sun, and fun."

"We are back from the land of people factories. They grow kids down there like we grow potatoes in Idaho. I want to talk to you about Research, Inc. I need to know everything you have learned about the company."

"Well, they are into cold fusion and are short of funds. They merged with a company that manufactures sophisticated medical equipment, which is supposed to produce a cash flow for research in cold fusion. The medical equipment business is off and the fate of Research, Inc., is in the balance."

"I like the idea of cold fusion. Call Dr. Klein and set up a meeting with him. I want to discuss the possibilities of investing in the company."

Mark looked puzzled. Jan had told him that they'd sold their villa and moved money into a Swiss bank account. "You sold your vacation home to create capital for an investment in a research company? But you both are retired."

"We are not retired from life."

Mary returned from her day of teaching. She looked great. Jan welcomed her with open arms; they hugged each other. "My, you look pleasingly pregnant."

"That I am. You and Jim are tanned and look so healthy."

Jim gave her a hug, too. He had never done that before. "I wish we could say that about the economy in this country."

"I know. Mark is showing the strains of unemployment."

"We intend to change that very soon."

Mark hung up the phone and said, "You have an appointment with Dr. Klein at two tomorrow afternoon in Boulder. I have the address and phone number written down for you."

Jan was leaning against the kitchen cabinets with her chin resting on her knuckles and breathing slowly. She was concerned about the business decision of investing in Research, Inc. Jim put his hand on her drooping shoulder and attempted to lift her spirits. "Jan, I have fiddled with my rotary engine in vain and will continue to do so, but tomorrow we shall become one of the building blocks in mankind's future source of energy, cold fusion. It is clean, plentiful, and will be produced at a very, very low cost. I need to have a drink on that. Besides, it is almost sunset." Jim was a sunset drinker. He almost never had a drink during the day, only at sunset. They toasted to his idea and the family investment. Excitement flowed again in the townhouse. Jim Clark's adopted family could not comprehend him, and they were not alone. Neither could his close friends nor his sister, who had always questioned his sanity.

Jim journeyed to Boulder, also known as the People's Republic of Boulder. He parked in a lot serving numerous hi-tech companies. He located Research, Inc., in a small building near the middle of the complex. Dr. Klein was in his office by himself. After a pleasant introduction, the two commenced to discuss the role of Research, Inc., in the search of cold fusion. Dr. Klein thought he and his four scientists would someday solve the riddle of cold fusion but it would take time, and time translated into money. "I appreciate your interest in our company, but I have nothing tangible to sell. My four associates and I are the company."

"What is your relationship with the stockholders in the medical equipment manufacturing part of the business?"

"They are my cash flow and they want out."

"If you spin off that operation with the stockholders involved, I will support your company and its efforts towards cold fusion until hell freezes over. I want forty-six percent of the stock in the company for myself and five percent for Mark Bailey. You shall have first right of refusal on my stock. I moved money out of the country before the president froze all assets in the United States. How much is your annual budget?"

"About five hundred thousand."

"I can handle that." He wrote a check in the amount of fifty thousand and handed it to Dr. Klein, "Here is my earnest money."

Dr. Klein accepted the check. They shook hands and the deal was made in principle. "We can close our deal at my attorney's office after you absolve yourself from the other stockholders."

"My associates will be delighted to hear that there is life after death." They parted with a second handshake and a smile. Jim had just made the most important deal in his life on a handshake. He was big on making handshake deals. It was the good old-fashioned way of doing business.

"Oh, I almost forgot a small matter. Mark Bailey wants to be part of your research team."

"I will give him a call right now." Jim was elated. He walked to the car and drove back to Denver.

He had already forgotten about his Mexican connection; his mind was on moving two bars of gold to Vancouver and then severing his Canadian connection. He had buried thirty bars of gold in Deerpoint and tucked away two bars with his ammo, which he'd later moved to the chalet. He'd hidden the two bars behind a panel in his workshop in the garage of the chalet. Jim found a new project to ward off boredom. By the time he returned to the townhouse, word had reached the family that Mark had a job with Research, Inc.

Jim was greeted with hugs and kisses from the girls. Mark roared, "Man, you don't fool around. A one, two, three, and bang!"

"What the hell, Mark, every now and then we have to gamble, I was born a risk taker." They had a jubilant evening.

Jim and Jan had so much luggage they decided to forego flying and drove to Deerpoint in Jim's car. As he drove across the little bridge and up to the chalet, he spotted the little juniper tree that was guarding his gold. It was undisturbed. He relaxed. They called the Crockers' house and invited them to have dinner at the Olde Steak House. They had much to discuss that evening.

Denver had shown signs of spring, but not Deerpoint. A herd of deer and a few elk were moving slowly across the twenty-two-acre mine-shaft property. The wild animals showed loss of weight and winter fatigue. "Honey, the deer are nipping on your juniper bushes and the elk are digging through the snow for grass."

"Let them do their thing; this is their territory." They unpacked their bags and tried to breathe life back into the dormant chalet.

J. J. and Betsy were full of stories ranging from Washington, D.C., and back to Deerpoint. "Jim, did you see where our former governor is taking credit for reducing crime in America?"

"Not recently."

"The knucklehead is in charge of violence and crime and denies instant capital punishment exists. The Attorney General's Office is investigating instant capital punishment in the South. What a bureaucratic mess we have in the capitol."

"I know. We spend billions of dollars on the war on drugs and today the fastest-growing industry in the country is the drug trade."

"You know, Jim, some congressmen are aware that crime is on the decline and are attempting to take credit for the decrease, but none have the courage to embrace instant capital punishment."

"J. J., politicians love to pass laws and appropriate money for their pet projects and therein lies the problem. Instant capital punishment is above the law and costs nothing to the taxpayer." They both had a hardy laugh.

"The president appointed your Denver mayor to a position in Washington, D.C."

"When did that happen?"

"This past week while you were in Mexico."

"What is his position?"

"Secretary of Public Awareness. His wife is the undersecretary."

"And her job?"

"Probably, public manipulator of misinformation." They had another laugh.

"J. J., we should not be laughing at our nation's problems."

"There isn't a helluva lot we can do about it. I did my part in law and order and it is working."

"It is sad how things turned out in this country. I could not fathom that you and I would be discussing our country in these terms forty-five years ago."

"Remember back when we discussed creeping socialism during our coffee breaks at the university. We feared the 'ism in this country."

"I had fears but never imagined Americans would become part of the liberal movement in a broad sense."

"The liberal movement never crossed my mind. When did you develop the bankruptcy phobia?"

"Phobia? During the eighties, the decade of greed. Benefits of deficit spending went to the rich and military industrial complex. The rest of us were supposed to benefit from such a largess. We didn't. The time to pay up is around the corner. Our national debit was one trillion dollars and now it is hovering around fourteen trillion dollars. Every American is on that fourteen-trillion-dollar promissory note. I wonder how many realize what they owe to their creditors."

"They probably think the debit belongs to someone else."

"You are right. Americans have become dependent on support from the federal government in many ways and probably will revolt before they will bite the bullet."

"Jim, it is time for us to go home, they are closing the restaurant," interrupted Jan.

"Yes, dear, we shall journey home."

Jim drove up the driveway in tracks he had made the day before in four feet of snow. Jan became excited when she saw the reflections of the light on the deer's eyes. "Oh, they are so cute. Look, they are lying beneath the juniper trees and only a few feet from our house."

"This is a safe haven for them." Jim closed the garage door. He spooked a few deer. Most of them didn't have the energy to leap through four feet of snow. It was a bright moonlit night and with his peripheral vision he saw a black dog leaping around down by the stream heading towards the deer. He went to his workshop, pulled out the .270, and put a round into the chamber. He quietly opened the side door and saw the dog was getting close to elk lying near a big spruce tree. Jim took a bead on the dog but kept losing him in the powerful scope. His weapons for the revolution were strange to him. He had never fired any of the guns. In his frustration he remembered the scope flipped down and allowed the shooter to use open sights. The M-1 he'd used in Korea had open sights. He felt more comfortable with them. Jim leveled the sights on the dog as he took a rest in the deep snow. He pulled the trigger. There was a thud; the dog was history. He stomped through the deep snow to the dog and covered him with snow. By morning he would be frozen solid.

Jan was in bed reading when Jim came upstairs to the bedroom. "What was all that commotion about?"

"I scared off a dog that was about to harass some deer."

"Those poor things."

Jim rolled into bed. Jan gave him a peck on the cheek and turned out the light. He slapped her fanny. They said good night to each other and fell sound asleep.

The next morning the chalet was ablaze with sunshine reflecting off the fresh snow. The chalet had windows on all sides except the rear, which was dug into the mountain. Jan was playing the radio and humming along with the music while fixing breakfast in the kitchen. Jim seated himself at the table and burst out laughing.

"What's so funny?"

"You are wearing sunglasses in the kitchen."

"I have sensitive eyes." Jim only wore sunglasses for skiing and sailing.

"Today I will crank up the old truck at the airport and do some errands around town. What are you going to do?"

"Well, there are no groceries in this place and I have other things to do."

"Wait for the snow plow."

"I can drive in snow just as well as you can."

"I forgot, you are a farmer's daughter."

"That's right, smarty pants."

Jim called his friend the mayor, also the sub-contractor who had the snow plowing business sewed up in town. "I will have lunch with J. J. Bye."

He drove down the driveway a short distance, plucked the frozen dog from the snow, and placed him in the trunk of the car. As he drove down to the airport he saw a deep track made by deer and elk from the chalet leading down to Joe Parker's meadow at the end of the airstrip. There were at least fifty animals scrounging for food around the airstrip. A plane had just landed so there was brief activity around the airport shack. Jim tossed the frozen dog into a large garbage dumpster and drove over to his lonely truck. He pumped the gas pedal three times and hit the starter twice before the truck finally coughed, chucked, squealed, rattled, smoked a bit, and then settled down to a slow rumble. He drove the truck around for about ten minutes to warm it up and recharge the battery. He went to the shack looking for Ace.

"Hello, Mr. Clark, how was Mexico?"

Jim stared at the fellow. He had never seen him around before but he apparently knew who Jim Clark was. "Mexico is great when Deerpoint is in the deep freeze. Have you seen Ace around lately?"

"Yeah, he is coming in on a flight this afternoon from Denver."

"What is he up to these days?"

"Flying freight out of Denver."

"Will you see him?"

"Most probably."

"Tell him I am looking for him."

"Will do, Mr. Clark."

"Thank you."

Jim drove back up the road to town, passing the chalet. The driveway had been plowed. The garage door was open. Jan must have gone downtown. He kept on driving and parked outside the Last Chance Bar, where he smoked his pipe in the car while watching for J. J. to arrive. There he was, marching along the sidewalk. He waved Jim to the bar.

When they entered the bar, Jim noticed a fresh poster on a wooden pillar which read, "Lab Dog Missing, Contact Ms. Molly Baker. Thanks Much."

"Look at this, J. J."

"That has been up there for a couple of days. People around here post notes there all the time."

"Holy shit! Who is Molly Baker?"

"You should know. You tangled with her at the town board meeting over your annexation."

"Don't tell anyone, but I think I shot her dog last night."

The judge roared with laughter. "That damn dog has tipped over every garbage can in town. He is a pain in the ass. You just became a local hero for shooting the bastard."

"Hold it down. I don't want to become a hero; I just want to live in peace. I am sorry I told you."

"Don't fret. It is legal to shoot a dog when he is harassing and chasing wild game or cattle. Joe Parker carries a 30/30 in his truck and shoots stray dogs all the time."

"I am not Joe Parker. He has clout. Forget what I told you."

"Don't worry about me. No one will ever find out from me."

"Did you ever take a look at my guns and ammo I had stored in your basement?"

"Nope."

"Someday I will tell you what I had stored with the ammo."

"What?"

"I won't tell you now. I don't trust you anymore." Jim went back to the chalet and tinkered with the rotary engine in his workshop. As the sun was setting a familiar car pulled up the driveway. It was that cursed old sports car, but it looked brand new. It was Ace.

Jim, with drink in hand, waved Ace to come upstairs. In the den Jim laid out his plan to Ace for moving the gold bars into Canada. They sat down to eat. Ace was dying to try Jan's cooking. "When can you fly us to Vancouver?"

"Next week, but be flexible with my schedule. I have to line up a twin-engine plane and make the necessary connections with the maintenance boys in Vancouver."

"What if our plan fails?"

"I have a backup plan."

"Like what?"

"I will carry the gold bars with my baggage through check-point charlie and take a cab to the condo. A bit risky, but I can pull it off." Ace thanked Jan for dinner and went home.

Jan had many questions, "Isn't it illegal to move gold out of the country?"

"It is, but it is the right thing to do, considering the circumstances. We need to convert the gold to Canadian dollars to fund our new project, Research, Inc. Think of it this way—we are doing it in the name of science."

"You make it sound so acceptable."

"Just kidding. We are doing it for a good reason and we surely are not the only ones moving money out of the country. I think we should sell the condo, our mining stock, and move all of our money into the Swiss account."

"Whatever you say."

"I want you to come along."

"I had planned on coming along; I am your . . . ah, partner."

"You are my unlawful wife."

Jan had to giggle at that comment. She found life with Jim exciting, scary, and sometimes too adventurous. A week later Jim removed a panel in the workshop and pulled out two gold bars and placed them into two large briefcases. It took three more weeks for Ace to charter a plane and find time within his normal freight-flying schedule to make the trip to Vancouver.

The flight started out like any other on a sunny spring day. After refueling in Idaho, Ace hit puffy clouds and then pouring rain. He pulled the plane up when a flash crossed the plane and everything went dark. The engines kept on roaring and pulling but there was no light. Ace was flicking away at switches reaching around the dash that held dozens of gauges. The lights came on again.

"What in the hell was that?"

"We were struck by lightning."

"It seemed like a lifetime in darkness."

"About fifteen seconds."

Ace was flying on instruments and by the seat of his pants. The plane growled, bounced, and dropped hundreds of feet at a crack. Jim looked around to see Jan sleeping through the entire storm. Ace was busy talking on the radio.

Jim looked at Ace and asked a burning question, "How much more?"

"Hang on. I am taking her down."

"What the hell. Let her rip, Ace."

Ace came down fast. Jim knew that this was the end of the line. Ace was going to bury him with the gold. "For Christ's sake, Ace, are you making a bombing run on instruments?"

Ace was glued to his job. He set the plane on the runway with water spraying and no visibility. Jim knew they would all be buried in the sea with the gold. He'd never learned how to swim. Ace throttled up to a maintenance hanger and killed the engine. "We made it."

"I don't believe it."

Ace had his headset hanging from his neck, laughing and joking. "The next part of this trip will be a piece of cake."

Jan woke up. "Where are we?"

"This is Vancouver, so I am told. About thirty minutes ago I thought we were flying to heaven on a one-way ticket." Jim would never know if the kid really knew his stuff or if he'd gotten lucky one more time.

They got into an aviation maintenance panel truck and hid in the back. The driver took them downtown right to the doorsteps of the bank. Ace and Jan took a cab to the condo. Jim converted the gold to Canadian dollars, sold the mining stock, and arranged for a sale of the condo at the bank. Dinner was a blast. They celebrated their successful smuggle.

The next morning Ace was up at the crack of dawn. He was going to fly out in the rain and did. They had been in the air for an hour when the sun came out and Jim fell asleep. He was tired. He awoke for the refueling and dozed off again. Even Jan was wide awake when they touched down in Denver. Ace returned his chartered plane to the hanger. Jim and Jan boarded the last flight to Deerpoint. The old black truck was waiting for them at the airport, a welcome sight.

They walked into the bedroom of the chalet with their bags and the two empty briefcases. Jan unpacked and put their clothes away. "Jan, no more wild episodes; I am getting too old for this kind of adventure."

"Me too."

Jim went downtown to buy the Denver newspaper and a Wall Street Journal. Jan watched TV from the kitchen while she was tossing together a light supper. Jim returned and fixed a couple of welcome home drinks. He changed the TV to another network. A reporter in Florida covered a story about a man who was planning a trip around the country. He advised U.S. citizens to stop paying taxes to a floundering mismanaged federal government. He was doing this as a patriot of the United States and for the benefit of its citizens. The crusader proudly wore an emblem displaying the American flag. America was listening to this man.

"Jan, the vice president at the bank in Vancouver told me about this man and the movement he has started. He said that if Americans stop paying income taxes, our government will go under within six months. He thought that Canada would be adversely affected when the United States took the plunge."

"Honey, we did the right thing. You were right on target again."

"A bit of luck. It was Mark who led us to Research, Inc. and that brought about a quick decision by us to create funds for the company."

"It was fate, honey."

"I guess so."

III

Jim and Jan settled into their new lifestyle in Deerpoint, away from the noisy, smoggy city of Denver. Ski season had ended on a down note. Business was off from the previous season and the economy across the country was deteriorating rapidly. High unemployment was a drag on the federal budget and did nothing for the economy. Disposable income was low. Manufacturing was off because of the Wage and Price Freeze Act. Production costs exceeded the selling price of goods. Purchasing power had eroded from years of inflation and foreign trade became a one-way street, imports to a consuming nation. Politicians in Washington, D.C., were the closest to the problem and were the last ones to recognize it. They were the problem. People's worst enemies were liberal politicians. A group in Washington, D.C., decided upon a band-aid approach: print more money to pay overdue bills and thus buy time to cogitate a long-term solution to the problem of a deteriorating nation.

Congress was in complete disarray. However, a few senators saw the storm looming on the horizon. The majority of congressmen had hoped to legislate their way out of the dilemma. They knew how to do that; they had done it before. A group of senators who tried to confront the situation head on were labeled by the media and their liberal opponents as the "Save America" gang of Washington, D.C. This small group of senators attempted to convince the president to shrink government drastically by selling off the military industrial complex in pieces, cut all wasteful projects, eliminate welfare programs, rebuild America's infrastructure, invest in the country's ability to become productive again. The president, being a positive thinker, liked some of the ideas but he balked at selling the navy to Japan and the air force to Saudi Arabia. Nobody was interested in the army. Germany reluctantly agreed to take some military equipment with its personnel. He told his cabinet and staff to go public and reassure Americans that he would lift the country out of stagnation and, over the long haul, it again would be a superpower of the world.

The former Colorado governor reminded citizens that the current White House's crime-prevention programs were indeed working. He did not remind people that the Attorney General's Office was investigating the phantom "instant capital punishment" in the South to appease the Black delegation in Congress. It was difficult to attack instant capital punishment because it was unorganized and originated at the top, starting with the CIA, the FBI, and flowing down through governors, judges, district attorneys, police departments, local sheriffs, highway patrol units, and into prisons and jails.

Willard Knight, the Florida crusader, appealed to people on a fixed income, those on social security with personal savings, military retirees, and other folks entitled to retirement funds. These people were caught between a fixed income that was eroding on a daily basis and inflation that was escalating at the same pace. They were scared to death of tomorrow and the day after, should they still be alive to see that day. The elderly were two steps ahead of the farewell pill; they had their own methods of euthanasia.

A local promoter in Florida foresaw the potential of Mr. Knight's message and set out to promote the man as a business entity. He sent advance people to cities to rent locations for the crusader. Tickets were sold for indoor events and revenue was generated from the sale of bumper stickers, sweat shirts, and banners bearing the message of the new savior. Mr. Knight had no financial or political aspirations. He performed out of personal convictions.

The crusader was an unofficial member of the silent generation, a Korean veteran who had walked in the shadows of WWII veterans. He had voted Republican all his life. He never stood up to the dropouts of the sixties. He had great respect for liberals but deep in his heart he knew they were leading the nation down a treacherous path of no return. This slight-built man with a fifties-style haircut came across to the general public as a nephew of their dear old Uncle Sam. The promoter tested slogans like, "Throw the Bums Out," "Down with the Liberals," and "Don't Elect Anyone" in the form of bumper stickers in Florida. The slogan that stayed with Mr. Knight was "Tax Revolt 2000."

Willard Knight and his company of promoters picked up momentum with every bus stop they made up the East Coast. His simply-put message was coined by a reporter, "The free lunch is over." Citizens were seething with vengeance. Mr. Knight came to their rescue. He identified an enemy for them, a government run by liberals. Mr. Knight was careful not to reveal who allowed democracy to fall (the very people he was speaking to on this tour). Instead he referred to his crowd as the victim of liberal Democrats, pseudo-environmental idealists, social safety engineers, and politically correct thinkers. The crowd related to his message; they became energized.

The crusade built steam as it left Detroit and headed for Chicago. Mr. Knight started pointing fingers to specific people in government. He labeled the king and queens of the welfare system and gave the location of their present residences outside of the United States. He reminded the middle class that they were doomed; the wealthy folks had already moved out of the country with their money and left them behind to do the suffering. He said over and over again, "They have abandoned you. You will have to fend for yourselves."

Mr. Knight became a polished speaker with a dynamic message. He was an educated man who sincerely believed in his country. He differed from Mr. Reverend, who represented a particular race of people and had a very personal agenda. The multitude of disgruntled factions that had sprung up around the nation were grouping together as followers of Mr. Knight.

Senators known as "the Save America gang" met and discussed plans for the government to declare bankruptcy. They hoped for approval by the president of the United States of America. The president's wife was not in favor of turning the country over to the bastards in the senate. She wore the pants in the family.

Jim and Jan were into their natural beautification program of the twenty-two-acre homestead. They planted Indian paint brushes, daisies, and spread grass seed by hand on the irrigated area. Jim enjoyed planting daisies around the juniper that guarded his cache of gold, the former outhouse hole. He cranked up the irrigation pump by the stream to wet down the newly planted grass and flower seeds. Jan became involved with local events, like the coming summer festival and other local activities. Jim, on the other hand, stayed out of the public eye. He preferred to fiddle with his rotary engine. He finally got the engine to run, which didn't prove much to the world, but to him it was a monumental accomplishment.

The engine was a crude-looking apparatus that injected air and fuel into a combustion chamber. The explosion within the combustion chamber placed a force upon the power wheel and thus he had a continuous motion of power. He envisioned 100,000 revolutions per minute and very high temperatures in the combustion chamber. He hoped that nearly all of the injected fuel would be consumed and thus have a low-exhaust emission. He rigged up a small compressor for air injection and used a propane tank for the fuel injection, and with this clumsy arrangement he proved to himself the basic theory of his rotary engine. He had spent the entire weekend without seeing J. J. The judge had gone to Washington, D.C., on short notice.

Jim and Jan enjoyed retirement. They lived life selfishly for themselves. Life was fun without social and business pressures. Jan was socializing with Peggy Roberts, secretary to the architect, who addressed her as Mrs. Clark. She didn't mind that at all. Deerpoint residents assumed that Jan was Mrs. Clark from the first day she set foot in the ski village. Jan had begged Jim for that title but was refused by the eccentric Jim Clark. Now a whole ski village bestowed the dubious title on her. Peggy and Jan became close friends. They liked each other from their first meeting. She enjoyed Shirley Parker. Everybody in Deerpoint liked the vivacious Shirley Parker.

Jim was sitting on a box in the garage smoking his pipe and admiring his new creation, the rotary engine. He had never had the luxury of time to do creative things. Making money always held top priority in his life.

Jan drove into the garage. "Hi, honey. Did you get it to run?"

"Yes. It runs like hell on wheels."

"I would like a demonstration."

"Coming up. Do you realize that I came up with this idea for a rotary engine about ten years ago but never took the time to build one?"

"That was about the time we met at the Gates Tennis Center."

"This indeed is a great day for me. Back out your car and I will rev up this little monster."

She backed out her car, left the garage door open, and took a

144

leaning position against the door leading up to the chalet. With folded arms she smirkingly looked on as Jim proceeded to demonstrate his invention. He spun the power wheel, which delivered a spark to the combustion chamber. He quickly turned on the air pressure and then opened the propane valve. The engine started to whirl and gave out a whine. Jan clapped her hands in approval. Jim lit his pipe and took a few puffs when all hell broke loose. Excessive heat in the combustion chamber melted a weld and the chamber blew off the engine, hitting the shop door and landing in a corner of the garage. Jim dropped his pipe and twisted the gas valve shut. Jan turned and ran out of the garage. He located the hot chamber smoldering by the exposed wall. He then made a large snowball and doused the flame.

"My God, you could have burned down the house."

"Not really. Well, the damn thing runs."

Jan walked over to him and said, "I am happy for you." She wanted to give him a kiss and a hug, but he held her off.

"I am full of grease."

"I don't care. I love you just the same. Why don't you patent it?"

"I tried. The patent attorneys failed me after the patent office turned down my application."

"Are you going to sell the invention?"

"Not without a patent."

Jan went upstairs. Jim disassembled the engine and stored it in his workshop. He walked upstairs, parked his dirty shoes at the entrance door, and washed up for supper. "Do you want to join me for a drink while supper is cooking?"

"Sure, I will watch the news with you. I would like to see your engine manufactured and used in cars."

"If I had graduated with a degree in engineering and gone to work for General Motors I probably would have invented a rotary engine back in the sixties."

"Why hasn't someone else done it by now?"

"Industry has been plagued with liability lawsuits, idiotic safety regulations, and little thought has gone into abandoning the dirty old piston engine. Research and development has taken a back seat in the auto industry."

"Cars are more efficient then they used to be."

"Smaller cars have less power and that means less fuel consumption. A catalytic converter does not increase gas mileage of an automobile, it is a band-aid approach to reducing smog. The piston engine is inefficient in converting gasoline into mechanical power. Foreign countries hire engineers; we hire more lawyers. A lawyer never invented anything but more laws."

"I noticed that you have removed the seat belts from the truck and your sports car. Why are you so antisafety minded?"

"If safety were my only criterion in life, I probably would be afraid to get out of bed in the morning."

"Occasionally you wear seat belts when I am doing the driving. Do you do that to intimidate me?"

"No, not at all. People who wear seat belts prepare themselves for a crash. I am a defensive driver. I have never had a major accident."

"Why did you remove the seat belts from your truck and sports car?"

"A prissy little jerk drove me to it. This nerd gave me static because I smoked my pipe in a hallway where he was renting an apartment. I told him in no uncertain terms who I was and asked him to move out of the building. He reported me to the city for not having smoke detectors in the hallways; that cost me thousands of dollars. So, on a hot August day I showed the jerk what I thought of his safety concerns. I tore out the seat belts in my truck and chucked them into the garbage dumpster. He watched me do this in the parking lot. His eyes grew big as saucers. I enjoyed myself so much I went home and ripped the seat belts out of my sports car. Never did like them. I took a shower, poured myself a drink, and celebrated. I called it my Ralph Nader Day."

Jan laughed, nearly spilling her drink. "What did you prove by expressing adolescent behavior?"

"That I am still alive and a rational human being. Haven't you ever done something out of character?"

"I once gave a principal the finger."

"You didn't, not the hazel-eyed, freckle-faced schoolteacher with that cute butt."

"Oh yes, that was me. He was a macho wannabe Romeo who made regular passes at me. As a divorcee he considered me fair

146

game. So I gave him the finger behind his back and he saw my lewd gesture. I embarrassed myself. The following day, after word got around about the incident, I became an instant hero. The other teachers disliked the guy immensely.

"In today's social climate you could sue him for sexual harassment. I turned in my boss for sexually harassing our secretary and damn near got fired for it. The corporate hierarchy told me to mind my own business. They said that secretary belonged to my boss."

"You did that back then? Well, you are different than most people. I overheard Doc say that you were on the endangered species list. I think you are one of a kind, all alone in your thoughts."

"I am not alone, there are others out there who feel and think like I do."

"Where are they? I never met them."

"Politically correct liberals have over-shadowed realists in our country. As the revolution progresses you will see and hear people express their true feelings. The realists will come out of the closet."

"You mean like the tax crusader from Florida?"

"Yes, Mr. Knight. He is anti-government, anti-liberal, anti-tax and has more followers than the liberal media reports."

"He is a radical conservative."

"He is a plain man who decided to stand up for what he believes in."

"I think he is a cross between a preacher and a politician."

"He is neither. He is not running for office and is intolerant of religious zealots. I think the guy is the icing on the cake, he is galvanizing the country for an uprising."

"Why, that is terrible. We are a democratic country. Can't we solve our dilemma without shooting at each other?"

"The president refuses to make the obvious move, to declare bankruptcy, and that leaves Congress in limbo. Someone has to make a move soon or a shooting confrontation will take place."

The news switched to a press conference on the steps of the United States Senate. It was the Senate leader with his cohorts, the Save America group. The leader said that if the president refuses to declare bankruptcy they will impeach him.

One senator said, "We must stop the bleeding of this country and return to a solid foundation. We have to rebuild our industry, our economy, our social structure and most of all our government."

"Jan, look at the guy behind the senator."

"My God, it's J. J."

"I wondered what the quick trip to Washington, D.C., was all about. He is one of the Save America guys. He never even hinted that he was connected to the Save America fellows in D.C."

"All along I felt that Betsy was holding back information about their association with Washington, D.C., through her brothers."

"Yeah, he started instant capital. . . . Ah, he is into law and order."

"What does law and order have to do with our country declaring bankruptcy?"

"Nothing. The judge has this thing about law and order."

The rest of the news was typical during these times: people on fixed income were near starvation, children were suffering from malnutrition, the dollar was worthless, unemployment was over thirty percent, inflation around fifty percent. Nobody really knew the precise figures because the economy was tumbling at a rapid pace. Commerce was dead in the water.

"Let's eat supper and shut out the rest of the world. Turn off the TV, I will put on some soothing music. There is nothing we can do about it anyway."

They ate supper as the sun set. Jim admired Jan as they ate supper together. She was more than a pretty gal he loved, she was a loving compassionate person who brought fulfillment to his life.

As usual they slept in the next morning. Jim would drag himself out of bed when the aroma from the coffee pot reached back into the bedroom. The phone rang.

"Honey, it is for you."

Jim answered it. "We will come down today. See you in your office tomorrow morning. Whenever we get there."

"Who was that?"

"John Price, my bean counter. He and the attorney have the Research, Inc., agreement ready for me to sign."

"How long will you be gone?"

"Aren't you coming along?"

"I would like to stay for the weekend."

148

"We will stay at the townhouse until we wear out our welcome."
She slapped Jim on the back. "What shall I pack?"

"The tennis gear and a few other things."

"Oh, that's great, I will get to shop at the Cherry Creek Shopping Center."

"Whatever."

"I have to start buying clothes for the baby."

"Aren't you rushing it a bit?"

"Jim, I was thinking of giving my car, your car, to Mary. They could keep it for us down in Denver."

"Why not?"

"Mary's car is about to fall apart. Mark spoke to me about it last time we were in Denver." They had established a rhythm in packing the car and driving to Denver. Jim drove the truck to the airport. Jan followed him in her car. They planned on flying back and therefore wanted the truck parked at the Deerpoint airport.

Jan got on the freeway and they whizzed over the mountains. Jim was taking in the scenery. "Did you call Mary and tell her that we are coming down?"

"No, I forgot."

"Me too. I keep forgetting that they live at the townhouse. It is nice to have them there. They have food in the refrigerator, Jim Beam on the shelf, and a car all gassed up and ready to go."

"There will be some inconveniences with this new arrangement."

"Who cares? I don't." Jan smiled and kept cruising along the highway. When they were within radio range, Jim tuned into a music station. They skirted the downtown area and drove up the hill to the townhouse. Jim noticed small groups of people hanging around street corners, not the usual street people he remembered from the past. These fellows were clean shaven, wore washed work clothes, and apparently had nothing better to do than stand in line at employment centers, food centers, clothing distribution centers, and at governmental aid offices. Traffic was light. Gasoline was so expensive people didn't drive around aimlessly from one end of the city to the other. Unemployed people stayed home, or near their neighborhoods. The city seemed much cleaner. There was less smog and virtually no trash floating around in the air or scattered in alleys and around buildings.

They unloaded the car, checked the refrigerator, and went to the supermarket for groceries. The supermarket reflected that times had changed. Everything was in bulk. The triple packaged food items were gone from the shelves. Customers at the checkout counter held food stamps in their left hand and government food coupons in their right hand. Half of the meat coolers were shut down, the produce department was almost bare; the overall scene was depressing. The supermarket was crowded with people. Entire families went on shopping trips. Apparently their lives had been reduced to the survival of one more day. Food, shelter, and clothing had become their main priorities. Jim hid the steaks in Mary's shopping bag; Jan carried a fresh loaf of bread and a pound of butter in her hands.

"Why did you do that?"

"I am not going to flaunt steaks in the presence of undernourished children. The pain and agony on the faces of those children reminds me of my childhood during the drought of the thirties. We had dust storms season after season. Grasshoppers ate the paint off our house. I have a fear of poverty. I remember my father and mother watching the sunset over their barren land one evening. They both had tears in their eyes. They didn't want me to see them cry. They tried to shield me from the depth of their despair."

"How old were you?"

"Six. Dad had wheat seed ground into flour for Mom to make bread. He was saving the seed for a crop in the future, should the rains come again. We lived on bread, black coffee, and syrup."

"I wasn't even born then."

"You didn't miss anything I want to remember. I took a personal vow that I would never be poor again and now I am reliving my past through these helpless people."

"You are too sensitive about other people, there is nothing you can do for them."

"I have deep empathy for these poor lost souls, the offspring of the selfish 'me generation.' That generation had the world by the tail and look at what they left for their children. This whole mess could have been avoided. Down with the damn liberals, the dropouts of the sixties, and the damn WWII hawks."

"How long do you think the depression will last?"

"The revolution will put an end to it. Let's be upbeat with Mary and Mark."

"Thanks, honey. You always worry about the other person."

"How about you? Don't you feel for these poor victims of the times? They are fellow Americans?"

"I have a duty to my family first and then I will worry about other people. Jim, you worry too much."

They parked the car in the garage, stowed away the groceries, and waited for Mary and Mark to return home. Jan hugged Jim. They kissed and hugged again, he slapped her firm fanny. She replied with a wrinkled-up nose and a smile. Jan finished unpacking in their bedroom and then went snooping around in the closets, like a typical mother-in-law. She dialed the radio to music, while Jim sat down in the living room to read Mark's newspaper. He flicked the TV to a news channel. He tried to shut out the world around him, but he couldn't. He was too much a part of it and always would be.

The news report was humiliating. Tourists from all over the world were visiting America because of the weak dollar and they wanted to see what the former superempire looked like. Business failures created a domino effect, real estate foreclosures multiplied, banks had over-extended on real estate loans, and factories shut down because of the wage and price freeze. The weak dollar made foreign goods expensive. Domestic prices rose. Government paid farmers directly to produce basic food. Jim thought the news resembled a freight plane coming in for a crash landing with no wheels to roll on. The regular news was interrupted for a special report. "Alaska seceded from the union. Hawaii will do the same."

"Jan, come in. You have to see this."

"I thought you were going to refrain from viewing the ills of the world."

"Watch this."

"My God, why would they want to do that?"

"Jan, Washington, D.C., has become an unbearable burden to its citizens."

Mary arrived. Jan and Mary hugged and then she patted Mary's tummy and said, "My granddaughter."

Mark arrived late. He was in a good mood, very upbeat. He was delighted with his new job and the 5 percent he would own in Research, Inc. He, like his mother, could stay focused on life and shut out the rest of the world.

"Dr. Klein tells me that as of tomorrow you and I will have controlling interest in the company."

"Not quite. He has forty-nine percent of the company and with my forty-six percent he will control the company. As far as I am concerned he will run the company as he sees fit. Research, Inc., spun off the medical equipment manufacturing business and now has no tangible assets. I made my first alimony payment to the company before signing a marriage contract and will continue to make payments until you fellows solve the cold-fusion riddle. Conceivably, the company can be worth millions of dollars someday or become a big tax write-off for me." Mark absorbed Jim's sobering message.

The next morning Jan had the opportunity to meet Jim's professional advisors, John Price, C.P.A., and Don Lawton, Attorney at Law. They had written Jan Bailey's name on legal documents before but had never met her. Jim introduced Jan to Mr. Price and then signed the agreement with Research, Inc. They both had to sign a deed to the condo in Canada.

Price scanned over Jim's books and said, "You have only three hundred thousand in your account; you are short two hundred thousand by your agreement with Research, Inc."

"I will hand carry this agreement to Dr. Klein and explain that I will make up the difference with the proceeds from the condo sale in Canada. How many U.S. dollars for two hundred thousand Canadian money?"

"About a million. All values have become so distorted with inflation at seventy-five percent. That is the picture today, hard to tell what it will be tomorrow."

The attorney walked into Price's office.

"Jan, meet Don Lawton." They shook hands.

"I see you sold your two safe havens just as the revolution is about to get underway."

"Jan and I found our sanctuary in Deerpoint."

"Not a bad idea." Price looked at Jan and said, "I would have kept the villa in Guaymas, Mexico."

She replied, "It was hard to give up, but we decided to invest in Research, Inc."

"Jan sold our villa to the welfare queen. How do you like that?"

Everyone remained silent. Price and Lawton knew the maverick Jim Clark quite well from his past dealings with them, but were hesitant to unduly judge Jan because of her association with him. "Thanks, guys. Jan and I will make a trip to visit with Dr. Klein."

Dr. Klein was excited to meet Jan and see Jim. He acted like a man who had just received a life-saving blood transfusion. He had no problem with the late payment; he was thankful that Research, Inc., was back on track. Jan suggested they drive through the Colorado University campus for old times' sake. She had received her master's degree in education from the university as an off-campus student. She spent a couple of summers on campus but never really felt like a typical graduate of the school. Jim had been a full-time student over a four-year period and took all of his courses on campus. He'd even attended football games to watch J. J. play.

"So you want to see our alma mater?"

"Yours, not really mine. I never was a rah-rah sorority girl on this campus."

"I was a student here a long time ago and left without honors bestowed upon me."

"I wore several hats when I took my courses from this school. I was a teacher, pregnant mother, and a wife. A master's degree meant more wages, pure and simple." They had difficulty in locating their former classrooms on campus so they went to a place known as "the Hill," a student hangout.

"I want to show you a shoe store I used to work in, if we can find it. There is the building, but it isn't a shoe store anymore," said Jim, disappointed.

"How sad."

"I have fond memories of that place. The store owner hired me on as a shoe salesman in my junior year. I was thankful to get the job, considering that I had no retail experience. There were large windows along this side of the store, people could see the entire interior from the sidewalk. We sold men's shoes only. It was fun working for this guy who was called the 'off campus professor.' All students who knew him held him in high esteem."

Jim was pointing at the former shoe store as Jan listened intently. "This end of the store was the entrance with a small counter that held a money drawer. Next to the counter he had a chess board set up. He beat every student who challenged him, except for one guy who majored in physics. The rest of the store was all shelving, with a small room off to the back corner. He made his bank deposits on a fly-tying table and used the room as a dressing room. He would change into his tennis clothes and hit the courts with his professor friends. The man loved individual sports, tennis, rock climbing, fly fishing, downhill and cross-country skiing. He would say to us, 'Learn how to think.' He was forever discussing philosophy with the students."

"He was your mentor."

"He was more than that to me at the time."

Jan put her hand on Jim's arm as they ambled along the sidewalk. Jim went on, "I recall selling shoes to alumni during homecoming days. They didn't need another pair of shoes, they stopped by to thank him for the memories. I am sure he is dead by now. What a good-looking man. He probably was in his forties, six feet tall, square-jawed, wavy gray hair, and a perfect set of teeth. He stimulated his customers with his charm and handsome features. Come to think of it, he didn't sell shoes; he sold himself. Because of him I took all of my elective courses in philosophy during my junior and senior year."

Jan squeezed Jim's hand and said, "That is a very touching story."

"You know, Jan, my two years in the army seemed like a lifetime in hell and my four years here were the most beautiful and memorable days of my life."

A man in his forties wearing baggy pants held up by suspenders stopped and asked, "Are you alumni?" Jim gave the guy a disdainful look. He wore horned-rimmed glasses, was bald, and had his gray hair in a pony tail. Jim knew he didn't want to talk to him.

Jan said, "Yes, we are."

"I dropped out of the university after the Vietnam War ended and stayed around Boulder. Love it here. Wouldn't live anywhere else." He continued on his journey to nowhere as he dragged his feet along the sidewalk in a pair of worn-out sandals.

"Did you get a whiff of him? He reeks of marijuana smoke."

"Jan, my guess is that he is an original chartered member of the People's Republic of Boulder."

"Honey, I want to go home."

They drove past frat-houses on the way back. "That is J. J.'s old frat-house."

"Was he a man about the campus?"

"Sure was. He was on a football scholarship, a frat-man, and a law student. I met him in the student union coffee shop at the beginning of my freshman year and we have been friends ever since."

They passed the business park where Research, Inc., was located. "Look, my new dependent. First I acquired you, then your two boys, then their wives and now I have Research, Inc. Oh, I forgot, and soon a granddaughter."

Jan smiled with pride. "Yeah, but I am a cheap date compared to Research, Inc., costing anywhere from three to five hundred thousand a year."

"In those terms you are a cheap date."

"Thanks."

The next day they played their husband-and-wife tennis match while waiting for Doc to show up. Jim served the ball gently to her forehand and she returned the ball to the center of the court. If he returned the ball with too much pace, she would stick out her tongue at him. Jim answered the tongue gesture by serving a hard, flat ball into the corner of the service area. He would ace her. She then retaliated by giving him her little finger from her hip. Their tennis was a mix of exercise and friendly intimidation. Doc arrived.

"Am I ever glad to see you, Doc. Beat the pants off him for me today."

"Hi, Jan."

"I have not seen you two mountaineers in some time."

"'I told you we would be back in Denver from time to time."

They played their friendly match and had a cup of coffee from a vending machine. They were sitting on a park bench overlooking the tennis courts when Doc lit up a cigarette and started to puff away. "Doc, they have no smoking signs posted all over this place, you can't smoke here."

"Times have changed; they are more interested in collecting court fees than harassing me about my smoking."

"Hell, I guess I will have a smoke." Jim reached into the tennis bag for his pipe, lighter, and tobacco pouch that he carried with him wherever he went.

"You were smart to buy gold; the country is going bankrupt. Now my worst fear is that Mr. Knight might start a shooting revolution."

"Ever since the national debit reached five trillion dollars and we were still importing more than we were exporting, I was convinced that the bottom would fall out of our economy. Our rise to a superpower and decline to a Third World country is classic. The final blow to our economy will be a textbook case. I don't know how we will handle violence. I am not sure how our population will deal with the economic effects in a social way. High gasoline prices, food rationing, and high unemployment are showing strains on our society's moral fiber."

"I fear the violence."

"How has the economic upheaval affected health care?"

"We don't keep crack babies alive so that they can die later. We allow people to die when there is no hope for their recovery. General practitioners are treating patients instead of shuffling them around to different specialists."

"How about you?"

"I keep on doing meaningful surgery."

"I think doctors are hypocrites. Their practice flows with the current of money."

"You should hear the cosmetic surgeons moan and groan in the cafeteria over lost opportunities."

"I never could figure out why our society is hell-bent on keeping everything alive forever at all costs when there is no hope."

"You are asking the wrong man. I have dedicated my career to saving sick patients who want to live."

"How do you feel about euthanasia?"

"I believe there is a time to die when all hope has evaporated for a productive enjoyable life."

"Have you ever helped a patient die?"

156

"Many times, but with the assistance of two other doctors, by request of the patient, and with the approval of the family."

"That is what I expected."

"That reminds me, you should come in for your annual physical. How is your condition?"

"Never mind my condition. I am enjoying life to the fullest."

"Have you seen your friend Bob recently?"

"How is Bob?"

"He is in the hospital. He is dying of cancer."

"How long does he have to live?"

"It is a matter of days. He thinks he will lick the disease and live forever. He asked about you the other day. I stop in to chat with him every day."

"I will go and see him. I believe in visiting a living person and not a dead friend at a funeral. I have not seen him in about five years. He never married."

"His brother visited him last week and then returned to Florida."

"I remember he had a lot of friends. Everybody liked him. He didn't have one enemy that I knew of."

"Nobody has been around to see him; you know how friends can be when the chips are down."

"Have you seen your tennis partner, Judge Schultz, lately?"

"No. He had to make an unexpected trip to Washington. He should be back this week."

"You know, Doc, something strange is going on. Judge J. J. Crocker made a trip to Washington, D.C., last week and just before Jan and I came down to Denver we saw him on TV with senators during a press conference. I think they are cooking up something."

"The senators threatened to impeach the president a couple of weeks ago."

"I know Judge Crocker has strong inside connections in Washington, D.C., through his wife's brothers. How are your daughters doing?"

"They will survive like the rest of us."

"Jan's boys are struggling with employment, a pregnant wife, making house payments. And Jan discovered what inflation can do to a static retirement income." Jim tapped the ashes from his pipe.

157

"Boy, that tasted good. I like smoking in a 'no-smoking' area. Did I tell you about the rotary engine I invented?"

"No. Did you get a patent on it?"

"Can't get a patent. It was an idea I had for many years. I recently took the time to build a model. It runs. I did invest in a company called Research, Inc., this week. A real gamble."

"Yes. That would be Dr. Klein in his quest for cold fusion."

"You are right."

"I think you are a frustrated scientist."

"A wannabe."

"How about an environmentalist?"

"If you mean picking up other people's trash and dog dung and washing down street people's feces, the answer is yes. I remember asking one of my younger tenants if he enjoyed the Earth Day celebration and he said that he had a great time, good food, great music, and lots of chicks. The next day I read in the Denver newspaper that the city hauled out nine tons of trash left behind from the Earth Day celebration."

Doc said jokingly, "You are an environmentalist?"

"I believe in going to the heart of a problem and not studying it to death."

"You would have made a great surgeon."

"Yeah, if I could operate on the brain, cut the bad parts out."

"You would put too many shrinks out of work."

"How about social engineers?"

Doc had to laugh at Jim's empirical approach to social problems.

"I don't miss being a landlord."

"You made lots of money in the apartment business."

"I made money for the sake of making money. The graffiti artist finally got to me."

"Now you are into gold."

"Did you take my advice and buy gold?"

"As a matter of fact I bought some shares in a gold-mining company."

"Good for you, Doc." Jan returned from her window shopping. "Did you whip the pants off Mr. Hard Ball?"

The question tickled Doc. He liked Jan. "No. We split sets." Doc had to make some visits at the hospital. Jim and Jan returned to the townhouse.

Judy Cox had left a message on the phone for Jan. "Please call me back."

"Honey, I just talked to Judy. She lost her job; she got fired."

"I was afraid she might get caught pushing the farewell pill. It could have been worse."

"Like what?"

"A law suit."

"The kids are concerned about how to make the house payments on Bill's salary."

"Their loan should be paid off with inflated dollars. Now is the time to do it. Find out what the loan balance is and pay it off for them."

"Oh dear, I guess we could do that."

"Make sure the money goes against the loan and not into Bill's account."

"I will give it to Judy; she is the responsible one in the family."

"She wears the pants in that family, thank God." After a shower Jim took a seat in the living room to watch the evening news.

The news instructed people how to obtain help from different agencies of the government to survive and ride out the depression. Violence was breaking out around the city. A curfew was put into effect. Citizens were encouraged to police their own neighborhoods block by block. Police were primarily on emergency calls around the city. Business people had already implemented security measures by hiring guards for their stores on a block by block basis. Snipers on rooftops backed up guards who patrolled along store fronts. Every store had at least one guard at the rear of the store and some had a guard at the front door. Few people wandered outside of their locale or neighborhood, folks just stayed home or remained near their home. Downtown was an area to be avoided. It turned into a war zone occasionally.

National news broke in with a flash from New York City. Middle East terrorists are suspects in the blowing up of the United Nations Building. They blew out the first five floors. Jan wrung her hands and grimaced.

159

Jim looked at her and said, 'It's only the United Nations building."

"The United Nations is our last hope for world peace."

"I fought in a United Nations peace-keeping mission. It was Harry Truman's police action. I called it the Korean War and General MacArthur damn near made WWIII out of it. Forty-five thousand Americans came back in pine boxes."

The president made his little speech denouncing the terrorist action. The senators and the Department of Defense were mum on the subject. Jan arranged for a gathering of the family. Jim went over to see how Fred Goldsmith was doing at the Fine Jewelry store.

"Hello, Jim."

"How are you getting along, Fred?"

"Thanks to the Director and Terminator tokens, my business is doing well. See those boxes over there? Twenty thousand tokens ready for shipment into the New York City market, the police department. Look at my latest."

"My God, you have them in onyx, turquoise, and every other imaginable color. What is going on?"

"I am preparing for the big event."

"Meaning what?"

Fred picked up a ring with the Director emblem on the face of it. "See this."

Jim examined the ring. It had "Revolution" inscribed on one side and "2000" on the opposite side. U.S.A. was printed on the front. Jim saw that he had a copyright and design patent on the ring. Jim looked up at him with a stare.

"Yes, Jim, you are entitled to part of the action; after all, you did the original design on the tokens."

"Have you shipped tokens to police departments in other cities?"

"Yes, recently I shipped to cities in the Northwest and Midwest."

"How about the South?"

"I have been shipping tokens into the South from the very beginning."

"To whom?"

"An all-white male fraternal organization. They like swift justice down there and they love capital punishment, instant capital punishment as it is now called across the country."

Jim looked at Fred and asked the painful question, "I wonder about people like you. What are your principles? Where are your morals? Don't you ever ask yourselves what will happen when these tokens get into the hands of a rebel in the South or a trigger-happy cop in Detroit or Chicago?"

"It is a free country."

"You say that it is a free country."

"I have a right to make a buck here and there. You are entitled to a share of the profits. I have them manufactured and sell them for a profit. What is really bothering you, Jim?"

Jim walked to the front of the store, put his hands into his pockets, and looked up at the building across the street. "The sniper on top of that building, the guard outside walking his beat, that's what bothers me."

"This would have happened anyway. You just jump-started it."

"I am sorry I ever designed those tokens. I hope you make a lot of money selling tokens and trinkets when the revolution comes. I don't want a single cent from your merchandising schemes. Do me one favor."

"Yes, Jim."

"Please don't associate me with the Terminator or Director tokens in any way. It shall always be your creation, your idea."

"If you feel that way about it, I agree."

"Bye, Fred." He left Fine Jewelry and drove to the hospital.

This was not one of Jim Clark's finest days. He had to prepare himself to visit a dying friend. He parked near the hospital and walked very slowly trying to collect his thoughts for his visit to a man he had not seen in a few years, and the man was dying. The probing question spinning around in his mind was, *What do you say to a dying man?* He sauntered through the emergency room. It was full of people with crying children. He was lost. He took a right turn and walked straight ahead. He passed rooms with patients connected to tubes lying in bed. This depressed him even more. As he walked to a dead end he turned and reached the front desk. Three minutes later he was in Bob's room.

"Hello, Bob!"

"Jim Clark, how nice of you to come and visit me."

Jim reached out to shake hands. He received a limp set of fingers. Bob's strong tennis grip was gone. He no longer was the durable, tough doubles partner he remembered. His mind flashed back when he and Bob were two young veterans attending the School of Business at the University of Colorado.

"Jim, I am getting out of here soon. I have a positive attitude about beating cancer."

Jim took a deep breath and walked to the window overlooking a parking lot. "Bob, do you remember when I had the shock of my life? I thought that I was going to die? I was so depressed I contemplated taking my own life. I asked you to find another tennis partner, which you did."

"Yes, I remember, but you are still alive."

"I was prepared to die. I always am. As you know, I believe in euthanasia. I am not afraid to die." Jim fingered the plastic box containing a farewell pill in his pants pocket that Bill Bailey had given to him.

"Jim, you are different, so damn practical. Sometimes you were a pain in the butt; nevertheless you were one helluva doubles partner. We beat a lot of guys out there in the hot sun. . . . I don't share your thoughts on the life hereafter. There is nothing out there beyond this life on earth."

"There is something out there after death, believe me. I still have the same medical problem and suspect that you and I will see each other in the promised land sometime within the next ten years."

"You're nuts. I am getting out of here alive, you wait and see."

"Whatever you say. If there is a heaven I suspect you will make it up there in your first ascent, to the land from where no man has ever returned."

Bob broke out in painful laughter.

Jim had hoped for this to happen. He abruptly changed the subject from the future to the past. They talked for two hours about their past escapades. Jim said good-bye in the most nonchalant way and promised to visit Bob the next day. Jim left the hospital feeling good about himself. The visit had turned out pleasant. Everything turned out pleasantly for Bob. It was his way of living, nothing to

162

distract him from enjoying life to the fullest. Bob was a rare, wonderful human being.

Jim stepped outside the hospital and it hit him that he had just bid farewell to his former classmate, tennis partner, friend, and pal. He became all choked up. He kept walking and walking until he was ten blocks beyond where he had parked the car. He returned to the hospital area and located his car and went home. He went into the bedroom, sat down in a chair, and stared at the wall until suppertime. Jan went for a walk in the park by herself.

The following day Doc called to tell Jim that Bob had died in his sleep early that morning. Bob's brother had made prior arrangements for cremation in anticipation of his death. The brother planned to sprinkle Bob's ashes on their parents' grave somewhere back East.

Jim enjoyed Jan's family gathering; it took his mind off Bob's death. "I am ready to go back to the mountains. This place gives me claustrophobia."

"Honey, I understand. You have been under a lot of stress this trip."

"We'll drive back tomorrow?"

"We are going to fly back, remember."

"I forgot. My mind is in shambles."

As they landed in Deerpoint, Jim pointed to the truck, "Look, Jan, he is waiting patiently for us." Jan smiled. She too was happy to see the truck. "Tonight I want to go out and celebrate my friend's departure into the other world."

"Honey, I am with you. Great idea. I remember meeting Bob during a tennis tournament at the Gates Tennis Center. I liked him immediately."

"Yesterday I had misgivings about myself because I had lost touch with him over the years and today I feel fortunate that I had the pleasure of knowing him."

"That is a healthy attitude. We shall make a toast to him this evening."

They drove up the slope to the chalet. Jim eyeballed the juniper that guarded his cache of gold and said, "Thank God, we are home."

Jan added, "Amen."

They carried their bags upstairs and dropped them on the bed.

Jan crossed her arms and said, "I am so happy to be home, happy that we have our own private hideaway."

"Home sweet home, Jan." She gave him a hug, he hugged her back and slapped her fanny. He walked out on the deck to scan their homestead. The ground was greening, but snow still covered the mountain tops. Ski season had ended and the most beautiful season, summer, was just around the corner. They did not call the Crockers, they wanted to share the evening with each other.

Jim was anxious to have lunch with J. J. at the Last Chance Bar. He had many questions for Judge Crocker regarding his debut on national TV.

"Hi, Jim."

"Hey, I saw you on TV last week."

"You are the only one in Deerpoint who saw me. Even Betsy missed the press conference."

"So you are in the loop, as they say in the capital city. Tell me, who all is in the Save America loop?"

"Mostly senators from the South, a few from the Northwest and Midwest. You should experience the power and excitement in Washington, D.C. I could feel it all around me. Things are happening in high places."

"Like what?"

"Impeachment of the president, for one."

"Well, that is not news; I anticipated that."

"We are drawing up plans for the recovery of this country after we declare bankruptcy."

"Are members of the House of Representatives in your group?"

"You mean the House of Spenders?"

"Yes."

"There are a few in our inner circle. The liberal Democrats have fled the country. They are hiding up in Canada or down in Mexico. This revolution is going to make endangered species out of liberal politicians. They fear their home turf. They are afraid of being shot on sight in their own districts."

"The past is haunting the liberals and their future in America is bleak. Either we make some quick drastic changes or we may be headed towards a shooting revolution."

"You are so right, Jim. This coming week the president will

164

announce that we are selling the air force to Saudi Arabia, the navy to Japan, and Germany will absorb most of the army stationed overseas. Germany will be the center of power in Europe; Japan will hold the line in the Far East, and Saudi Arabia expects to maintain peace in the Middle East."

"Where is the vice president these days?"

"He is hanging around waiting for a miracle to happen. We're working on a successor to the president and it is not the vice president."

"One of the senators?"

"Can't tell you, top secret at this point."

"When are you fellows going to call for bankruptcy?"

"First, we have to get rid of the president, then we can move on with our short-term and long-range plans."

"J. J., the president was not alone in this grand debacle, how about the 535 congress-people with their massive entourage of attorneys and bureaucrats who have become permanent fixtures in Washington, D.C.?"

"I saw so many bureaucrats, attorneys, lobbyists and other briefcase-toting people swarming around the capital, it reminded me of ants going after a discarded fruit seed."

"I see them as ants who are gnawing the last piece of flesh from the bones of Uncle Sam."

"Ah, well put indeed."

"I once saw the same scene on Wall Street. We have to get rid of those damn blood-sucking parasites, lawyers."

"We will."

"You and Jan should go to Denver next week and listen to Mr. Willard Knight give his speech from the steps of the state capitol."

"I see him on TV occasionally."

"The media is holding back part of his message. The president called the man a quack. Your former Denver mayor is trying to smear Mr. Knight with false accusations."

"You mean our Secretary of Public Awareness and his wife?"

"The capital is full of people like the former Denver mayor and our former governor, professional politicians, I respect Mr. Knight. He started out by himself in Florida and no one took him seriously. Now he is preparing his followers to march on Washington."

165

"How do you fit into the scheme of things?"

"I became involved through the Director and Terminator tokens, law and order. I took your original idea and put it into motion. It worked. The country was ripe for the idea of putting authority back into the hands of law-abiding citizens. Now the criminal no longer has the upper hand; the victim has more rights than the criminal for the first time in years."

"Are we laying the foundation for a police state?"

"Probably, until we get the country back on its feet again."

"I first questioned the weakness of our society when we tolerated the use of social drugs and allowed our youth to defy authority. Parents expected the public to raise their children for them. Individual responsibility versus social responsibility."

"We will legalize social drugs, and that will put drug dealers and drug pushers out of business and reduce crime."

"There will be opposition to that idea."

"Citizens will like the idea of controlling the sale of social drugs and the revenue it will produce. And on the other side of the coin we will reduce our policing expense enormously. Recently we were a superpower, now we are trying to avert a civil war in this country, a Third World country at best. I hope no dictator decides to invade us."

"J. J., who would want to invade a country with the problems we have? We are a liability and not an asset."

"Why didn't Americans exercise their right to a peaceful revolution in the polling booth?"

"I recall that protesting in the sixties became a substitute for voting."

"I think, Jim, that the march on Washington, D.C., will be a peaceful one. Trust me, the country soon will be in good hands. I have to return to the courthouse. I am not retired like you."

"See you tomorrow, Judge."

"Thanks for the lunch, Jim."

Jim returned to the chalet, Jan was gone. He remembered that she was out scrounging for meat, spare ribs, ham hocks, and a roasting chicken. She didn't encounter much of a problem with food stamps as long as she had cash in hand. It was the working stiff who suffered on all counts and at both ends of life, no job, no money, only handouts. Residents of Deerpoint fared reasonably well because

166

foreign tourists took advantage of a weak American dollar. However, the forthcoming ski season looked bleak. The United States was developing a reputation of domestic violence that eventually would drive visitors away.

Jim walked over to the juniper that marked his buried gold and admired the daisies he had planted beneath the bush. He knew that after the country declared bankruptcy his gold would buy a sizable hunk of stock in the Bank of Colorado. The phone rang. He shuffled upstairs and interrupted the incoming message. It was Bill Bailey.

"Bill, this is Jim."

"Is Mother there?"

"No, but she will be home soon to cook supper."

"Have her call me at work or at home."

Jim left a note for Jan and drove his truck downtown for an oil change. When Jim returned from downtown Jan was still out shopping. He proceeded to rake the gravel in the driveway and tidied up around the chalet. Jan drove her Mercedes into the garage.

"I left a note upstairs for you. Your number-two son called."

"What did he want?"

"I have no idea. You are to call him back." He took a break from his raking, leaned a chair against the garage, and smoked his pipe. Jan came back downstairs.

"Bad news. Bill and Judy are having marital problems."

"So what are you supposed to do about it?"

"When are we going back down to Denver?"

"We just came back."

"I know. I need your help in dealing with Bill and Judy. I don't communicate too well with either one."

"What is the problem?"

"Ever since Judy was fired from the State Department of Health over the farewell pill, they have been at odds with each other."

"She needs a challenge."

"Bill wants her to contribute to the family budget."

"I will talk to them. The judge suggested we attend the rally in Denver. Mr. Knight is giving his last speech before he marches on Washington, D.C."

"I think I would like that. Reminds me of protests I attended during the sixties."

167

"I doubt that smoking grass and having free sex is on Willard Knight's agenda."

"Smarty pants."

"What's for supper?"

"I lucked out. We have spare ribs. Fire up the char-broiler."

"Thanks. I can always count on you." He gave her a hug and slapped her left rear.

They flew to Denver. On their ride to the townhouse in a cab they saw long lines at the gasoline stations. There was a temporary shortage. Jan and Jim made arrangements to meet Judy and Bill at a restaurant.

Jan tried to be counselor, mother, and mother-in-law all rolled up in one. She proceeded to establish neutral ground and attempted to attack the marital problem. Jim listened patiently to half an hour of empty words, and then addressed the matter in his own way.

"Look, if you two can't resolve your differences I suggest you get a divorce before you have children." He looked right at Judy and said, "I will continue to work with you on the farewell pill. First we must get FDA approval and then go for a patent. Bill, I will take your interest in the pill since I already paid you twice for your efforts. Does anyone care for dessert?"

Three gaping mouths declined.

"Well, let's get the hell out of here so I can have a smoke."

They left the restaurant. Jan was perplexed. She had made her best attempt in trying to save her son's marriage but had resolved nothing. In parting, Jim gave his farewell and said, "Let us know of your decision." They all went home.

"Jim, I can't believe you solved their problem in such a simple manner."

"I didn't. They will have to do that; I just told them what I intend to do. There is nothing more you and I can do."

"Bill's father never took him to the wood shed. I think you just did, and he needed that."

Mary was expecting her child in June and that meant Jan had some serious shopping to do for her granddaughter. She dropped Jim off at the tennis center and went shopping. Jim was just finishing his pipe when Doc showed up with his friend.

"Jim Clark, meet Judge Schultz."

"Well, I will be damned. Judge Crocker's counterpart in Denver."

"That I am. Nice to meet you, Jim. J. J. speaks frequently of you."

Doc looked around for a fourth. He wanted to play doubles. "Hang on, guys. I think we have doubles coming up."

After one set of doubles, Judge Schultz excused himself and left.

"Schultz is all business, he is not like Judge Crocker. J. J. likes to shoot the bull, have another drink, and show up late for court," said Jim.

"Schultz is a well-intended man; however, there are times I think he missed his calling. He would have made an excellent SS officer."

"Are you coming out to play tomorrow?"

"Yes," said Doc.

"Between tennis and hospital calls, does your wife ever see you?"

"Doc smiled. We have been living like this for forty years. We have a compatible relationship."

Jan returned from her shopping. "Do you want to hit some tennis balls?"

"I need to work out the winter kinks."

On their way back to the townhouse they passed by Denver's oldest country club. "Honey, I always wanted to belong to a private club like this. Have you ever belonged to a private club?"

"No, and I never will."

"Why not?"

"People behind those white walls inherited their wealth. They are a bunch of pseudophilanthropists . . . I have nothing in common with them."

"I play tennis with some of the ladies who belong to this club; they are nice people and very interesting. I see them pictured in the society section of the Denver newspaper. They attend fund-raising dinners, hold fashion shows, and play golf and tennis at this beautiful club."

"Their great-grandfathers invented and patented valves, batteries, v-belts, and turned a little brewery into a giant industry. Those fellows were real men; they smoked cigars and drank good whiskey. I bet the old gents would turn in their graves if they could see their

169

offspring prancing around with liberals. A bunch of misguided reborn liberals. Victims of affluence."

"Well, so much for that idea."

"Jan, we no longer live in Denver. Deerpoint is our home."

Jim had his usual chat with Mark about his work at Research, Inc. Mark was hopeful for the project and so was Dr. Klein. He had recently received his master's degree from the University of Colorado, based mostly on his work at Research, Inc.

"Dr. Klein is encouraging me to work for a doctorate degree."

"Mark, if you like what you are doing, go for it and never look back."

"Thank you, Jim. I appreciate your support."

The big day arrived. Mr. Knight was going to give his speech in Denver. Jim was apprehensive about attending the function. Jan on the other hand was excited to witness a mass cultural event. The last time a large gathering was staged in Denver, Mr. Reverend was assassinated. They walked over to the large crowd of people. Men in uniform seemed to be everywhere. Ambulances and squad cars were lined up in formation. Colorado National Guardsmen were posted by the stage and beyond in single file around the perimeter of the spectator area. Young men dressed in plain tan military uniforms extended the file beyond the National Guard troops. These men in plain uniforms wore an emblem signifying their organization as the "Aryan Nation" on their left lapel and the emblem, "Save America," on the right lapel. Above the flap of the left breast pocket they wore a pin with the design of the Terminator token. Jim choked when he saw that emblem displayed in public for the first time. He still carried his tokens in his billfold.

The crowd was a mixture of young men and women wearing sweatshirts bearing the "Save America" theme. Others wore shirts that read, "Down with Liberals," and there were those who wore "Colorado Rockies" shirts, denoting the local baseball team.

Baseball was played on weekends and a few games during the week. Baseball players preferred partial pay over no work at all, so they continued to entertain spectators. Men in the Colorado National Guard were lucky; they were on a payroll. The Aryan Nation paid their men a base salary from funds donated by private contributors who sanctioned the grass roots organization. A regular paycheck was the desire of everyone during these times. Young men and women wanted to have the self-respect, dignity, and the pride that came with being self-sufficient and independent. Dependency no longer was a choice but rather became a fact of life for people who hd previously been proudly in command of their own destination. Basic survival had replaced the wasteful frivolous ways that America had become so famous for throughout the world.

A man from Colorado introduced himself as a retired general of the United States Army and he in turn presented a retired general from Montana as the head of the newly formed organization called the Aryan Nation.

The police chief of Denver rose and informed the crowd that he was in charge of law enforcement. He pointed out to the folks attending the rally that he would not tolerate rioting. "We will shoot anyone who reaches for a weapon."

Most of the young people carried guns in their jackets or had one tucked into their belts beneath their sweatshirts. The Denver police chief went on to explain that each police officer was backed up by a plainclothes lawman from a Colorado organization called the "Enforcer," which was under the command of a retired Colorado general. He made reference to the colonel, seated between two retired generals, who was in charge of the Colorado National Guard. Law and order were present at this meeting of disgruntled Americans and there was no doubt about it.

Mr. Willard Knight walked up to the microphones and told the crowd that a group of young ladies would sing the new national anthem, "America the Beautiful." The girls, accompanied by some wind instruments, had the crowd singing along with them.

Mr. Knight presented his speech: "My dear fellow Americans, we are gathered here today to change government in Washington, D.C., as we have known it in the past. It is not the Constitution of the United States that has failed us but the politicians who are supposed to represent us. The liberal spirited politicians in Washington tax us on our labors and then give away our money. I say to you, stop sending money to Washington and we will put the corrupt politicians out of business by midsummer. Look at the mess we are in, children suffering from malnutrition, elderly folks starving in senior citizens' homes, and look at yourselves, unemployed, underemployed, barely eking out a meager living. What about your parents who have been stripped of their hard-earned savings by inflation? The president put into effect a Wage and Price Freeze Act to curtail inflation and that effectively shut down production in our country. He printed more money to pay for the interest on our national debit. He sold off the navy, army, and air force to pay off foreign debit. In disgust, Alaska and Hawaii have left the union. He is a foreign policy president with a large defense budget to force his will upon the free world. He supported dictators with foreign aid that you and I paid for. Who looked out for you when all this was going on in our capital? No one. Did they ever ask for your advice? Never. They just went ahead and spent your money as they saw fit. When one out of five citizens works to support four out of five members of our society on the government dole, socialism has gone amuck.

"Crime is a drag on society. Liberals have permitted crime to become a profitable business. Liberals refuse to execute killers; they prefer to put them into a retirement home that you and I can't afford, fancy hotels, health spas, institutions they called rehabilitation centers. You pay to comfort the criminal; they reward him. We need more capital punishment. Instant capital punishment has proven that crime does not pay. We have to make everyone responsible for his actions, do his share as a citizen, pay his dues to society on an equal and fair basis. We need more engineers in production and less attorneys sucking off of our economic system. Who needs a social engineer telling you how to live a politically correct life? Have you ever seen an attorney or a social engineer with callused hands? The power of government must be moved back to the taxpayer on a local level. We must do this ourselves, no one else is going to do it for us. We have to march on Washington, D.C., remove the president from office, and reduce the size of Congress." This brought applause.

"I recommend that we legalize the social use of drugs and take over the drug industry." This brought a loud roar from the young crowd. The slow economic decline and gradual deterioration of America's social fiber had created apathy among the younger generations. They languished in hopelessness. Mr. Knight struggled to arouse his young crowd into action. He was successful with his previous older crowds, who were better informed on current events and had memories of better times.

"I want a brave new country for you young folks. We should not keep crack babies alive at an astronomical price only to see them die a few years later. We should give folks the right to a decent life or let them choose to end it in a peaceful and respectful way. Let them make the choice." He finally hit the young crowd's hot button. They roared to life; they felt like they had just scored a touchdown.

"We have lost our common sense about the quality of life. We should not weaken the strong to support the failing weak, that will destroy an society over a period of time." He had another round of applause. "The Save America boys and I will recommend to our new president that we put America back on a new road to prosperity unlike anything you have ever experienced in your life. March with me to Washington. Down with the liberals. Thank you for your support."

The police chief noticed Blacks flashing their phones. He knew they had plans for a riot. The chief put all units across the city on alert. National Guard units were posted at shopping centers and in downtown business areas. Jim and Jan walked hand-in-hand back towards home.

"Well, Jan, how did this crusade compare with your past experiences?"

"Same idea, to bring about a change, with a sight difference; this rally will bring about change."

"Did you see the harmony and respect between the military force and the young crowd?"

"Yes. The young people seemed to respect authority rather than defy it."

"Your generation hated authority!"

"We were idealistic college students looking for a cause. The people I saw today at the crusade have a cause, a real cause. I think Mr. Knight pointed them in a direction to do something about their plight."

"That he did. Let's go have lunch at one of your favorite restaurants and then hit some tennis balls."

"Honey, you are reading my mind again."

They spent a pleasant afternoon doing what retired people should do, enjoying life. When they returned to the townhouse Mary had returned from her day of teaching.

Jim gave her a quick look and said, "Mary, you look like you are going into labor any minute."

"One more week of school and then I can just lie back and wait for the baby to come."

Helpful Jan was always available. "Go lie down now. I will fix supper."

Jim fixed himself a drink and sat down to see how the media covered Mr. Knight. The police had squelched the Blacks in their effort to start riots all across town. The fire department had doused some fires in downtown Denver. Fine Jewelry had been robbed and the owner shot. Other attempted robberies had been thwarted by hired guards and sharp shooters.

"Jan, did you hear the news from the kitchen?"

"Some of it."

"Fred Goldsmith was robbed and probably for the last time."

"Oh, no. Was he shot?"

"Yes. He refused to hire inside guards like other merchants on his street did. Fred was counting on others to provide free protection. He may have made his last mercenary American dollar. The Black rebellion lost a battle today. Denver stood up to their violence and won."

"The crusade ended so peacefully. I don't understand."

"Blacks received a proclamation today on their exclusive business, the drug trade. They lost more than a battle in rioting. Jan, they are planning the crusade."

"Am I in the picture?"

"Among fifty thousand, hardly. The general from Montana is taking applications for his organization and so is the general from Colorado. See those young Mexicans signing up? They want to be part of the American revolution. I don't see any Blacks in line to sign up."

"Probably nobody asked them."

"Blacks don't fight for other people's rights; they demand rights for themselves. They are bona-fide dependents of the state."

"Hello, Jim."

"Welcome home, Mark."

"What's new on the tube?"

174

"Mr. Goldsmith was robbed and shot after the rally, probably dead by now."

"I'm sorry to hear that."

"I am surprised that he lasted this long, considering that his store is located on Colfax Avenue in the rough part of town. I visited with him a couple weeks ago. Fred was bound and determined to make his last almighty buck. He stayed too long."

"How did the crusade come off today?"

"Pretty good. I don't know if he reached the younger crowd. I am too far removed from your generation to understand where they are coming from."

"Some of my softball team said they would attend. Those guys were ready to shoot somebody today. Was there any violence?"

"Not at the rally."

"You and Bill play mostly team sports?"

"Yes. Our dad had us playing every sport in the book. You know athletic coaches, practice and play, practice and play some more. Never played tennis. After Mary has the baby we plan on taking tennis lessons."

"Good idea. I love the game."

"Is Mom a good player?"

"Nice player. That's how we met."

"Yes, I know. The Rockies won today. I would like to see a game sometime."

"Why don't you locate four season tickets? I will buy them."

"I see tickets advertised in the newspaper from time to time."

"I want four tickets behind the batter's box, slightly to the right and about three rows up."

"I have never seen tickets like that for sale."

"Run an ad and ask for them, they are out there, times are tough."

"Boy, wait until I tell Bill about season tickets for the Rockies."

"Have you talked to Bill lately?"

"Yes. I guess you set him on his ear."

"Mark, I did your mother a favor. I am not a marriage counselor."

The national news overshadowed the crusade in Denver. A commentary report on the state of Israel was coming on line. "This

175

little nation has been living in fear ever since the United States ceased to support it with foreign aid. No other nation has come forth to support this small Jewish nation in the Middle East. Israel is like a little rabbit dashing about in an Arab desert, while the wolves are waiting to make their kill. Israel will not survive in an Arab world."

"I saw that coming. Uncle Sam is no longer the protector of the world. We will see uprisings in Africa and all over the world."

"The United Nations is defunct. There is no hope for world peace."

"Mark, the United Nations is a mere shell without a superpower backing it up. We should send a note of thanks to Libya for blowing up the damn place."

"Do you converse with Dr. Klein occasionally?"

"We discuss finances on a monthly basis."

"I recently received clearance from the Department of Defense. I'm not sure if I should be discussing internal matters with you, but since you are the sole supporter of the company. . . . "

"What is so secret about cold fusion?"

"Well, there are other people working on cold fusion and the defense department is keeping tabs on all of us. They think we are more advanced on our work than the others and fear that a foreign country might want to extract it from us."

"Terrorist approach?"

"That, or because we may sell our research conclusions to a foreign entity. Dr. Klein is flying to Washington, D.C., to meet with the Department of the Army."

Jim knew all about Dr. Klein's trips to Washington, D.C. The Department of the Army wanted to buy out Research, Inc., but Jim refused to sell unless Dr. Klein was in full agreement. Dr. Klein had told him that all their phones were probably bugged so they met at airports, parking lots, and restaurants in Boulder. "How are the scientists reacting to the defense department's interest in cold fusion?"

"Those guys are so steeped into research they are unaware of our revolution. Last month we ran tests for three days. We wanted to prove our discovery. Three scientists remained in the laboratory for two days, with no sleep, little food, and they never shaved or showered during that time."

"Dedicated fellows."

"They live for research. There is nothing else in their life except research. Dr. Klein said that those fellows would die from personal neglect if it were not for their loving wives."

"Feel free to discuss your work at Research, Inc., with me. You need someone outside the office to talk about your work."

"Don't say a word to Mother about our discussion."

"Don't worry. I have secrets I share only with myself."

"Good, I feel better."

Jim had not told anyone where he'd buried the gold. Everyone thought he had it stored at the Bank of Colorado, and no one would know the burial place until his death.

"Jim, when do you think life will be normal again?"

"I hope in about a year. They will declare bankruptcy, issue new currency, and then toss out all of the past failed programs and start fresh, anew. My friend, Judge Crocker, and his cohorts are working on a reorganization plan."

"The other day I was in the supermarket and saw people buying dog and cat food. I suspected that they didn't even have a pet. One of the guys on our softball team said the Orientals stir-fried all the pets in his neighborhood."

"I don't doubt that. I think some of the hamburger I saw in the store was horse meat. I didn't have the heart to tell Jan. It looked very red to me and a bit coarse. Folks can't afford to feed their horses so they sell them, and horse meat finds its way into the store. Survival has become the number-one priority in this country."

"I can't bring myself to live like that."

"You can and will if you are desperate enough. Believe me, I know."

"We probably are having our baby at a bad time."

"Some of my best plans led to failure and the best things in my life just happen, like meeting your mother."

"I am happy for Mom and you. I know she feared growing old by herself."

"I never knew that."

"I know she is happy with you."

They sat down to eat their evening meal, spaghetti and meatballs, lots of spaghetti with sauce, but too short on meatballs for Jim's tastes. Meat was difficult to obtain in the marketplace. Farmers had down-sized their herds over two years. There was a shortage of nearly everything for a multitude of reasons. Jan gave her Lutheran prayer. She asked blessings for the family, for her granddaughter, America as a whole, and all the poor deprived souls out in the street. She glanced up to Mark, who gave her a negative look, then she glanced towards Jim. He rolled his eyes. She said, "Amen."

"Jan, I feel for those people out there not belonging to anything, not needed. It must be an empty life. They wake up to the same kind of hopelessness they bedded down with the night before. Every day is the same for them. I saw that longing look in those children's eyes . . . the true victims of our demise."

Jan gave the remarks some thought and said, "I saw that lost expression in the eyes of people at the crusade today. My heart sank to my knees."

Mark had his slant on the day's event. "People at the crusade today have no idea how they've arrived at such a miserable junction in their lives. They are about to turn violent."

No one commented on Mark's suggestion, they kept on eating. Nobody wanted to entertain the possibility of a shooting revolution.

"Liberal politicians will be the target; they are the enemy."

They refrained from comment on Mark's opinion of the revolution. He continued, "We could fight amongst ourselves, society turning on itself, which would accomplish nothing."

After supper Mark and Jim withdrew to the living room, also the TV room and the family hangout, and it was the family room for all purposes.

"If we resolve cold fusion we will put holes into the Arab tankers. I am looking forward to that day."

"You are right about that. It would change the lifestyle of the privileged in the Middle East. They may have to trade in their Mercedes for a couple camels and go back to selling figs."

"The electric car never made it unto the big highway. I was hoping your rotary engine would replace the piston engine."

"I think that the electric car, aside from its technical problems and practical limitations, would merely shift the brown cloud of fossil fuels from the city to coal fields in the mountains and wilderness areas."

"Jim, the electric car will serve us well in the city after we come up with a clean, plentiful source of energy, like cold fusion."

"Someday an inventor will find a replacement for the universal piston engine."

"I will continue to work on cold fusion and you should continue to work on your rotary engine."

"Cold fusion is a new frontier, my spinning little engine is something out of the fifties. Do you want to watch the late news?"

"Sure."

Late reports indicated more violence than had been reported earlier but nothing compared to what Los Angeles goes through every week. Approximately thirty people were killed after the crusade ended. Mr. Goldsmith died at the hospital.

"I will go over to the store and visit with his daughter. I have never met her, but Fred spoke of her frequently. An only child," remarked Jim.

The reporter explained that New York was on the other end of the spectrum from Los Angeles; it had become a police state. They showed three New York police officers making an arrest.

"Look at that, Jim, the officers are wearing pistols with twenty bullets clipped on their belts, no night sticks, no handcuffs. These guys didn't come to arrest; they came to shoot."

"Looks like they are enjoying their work."

"Too much so."

The news switched to Los Angeles. The Blacks were burning and looting the city, block by block. The Mexican government was complaining that too many people were emigrating back to Mexico. They were unable to handle the sudden influx of people. Life for Mexican-Americans in California became impossible. They were leaving by the thousands daily.

"Mark, I didn't think I would live to see this happen, Mexicans fleeing back to Mexico."

"Boy, what a switch for California."

"I bet the Hollywood glamour boys are already down there rubbing elbows with their liberal cousins."

"Right after I graduated from engineering school I applied for a job in California. I envied their laid-back lifestyle and now they are

179

drowning in their self-styled liberalism. Strange how things play out sometimes."

"I have no empathy for them. They asked for it. I remember Hollywood singing the song, 'We Are the World.' They raised funds for food that was shipped to a small country in Africa. The food rotted on the docks while two dictators were fighting over control of the country. The United States got sucked into the fracas at a heavy cost. A few years later the U.S. soldiers left and the two dictators went right back at it again. All is forgotten and nothing was resolved."

"I may be wrong, Jim, but I believe liberals are driven by a guilt complex.'

"That is an interesting supposition. That explains why some of my friends of years ago were so compassionately concerned about people on the lower level of the economic ladder. It was a guilt trip."

The last news item dealt with Mr. Knight's march on Washington, D.C. They had video shots of the Denver crusade. They zeroed in on sweatshirts carrying slogans like, "Kill Liberals," "March on D.C.," "Save America," "America My Country," "U.S.A. 2000," "Fight for America," "No Taxes 2000," and "Revolution—USA 2000."

"I saw something strange the other day at the Bank of Colorado. A cashier was wearing a ring that had U.S.A. on the front, Revolution on one side, and a strange cross on the face of the ring. I asked him about the ring and he said that the ring reflected the spirit of the revolution. He'd bought it at the Fine Jewelry store. He wore it to show his support for a change in America."

"Well, Mark, I think I will hit the sack. I am tired. Too much excitement for me today."

"I hope I will think young and play tennis when I am your age."

"Thank you, Mark. Now I will call it a day."

Jan and Mary had gone to bed. They both had the habit of reading themselves to sleep. Jan had fallen asleep wearing her glasses with a book on her lap.

Jan helped Mary with domestic chores. She shopped for groceries, waited in gas lines to refuel Mary's car, cleaned the townhouse, and cooked for a family of four. She had trouble adjusting to the larger bills everyone was carrying, fifty- and hundred-dollar bills. Inflation had torn the guts out of her retirement check. Without the cash flow from Jim's Swiss bank account she would have been at the mercy of her two sons, who were scraping along with Jim's help. She shuddered as the thought of having to make it on her own crossed her mind while sitting in the car waiting for her turn to refuel.

Jim walked to the Fine Jewelry store to find it all boarded up. He could see movement in the back of the store, he knocked on the glass entrance door. A lady approached him and said, "We are closed."

"I know. I am a friend of Fred's. May I come in?"

She reluctantly let him in. Jim introduced himself and extended his right hand, she acknowledged the handshake with some trepidation.

"I was sorry to hear about Fred on the news. Only a few weeks ago I visited with him. Many a time I suggested that he retire, but the store was his life."

"I suppose he changed the subject on you like he did with Mother and I every time we spoke to him about retiring."

"He told me that he was making money again with the tokens. He was very happy."

"My husband and I are going to sell off the merchandise and the building for Mother."

"Hang onto the patents and copyrights of the Revolution—USA 2000 tokens."

"We found the papers in the safe. You must have known my father quite well."

"We knew each other for many years. I used to own apartments in Capitol Hill. We had many a cup of coffee together and debated world affairs."

The lady lightened up. "Oh, you must be the man who bought all that gold."

"That's me. It looks like you have things under control here so I will move along." They said their farewells and Jim went to the café they used to visit for old times' sake. He recalled the head games they used to play on Max. Max was young and vulnerable. He didn't have a chance of winning an argument with the two old pros. Jim left the café feeling good despite the mayhem that surrounded him. He did lose another friend but he was still alive, like Bob had said.

He went back to the townhouse to read the morning newspaper and the *Wall Street Journal* he had bought from a vending machine.

Jan returned, exasperated from her morning of waiting in lines and searching for bread, butter, Crisco, coffee, and meat. "Honey, I long for the good old days, and I am not talking about the fifties or sixties. Just take me back five years when life was fun and easy."

"Shall we fly back to Deerpoint?"

"Yes. I think Mary and Mark want to have the weekend to themselves."

They landed in Deerpoint on a beautiful day. "Guess who is waiting for me over there?"

Jan smiled; she showed her compassion for the dirty old truck. "Honey, why don't you ever wash that poor thing?"

"If I washed that truck it would go into shock."

Life at the chalet was a contrast from the townhouse. Here they had open space, sunshine, and the absence of impoverished people on every street corner. Deerpoint residents were not insulated from the outside world by any means, but they managed well by themselves. The town was one big family. Summer tourists activities were canceled. This saddened Jan. She lived for summers in Deerpoint. Jan had her small circle of tennis friends she socialized with daily. Jim fly-fished every stream in the county and even made trips into the wilderness areas with his fly rod.

National and international news progressively over-shadowed local violence and disruptions in Denver. Problems in California multiplied as the wealthy moved to Mexico and other places with their money tucked safely away in a foreign country. Mexican Americans moved back to Mexico with the clothes on their backs just like they had entered the United States illegally years before. Middle-class people with some means left California for Oregon, Washington, Utah, and Colorado. Utah threatened to call up the National Guard and seal off its borders. Utah was a relatively peaceful state. They had followed Colorado in the practice of instant capital punishment. The big news was that Israel had been annihilated by Iraq. They did it secretly and cleanly; they gassed the major population centers. Israel vanished as a country. The United Nations was defunct. The United States had reduced its military machine to the Coast Guard, Marines, National Guard, and a few reserve units scattered around the remaining forty-eight states. Nations with economic and military power at their disposal avoided the Middle East crisis. The president of the United States addressed the world regarding moral obligations as if he still was directing world affairs. The world listened and did nothing.

Jim didn't see much of J. J. He had dashed off to Washington, D.C., for another meeting with the committee who was going to save America. Events were unfolding quickly around the globe as Uncle Sam trembled. The national debit rose to $16 trillion. The purchasing power of the dollar was somewhere between five and ten cents. Nobody cared at this point in time. It was too late for any minor corrections. It was time to start all over again with a new format. Judge Crocker, Judge Schultz, a racist from Louisiana, a group of senators and military leaders laid the foundation for the rebirth of America. No one specifically knew what this collection of saviors had in their plans for the country.

Jim Clark patiently waited for the country to declare bankruptcy; then he planned to dig up the gold and make his investment moves. The time was not now. The revolution was still in motion. Jim was a prisoner unto himself. He read newspapers and watched too much TV. He communicated only with Doc and J. J. That evening he watched the president address the nation. The president was faltering, indecisive. The man was at the end of his political career. He accused the Senate of undermining his plans for a recovery. He lied. He didn't have any plans; he didn't even know the source of the country's problems. He considered himself the leader of the free world. America came second in his mind. He always assumed that America would take care of itself. The downfall of the United States was not caused by this particular president or the present Congress; the seeds of destruction had been sown by numerous presidents and many members of Congress from both parties, and of course, the nonvoting citizen, years ago. The president feared Mr. Knight's upcoming march on the capital, and rightly so.

Jim and Jan had a drink on the deck at sunset. "Jan, here is to better times after this long, turbulent summer."

"Thanks, honey. Do you see the beginning of the end?"

"Yes, I do. I will know more after seeing J. J. He is due back tomorrow, according to Betsy."

The phone rang. Jan said, "I'll get it. Honey, it is Judy Cox. She wants to speak to you."

"Hello, Judy. Is this good news or bad news?"

"Both."

"Give me the bad news first."

"Very well. I need forty thousand francs for the farewell pill."

"And the good news?"

"The pill is selling so well I am going to push the FDA for approval and obtain a patent on the pill. I have to come up with a distinctive name for the pill."

"Judy, to me that is all good news. Go for it. I will transfer the money into your account within a day or two."

"Times are changing. Last year the Colorado Health Department canned me for pushing the farewell pill and now they are promoting it for me."

"I'll be damned."

"You should have been at the Sunset Senior Citizens' Home the other day. A little ninety-five-year-old woman took the pill in the presence of about ten other residents. She sat down in a chair, swallowed the pill, closed her eyes, and joyfully made her journey to the promised land. Later five more residents took the pill. Families are committing suicide every day. There is so much stress and parents are unprepared for it. Elderly people and the very young are helpless victims in circumstances they cannot alter or control. The idea of euthanasia is definitely catching on."

"I think the need for a pill has been there all along. We provided a means to satisfy an existing desire. How is Bill doing?"

"He is doing his thing and I am doing mine, Thanks to you, Jim."

"I will transfer the money tomorrow."

"Thanks again, Jim. Say bye to Jan for me."

"Will do."

"Good news, Jan."

"What did she want?"

"Forty thousand francs."

"For what? The pill?"

"The farewell pill."

"I wonder how she and Bill are getting along?"

"OK, I guess. She said that they both were doing their thing."

The sun had dropped behind the mountain. An instant chill hit them. "I am curious as hell to know what J. J. and his buddies are cooking up."

"Will he give you the details?"

"He won't reveal all of his secrets but he gives me enough to stay a step ahead of the news. How was your tennis match today?"

"The gals around here are real jocks. I have to take some lessons or they will refuse to play with me. How many rainbows did you hook today?"

"A few, I don't remember. I spent most of the day thinking about America's future. Judy is doing an excellent job with the pill. Research, Inc., runs by itself on our money. I have nothing to do."

"What about your whirling motor?"

"It is collecting dust in my workshop downstairs."

"I am happy to see you relaxed in retirement."

"'I feel kind of worthless."

"Jim Clark, if you don't have something to stew about you are unhappy."

"I am that I am."

"Oh my, now you are quoting the Bible."

"Philosophy, not the Bible."

"That is my book of philosophy. You do believe in the Bible?"

"The Old Testament. The Old Book was written by thinking men who laid out a great philosophy for mankind to live by."

"So what is wrong with the New Testament?"

"That was concocted by a whole bunch of people who figured out a way to hook people on the Old Testament."

"I don't have any idea what you are talking about. Do you?"

"The idea of original sin and the other mythical stuff they hung around J.C.'s neck are a means to hook and hold a person."

"I have faith in God and if you don't, you are a nonbeliever."

"I am no such thing. Everything God created is unique. Men are not created equally. Perfection exists only in the mind. Positive thinking stinks. Constructive thinking is glorious. Do you get my drift?"

"Yeah, you floated down a river in your raft after managing white water and now you are swirling around in a large eddy. You have lost your paddle and now must remain in the eddy forever. You are left all by yourself sitting in a raft."

"Boy, you shot me down."

"I know. I had a good teacher."

"Touché."

Jan shivered. "It's cold out here. Let's go in and have supper."

Jim could barely contain himself when he walked downtown for his coffee break during midmorning. He was dying to converse with J. J. He seated himself at his favorite little table and ordered coffee. J. J. eventually arrived.

"Well, well, the messiah returns from the East."

"Hi, Jim. It's great to be back. This nation is loaded with problems."

"I know. I watch TV every night. I read the Denver paper and the *Wall Street Journal* every day."

"The media only scratches the surface of the real news."

"Well, great one, I am all ears. I have been waiting for a report from you."

"You are right, Jim. Law and order by itself is not the solution to the problems in our country. Our economy is shot to hell."

"When are you guys going to declare bankruptcy?"

"As soon as we take over the government in Washington, D.C. We will get rid of the president and then take over the White House, all in one day. That is the easy part. Rebuilding the country is the tough part."

"Who do you have in mind to replace the president?"

"Top secret; still can't tell you until it happens. I have my ideas on law and order and I suppose you could help me on the economic side, but how do we restore the family unit and address family values? None of our efforts will be rewarded without social changes."

"Let economics dictate society's lifestyle. After bankruptcy, money will flow back into the country and business will crank up to satisfy a pent-up demand. It is conceivable we could reach a high level of prosperity within five years. I cannot help you on the social-behavioral side of the equation. Remember how we got into this mess . . . more and more government. Think in terms of less

186

government. Let society find its own way with the guidance of law and order."

"Sounds simple enough. It gets complicated in Washington."

"When I was in the apartment business, I wanted to corral the street people and give them a do-or-die alternative. I wanted to kill graffiti artists and drug users with a machete."

"Fifty senators and the rest of us have a similar plan we are working on. We have a three-year rehabilitation plan for the country that will require a lot of authority concentrated in a single place. Why don't you join me on my next trip to Washington?"

"It is not my cup of tea. I intend to do things with my gold after bankruptcy that will blow off your socks. I expect to buy part of a bank and pump blood back in the veins of industry."

"You probably will do that and more. I sure would like to have you present at our meetings."

"J. J., I loathe meetings. I hate them. I have one question."

"Shoot."

"On what day are you going to take over the country?"

"The day after Mr. Willard Knight makes his march on the Capitol, I think."

"I cannot bear to watch this country drag itself any farther down the black hole."

"My heartburn just dissipated. I am very tired, I wish it were all behind me. A few weeks ago I was in awe of political power, now I am fatigued from responsibility. Betsy and I are going to move to the Maryland this fall. She longs to go back and I have been offered a position with the new government."

Jim was stunned momentarily. "After you end the revolution get some advice from the Federal Reserve Board, bankers, economists, and industry at large; they can help set you fellows on a new course. Allow industry and the working people to do their thing for a change. Government has been a burden on the backs of its citizens for decades. And above all else, keep the damn liberals out of Washington, D.C."

"That may have been the best advice anyone ever gave to me. I will carry that with me to the capital on my next trip."

"When are you going back?"

"On the day of the big march. I have to go back go to the

187

courthouse. I am not retired yet, but pretty soon I will be. Thanks again for your advice and encouragement. I appreciate you sharing your thoughts with me." They parted.

Jim trudged upstairs to the living room. Jan was in the bedroom packing her suitcase. "You are packing. Are you divorcing me?"

"I am not married to you, remember." She hugged him and gave him a big kiss. He didn't respond with his usual pat on the fanny. He was dumbfounded. "Going to Denver. I became a grandmother early this morning, Mark just called."

"Grandmother to what?"

"A baby girl, what else? I think I will drive down."

"No, you are not. Just yesterday there was a massive highway holdup on I-70, a trucker saved the day."

"You are making this up."

"No, I am not. It happened just outside of Denver yesterday. A trucker picked off two guys with a sniper rifle and others jumped in and mowed down the holdup men. The revolution is moving our way. They shot innocent people and wounded each other. Too many guns."

"I didn't see that on the news."

"I read it in the paper this morning. Hell, I have nothing better to do. I will come along. Let me pack my bag. I will take my tennis racket. Make reservations on Eagle Airways. We should be able to make the last flight to Denver."

"Aye, aye, sir."

They packed fast. They had become proficient travelers. Jim spun the wheels on the old truck, dropped Jan and the bags off at the shack, and parked the truck. The plane was landing as Jan bought the tickets. They boarded and were welcomed by the copilot, Ace. "Hello, Jim. Hello, Jan."

"Ace, I didn't know you were flying Eagle Airways."

"They signed me on and now it's passengers and no more freight." Ace returned from the cockpit and said to Jim, "I want to talk to you about Eagle Airways when we both are back in Deerpoint."

"What about Eagle Airways?"

"I have an investment idea in mind."

Jan squeezed Jim's hand. She dreaded the five-hundred-foot

drops the plane sometimes made going over the Rocky Mountains. Jim didn't bother to brief Jan on Judge J. J. Crocker's report. She was on a high. Her wish had come true . . . a healthy granddaughter. Jan had been preparing for this occasion for seven months; to Jim this was just another day.

At the townhouse Jan got out of the cab and went for the keys to Mary's car. "Honey, I am going over to the hospital to see Mary and my granddaughter. Are you coming?"

"No. I will stay and wait for Mark."

Six o'clock came and passed. Jim's stomach was growling, so he fixed himself supper. Much later Mark and Jan returned from the hospital. Jan was off the ceiling.

She squeezed Jim with a hug and said, "It's amazing. She looks just like me." Jim went back to watching the late news.

A report came in from the Middle East. Saudi Arabia was bombing Iraq. Syria, Iran, Turkey, and Jordan were moving ground troops with tanks and artillery into Iraq. They joined forces and set out to pulverize Iraq. It was reported that the Middle East countries wanted to save face for what Iraq had done to Israel. More specifically, the nonproducing oil countries wanted the oil fields in Iraq. Oil had always been a bone of contention between the producing and nonproducing countries. Palestine was marching with Syria in this attack against an Arab brother. The other news was a repetition of uprisings in America.

The Black caucus put pressure on the Attorney General's Office to investigate the New York Police Department. The police in New York City were winning the war against crime. Unofficially, different precincts were running contests on their daily kill. In New York, the police had taken over the city and given it a chance to survive. In Los Angeles, the rioters controlled the city and had set out to destroy it. The Civil Liberties Union, Civil Rights Activists, Coalition for a Sane America, Individual Rights Organization, Liberty for All, and many other liberal groups were up in arms over the rapid deterioration of their liberal work. It was going down the tubes fast. There was no turning back the pages of history; instant capital punishment was a fact of life, and the liberal movement was destined to become extinct. Liberal Democrats had either fled the country or gone underground. Some brave, die-hard liberals secretly remained around Washington,

D.C. Liberal politicians feared returning to their home districts; it was too dangerous for them.

Florida was a mixed bag of turmoil. The rich moved their money to the islands before assets in the country were frozen and subsequently made their departure. Thousands of retirees departed to the islands with whatever they could smuggle in a mad dash. Jewish women hocked their diamonds for passage on a cruise ship to the islands. A violent uprising was anticipated in Florida. Caribbeans were warring amongst themselves and invading cities with widespread rioting, which soon was expected to escalate into a civil war. Many of the senior citizens had lost their savings to inflation and therefore were forced to remain in Florida. Brown people had never had any money; they were stuck for the duration or had the choice of returning to their former homelands as they had arrived on the shores of Florida, via a shabby boat or raft. It was ironic that the very people who aided and abetted the social revolution through the years suffered with the victims of too much liberalism, the poor, particularly the black people who had been promised so much by their government in Washington, D.C.

In California, American-Mexicans had an escape hatch, holes in the fence along the Rio Grande River. The Mexican government was making preparations to close its borders. They wanted to stop the reverse migration. Canada was getting concerned over the number of Americans entering their country. They were making plans to close their border to the south, but how? Canada and the United States shared a border thousands of miles in length and it would be impossible to seal up. During prohibition days, liquor flowed freely from Canada into the States; likewise people moved freely across the border to the north.

Jim Clark was no longer alarmed over news he received on TV or through the newspapers, he knew D-day was near. He took a cab to the tennis center and waited for Doc to make his presence.

"What, you back down from the mountain again?"

"Jan became a grandmother to a granddaughter. In that order. Have you seen Judge Schultz recently?"

"Yes. Did you get to talk to Judge Crocker?"

"I sure did. The manure is going to hit the fan during or after the march on the Capitol."

"Schultz tried to recruit me to a postrevolution position. I have second thoughts about his rehabilitation program."

"You sound like me. J. J. Crocker asked me to accompany him to Washington, D.C., and I refused. I figured he was trying to rope me into something. Doc, we are members of the silent generation and are doomed to die that way."

"The WWII guys kept the country in a Cold War and the social revolutionists of the sixties got their wish. We watched the parade as it passed us by; we never lifted a finger."

"What the hell! It's history now or soon will be. Let's hit the tennis court. Today I will beat you."

"I have an opening tomorrow, come in for a check-up."

"I will be there. Do you have a young sexy nurse?"

"I have had the best nurse in town."

"That means the same bland old lady." After their match Jim asked Doc to drive him over to a GMC dealership.

"Are you going to buy a truck?"

"Yes. I saw an ad on TV that caught my eye."

Jim bought a neat little white truck that reminded him of a truck out of the past; he liked it.

"You bought the truck in thirty minutes."

"How long does it take you to do a minor operation?"

"Depends. About fifteen minutes."

"There is your answer."

"Jim, you are right about yourself; you would be completely out of sync with the boys in Washington, D.C. Is Mark Bailey one of Jan's sons?"

"Yes. I am putting the title in his name. He will take care of it for me. How about a ride to the townhouse for a drink?"

"Sounds like a good deal to me."

"Doc, you have five years on me. When are you going to retire?"

"This fall, maybe. I might work part time for Judge Schultz."

"I thought you turned him down."

"I did, but he will be back. I have to work for monetary reasons. Can't say that I am keen on his rehabilitation program."

"What is the rehabilitation program about?"

"They plan to take people off the street, off welfare, and retrain them, prepare dysfunctional people for the structured world."

"Meaning what?"

"To live like you and I, like most of us. Make them self-sufficient. I have second thoughts about their draconian plan, but it is a chance to make a difference, and besides, I need the money. So this is your Denver hideout?"

"Jan's townhouse. Mark, Mary, and their baby live here; it gets a bit crowded. You and your wife should visit us in Deerpoint. I will show you nothing but blue sky and mountain scenery as far as the eye can see. Do you fly-fish?"

"Surgery and tennis is all I know."

"They have tennis courts up there."

"Helen and I lost most of our retirement funds, U.S. securities. Inflation destroyed the bonds and you know what will happen on bankruptcy day."

"I am sorry to hear that. Yes, I know. The federal government will write off its debit, cancel your bonds and notes."

"I have had substantial earnings throughout my working career and should be able to retire in style, but I can't."

"It is no consolation to you and Helen, but the younger generations will have an opportunity to make a fresh start in life. I feel for you, but I also have empathy for your daughters and Jan's boys. Remember when the president sold our army, navy, and air force?"

"Yeah."

"Seventy percent of our federal budget went towards paying the interest on our national debit at that time. The president gave the military operations away because he couldn't meet the military payroll. The senators advised him to let our personnel go with the equipment because we had such a high rate of unemployment."

"Interest rates were so high we bought more securities."

"The government was competing against industry for dollars. Things really started to unravel fast at that juncture."

"I know. I should have bought gold."

"Not necessarily gold but something other than U.S. bonds and Treasury notes."

"Thank you for the drink. Helen is waiting for me."

"Bye, Doc."

Mary was sleeping with the baby, but they had awakened. Jan returned from her dismal grocery shopping trip.

"How did you get back?"

"Doc dropped me off." Jim looked out of the living room window and smiled. Mark had driven up to the townhouse. He had a surprise for his favorite adopted son.

"Hello, Jim."

"How is cold fusion progressing?"

"Frustrating day. We took three steps backwards. Dr. Klein told us to stay away from the laboratory until Monday. We are all burned out."

"I bought a GMC truck today, put the title in your name."

"Hurrah! I have a new truck to drive and it isn't even my birthday."

"I got tired of waiting around for taxi cabs. We are to pick it up when they call us."

"I will park it in the garage and take good care of it for you."

"It is your truck; I just want to drive it once in a while. We need a third vehicle for all of us to have transportation."

"You have bought a new vehicle for everyone in the family and you are still driving that old truck in Deerpoint."

"Wheels are wheels to me, except for that old truck; it is special to me. That truck and I have come a long way."

"How about your sports car?"

"Please don't bring that up."

"Speaking of new cars and trucks, I saw drawings of a rotary engine in a scientific magazine."

"I'll be damned. Is it like mine?"

"They went a step further: two explosion chambers, two exhausts, and the fuel is injected ahead of the combustion chambers."

"Who invented it?"

"Engineering students at the University of Pennsylvania. They turned the invention over to General Motors. I think they were on a grant from General Motors. According to the article this is a breakthrough for the auto industry."

"I hope you are as close to cold fusion as I was to the rotary engine."

"About twice a year we think we have it solved and then we can't prove it. Nothing, no cigar."

"Have patience, it will happen someday."

193

"The defense department thinks so. I think of you often, footing the bill for this exercise in futility."

"I am making my selfish contribution to mankind."

"I am sorry you lost out on the rotary engine."

"I didn't lose. I tried. I am encouraged that young people in this country are still dreaming and trying." They had their family supper.

Jim gave Mary a fatherly look and asked her, "How does it feel to be a mother?"

"About one hundred pounds lighter." They enjoyed each other at dinner, they had adjusted to the times like everyone else.

"Jan, are you ready to return to God's country?"

"'I am ready to go home."

"Mom, Mary would like to skip teaching for a couple of years and spend time with the baby."

"I think that is the proper thing to do."

"But, we need to continue living in the townhouse."

"What do you think, Jim?"

"Don't even ask me, do it."

"Honey, Mark said you bought a new truck."

"Yes."

"I don't believe it. What about your old truck?"

"It will stay at the airport in Deerpoint."

The next day Mark gave Jim and Jan a ride to the airport. They made another thirty-minute flight to Deerpoint. The judge had left for Washington, D.C. The following day Mr. Knight was scheduled to make his grand speech on the steps of the Capitol Building. His speech had its origins in Florida with a theme of "no taxes" and now had become a rebellious message. International news focused on the invasion of Iraq. Countries who participated in the destruction of Iraq expected to share in its oil revenues. They divided Iraq and drew new border lines. The Palestinian army returned to its newly acquired homeland, Israel, thanks to Iraq. Middle East oil was still fueling industry throughout the industrial world and therefore was watched with a critical eye. Every time Arab leaders dressed up in white bed sheets and checkered tablecloths the world was on edge for fear of what they might conjure up out in the middle of the desert. The last such meeting produced the invasion of Iraq. Germany and France supplied the Middle Eastern oil producers with war toys in exchange for the precious black stuff. The fall of the United States left a vacuum in military police power and upset the world trade markets temporarily. It was in the best interest of the industrial world for the United States to become a producing and consuming nation again. The upcoming events in Washington, D.C., would mark the end of a long, good life in America and hopefully erase the recent years of hell people were forced to endure.

The next morning Jim and Jan had a late breakfast. They were back in rhythm with their life. "Jan, the open space around our chalet makes the townhouse seem like a prison cell."

"It was perfect for me when I was single and working. Certainly it was more practical than you living in a four-bedroom house by yourself."

"I made two hundred thousand dollars on that house."

"What do you have planned for today?"

"Watching TV. I want to see the fireworks in Washington, D.C. J. J. is beginning to sound like a politician, telling half-truths, mumbling innuendoes, and contradicting himself every other sentence. Even Doc shifted positions on me when I quizzed him on the subject of rehabilitation. Did I tell you that J. J. and Betsy are moving to Maryland?"

"No. When?"

"This fall after he retires from the bench. He is taking an advisory position with the new government. He is in Washington, D.C., right now."

Jim went out on the deck and peeked around the corner to check his juniper bush. It was still there, undisturbed. After reading the morning paper he flicked on the television. TV cameras panned the gathering crowd.

Jan came in from the kitchen, "This is bigger than I imagined."

"We are about to witness the most important mass gathering in our lifetime." The crowd was a mix of people, young and old, a cross section of America. "Guess they are going to maintain law and order, look at the military men lined up along the sidewalk, and the men in uniform marching in the parade."

The reporter was describing people in attendance, where they came from, who they were, and why they were attending the Revolution—USA 2000 event. Reporters had dubbed the event as such.

Motorcycle policemen escorted about three thousand men, in uniform, armed with rifles and side arms. They wore khaki uniforms and dark brown baseball caps with tan visors. A closeup showed that they wore a patch with the U.S. flag on the left upper sleeve and an oval emblem denoting "Save America" on the left lapel. On the right lapel they wore a Terminator emblem. The militia men looked and acted more military than the National Guard, who were supposed to be guarding them. The Aryan nation of the Northwest was followed by a southern group of about six thousand men dressed in rebel hats and khaki uniforms, also armed. Leaders of these units marched their men in formation to music by a marching band. American flags fluttered everywhere.

Jim switched channels for better coverage. Blacks who had planned on making a statement receded to their ghettos, it was reported. The demonstration was well orchestrated and had law and order stamped on it from stem to stern. This gathering was similar to the one in Denver, only much larger. The Black caucus was not in sight at this event. The Save America boys attended in full force; about fifty people surrounded the podium. Ten high-ranking military men moved in the midst of advisors and the senators.

Mr. Willard Knight approached the speakers. A naval cadet choir sang "America the Beautiful" and the speeches commenced. Mr. Knight introduced himself as the man of the hour. He pointed out how working Americans defeated liberal politicians and bearded faceless parasites, the bureaucrats, by stopping the flow of money into Washington, D.C. This brought a loud cheer from the crowd. He thanked everyone in advance for supporting the new regime that would take over the country.

He introduced a senator from Utah, who spoke of reorganizing government in Washington by only funding basic government functions and letting other programs die a natural death. People gave him a cheer. He made reference to liberal Democrats, who had fled the country with money stolen from its citizens. He said, "Someday they will return and we shall be waiting for them. We shall not forget what they left behind." He had the crowd enthused.

The Utah senator introduced a senator from North Carolina, who promised to impeach the president the following day. This brought the loudest cheer of all. He said, "We will repeal all liberal laws from the books in one fell swoop. We will live by law and order, period." Folks were pumped up with new vigor.

The speaker of the House of Representatives took his turn at the podium, "We will have a fair and equitable tax, a flat tax with no deductions. Local governments shall provide for themselves through sales tax and property tax for revenues. We no longer will redistribute a man's savings to the nonworking American. The free ride is over."

A senator from Indiana made his talk on the mysterious subject, rehabilitation of America. He said, "We will establish rehabilitation centers in all major population centers. There we will educate, train, and reform citizens who are incapable or unwilling to providing for themselves. Everyone in this country will support himself and contribute to society according to his ability. Women will no longer be paid to perform reproductive services. Fathers will be responsible for their families. No one will live off another man's efforts." An applause interrupted his solemn message; it was what the crowd wanted to hear.

The governor of Texas gave his talk on how immigration would abruptly change. "No one will enter this country illegally. Whoever violates our immigration laws shall be placed in a labor camp and forced to earn his redemption. We will defend our borders with guns. Death be to the trespasser." Cheers roared.

Mr. Knight closed the rally by instructing folks to return peacefully to their homes and prepare themselves for the rebirth of America. He gave a short prayer and said, "God bless you, God bless America."

The reporter wrapped up his coverage with a commentary, "Ladies and gentlemen, tomorrow a new regime will take over our government. You have witnessed the last day of a failed democracy."

"Honey, I am astounded over what is going on in our capital."

"I am not. Anything is better than a civil war. We have been on the brink of one over the past three years."

"They didn't declare bankruptcy."

"Give them a few days."

Jan dished up the evening meal, a few morsels of meat with noodles and vegetables. Later they watched newsmen skip around the country interviewing people on TV. They were seeking out public

197

reaction to the day's event. Jim showered and sat on the bed next to the night table. He removed the Director and Terminator tokens from his billfold and placed them in the drawer. "I see you bought some revolution buttons."

"Fred Goldsmith gave them to me as a gift." He opened the plastic box with the new farewell pill in it.

"Why don't you put that damn pill away; it reminds me of death."

"Where is yours?"

"I ground it up in the kitchen sink."

"This is a new one. Judy gave it to me."

"It is shaped like the Star of David."

"Judy decided to change the shape of the pill, make it distinctive. A star carries the connotation of a heavenly trip. This pill can serve a person well if taken when all else fails."

"I hate that pill. It is dangerous to have around children. They may think it is candy."

"After euthanasia becomes legal, doctors will prescribe it and exercise complete control over the use of the pill."

"You are sure?"

"Yes."

"Hmm, Star of David. Sometimes I think you and Judy are Jewish."

"I am not Jewish. Hell, I am not even circumcised. You should know that."

Jan dropped into her chair and convulsed with laughter. She threw her head back, kicked up her knees, then slammed her feet on the floor. With hands cupped around her face, she said, "Jim Clark, sometimes I just don't know about you. You oscillate between extremes. After knowing you all these years, I am still trying to second-guess you. You say one thing and do another. Oh, God! I will go to sleep on that one."

Jan read herself to sleep and Jim cogitated himself into a dream, the usual rough one. He pondered the tokens. He'd conceived the idea of the tokens. He'd designed them, had them produced, but never used a token himself, and now millions of people were wearing them in public. This dwelled on his mind.

The next morning's newspaper had a bombshell of a headline, "President Commits Suicide."

"Jan, the president shot himself last evening. Security guards reported the suicide."

"Oh, no."

"Insiders were quoted saying that he never wanted to be president of the United States; it was his wife who yearned to reside in the White House. She made him do it; she drove him beyond his limits."

"She didn't do that, did she?"

"I don't agree entirely with that either. Would you believe this, Jan? The vice president is hiding out in Montreal, Canada. He left yesterday during the rally. He is more of a coward than his mentor."

Jan was putting breakfast on the table. "I am hungry."

"I will turn on the TV so we can watch the news from the kitchen."

A reporter was discussing the vice president in hiding. "The vice president and his wife have abandoned the White House for Canada. The president's wife will remain in the White House until the vice president returns from Canada. This is her last hope to succeed in the White House."

"I bet the senators and their revolutionary friends have other plans for her and the vice president."

After breakfast Jim gazed at the mountain behind the chalet through the kitchen window. A tiny stream had developed from the winter's snow melt. It was oozing out from the mine shaft. He went out on the deck to smoke his pipe. Wild flowers had popped up all over the twenty-two acres. Deer had moved up the mountains seeking solace from humanity; they were tending to their fawns. Ducks gunned up and down the stream. They were a busy bunch, nesting, feeding, and flying from the river to ponds near the chalet. Nature had a way of doing its thing in defiance of mankind. Jim was looking at God's world that man was constantly screwing up. He went inside to join Jan watching TV.

Television cameras concentrated on the steps of the Capitol Building. Senators emerged with their entourage and approached a battery of microphones at a podium. This was the moment. The senate majority leader addressed the nation. "The president of the

United States is dead. He committed suicide last evening and the vice president has fled the country. We have been without a leader for the past twelve hours. The senate convened this morning and elected retired general Maxwell Puckett as president, and the speaker of the House of Representatives is our vice president. A justice of the Supreme Court swore in the president and vice president. It was clumsily done, but it was done. There was no further fanfare."

"Well, Jim, I guess the revolution is over."

"Not quite. There are bullets flying around in different parts of the country. I don't envy the bureaucrats fleeing the White House."

"There will be work for them in government."

"Not the new government. I am going to lie down for a while, I don't feel well."

"Do you want lunch?"

"I don't think so."

"I will go downtown."

Jim felt chest pains, so he took a nap.

IV

Lately Jim took short naps after lunch, but rarely slept for two hours. He awoke and was confused. Jan was not at home. He knew he had been napping and that was the extent of his comprehension. He had lost his bearings. He checked his watch for the time and date. He felt refreshed but tired. Physical movement was necessary.

He went downstairs to his workshop. The work bench was clean, his engine was boxed up and packed away. He mumbled to himself, "That damn patent attorney let me down." Scanning the workshop, he noticed the boxes containing his ammunition and weaponry he had bought for the revolution. He'd fired one shot from one rifle and killed a black Labrador dog. He placed a chair on the south side of the garage and smoked his pipe as he collected his thoughts. The juniper bush was still guarding his cache of gold. He would dig it up and put the gold to work. The phone rang. He slowly made his way upstairs and intercepted the call.

"Hello, this is Jim Clark."

"Dr. Klein calling. Did you watch the swearing-in ceremony?"

"Not much of a ceremony, but we have a new president."

"I think the secrecy of our project in Boulder is a thing of the past."

"I hope so."

"We need some more funds. About two hundred thousand Swiss francs."

"That is down from the previous amount."

"We tightened our belts."

"Can you wait a couple of weeks?"

"Sure."

"I think the new regime will declare bankruptcy and issue new money. I want to wait for that to happen."

"That is acceptable to me. I hope the FBI stops following us around."

"If they followed me around I never was aware of it."

"The defense department still wants to buy us out."

"My answer is the same."

"Thank you, Jim."

"Good-bye."

Jim's mind was functioning again. His thoughts were on Research, Inc. He recalled providing for them in his will.

Jan returned all excited. "Honey, folks are cheering the end of the revolution."

Jim gently embraced her and gave her a long hug.

"I saw Molly Baker downtown. Do you know she is still washing dishes, cooking, and struggling to make ends meet?"

"Her family corporation probably shut down for lack of business. Wall Street all but closed down last month. Times have been tough on everybody."

"Not everybody. You have done well in taking care of me and my family; I am proud of you."

"Thank you, dear. I needed that."

"Honey, I feel like going out for dinner this evening."

"Great idea. I will shower and have a drink." His purpose for living came to the forefront, Jan Bailey. Jan lived from one precious moment to the next. He admired her for that. He'd grown to dislike himself. His constant quest for perfection kept his emotions in turmoil.

At the Olde Steak House Jim decided to reunite himself with Deerpoint without J. J. He struck up a conversation with Molly Baker, who was employed at the restaurant. "Who is supplying the restaurant with steaks?"

"The owner has an arrangement with a rancher to supply us with steaks; the grocery store gets the roasts, soup meat, and hamburger."

"Life will return to normal again."

"I hope so."

"Molly, do you know if the corporation will crank up the chair lift this coming ski season?"

"I heard that they will."

"Jan, we have to get our art and music festival organized for next summer."

"We will. We have all winter for that."

Molly excused herself, she was waiting tables that evening.

"I think I will get involved in Deerpoint's summer activities."

"That's great, Jim. What do you have in mind?"

"A thinkers' convention."

"You are teasing me."

"I will bring bearded professors out of their ivory towers and turn them loose in a tent next to your music pavilion."

"Be serious."

"I will come up with something, I can't let you girls outdo me."

They had a delightful time without the Crockers. Jim did miss his old friend, Judge J. J. Jan didn't miss the Crockers, she tolerated them. They paid their check and were departing when Ace appeared with a buxom blonde.

"Hello, Mr. Clark. Mrs. Clark. I have been hoping to see you around town."

"You should have called the house. We usually are around unless we are in Denver."

"Could we have a drink? I need to discuss something with you."

"How about a short one, Jan?"

She replied, "One short one."

Ace introduced his female friend and broached the subject of Eagle Airways. "You should invest in Eagle Airways. We have growing pains. I have faith in the operation, but it is mismanaged by the owner."

"And you know all about running an airline?"

"Better than he does."

"How much will it take to buy him out?"

"I don't know, but I will investigate that."

"What is the owner's name?"

"Don Dugan."

"Does he own the company by himself?"

"So I am told. He needs capital infusion to grow but doesn't know how to go about it."

"How is your mother?"

"Getting along. I help her out now that I have a monthly paycheck coming in regularly."

"I will be in touch, Ace."

"Thanks, Jim."

Jim and Jan said good night to numerous people they had befriended since living in Deerpoint. Local folks were friendly and Jan took advantage of that. Jim was still adapting to the intimate environment of a small town.

The late news covered the new president, the former president, and the vice president's announcement, which he had made earlier in New York. He said, "I am too distraught over the death of my beloved friend, the president, to return to the White House."

"Jan, read between the lines of this guy's explanation for deserting his office, the damn coward."

"I can't blame him under the circumstances."

"I bet J. J. and his boys gave him a choice of stepping down or staying in Canada. Those fellows play hardball. I have empathy for the guy, however, he has to be realistic. They were going to impeach the president for good reasons and this weakling did not fit into their program."

"Are you going to invest in Eagle Airways?"

"I like the idea of owning part of an airline that services Deerpoint. Like a local investment with regional potential. Dr. Klein called this afternoon for his annual allowance."

"How much this time?"

"Two hundred thousand Swiss francs."

"How is our money holding out?"

"Good. I am anxious to put our gold to work, it isn't making any money buried . . . in the Bank of Colorado."

"When are Betsy and J. J. coming back from Washington?"

"I don't know. He has changed. He is not the same guy I remember through the years."

"Maybe you have changed."

"How about you?"

"I never change."

"Good night, sweetheart."

The following day at noon Pres. Maxwell Puckett made his speech to the American people. He sat like a ramrod behind a large desk in the Oval Office. He looked like the retired four-star general that he was. "Ladies and gentlemen, I am your president for the next three years. My first order of business is to establish law and order in every state of the union. Congress will put America back on a productive course. We are declaring a bank holiday tomorrow. Old currency may be redeemed for new money at the rate of five cents on the dollar. All debits of the United States of America hereby are cancelled. We have declared bankruptcy. We will provide equal opportunity with equal responsibility for each and every citizen in this country. Capital punishment will be carried out by every state in the union. Executions shall take place no later than ninety days from the date of conviction. Each state may choose its method of death. If states fail to abide by the new law, I will have my military police force execute that mandate. All inmates on death row shall be executed within ninety days and the other inmates will be transferred to respective rehabilitation centers. We will convert former military installations, vacant prison systems, and other unused facilities to retrain, educate, and reform people who have been disabled by our former welfare state and liberal judicial system. I will make a motorcade trip across the country and survey firsthand our problems in the different regions and will make my report with recommendations to Congress. Every person in this country desires a job and equal protection under the law. Congress and I will provide that for all citizens. I thank you for your cooperation in rehabilitating this country into a proud and productive nation. God bless America."

"Well, Jan, there you have it in a nut shell. I knew something harsh was coming down, but I didn't anticipate this kind of draconian approach."

"What does it mean to the average citizen?"

"Many different things. Depends on your behavior, your lifestyle. Innocent people have nothing to fear; they no longer will be helpless victims of crime."

"It sounds scary to me. He is taking over the country like a dictator."

"You got that right; that is exactly what is taking place. It is only natural that a failed democracy be rescued by absolute authority."

"I wonder if J. J. had his hand in this."

"We will find out eventually."

Shortly after the president finished his address to the nation, the Black delegation was knocking on his door. Their leader and spokesman said, "Brother, we need your help and assistance while you are in office."

"You will be treated like any other American; I can assure you that. Now let me set you straight. I am not your brother. As president of this country, no productive American will be enslaved to support the nonworking. I suggest that you fellows find honorable jobs. I don't condone begging. Excuse me, but I have other people to see."

"But, brother, you are as Black as us. You owe it to your people."

"My people are all of America. I do not belong to any special group. I am the new America. Spread the word among your brothers. Now, get out of here before I lose my patience with you."

He had his motorcade organized with a company of Military Police, Secret Service people, and his advisors, who knew the cities they would be visiting. Save America senators, the vice president, and the head of the FBI met in conference before he embarked on his "See America" trip. He arrived in Florida in the midst of a civil war. He put that down by assigning a U.S. Marine regiment to shape up a lackadaisical Florida National Guard. His orders were always to coordinate efforts with local law-enforcement agencies and if that failed to take matters into their own hands. Shoot first and ask questions later. He kept reminding his men to show force in order to establish respect. "Remember, law and order is our mission."

As the general trekked across the South, he saw that respect for the law was very high. He informed each governor that he endorsed their diligent effort in maintaining law and order. Southerners meted out justice in a very sensible manner. They still had vivid memories of federal troops guarding liberals in their front yards during the sixties. In Alabama he met with the general in charge of the rebel brigade who marched with his men in Washington, D.C. The general asked that his rebel brigade receive federal recognition. President Puckett united the brigade with the state National Guard. The motorcade moved across Mississippi, Louisiana, Texas, and Arizona. They swung into southern California and moved towards the war zone, Los Angeles.

A section of the Pentagon was blown out by terrorists. The FBI had arrested the terrorists from Libya who had blown up the United Nations Building and assumed that Libya was behind the bombing of the Pentagon. The general was ticked off; the Pentagon was his office at one time. "Give the Libyan terrorists a swift military trial, then execute them by a military firing squad. Make sure this will be televised. Find the terrorists who bombed the Pentagon and do the same to them."

The general entered Los Angeles; he was aghast. The city was smoldering with smoke. It was a war zone on American soil. He set out to rescue Los Angeles from itself. He ordered the Marine Corps stationed in the West Coast to converge on Los Angeles with the National Guard and an Army Reserve regiment. Martial law was imposed on the city until further notice. The Mexican border was sealed off with armed guards from California to Texas. He shut off all immigration after the Pentagon bombing. A new problem arose. Americans were taking pot shots at foreigners who had entered the country during liberal times and taken away their jobs. Foreigners parading around in their native garb raised the ire of Americans for America. Arabs had the choice to adapt or go back to their homeland. Arabs were a thorn in the general's side. After the execution of the Libyan terrorists, Libya threatened to bomb the White House and then the Capitol Building. General Puckett had to return to Washington, D.C., and tend to presidential affairs. His sight-seeing tour as commander in chief of the United States federal police force ended. He had spent most of his military career overseas, in the South, or in Washington, D.C. He had much to learn about his country.

He met with his small cabinet, senators, and their advisors. The quandary was, "What shall we do about terrorism?"

His reply was, "Drop the big one on Tripoli."

The senators murmured, "We can't do that. We will start a nuclear war."

"Senator, they will never know who or what hit them. Maybe they will fight amongst themselves for a while and leave us alone. We have to send a loud and clear message to the Middle East."

One of the senators asked the question, "How will we deliver the bomb?"

"The Black Birds."

"Black birds?"

"Yes, our orbital plane we developed secretly; only a few know about them. Our late president didn't know about the Black Birds."

"Where do we keep them?"

"Secret. The fewer who know the better for all of us. The Black Bird cannot be detected in flight. They may pick up the bombing run, but that's all."

The Senate majority leader said, "Let me discuss this with the others."

"Very well."

It was time for Jim Clark's gold to return to a productive life; he had to dig it up. "Jan, I need to go to Denver. I have to transfer money to Research, Inc., close our Swiss bank account, see the C.P.A. and my legal counsel, check out Eagle Airways, and take some tile back to Denver for J. J."

"My, my, but you have a long list of things to do."

"For a change I really have something worthwhile to do. Do you want to come along?"

"You don't have to ask, I am packing right now. When are we leaving?"

"How about sometime in the morning?"

"OK. I will pack for a week's stay." Jan went downtown.

Jim dug around the juniper bush, put a chain around the base, hooked the chain to the truck, and pulled the bush out of the ground. Feverishly he scooped out the dirt; it was easy digging. He hit the tarp with the shovel. In his fervor he pulled up the tarp and there was the gold. He placed the bars one by one into crates on the truck, covered the gold with the tarpaulin, and backed the truck into the garage. He pondered the outhouse hole, what to do with the juniper bush. He had grown fond of the bush; it had become a sacred living symbol of the burial site. There really was only one choice; replant the bush. He reset the daisies the best he could and ran some water around the bush to settle down the loose soil. This had been a feverish hour for him. He took his chair and leaned back against the garage to smoke his pipe.

Jan returned and parked her car in the garage. She noticed immediately that he had dug up the daisies. "Honey, why did you dig up the daisies?"

"I realized that my little spruce tree won't arrive for a few days so I discontinued digging up the bush. I will transplant the bush."

"Mr. Clark, sometimes I think you are losing it."

208

"I lost it a long time ago, right after I met you."

Jan smirked and went upstairs. Jim continued to puff on his pipe. He was exhausted; the climax of this long-awaited event finally hit him. A trip to the Bank of Colorado and the saga would come to an end.

The next morning they drove the truck to Denver with a load of gold. Jim's efforts were in vain. On the day of bankruptcy the banks did not confiscate all bank deposits like Jim had expected; he could have stored the gold in a vault at the Bank of Colorado. Jim's grandparents had lost all of their savings during a bank closure in the thirties. He had carried this fear with him throughout his life. He dropped Jan off at the townhouse and drove to the docks at the Bank of Colorado.

Pres. Charles Kingsley himself supervised the unloading and storing of the thirty bars of gold. "Where did you have it buried?"

"You will never know and neither will anyone else."

"What do you intend to do with it?"

"Buy forty-five percent of this bank. I am closing my Swiss bank account today and moving my money back here, a fair amount of money."

"We could become the largest bank in the region with your gold."

"That is what I had in mind."

"I will call a board meeting and we will have an answer for you tomorrow at the latest." Jim went up to the second floor of the bank building and visited with John Price, his C.P.A. John Price was in his office like always.

"Jim, it is great to see you back. Are you going to make some investments with your precious pile of gold?"

"News travels fast. I just unloaded it thirty minutes ago. The answer is yes. That is why I am here to see you. I asked Kingsley if he would give me a forty-five percent interest in the bank for my gold. What do you think of my proposition?"

"I doubt that he will give you that much, maybe twenty-five percent."

"Could you check out the figures? I want your opinion."

Don Lawton, his legal counsel, walked into the office. They shook hands. They had not seen each other in months. "You were right about the country going bankrupt. What are you going to buy with the gold?"

"Forty-five percent of this bank."

"Good investment, safe, secure, and no management required on your part."

"I like that. I am going out to visit with Don Dugan, owner of Eagle Airways. Do you know anything about him or the company?"

"Nothing. Can't help you on that. Are you still funding Research, Inc.?"

"Yes, I am."

"How are they doing?"

"Still searching, I guess."

"Judy Cox was in for legal advice. She is negotiating with drug companies for the manufacturing and distribution of her pill."

"She is a winner."

"Her husband, Bill Bailey, is lucky to have a savvy gal like her."

"Bill is a overgrown playboy. She wears the pants in the family."

"I noticed that. She said you have been funding her project."

"I am funding too many wild projects. I need to start making money again. John, give me a call after you run some numbers on the Bank of Colorado."

"How is Jan?"

"She is in seventh heaven. She became a grandmother. The granddaughter is a new extension to her life. Do you still have all of my account numbers and code numbers to transact business for me?"

"Yes, I do."

"Move my money from the Swiss bank account to the Bank of Colorado and credit Dr. Klein's account with seventy-five thousand dollars."

"I will do that."

"I will be back in a day or two."

Jim started to leave when John said, "We missed you around here."

"Thanks."

He drove back to the townhouse and placed a call to Doc. Doc answered the phone. "What are you doing home this time of the day?"

"The same thing you are doing. I am retired."

"How about some tennis?"

"You are on."

"I will be at the courts in thirty minutes."

Jim missed tennis with Doc and the social exchanges they had after their matches. Deerpoint was a wonderful place to live; but, socially, life left much to be desired, especially with Judge Crocker moving to Washington, D.C.

"How are you, Doc?"

"Great, and you?"

"I can't imagine you not going off to your office or the hospital. So you are retired?"

"Not quite, I promised Judge Schultz to set up and organize the first rehabilitation center, called "Rehabilitation Center I," at a former military base here in Denver."

"Schultz is going to rehab Denver?"

"This will be a regional center."

"President Puckett will inspect our operation when he swings through here."

"My buddy in Deerpoint, Judge Crocker, is taking a position in Washington, D.C., doing something for the administration."

They finished their match and had a soda pop on the bench.

"Cigarettes taste much better these days, all pure tobacco and no taxes."

"I think I am beginning to enjoy life again. We are back to real values and decent virtues."

"What are you going to do with your pile of gold, King Midas? Eat it?"

"You are the third person who had asked me that question today. I am going to invest in the Bank of Colorado and buy into a small airline, Eagle Airways."

"Bank of Colorado, hmmm. I bank there. Good luck in your new ventures."

Jim walked into a building that was used for many purposes in the airline business. At the rear there was a sign hanging over a door. Eagle Airways. He opened the door to find a cute gal at the front desk and a husky fellow with rolled-up sleeves, tie hanging from his neck, seated behind a messy desk. On the back wall was a picture of a younger version of the same man posing with a jet fighter. "May I help you?" he asked.

"I am Jim Clark. I am looking for Don Dugan."

"Ah, that's me, in the flesh. Have a seat."

Jim sat down and proceeded to tell him about Ace and how he was directed to this air hanger. "Ace told me about you. I am not very good at begging for money and the banks won't touch me."

"How much would you want for fifty-one percent of the company?"

"Oh, I don't know if I want to give up control of my company that I built on a shoe string. I did well until inflation set in, the recession came, fuel prices went up, and then the depression hit. I found it difficult to keep up with the wild pace. Almost filed for bankruptcy."

"I used to own apartments in the Capitol Hill area. Sold out and bought gold before the economy started to gyrate out of control. I need to reinvest my money."

"I sure could use some capital right now. Need to expand, lease some more planes. The ski areas are going to open again this year."

"I would like forty-six percent for myself and five percent for Ace. I have no interest in running an airline. Call me a passive investor."

"I have to give that a lot of thought."

"I am buying into the Bank of Colorado tomorrow. Probably could arrange for a loan through that bank for you, a loan you have to repay. My investment comes without strings attached."

"I have to think about it."

"Here is the phone number of my C.P.A. Call him if you can't reach me in Denver or Deerpoint."

"Ten years ago I almost got over the hump and now I find myself in the same position."

"How much does it take to get you over the hump?"

"About one and a half million right now."

"I have no problem with that. I can see you in a nice office in the Bank of Colorado building right in downtown Denver." Jim glanced towards Don's secretary. She smiled and gave him a nod. He stood up and said, "Thank you for your time. I hope to hear from you." They shook hands.

Don Dugan was an informal person. It never crossed his mind to introduce Jim to his secretary. Jim did that on his way out. He had that intuitive feeling that she was more than a secretary to Mr. Dugan. Jim walked out to his old truck, knowing that he wanted to invest with Dugan and that Dugan would take him up on his proposal.

Dugan's daughter, also his secretary and partner in the business, didn't waste any time in prodding her father to place a call to John Price, C.P.A. John rushed into the attorney's office. "Lawton, you won't believe this. Clark is at it again. He just made a handshake deal with Don Dugan to buy half interest in Eagle Airways for one and one-half million dollars. How does he do it?"

"Don't knock him. He bought gold and look at him."

"I bet he didn't even look at Eagle Airways' books."

"He has that innate ability to profile a person. It is amazing how he makes decisions based on the character of a person. He should have been an attorney."

"He sure as hell would never have made it as an accountant."

"What are your recommendations on the bank stock?"

"I will suggest that he ask for thirty percent and go as low as twenty-five percent. My guess is that Kingsley will not give him more than twenty-five percent. He probably will double his investment within five years, with handsome dividends."

"You mean Mr. Kingsley, the fish face, don't you, John."

"Mr. Fish Face." John Price left Lawton's office laughing. They both got a kick out of Jim Clark. Jim bought into Eagle Airways, and Dugan eventually moved his daughter into a neat office at the Bank of Colorado's building.

Jim played a cat-and-mouse game with Charles Kingsley. He didn't return his calls for two days. Kingsley desperately wanted cash infusion, so he met Clark's demand, 30 percent of the bank. Unfortunately the two men got off to a bad start and that animosity would persist through the years.

"Jan, how about some tennis; then you can go shopping. There must be something your granddaughter needs urgently."

"How much money did you invest?"

"I don't know exactly. Feels good to have our money working for us instead of the other way around."

"Hey, I like that."

"Change into your tennis clothes and I will give you a ride by the country club in my dirty old truck. You can wave to your girlfriends as we pass by."

"Sometimes you can be a real jerk." She gave him a hug. He slapped her fanny. "But I love you and I wonder why?"

That evening Jim was watching TV while Jan and Mary cooked supper and fussed over the center of attraction, little Jan, so named after Jan Bailey. Tripoli was bombed, wiped out. Speculation erupted in every corner of the world. "Who bombed Libya?" Arab nations were the first to point fingers.

Pres. Maxwell Puckett returned to Los Angeles to pick up where he had left off. He saw improvements in law enforcement in a short period of time. Puckett called his generals together for a meeting and addressed them. "Let's have a show of force. Gather every available piece of military equipment we have on the West Coast and we will parade through Los Angeles. Goddamn it, we will give them law and order if it means killing half of them."

They had a parade of helicopter gunships, jet fighters, artillery pieces, troops marching, troops on trucks, troops on troop carriers, and troops perched on tanks. President Puckett led the way standing up in a jeep, wearing his overseas cap that bore his title, "Commander in Chief." Flags abounded, some had fifty stars and others forty-eight stars in the field of blue. Everything the Marine Corps, National Guard, and Reserve units had was in the parade. The media sucked up the event; they called it a display of power. That it was. They referred to President Puckett as a military dictator. That he was. He had complete authority over U.S. military forces, with specific powers from Congress to establish law and order. Puckett's small caravan moved up the coast to Portland, Seattle, and then crossed into Salt Lake City. Denver was the next stop. General Swanson, Puckett's defense minister, met with the general who commanded the Northwest Aryan nation. He wanted his men to go on active duty and serve their country along with other military units. Puckett asked General Swanson, "Do you think it is a good idea to activate the Northwest Aryan nation?"

"They are deserving. They came to our aid in Denver for Mr. Knight's rally and they made a good showing in Washington, D.C. It is far better that they be with us than against us."

"Very well. What should their assignment be?"

"Let's make them the elite corps in Washington, D.C."

"Good idea, Swanson. I concur. Don't you think the general has strange laissez-faire ideas that are out-dated?"

"Look at yourself, a military dictator with Congress as your tribune. That's out of the past."

"Swanson, you are a realist; that's why I chose you as my defense minister."

"Puckett, I am ready to retire when this job is finished. What an ironic ending to my military career."

The next morning was a red alert day for the president. Self-styled saviors of America broke into the Senate, killing twenty-five members. Ninety-three members in the House of Representatives were killed or wounded. The president had to return to his proper post, the Oval Office. Puckett's center of power was partially destroyed. The House was not critical to him; they rubber-stamped the Senate. His task as president, or director of law and order, as the Senators regarded him, just became more difficult.

Young men replacing the assassinated senators were adamant about getting the country pointed in the right direction. They passed a flat income tax, legalized social drugs, and pushed rehabilitation into high gear. Off the record, they approved of President Puckett's approach to law and order but with some reservations. The revolution gave the younger Congress a second chance at life, and they pushed with all their might for a new and better America. They approved free educational benefits through college for all who qualified in the field of science. All savings were exempted from income tax. This stimulated the desire to succeed, save money, and invest it. The work ethic was restored, and dependency became an undesirable stigma in rehabilitation centers. Government vowed to stay out of people's lives if they functioned responsibly. It became readily apparent that those who worked hard and remained self-sufficient would never reside at a rehabilitation center. Dependency changed from a choice of lifestyle to a mandatory stay in a rehabilitation center for many citizens.

The new Congress immediately made provisions, though not in the grand style of the past, for the elderly and retired civil servants who had gotten lost in the shuffle. The philosophy of everything living forever at any cost gave way to euthanasia and a cost-effective health care program with practical applications. The new Congress had little sympathy for liberal Democrats and had nothing in common with the war hawks, whether Republican or Democrat. They teamed up with their peers and did the inevitable, formed a new party, the Independents. The gap between the old guard and the young in Congress dissipated. The revolution resolved that festering problem. Older senators and representatives were killed or scared away from the capital. Liberals vanished. Brave young men and women took control of government. It no longer was business as usual. The absences of unlimited funds at the disposal of Congress eliminated the army of ants, mostly attorneys, from feeding at the public trough. The revolution cleansed Washington, D.C., beyond comprehension. Young dedicated men and women served citizens across the country. A lean budget kept Congress from serving itself through corruption.

America had a pent-up demand and foreign investors took advantage of this opportunity; industry cranked up rapidly. Middle East oil producers extended credit on oil shipments in hopes of igniting a weak economy in the United States and other industrialized nations. Oil was still an integral part in the cost factor of nearly every item manufactured around the globe. President Puckett had to forego his trip across America as commander in chief and remain in Washington, D.C., to fulfil his duties with a fast-moving Congress. At the president's request, General Swanson stopped by to discuss developments of cold fusion with Dr. Klein at Research, Inc. Puckett prayed for cold fusion. He was obsessed; he wanted to see the Arabs drown in a sea of oil.

Jim attended his first board meeting at the Bank of Colorado. It turned into a catastrophe. He had been naive in his wishful thinking. Sir Charles Kingsley called the meeting to order, moved through a short formality, and then adjourned the meeting. It appeared to Jim that the real meeting had taken place before the formal one. He put his hands into his pockets and slowly shuffled his feet along the polished marble floor. He sauntered down to the loan department. His visit with the vice president of the loan department further aggravated his heartburn. The man was a pigeon for the board of directors. On his way out of the bank a man in his early forties introduced himself and asked him to sit at his desk. The junior loan officer spoke with great aspirations about the Bank of Colorado. He indicated how the bank could buy out smaller banks and become the largest bank in Colorado. After listening to the man, Jim perked up and said, "I wanted to encourage the board to lend out more money to businesses but they shut me off at the meeting. It was a slam dunk meeting. I feel left out."

"Mr. Charles Kingsley is content to roll with the times. He is very conservative in granting loans to businesses."

"I would say lazy. He reminds me of a stuffed bird, but he has the face of a fish, a sucking fish." His disparaging remark drew a chuckle from the loan office. 'I should not be talking to an employee like that about Mr. Kingsley, even if he is a fish."

"Nice to have met you, Mr. Clark. We will see each other again."

"Honey, how did it go at the board meeting?"

"Not worth a damn. They shafted me. Kingsley took my gold and now treats me like a fifth wheel. I am dead in the water."

"It can't be all that bad. You are a major stockholder."

"Minor stockholder."

"I have seen board members and their wives in society pages of the Denver newspaper; they are high-class people."

"Those phony birds inherited their money. They are a bunch of gutless wanderers. You should have seen them at the board meeting. It was hilarious. They were seated in a pecking order, all dressed alike, white shirts, dark suits, black shoes and black socks. They wore different-colored neck ties. I think they were planning a group picture until they took a look at me."

"Let me guess. You were dressed in your tennis shoes, tennis shirt, and blue jeans."

"My favorite sweatshirt, the one with the big sunflower."

"I bet you stood out like a sore thumb." She gave him a hug. He didn't respond.

"I will never attend another board meeting ever."

"Are you going to sue them?"

"There is nothing to sue over."

Mary was taking a nap with the baby. Jim looked at her and said,

"Jan, this place is overcrowded; give the kids money to buy their own house."

"That very thought crossed my mind this morning. We are buying into banks, taking over airlines, and live like paupers."

"Do you want to go to Deerpoint?"

"Start up the truck and we will be on our way."

He listened to the radio until the signal faded. Jan likewise had faded; she was sound asleep.

Jim drove the truck for the last time across the Continental Divide and down into Deerpoint. He pulled up to the garage door, clicked it open, and Jan jerked up, "Are we home?" Jim chuckled as he turned from her and peeked at the lonesome juniper bush that had nothing to guard. Fall was in the air, leaves were about to fall, and the ski lifts soon would be running again. J. J. was back in town. Jim went to the Last Chance Bar.

"How is Washington shaping up?"

"Real good."

"What kind of an assignment do you have at the capital?"

"Advisor to the president."

"When are you going to move to Maryland?"

"Next month. Which reminds me, Joe Parker bought out my share in the sand and gravel operation. He needs an investor for his land development. I told him to contact you."

"He did. I will get with him in a few days. I need something in Deerpoint to keep me occupied."

Jim told J. J. about his ventures in Denver. J. J. liked the idea of buying into Eagle Airways and did a belly laugh over Jim's first board meeting with the stuffed birds at the bank. "You don't belong in a board meeting with those guys, and you would look out of place at a country club."

"You got that right. Do you remember when I had Ace fly Jan and me to Canada?"

"Yes, I remember."

"Did you know that I stored two bars of gold in your basement with the ammunition?"

"You did?"

"Ace snuck Jan, me, and the gold in a maintenance van from the airport to downtown Vancouver. I exchanged the gold for Canadian dollars and then transferred the money into a Swiss bank account along with proceeds from a condo and mining investments I had in Canada."

"You hedged against inflation."

"And bankruptcy."

"You stored two bars of gold in my basement and I never knew about it. Why didn't you tell me about it?"

"Your father lost his life over gold. I didn't want to bother you with my crazy idea."

"As it turned out you were not so crazy after all. I guess you know that I initiated instant capital punishment."

"Yes. I figured that out with the help of Fred Goldsmith."

"I am glad the revolution has ended."

"Has it?"

"Pretty much so. Military forces have control of the country and soon should be pulling out."

"Do you think Puckett went overboard?"

"No, Jim. The poor man was conned into a difficult job, and I was part of that."

"And now you are an advisor to him?"

"I will help him any way I can; I owe it to him."

"How are the East and West Coasts doing?"

"We finally put the revolt down in California, and New York is quiet."

"How about Florida?"

"They are settling down. As industry cranks up, violence disappears. When people have work and money to live on, their behavior changes. We are taking people off the streets and placing them in rehabilitation centers. That is a slow process but well worth the effort."

"I hear your buddy Schultz is in charge of the Rocky Mountain region on behalf of the Department of Rehabilitation."

"We expect him to set up a complex that will be used as a model for the rest of the country."

"I hate to see you leave Deerpoint. I will be alone with Jan and her friends, and I don't think that will cut it for me."

"Silverman is an astute, classy type of guy. I enjoy him in and out of the courtroom. There is Joe Parker. He and Shirley are a kick in the head. Betsy and I may not stay in Maryland very long. Going there is her idea. I have had a change of heart about Washington, D.C."

"Why?"

"I was at the White House when the slaughter took place in the Senate and House. I went over to see the carnage. I knew most of the senators intimately. My stomach turned. I sat on the steps of the Capitol Building for an hour before I collected myself. That evening I thought back to the student union in Boulder, where you briefly told me about Korea but spared me from the gory details. Now I understand what you must have gone through as a young man."

"That was different, I was trained to kill. They ordered me to kill. I was paid to do a job for the United States of America. After killing the first Korean, it became easier every time; then one day I woke up and hated killing. I learned to hate myself for doing it. If you stay on the front lines long enough, you either become a hero or you get killed. In my case, I went psycho."

"I can relate to that, Jim."

"I hated the bastards in Washington, D.C., who'd made me do it. My first voting booth was a foxhole, and Harry Truman didn't get my vote. That is why I don't hunt anymore; I can't kill for the sake of killing. I have to have a valid reason to do what I do."

"I find that very interesting. The revolution changed my thinking about life."

"I reached the end of my rope when I bought my weapons for the revolution and designed the tokens, Terminator and Director. At that time you professed the law to me."

"Yes, I remember. That all changed later."

"The gang that killed the senators and representatives were wrong in what they did. They used bullets where the ballot box failed them. They had a cause and believed in it. They fought for it."

J.J. said, "I see the massacre from a different perspective."

"That doesn't make it right; it merely justifies the deed. That was not killing for the sake of killing."

"I often wondered what you thought of my involvement with instant capital punishment. You made the tokens."

"I prepared myself to take up arms to defend my property and my rights. The criminal had more rights than the victim. Out of frustration I reduced myself to the last line of defense: kill, destroy, vengeance."

"That is how I felt when my father's killers were released to roam about and kill again. Something inside me snapped. I went against everything I believed in and took the law into my own hands."

"We are lucky that we didn't have an all-out civil war in this country."

"But, Jim, you didn't kill the graffiti artists."

"I came damn close. Jan noticed a difference in me after I sold my last apartment building. She said that I was a new man. I became passive. The enemy won and I lost. The scales of justice were tilted to favor the criminals. I was the culprit. And you used to lecture me on how your hands were tied. Who said, 'The law is the law and I must mete out justice accordingly.' "

"I did my job as a judge and upheld the law of the people."

"You found a way to win. You took the law into your own hands. You used the tokens."

"You should come to the White House with me."

"I have faith in the younger generation who have taken over government. Let them show us the way, it is their turn. Who are we to lead them? . . . We have failed them. Give them a chance. If we maintain martial law over the next twenty years, the country will face another rebellion; and this time it will be the people against a standing army, a real civil war."

"It is good to return home and touch base with reality. I had gotten so caught up with power that I forgot the responsibility that goes with it."

"J. J., stay out of politics; it is not your cup of tea."

"You are right, Jim. It is time to let go. We should not make the same mistake WWII veterans made. They refused to turn over the reins and stayed too long. Look at the mess they left behind."

"Look up Schultz. He will give you a tour of Rehabilitation Center I. He told me that the center is going to reprocess waste water of the entire region. He said, 'Think of Rehabilitation Center I as a sewer plant that will clean up the polluted waters of yesterdays' years.' "

"I used to dream of doing that in my wild fantasies while living in the Capitol Hill area."

"Swift capital punishment and rehabilitation of our citizens will have an immediate effect on our society. Our post-revolution experiment should work by all calculations."

"Judge, so you admit that you are running a social experiment?"

"Children of parents at the centers will receive proper health care, shelter, education, and social direction that they had lacked previously."

"Was there a connection between the bombing of the Pentagon and the bombing of Tripoli?"

"I don't know, and if I did I wouldn't divulge it to you. The Middle East will settle down now that Israel is gone and Iraq has been divided up by the desert wolves. We expect them to fight amongst themselves occasionally. When cold fusion replaces large amounts of Middle East oil, we will have a new scenario."

"What is the fate of the United Nations?"

"The president said he will leave the building like it is, with five floors blown out. He thinks it makes a neat monument to the Cold War."

"I had never heard of Gen. Maxwell Puckett until you fellows appointed him to run the country."

"He earned his first star in the field and the other three stars were political gifts, he told me. I almost forgot; the courthouse employees are throwing a retirement party for me. You are hereby ordered to attend."

"Jan and I will be there for your grand departure, Judge."

"See you tomorrow."

"Thanks, J. J." Jim arrived late for supper, something he seldom did without calling Jan.

"Honey, I am home, however late."

"That's OK. The roast is in the oven. We have time for one drink."

"I will fix them. I lost track of time. J. J. had so much to talk about."

"You had a phone call while you were socializing at the Last Chance Bar."

"From whom?"

222

"A gentleman named Milton Perry. He asked that you call him back."

"He is not a gentleman; he is a mouse."

"Who is he?"

"One of the stuffed birds, board member of the Bank of Colorado. I will call him tomorrow, maybe. Screw those guys. The courthouse employees are giving J. J. a retirement party."

"Are we invited?"

"He invited us this afternoon. Could you bird dog for me?"

"Do what?"

"Well, times are still tough around here and it takes bucks for booze to throw a good party. And you know folks around here like their juice. Seek out a way that we can pay for the liquor."

"I can handle that."

"I could set it up with our liquor store to have an anonymous donor supply the booze. I don't want to embarrass the locals; they have their pride."

"Honey, you are too sensitive."

"I am that I am. God knows this town could use a good bash to kick the new ski season into gear."

Jan finished her drink, sat on Jim's lap, and gave him a kiss on the forehead. "I love you," she told him.

After supper, Jim smoked his pipe on the deck. It was a cool, beautiful full moon evening. One side of the valley was a dark silhouette and the other was lit up brightly. Old habits die hard; he gave the juniper bush a glance before retiring to the television set. The next morning they slept late. The phone rang as Jim was finishing up in the bathroom

"Honey, it is for you."

"This is Jim Clark."

"Milton Perry calling here. I need to see you in private."

"About what?"

"I can't discuss the topic with you on the phone. When will you be back in Denver again?"

"I don't know. We just came back a few days ago."

"It is very important to me and I think important to you that I converse with you."

"Look, Thursday morning I will be at the airport. You come out and meet me there. I don't want to take a cab from the Kansas border to downtown Denver just for the hell of it."

"That would be superb."

"I will be on the first flight Thursday."

"Good-bye, Mr. Clark."

Jim hung up in disgust. He was going to fly to Denver on the spur of the moment to meet with a mouse.

"What did he want?"

"I don't know. I am not sure he knows. We are to meet secretly at the airport on Thursday morning."

The day passed quickly. The retirement party was a success. Many had too much to drink, thanks to Jim Clark's generosity. The following morning Jim drove his old truck to the airport and boarded another flight to Denver. He was greeted as Mr. Clark. Word had spread that he held a controlling interest in Eagle Airways. He didn't mind. His thoughts were on Milton Perry and the urgent meeting he had set up.

Milton reminded him of a retired accountant, the neat blue suit, the pencil-thin mustache, bald, short, only about five feet and six inches tall, with steel-rimmed glasses, polished nails, a luster shine on his black shoes. He was so neat he squeaked. Jim recalled Milton sitting at the end of the pecking order across from him at the bank board meeting. He reminded Jim of accounting students at the University of Colorado. They all seemed to be cut from the same cloth. Milton fit the mold of a retired accountant who dressed up in a suit every morning with no place to visit and nothing to do, so he would tally up his net worth and then initial his own report to himself every day. Milton was fastidious.

The plane bounced a couple of times and taxied to a spot near the airport. Jim walked into the lobby dressed the same way he had attended the bank board meeting, tennis shoes, blue jeans, white sweatshirt with a colorful sunflower printed on the front, depicting his eastern Colorado farm heritage. Milton was dressed in his customary uniform, suit, tie, black shoes, all for an informal meeting in a coffee shop at the airport. Jim was carrying his jacket with a pipe, tobacco pouch, lighter, checkbook, and pen in the pockets. He had cash and one credit card in his billfold. Jim liked to do business in cash. Milton insisted on shaking hands. They found a table off to the corner in the coffee shop and seated themselves.

Milton commenced to tell his life story, the position he had at the bank, how he met his wife, the daughter of the president of the bank. His father-in-law never liked him. He promoted Mr. Charles Kingsley over him as president of the bank. He retired as head cashier. His wife and her sister owned twenty five percent of the shares in the bank.

"I thought you owned the twenty-five percent."

"My wife and her sister inherited the twenty-five percent stock from their late father."

Jim ordered his second cup of coffee and was thinking of making a trip to the bathroom; his prostate gland was acting up. Milton Perry continued his meticulous confession of his pitiful career as a banker that could have simply been summed up, Mr. Inept marries boss's daughter. Jim went to the bathroom to relieve himself and returned to the table. He was about to lose his patience.

"Milton, why am I here today?"

"Mr. Clark, my wife and her sister wish to divest themselves of their interest in the Bank of Colorado."

"So, what does that have to do with me?"

"A large bank wishes to buy controlling interest in the bank and they will not buy us out unless they have your thirty percent."

"At what price?"

"I can't discuss that with you. The bank vying for our stock will contact you in a few days. The price will between you and them." Milton became very nervous at this point. This was the apex of the meeting for him. It appeared to Jim that Milton wanted to sell out years ago but couldn't because he was locked in. Fish Face had him by the tail. Jim was exhilarated, he too wanted out of a no-win situation after a brief encounter with Kingsley. Milton on the other hand had despised the man for years, even had to work for him at one time.

"What kind of a payoff do you anticipate?"

"Can't discuss that with you. The corporation will contact you in a few days. They will deal with you privately."

"Very well, I will sell to them if the deal is acceptable to me."

"Please keep this confidential for my sake. If Mr. Kingsley finds out about this he will make life miserable for me. His wife, my wife, and her sister socialize at the same country club."

"Don't you worry about that. I dislike Fish Face as much as you do." Milton cracked his first smile, he was relieved, he trusted Jim. Jim said, "Let's have lunch. I am hungry."

"I'm too excited to have lunch. I want to call the girls and present the good news to them."

"Milton, I have not made a deal with them yet."

"You will, Mr. Clark. They want the bank without Mr. Kingsley, and they are willing to pay for it." Jim got up from the table and shook the departing man's hand and then had a pastrami sandwich with a draft beer. He dashed to the Eagle Airways counter to make the next flight to Deerpoint. Seated in the waiting room his mind shifted to the cute golden-haired, freckled-faced, lovable, beautiful bouncing woman who would be waiting for him at home. Ace was the pilot on this flight.

"Mr. Clark."

"Ace, did you put the Eagle Airways stock in trust for your mother?"

"I did."

"Good."

"She was happy to have a real security blanket to wrap around herself."

"Ace, I want to see the paperwork on that, I don't trust you."

Ace grinned, he could charm the pants off a stewardess in broad daylight. "I am dating Dugan's daughter."

Jim passed on that pronouncement. Ace was always scheming for a short cut to the brass ring. He would marry the boss's daughter. The sandwich and beer made Jim sleepy. He awoke as Ace put the plane down on the tarmac.

Ace waited for Jim to make it down the ramp. He put his hand on Jim's shoulder and walked with him to the terminal. "Thank you for the nice retirement stock for my mother."

Jim turned and looked straight at him and said, "Young man, you earned it. The flight to Canada. Those two bars of gold were my salvation through the revolution; they kept one company alive and provided the down payment for another. I needed to thank you for your daring guts and integrity."

Ace stuck out his hand and then slapped Jim on the back and said, "Thanks, partner."

Jim added, in parting, "With needed cash in the hands of Don Dugan, Eagle Airways will do well over the years."

Jim walked over to his truck. He considered Ace a good, clean-cut fellow, pleasant company, a charming person with a tolerably inflated ego. Jim trucked his way up to the chalet, today he beeped the horn, something he rarely did. Jan peeked out of the window. He waved to her and gave the grounds a survey, including the juniper bush, before he went upstairs.

"Honey, what was the secret meeting all about?"

"Milton Perry has an offer for his twenty-five percent of the bank; he needs our thirty percent to swing the deal."

"Are you going to sell?"

"You're damn right I will. I am going to ask twice what we paid for that thirty-percent interest, and I personally want to kick Sir Kingsley's butt out of the window from the top floor of that bank building."

"Who is buying you guys out?"

"Don't know. They are supposed to be calling me within a few days."

"Why all the secrecy?"

"The buying corporation wants to make a clean shot at the bank. Leaks could foil the deal."

"Judge Crocker's retirement party was a success. The locals are all talking about it. I think Deerpoint shed the emotional veil of the revolution."

"Soon the ski lifts will ferry tourists up the mountain and everything will be back to normal."

The mysterious phone call came through on a snowy afternoon one week before Thanksgiving. "Is this Mr. James Clark?"

"Yes."

"Mr. Norbert Nogard, president of Midwest National Bank in Minneapolis, Minnesota, is on the line, Mr. Clark."

"Hello! Mr. Clark?"

"That is me."

"We have Mr. Milton Perry's bank shares under contract, contingent upon purchasing your thirty percent. Do you want to sell?"

"Yes. What are the price and terms of payment?"

"Our offer is fifty percent over what you paid for the share with your gold. We own three major banks with thirty branch banks."

"Double the price I paid for my thirty percent and you have a deal."

"I have to meet with the board to do that."

"I should give you my Denver phone number in case we will be down there for Thanksgiving."

"We have all your phone numbers."

"My attorney's name is Don Lawton. He has an office in the bank building."

"We know all about him. He is on the second floor of the bank building."

"Well, I have nothing else to add or ask about."

"We will be in touch."

"Did you sell or is it premature to celebrate?" asked Jan.

"We will know in a few days."

"What if they don't call back?"

"They will call back. Milton told me that they want the bank, period."

"So your trip to Denver was not in vain?"

"I think it was the most profitable meeting I ever attended."

"What did they offer?"

"One and a half times what we paid for our share."

"You should have accepted the offer. It is not like you to haggle."

"They gave me the opportunity to play hard ball, so it's hard ball with the bankers."

"Why do bankers make a difference?"

"Invariably they are rich cheapskates and I am in a position to make them pay the price. What is on the agenda for Thanksgiving?"

"I wanted to have the family gather here, but Mary is reluctant to make the trip with the baby in bad weather."

"Mary is a sensible woman. Let's go to Denver."

"Mark and Mary are moving into their new house on the first of December."

"When did you find out about that?"

"While you were at the Denver International Airport. We could spend some time down there. I want to redecorate the townhouse, wallpaper, paint, buy new furniture and appliances."

"I want to fly down. I am tired of driving over the Continental Divide in bad weather."

"I need a car in Denver to get around."

"I will give you another hundred thousand for your account. Buy yourself a car and I will keep the truck. Give Mark money for a truck. Let him buy his own truck."

"Thanks, honey."

"Don't mention it. I am glad we have it to spend."

D-day had arrived for Mr. Charles Kingsley, Jim closed on the bank deal. They met his price with stock in their corporation. The new president was the loan officer Jim had befriended. He was a mole in the Bank of Colorado. Now Jim knew why the Midwest National Bank in Minneapolis, Minnesota, had such accurate information on him. Kingsley told the press that he was retiring and pursuing philanthropic endeavors.

"Jan, have you read about me in the business section?"

"Yes, I did. They say you are a rich man. You did it with gold."

"The press doesn't know how much we are worth."

"Did you read the article on Kingsley? He is quite a man."

"He is as phony as a three-dollar bill, feeding the press his big ego. He no longer has access to the bank for excessive donations."

"You are ticked off because you couldn't push the board of directors around."

"You are partly right. Milton Perry had been associated with the bank for over forty years and he wanted out in the worst way."

"He didn't fuss like you."

"Jan, I am not Milton Perry. Do you want to trade me in for a puppy dog like Milton? His wife keeps him on a leash."

"By the way, the last time you bought a car we killed a whole day looking at cars you didn't want to buy; this time you are on your own."

Jan had no rebuttal. He had given her money for her account and she knew exactly which car she would buy. She even knew what color she wanted.

Thanksgiving at the townhouse was an overdue gathering. Jim and Jan had not seen Judy Cox and Bill Bailey in a while. On the other hand, Mark and Mary had seen too much of Jan and Jim. The Bailey couple arrived with little Jan. They were euphoric. They had been out to see their beautiful house in a suburb outside of Denver. Judy and Bill lived in a nice, established neighborhood within the city limits. Judy wouldn't be caught dead in a suburb; she wanted to be at the center of cultural activity. This would be the last time they all gathered at the townhouse.

"Judy, how is the farewell pill coming along?"

"Great, Jim. We are legitimate. Doctors are prescribing the pill."

"Jan used to worry that children might mistake the pill for candy."

"Not anymore. The pill is administered by medical people in hospitals and nursing homes. Guns are still a hazard in the homes of our citizens. I am glad to see that pleasure drugs are not distributed to children by drug dealers."

"I read where the Black caucus raised hell because social drugs were legalized. Put too many of their brothers out of work."

"The pope is up in arms over the farewell pill, new birth control methods, and, of course, capital punishment."

"Why doesn't somebody explain to the old man that America does not want to become a lucrative Third World nation for him?"

"Oh, Jim, you know organized religion thrives on mankind's ignorance and misfortune."

"Mark, how are your efforts in research progressing?"

"We are very close to solving the riddle."

"I hope I live long enough to see the Middle East oil-producing countries drink oil for breakfast."

Jan was playing with the baby. The little girl had Jan wrapped around her little finger. Bill emerged with a drink in hand and said, "Jim, you scored another one, upsetting your archrival, Sir Kingsley."

"That is the hallmark of my career, and it all just fell into my lap."

"It reminded me of the good old days, the graffiti wars, but we gave up too soon."

Mark gave Bill a stern look. "My dear brother, had we kept up the pursuit, we would have been in trouble with the law."

"You are right, but it was fun while it lasted."

230

Jim walked over to Bill, put his hand on his shoulder, and spoke to the boys like a father. "Guys, those were exciting days but frustrating times for me. I had all but forgotten about our vigilante escapades. Do you fellows realize we were the forerunners of instant capital punishment?" Jim briefed the boys on the subject but never mentioned his involvement with the tokens. He kept that to himself.

Bill spoke to Mark. "Have you noticed the absence of street people in the city?"

"I hear they are rounding them up and processing them through a rehab center on an old army air base."

Mark had an interesting observation for Jim. "The other day, on my way over to the supermarket, I saw parents with their delinquent boys cleaning off graffiti under the supervision of a cop."

"I would relish seeing that. God, how we used to fight that menace."

"I saw a cop arrest a juvenile the other day. He kicked the punk in the butt as he got into the squad car. Times have changed."

Bill was quick to further Mark's comments. "He was lucky he didn't get shot on the spot."

"Do you boys think the revolution will produce a new society?"

Mark had the thoughtful mind. "We were forced into rapid changes that otherwise would have come more slowly. It has been hard on folks. I often wonder how Mother would have made it on her retirement check."

Bill spoke of his father. "Dad is still working and so is his wife. They may never retire." They ate as barbs were exchanged. It was Jim Clark's way of communicating with the family and they liked it.

Life was almost normal for the boys and their wives. However, most working people were still struggling to recover from the shakeout left behind by the revolution. A younger generation had taken over the federal government, with the help of a few tough old conservatives, and their counterparts were doing the same on a local level. There was little tolerance towards dependency in the new direction America had taken.

The army, formerly the National Guard, was still posted throughout Denver. Police used their guns indiscriminately, and martial law was more or less in effect. Local liberals wanted the firing squad moved out of the downtown civic center. They found it very disturbing to hear shots fired during their lunch hour. Evening television always showed the slumping body tied to a post. It left a vivid impression on people's minds. President Puckett insisted that a clear message be communicated to the would-be perpetrators until criminal activity fell to zero. Leftover liberals bravely emerged from hiding and attempted to halt the drastic changes that had come about. The president forbade all protests, marches, and parades under martial law. He had dictatorial powers and the liberals knew it. The East Coast and West Coast were still a thorn in the side of America. Radio talk show hosts had a field day with Los Angeles and New York. The callers suggested asking the Arabs to gas those problem areas; radical thinkers were still around. The boiling point of the revolution was reached when a group gunned down senators and representatives out of frustration in Washington, D.C. Every passing day showed signs of a recovery from that fatal day.

The Sunday after Thanksgiving Day was perfect for tennis; Jan and Jim took advantage of the beautiful day. Doc, as usual, showed up for his match with Jim.

"Hello, Doc."

"Hi, Jim. Hello, Jan."

"Doc, this might be our last match in Denver for the season. I would like for you and Helen to join Jan and me in Guaymas for a week or two."

"We can't do that. Short of cash. Our corporate stock has not rebounded."

"Between you and me, I will foot the bill. I make more money than I can intelligently spend. After my power play with the bank, I am loaded."

"Well, I didn't invest in gold like you did."

"I also got lucky. Come down to Guaymas as a favor to me. I want someone other than Jan to play tennis with and shoot the bull. It would be nice for Jan to have someone to socialize with besides stray liberals hanging around Mexico."

"I will have to discuss it with Helen."

"Despite my generous contributions to Research, Inc., and my purchase of stock in Eagle Airways, I still have excess cash flow from my stock in Midwest National Bank Holding Corporation."

"I read about you in the Sunday newspaper. It was interesting to read an article that was secondhand news to me. Reporters never quite get the story straight, do they?"

"I set them on the right course regarding Charles Kingsley. He told the press he resigned. I told them he got booted out, but they didn't print it that way."

"You never liked him?"

"Do you know that he will make more money off his stock in Midwest National Bank than his salary was at the Bank of Colorado?"

"How is that?"

"The bank will expand and grow faster without him."

"How would you like a tour of Rehabilitation Center I?"

"I don't know if I want to subject myself to that; but since you are one of the architects of the center, I'd best go. I read in the newspaper that liberals are vehemently against the program. They call it dehumanizing."

"That it is. The question remains, How do we change social behavior of a lost society?"

"I don't have the answer. After years of fretting and worrying over other people, I have resigned myself from problems of the world."

Jan returned from her social break. "Jan, I asked Doc and Helen to be our guests at Guaymas over the holidays."

"I think that is a great idea. Helen and I can go shopping together. Oh, I think that would be real fun."

"Well, that's settled. You are coming."

"I have to discuss it with my wife."

"Good enough."

Jim dropped Jan off at the townhouse and went to see Don Dugan. He had conjured up a new idea for Eagle Airways.

"How are you doing, Don?"

"Come in, Jim."

Jim passed the smiling young lady, who was the other half of the operation. "Don, I have been thinking about the financial structure of this company."

"Did I goof up?"

"No, not at all. I was thinking of how I became involved with you and how that same problem may arise again. I was wondering

233

what you thought of taking Eagle Airways public and listing it on the regional stock market. You and I have controlling interest in the company, and most likely that will not change. It will be easier for us to raise capital as you expand the company, and the public would be involved with our operation."

"I would have to answer to stockholders? I will have to think about that for a few days."

"No hurry, take your time. If the company keeps on growing we will have to take it to the public sooner or later."

"Thanks, Jim."

When Jim arrived at the townhouse, Jan was on and off the phone continuously.

"Honey, I made arrangements with an interior decorator to redo the townhouse while we are in Mexico this winter."

"Smart girl. Very good."

"I have a surprise for you, Jim. I am so excited I can't help myself."

"What is it?"

"Did you like our villa in Guaymas, Mexico?"

"Yes. I am sorry that we sold it, after the fact. Yes, I am waiting with bated breath."

"Remember who bought it from us?"

"Yes."

"She wants to sell it back to us, at half price. What do you think, Jim?"

"Go buy it."

"Really?"

"Go buy it today. I will transfer two hundred thousand dollars into your account this afternoon."

"The villa is not that much."

"Set up an appointment with John Price and Don Lawton to close the deal with her. I want you to do this by yourself. Get a little business experience."

"Oh my, I am so excited."

"Why is she selling?"

"She told me that her government retirement money is insufficient to live on, so she is practicing law on a part-time basis. In other words, she needs the money and can't afford to maintain it as a vacation home."

"On second thought, close the deal with her after we have a look at the villa over the holidays."

"Great. Honey, I love you." She hugged him and gave him a big kiss. He slapped her firm left fanny. "I think she remembers how I cried when we sold it to her. We both were desperate that day."

Jim snapped his head; he was stunned. He didn't realize how much the villa had meant to Jan. "Take the title to the villa in your name. It is your love nest."

Jan confirmed the offer with the former congressman over the phone and then sealed the agreement with a letter of intent to buy and good-faith money over lunch at the Cherry Creek Shopping Center. This was not a buyer-and-seller negotiated deal; this was a meeting of two happy women.

Jim drove out to the old army air base to tour Rehabilitation Center I with Doc. A rude awakening was in store for him. He liked the changes the new regime had brought about in the streets, neighborhoods, and in government. Now he would witness the reformation of a society. The guards at the outer gate let him enter, as had been requested by Doc. He had written down the building address to locate Doc. They admitted him to the front desk in a large waiting room. He was in some kind of admissions room.

Doc appeared. "Are you ready for a tour?"

"I guess so."

"We will take my car."

Doc and Jim got into an army vehicle marked "Rehabilitation Center I" on its doors. Doc drove to the far end of the base and began the tour by identifying various buildings and explaining different functions that took place inside.

Jim started asking questions. "Those guys marching over there look like raw recruits. Reminds me of basic training at Camp Carson with the 196th Regimental Combat Team I was assigned to back in 1950. Who are those men?"

"Some are from our jails, some from prison systems, and some are here under court order. Others have been picked up by the police in neighborhoods where the block chief turned them in for loitering."

"What will you do with them in this place?"

"We are a regional processing center. From here they will be reassigned to different rehab centers for specific training. This building houses women and their children. They have a nursery next door and down there in that large building are classrooms for the gals and over here is the job training center."

"Where do these women come from?"

"All over the region, mostly from the Denver area. They have been referred to us by social service offices. Our job is to reeducate them, train them for a job in society, and change their social behavior. There is the old base hospital where I spent most of my time. We do surgery in there."

"A rather large hospital for surgery with so few people in the confines of this place. Doc, you sterilize people in here."

"That is correct. Under court order or by direction from the Social Review Board."

"I never heard of a Social Review Board. What is that?"

"A group of people who pass judgment on who should be sterilized or receive birth-control injections."

"Meaning?"

"We inject women to control birth for periods of three, five, or ten years, and others have permanent sterilization done on their reproductive organs. Obese women who come in here with three or four illegitimate children that they cannot provide for are sterilized permanently. We vasectomize men who have not met their responsibilities as a parent. It is easy to father a child but another matter to care for that child. A lot of Black children have no idea who their father is and, oftentimes, neither does the mother."

"Sick, sick. That is what the War on Poverty of the sixties left in its wake."

"We castrate men who have raped women or molested young boys."

"What about a more violent crime?"

"The firing squad downtown is a constant reminder that violent crime has its consequences. We do castrate men for abusing children or if the man is beyond rehabilitation. Some men have an abnormal aggressive behavior that can only be put into check by castration. We call it 'crime prevention' or 'eradicating the source of violence.' Under certain circumstances a man has a choice, castration or the firing squad. Women on welfare who have had children are sterilized. Many women desiring a better life request that their reproductive organs be shut down. Not all of our work is dictated by decree. There are women who request birth control or sterilization. It is surprising the number of women who strive to become self-sufficient. Now the law allows them a choice."

"How do you expect to reestablish the nuclear family?"

"In here we try. The mother gets up at six, feeds and dresses her children, and then takes them to a school. Mothers attend study classes to complete the equivalent of a high school education. At noon they have lunch in a cafeteria next to the nursery. In the afternoon they attend workshops. Trade and tech schools abound in this place. They spend the evening with their children at home, in their apartments. That is family time. The mother helps her children with schoolwork and does her own homework. Large group meetings are held to lecture them on social behavior and the finer things in life, including movies, music, and plays in the theater over there."

"Behind these walls you teach parents what their parents neglected to teach them. The 'me generation' dropped out and we lost a generation."

"More like two generations. We stress discipline with the understanding that it will help them develop a more structured life. For past generations it was too easy to drop out and never return, due to governmental programs and civic groups supporting dependency. When dependency became socially acceptable, we were in real trouble. Rehab centers will attach a stigma to life in welfare lane."

"Do you have addicts come through the center?"

"Nearly all of our residents have tried drugs at one time. However, after leaving their old environment, they stay drug free. We attempt to replace despair with hope for a better life. The severe drug abusers are shipped to a nearby army hospital that has rough recovery program. Some will never recover, so we let nature take its course with those people. We can't save everyone, but we intend to clean up our communities. Now that drugs have become legal, we see fewer younger people introduced to drugs."

"The drug salesmen are out of business."

"They sure are. It is time for lunch. I will treat you to a home-cooked meal in our cafeteria."

"How can I refuse? Why do I feel like I am back in the army in this place?"

"This definitely is an institution."

Jim's mind was growing numb. He was facing reality. Words could never describe what was taking place at this rehab center.

They went through the cafeteria line and sat opposite two young surgeons.

"Midday to you, Doc."

"Bill and Phil, this is my tennis partner. Jim Clark."

"I didn't know they allowed visitors in this butcher shop."

"Don't be so down. Think of it this way; you are at the heart of the country's social revolution."

This did not satisfy Bill. "We dismantle reproductive organs day in and day out; what is so great about that?" he asked. "You guys are spoiled, doing breast implants, cosmetic surgery, working part-time, and pulling down twice what the average general practitioner makes."

Phil spoke, "I didn't know a little body had so many parts and carried so many diseases."

Bill was eating a sandwich, elbows on the table and eyes scanning the ceiling. "How I long for my practice, my tennis matches, and the golf links. I have not seen my condo in Vail during this lifetime. I go to bed at night seeing all those big rumps and somewhere inside that mess of lard are tubes I have to tie off. God, what a waste. Why do obese women have children they cannot take care of?"

Phil looked at Doc and said, "Ask him. I haven't the foggiest notion."

"I guess they need love, that leads to pregnancy, childbirth follows and the child becomes an extension of themselves. Unconditional love from a child. If the government rewards them for producing children they will have more children. It becomes a way of life."

Bill looked at Jim. "Mr. Clark, too much thinking will drive a doctor nuts, particularly in this slaughterhouse. I never dreamt that I would be reduced to this kind of life. Did you, Phil?"

"Never. This place is dehumanizing, devoid of compassion, a trip to hell without a return ticket." Phil was looking at the cafeteria line, "Look, Bill, see who just walked in to have lunch. The psycho, master mind of Save America in the flesh. The potentate of sterilization."

Doc tried to calm down his surgeons. "Easy, guys."

"Hello, Doc. How are you, Mr. Clark?"

"Sit down and join us."

Phil and Bill always needled Schultz. He was a convenient target. Bill was the first to bite into Schultz. "Where is your black leather coat, your black leather high boots, and the swastika?"

Phil took his turn, "Yeah, Schultz, what is the latest scoop coming down from the Department of Genocide?"

"Scuttlebutt has it that you two surgeons are doing great things for mankind. I shall recommend you both for a medal," said Schultz.

Bill looked at Phil. "Do you want a medal?"

"I would rather drill an extra hole into my head."

At this point Doc and Schultz were snickering. Judge Schultz had stopped lecturing the day he left district court as a judge, but today he was in the mood to give two young doctors a piece of his mind. Doc always tried to keep the peace among his men but today he had to let Schultz have his say. "Schultz, forgive these two young doctors. Their mothers never spanked them, and they are still suffering from a lack of discipline."

"What did you fellows do to prevent the country from going bankrupt? Did you vote for our former liberal governor and our politically correct former mayor? Or did you even bother to vote at all? You fellows were preoccupied with greed. Your greatest concern was liability insurance to save your butts in a malpractice suit. You were concerned if there was enough health insurance and government funding to support excessive meaningless health care. Before the advent of the farewell pill, doctors sucked the elderly and their financial support systems bone dry and you fellows call that delivering good health care, saving lives, curing people. I call it lining your pockets at the expense of society. You fellows are paying the ultimate price, caring for people at a reasonable cost."

Doc interceded. "There are two sides to every story. The health organizations responded to the needs of society, and patients were able and willing to pay the price. How about all the attorneys hounding us with law suits?"

Phil said, "It is all a matter of perception."

Judge Schultz wouldn't give up the battle. "Your perception. You both are against capital punishment. You have no empathy for the victims of crime. You two remind me of the 'me generation.' A few years ago I let a man off who booby-trapped his repair shop. He killed one kid and maimed two others. The man was exasperated because the kids terrorized him."

Bill looked up from his tray. "He should have called the police."

"He did. A liberal judge would have sent the man to prison; I let him go free. He moved to Kansas and joined the militia, and I can't blame him for that. Many Americans got fed up and took the law into their own hands. We all are to blame for what happened in our country, and now we have a chance to rebuild it."

Phil and Bill picked up their trays and left. They were bored listening to Schultz. For them the revolution was a bad dream; for others it was a living hell and the wounds were still healing.

"Schultz, I will put the American Bar Association on trial."

"Hey, I have attorneys working as administrators, counselors, and teachers in this center."

"Do they give legal advice to the residents?"

"The best advice a former public defender can give these people is to obey the rules and work on self-improvement."

"That reminds me; we lost another patient this morning."

Schultz strained for a moment. "I thought I saw a picture on TV last night of a guy who was on the police hit list for escaping."

"The police shot him this morning."

"Why was he committed to the center?"

"He beat up his wife and threatened the family with a gun. She turned him in and the judge hearing the case issued an order for his castration. He was scheduled for the operation this afternoon."

Schultz mused. "He would have faced the firing squad eventually anyway."

"Most likely."

Jim didn't say much throughout Schultz's lecture. He didn't feel well and no longer carried the world's problems on his shoulders. Life had taken its toll on Jim Clark. Schultz was a few years younger than he and still had the desire to push his ideas on rehabilitation forward. Doc, on the other hand, was older than both of them; he continued to work because he'd lost most of his retirement money to the United States government in U.S. Treasury notes and bonds.

Schultz suggested to Jim, "You should have J. J. show our boot camps to you. We converted prisons into reforming centers for men."

"I don't think I am up for that. I did my thing and am willing to let the younger generation take care of the problems that are still haunting the country."

"We are trying out an new idea on the western slope of Colorado, rehabilitation without walls."

Jim perked up for a moment. He had never heard of that program before. "Just what kind of rehabilitation experiment are you talking about?"

"I got the idea from President Puckett. He started taking the troops off the Mexican border and resorted to capturing illegal aliens and placing them into the custody of an employer."

Jim had to identify this new plan for what it really was. "You mean, you place the aliens in bondage?"

"That is another way of putting it. They have to earn their way back to Mexico if they want their freedom. In America they will be confined to labor at minimum pay, which they receive in a lump sum upon their return to Mexico."

"I don't see the correlation to a rehab center?"

"We house our men in a military-style barracks and deliver them to various factories in an industrial park; at the end of the day we pick them up. They earn their keep and learn a trade at the same time. We also recondition them for a structured life. Upon graduation they become free men again."

Doc knew how men constantly escaped the Rehabilitation Center and so he asked the question, "How do you keep the guys from running away?"

"The same way we keep them here. Police have a duty to shoot escapees on sight and now a new force has evolved: the bounty hunter. They get paid for each captured man, dead or alive."

Jim was wondering if Colorado was exclusive to rehab programs. "Does the rest of the country participate in these programs?"

"The East Coast, West Coast, and Florida are in various programs to rehab their people."

"How about the South?"

"The South got started on the right foot. They implemented the tokens and moved into a rehab system before we got into it. We actually got the idea for rehabilitation centers from them."

Schultz had to return to his office, he was a busy man.

Doc nudged Jim. "Do you want to see some more of Rehabilitation Center I?"

"Not today. I will go home."

"When will we play tennis again?"

"In Guaymas over the holidays. I insist you come for old times' sake."

"I talked to Helen. She is anxious to make the trip. We will come."

Jim pulled out his checkbook, and wrote a check to Doc, and handed it to him. "We will have a good time."

"Thank you, Jim."

"Bye."

Jim drove back to the townhouse on the cold bleak day. Jan was bouncing around the townhouse; she was as chipper as always.

"Hi, honey. How was your sight-seeing trip?"

"All right. I am tired. I think I'll take a short nap."

Jim didn't bother to discuss the morning with Jan; he had learned more than he cared to reveal.

The next day they flew to Deerpoint. The old black truck was faithfully waiting for them. It had snowed. Everything was white. The mountains gave Jim a lift; he felt at home again. They skied a few times, all easy runs, and prepared themselves for their trip to Mexico.

They took a flight to Denver and from there flew directly to Guaymas. Jan talked through the entire flight. She was excited, getting her villa back. She would have to buy a little car. She reminisced over past trips, particularly their first one. That trip was very special to her. She was going to buy back her love nest on this trip.

Mexico was warm and beautiful this time of the year. The bleakness of Denver vanished from Jim's mind as the plane taxied to a stop. They remained in their seats holding hands until the plane was empty. They arose, hugged each other, and deplaned.

Jim immediately quizzed the manager he had befriended years ago and he concurred that they should buy the villa at the agreed-upon price. The villa was just as they had remembered it; a little soiled here and there, but otherwise it was still the same love nest. "Jan, do your thing. Buy the villa."

"Yes, sir. Your wish is my command." She gave him a Girl Scout salute. He embraced her. They missed Jan's little convertible, so they went and bought a new one just like the one she used to have.

Doc and Helen arrived overdressed for Mexico. They soon shed their winter clothes and changed into short-sleeved shirts and tennis shorts. Helen had a weak tennis game, but they managed to have fun playing mixed doubles. Jim had rented a villa for Doc and Helen a few doors down from Jan's place. Christmas was fun for Jim and Jan. They were sharing their Mexican holiday with friends.

Jan remarked to Jim one evening as they went to bed, "Helen is a lovely, delightful, and intelligent person. I have missed knowing her all these years. I think Doc is the greatest friend you have."

"Not much to choose from, besides J. J."

"J. J. is too gruff for my taste and Betsy thinks she still lives in Maryland, if you know what I mean."

"I know what you mean. We all have our hangups and idiosyncrasies."

The trip was a renewal of the past without disruptions. Doc and Jim hacked away for hours on the courts while the girls read novels by the pool or dashed around town in Jan's new convertible. Helen was like a little girl, living out a dream with a younger woman who knew her way around in a foreign country, Mexico. Every evening they had a drink by the pool at sunset.

One evening after dinner they turned in early. Jim held Jan's hand until he dozed off. He had had strange dreams lately. Jim was too pragmatic for the interpretations of silly dreams. Besides, most of his dreams were dreadful ones.

The next morning Jan prepared a Mexican breakfast, scrambled eggs with peppers, bits of bacon, onions, and a few other tasty vegetables. They read the morning newspaper that they purchased at the front desk. Jan decided on a do-nothing day. Doc and Helen were flying out the following morning. They had done the gamut, deep-sea fishing, sailing, tennis, swimming, and many walks around downtown. Jan made Helen feel like a local. She took Helen for a last drive through downtown and then made a farewell drive past the bay area. She and Jim always did this on the day before they departed Mexico. They parked the sports car in Jan's garage and walked over to the ambulance and police car that were parked at the entrance of the complex. Doc was talking to the police officer.

Helen asked him, "What is it?"

Doc walked over to Jan, put his arm around her, and said, "That is Jim in the ambulance."

"Oh, my God! What happened to him?"

"He had a heart attack on the tennis court."

"Will he be all right?"

"Jan, he died about fifteen minutes ago, massive heart attack."

Jan went into convulsions. They took her to the villa and spent most of the day consoling her.

"Why didn't he tell me about his heart condition?"

"He wanted to enjoy life with you until the very end without the threat of a heart attack on your mind. He shared his life with you. He loved you very much."

Later in the day Jan settled down and started to rationalize the situation.

"What now?"

"We will ship the body to Denver."

"He wanted cremation. I remember. It is in his will. He told me to spill half of his ashes on the east side of the Continental Divide and the other half on the west side. Come to think of it, he was anticipating this."

"Jan, I will drive downtown and make the arrangements to ship the body."

"Helen, I think I should make some phone calls. His sister ought to know."

Helen was the saving grace for Jan. She knew how to react to this kind of situation; she had been through it before. She was a nurse in intensive care when Doc was in residency at the same hospital back East during their courtship days.

The phone call to Jim's sister turned out a shocker. "Is this Vera Buckner?"

"Yes, that is me."

"This is Jan Bailey. I am calling from Guaymas, Mexico."

"Oh, yes, you are James's girlfriend."

"Jim died this afternoon from a massive heart attack."

There was a pause. Jan didn't know if Vera was still on the phone. Finally she spoke, "Yeah, I always knew this would happen. His father died the same way while he was at school in Boulder."

"He told me that he wanted to be cremated."

"Yeah, that sounds like my brother, James. Are you going to have a funeral?"

"No. Jim was short on religion. He said he didn't want a stranger selling religion over his dead body."

"Yeah, that sounds like my brother, James. Well, thank you for calling."

"I will be in touch with you when I return to Denver in a few days. He has a will on file with his attorney at the Bank of Colorado."

"Oh, I thought he would leave everything to you."

"He told me several times that you and I will share his estate."

"I didn't know that. Well, you give me a call. We are always here."

"Bye."

Vera hung up the phone. Jan sat back in the chair and started to giggle. "Helen, did you hear the conversation I had with his sister?"

"Sort of."

"I can't believe how nonchalant, how indifferent she is over the death of her brother, James."

"Have you ever met her?"

"Never. Jim rarely spoke of her. He did mention to me that his nephew hates the damn farm as much as he did. His sister kept her son on the farm. Jim got away from the farm despite his father. The two never got along too well."

Jan pulled out the drawer on the telephone stand and saw the new farewell pill in a light blue box. "Look at this, the damn pill that he never needed. Thank God for that." She took the pill and ground it up in the kitchen sink.

After flushing the powder down the drain, she said, "I hope this cleans out the sewer line." The girls embraced each other in a lighter mood. "I will call John Price and Don Lawton and let them contact Don Dugan and Dr. Klein. They know each other better than I will ever know any of them."

"Did he confide in them?"

"This past year he handled everything through John and Don. That is how I met them."

The most difficult phone calls Jan made were to her two sons. Jim was a second father to them. The boys didn't take Jim's death too well. They thought he would always be there for them.

Doc returned. He was exhausted; a delightful vacation had turned into a nightmare. It had finally hit Doc that he had lost one of his best friends. They had met on a tennis court and parted on a tennis court.

Doc stood gazing at the setting sun over the bay in deep thought. It was a gorgeous sight but a somber moment. "The sun is setting. I am going to have a drink by the pool. Do you girls want to join me?"

Jan moved quickly. "By all means. A toast to James Clark. How about it, Helen?"

"Thanks, Jan. I am not much of a drinker, but today I need two before dinner."

They went through the motions of communicating with each other, but Jim's death was foremost in their minds. As they nibbled through their dinner, Jan asked Doc, "Are we flying out tomorrow?"

"I want to make sure the body is shipped out before we board ourselves."

"Thanks, Doc. I will reimburse you in Denver."

"You don't have to. He wrote a sizable check to me for this trip the day I showed him around Rehabilitation Center I."

"I don't know how to put it delicately, but I think he knew the big one was coming. I sensed something was not the same with him."

"So did I, Jan." They had a sleepless night.

The Mexicans were on the ball for a change. The body was shipped out early in the morning. They said good-bye to Guaymas and flew into a terrible snowstorm in Colorado on New Year's Day, 2001.

V

New Year's Day was not a day of celebration but one of mourning. Jan called Mark and asked him to pick up Jim's personal things at the townhouse. She wanted to get rid of all physical reminders of Jim. Mark struggled to keep from breaking down emotionally. He talked to his mother as he packed mindlessly. He spoke of the time he'd helped Jim move his belongings to an apartment from his house. They had used the dirty black old truck. That day he'd inherited Jim's furniture.

Listening to her sensitive son, Jan began her therapy towards recovery. Mark called his brother and asked him to come over for the evening so that their mother would not be alone on this trying day. The family reunion was welcomed by Jan; she needed family support. Little Jan stole the evening and saved the day. They all spent the night at Grandma's house.

Don Lawton set up a meeting with Jan and Jim's sister the following week to read Jim's will and divide the estate accordingly. Jan arrived late. Don Lawton was seated next to John Price and at the end of the table was Vera Buckner. Opposite John and Don were Henry Buckner and his son. Jan sat down the end of the table facing Vera. The meeting started awkwardly. The family didn't know each other. Jan introduced herself to the Buckners, which embarrassed Don Lawton. Don opened the envelope, removed the papers, and proceeded to read the short will. He was acquainted with the will; he had written it. A recent addition to the will dealt with funding Research, Inc. There was a small envelope with a partial map in it.

Don passed it on to John Price and asked, "What do you know about this?"

John studied it for moment. "I think this is where he buried the gold."

Jan spoke up. "He stored it in a vault in this bank; he told me so."

"I disagree. I know the exact date he removed the gold bars from the bank and this concurs with that date." Jan was confused momentarily.

"Here, Jan, look at the map. Does it mean anything to you?" She saw from the drawing where the chalet was located and a small rectangle was identified as the outhouse. She looked up and said, "He buried the gold in the outhouse hole. Then he planned a juniper tree over it and then planted his favorite flowers, daisies, around the bush. Here he indicates thirty bars of gold with a date of the burial. He gives the direction and distance from the southwest corner of the chalet to the outhouse hole."

Don chuckled, "So that's where he buried the gold."

John looked at Vera, her husband, Henry, and Charlie. "He returned the gold bars about two weeks after the United States declared bankruptcy."

The Buckners were stone-faced. They only knew that Jim had sold his apartments, retired, and later they'd read in the newspaper that he'd bought into the Bank of Colorado and Eagle Airways.

Jan confirmed John's supposition. "I remember Jim digging up the juniper tree. He was going to plant a spruce tree in its place but never did. The next day we hauled tile back to Denver for Judge Crocker. It was the gold we hauled back to Denver, all thirty bars. I'll be darned."

Don Lawton continued to read the list of assets John had assembled. When he finished, Vera said, "I want the airline stock for my son, Charlie. We don't care about the other assets."

Jan looked at Charlie, who was seated to her right, and saw a young Jim Clark, with brown hair. Jim had always been gray to her. With the light blue, penetrating eyes and that tan, he looked like a younger copy of Jim. Charlie had a farmer's tan. She could see the line where he wore his cap out in the blistering sun and wind. The young man was sitting on the edge of his chair with a pensive look about him. Jan said to him, "You don't like the farm any more than Jim did?"

He replied, "I want to be a part of Eagle Airways. I want to get off the farm just like Uncle Jim did."

"If Jim were here today he would give you the stock in Eagle Airways, so I will make a deal with you. You take the Eagle Airways stock and I will take the Research, Inc. stock." Vera smiled and nodded her head in agreement.

Lawton wanted to do it by the book, but Jan intervened. "I recommend we give Doc one million dollars of bank stock. He was Jim's tennis friend. And I want to give Jim's recent land investment with Joe Parker in Deerpoint to Judge J. J. Crocker, his life-time friend. Vera and I will split the remaining bank stock."

Don Lawton cleared his throat. "We are not following the will."

Jan was determined. "John, how much is the bank stock worth today?"

"About one hundred million and pays about five percent in annual dividends."

Vera cupped her rough, calloused right hand and tapped the table in front of Lawton. "We will do as she says."

Lawton said to her, "Very well, you are the administrator of the will."

Jan rose from the table and addressed Charlie. "I want to personally introduce you to your partners in Eagle Airways, Mr. Don Dugan, the founder of the company, and his daughter. They have an office on the first floor of this building."

Price asked, "What about the cars, the chalet, the truck?"

"They are mine. Transfer them into my name. Do the same with Jim's checking account."

Charlie, Vera, and Henry followed Jan in tandem. The Buckners had come to Denver expecting nothing and had received everything. Vera was anxious to see what her son inherited. Dugan was relieved to meet Charlie. He expected two women as his new partners; instead he met a young man who could have been the son he'd never had, or a son-in-law he was hoping for. Charlie told Mr. Dugan that he wanted to learn the business from the bottom up. This was music to Dugan's ears. Jan was impressed with Dugan's daughter. She had her wits about her. She was neatly dressed, very sharp, and pleasant. She could not envision Ace scoring with this gal. Ace made out with bimbos and innocent young girls.

Don Lawton and John Price collected their paperwork off the conference table in their joint meeting room and rehashed the reading of Jim Clark's will. "John, I think these people are definitely related to Jim Clark."

"Sure looked that way, headstrong and determined. Did you notice how quickly they agreed on the division of the assets?"

"Not one squabbled. They just went ahead and did it the way they wanted to do it, and that was it."

John paused for a minute in thought. "And not one penny in inheritance tax. The new tax law is putting me out of business."

"I think we just picked up the Eagle Airways account, and we still have Jan as our client."

"Don, I am going to miss Jim. He added spice to life. He had such a unique way about him. All business with a wry twist; never knew anyone like him."

"Do you remember how he rubbed salt into the painter's wound?"

"That was a fun day."

Jan went back up the hill to her townhouse. There was a message from Doc. He was bringing over Jim's ashes.

Doc brought the container with the ashes in a bag. He removed the vessel and placed it at the end of the kitchen counter.

"Would you like a cup of coffee?"

"I could use a cup of coffee, thank you." He sat down at the kitchen table. "Jan, you know how obsessed Jim was with gold."

"One of many obsessions."

"Do you recall the gold caps he had on his teeth and the extensive gold bridge work?"

"I used to kid him about having a gold mine in his mouth."

"There is gold in that urn with his ashes."

Jan slapped her hand on the kitchen table and laughed. "That's so appropriate. Doc you are a genius."

The two exchanged stories of the eccentric man. They reflected on how both of them met him on a tennis court.

Doc excused himself and put on his coat and cap to leave as Jan said, "By the way, Jim's sister and I have a retirement present in the mail for you. It is in memory of Jim, your tennis partner and best friend."

"Thank you, Jan."

Doc left not knowing how much the gift would be, but he knew it was money. Jan was a generous person with or without money.

She stayed one more night in Denver before flying to Deerpoint.

Sitting in the plane by herself, she gripped the arm rest with her left hand and clutched her carry-on bag with the ashes in her right hand. She didn't experience any sudden drops that she feared so much in flight and she didn't fall asleep. The pilot taxied up to the terminal. It was a cold day in the mountains, twenty below zero. She saw the truck covered with two feet of snow. It was waiting for Jim, but he would never be back. It was as if the truck knew this. She couldn't take her eyes off the truck parked all by itself away from the terminal. She broke down and started to sob. The attendants came to her aid, they knew her as the widow of Jim Clark.

Jan made her way down the ramp steps with tears flowing. At the bottom she slipped and fell. Her eyelids froze. She could barely see. The world caved in on her. She was lost and alone. A man reached down and lifted her up. Through her blurry eyes she could see it was Ace. She grabbed for him; he gave her comfort.

"Would you please start the truck for me?"

"It probably wouldn't start for me. It has been parked out here in the cold for a month."

Ace escorted her to his truck and loaded her bags into the back.

"How did you know I was on this flight?"

"Denver called our terminal here and they located me at the Last Chance Bar. I was having a beer with Judge Crocker."

"Oh, is he back?"

"Just for a couple of days. He is coming over to see you."

Ace drove up the plowed driveway and parked in front of the garage. Jan regained her composure. "I see the mayor plowed the road."

"He was in the bar when the call came in for me."

Ace carried her baggage upstairs.

"Ace, could you come by tomorrow and pick up Jim's things, like the rifles, tools, and his clothes? I want to get the stuff out of my sight."

"Sure, how does nine in the morning sound?"

"Fine."

Ace had no sooner left when J. J. drove up to the chalet. He pushed the buzzer and Jan let him in. "How are you holding up?"

"Pretty good until I saw the truck at the airport, and then I fell apart. Thank God for Ace; he was there to rescue me. I am going to give the truck to our mayor. What do you think?"

"He would be delighted to have the truck."

"Where is Betsy?"

"In Maryland."

"I was surprised to hear you were back."

"I flew in from Oregon yesterday. We had a problem with capital punishment out there."

"Could you help Ace clean out Jim's things tomorrow? I thought you might be interested in some of them."

"In the morning?"

"Yes."

"Are you staying in Deerpoint?"

"This is home. Life goes on and I will regroup myself in Deerpoint. Is Betsy happy in Maryland?"

"She discovered that Maryland is not as she remembered. Betsy tried to relive the past and that is not possible. She is ready to come back to Deerpoint. I never wanted to go in the first place. It was her idea."

"You will have things to do around here. Jim's sister and I willed our interest in Joe Parker's project to you."

"You ought not to have done that."

"You were Jim's best friend. Let's be candid, J. J. What we gave to you was only a fraction of the estate. I am not exactly poor, you know."

"Jim told me that after his power play with the bankers he was worth over one hundred million dollars."

"You are pretty close."

"My retirement pay from the state is not enough for Betsy and I to live on and the Last Chance Bar is barely breaking even."

"I am in competition with you. I put up the cash for the Buckskin Café."

"So you are in business with Molly Baker? She and Jim never hit it off too well."

"I know, but she is my friend. She fell on hard times when her family corporation shut down during the revolution. She scrubbed floors, waited tables, and washed dishes to survive. I felt sorry for her."

252

"I think she will do well. She is a smart and capable woman. Did Jim know you invested with her in the café?"

"No. Jim kept giving me more money for my account than I needed, so I started to make investments on my own. He encouraged me to do so. I keep thinking he planned on dying."

"Maybe he did. He had a plan for everything else in his life."

"You knew him much longer than I did."

"Jan, we both knew the same Jim Clark."

"Did you fellows come up with a plan for the summer?"

"We discussed world affairs between drinks. The answer is no."

"Molly Baker, Peggy Roberts, and I are going to make our maiden voyage this summer with the Music and Art Festival."

"Let's go to the Olde Steak House and have dinner. I am starved."

"Great idea."

Dinner with J. J. was an opportunity for Jan to shift from Mrs. Clark to Jan Bailey in Deerpoint. J. J. sympathized with Jan. He knew what it was like to have a death in the family in this small town.

Joe and Shirley Parker were having dinner at the café. They joined them. Jim's death was the topic of discussion, but Jan abruptly changed that. J. J. jumped right in and led the way for her, "Joe, I am your partner again."

"I thought Jan was my partner."

"She and Jim's sister conveyed their interest in your land to me. You will receive the paper work in the mail next week."

"Well, that was downright generous of you gals."

Jan gave him a wink. "Don't count me out just yet. I have plans for some of your land, and you are going to need me as a partner sooner than you think."

"I will hold you to that."

"Trust her, Joe."

"Hell, Judge, it's you I don't trust. I have to watch you like a hawk."

They had a laugh. Joe was straight as an arrow, the western man personified. "Recently I was working on my plans for my property with Peggy Roberts and she told me that you girls were going ahead with a summer program."

"We are going to make a trial run."

"With a Music and Art Festival on the agenda I feel more confident in developing a golf course with home sites."

Jan was waiting for this opening. "I think the two will complement each other."

"I have the land free and clear but need money up front to put in the infrastructure before they will let me sell building lots."

Jan stood up and extended her hand. "I am your new partner."

They shook hands on a preliminary deal. Shirley Parker stood up and congratulated Jan.

"Thank you, Shirley."

Joe ordered a bottle of champagne to celebrate the occasion; Shirley liked her champagne.

"By the way, Judge, what were you doing in Oregon?"

"I had to persuade the governor to discontinue their method of capital punishment."

"I thought President Puckett required execution by firing squad?"

"He does, but he allowed a few states to experiment with a new idea and it backfired. In Oregon the victim may choose the method of execution."

"And you say it backfired?"

"A gal whose female partner was raped and murdered by a two-legged animal insisted on having her revenge. She had them tie the guy to the post and cut off his testicles. She flipped the testicles to her dog. He gulped them down. The dog got excited and went for the groin. The attending policeman shot the dog. The entire scene made national television and caused quite a stir in the White House, so they sent me out to bring the state into conformity with the rest of the country."

Jan cringed. "How horrible."

"Look at it this way, the victim who was raped and had her throat slashed didn't deserve to die at the hands of an animal. The rapist/killer is no longer a menace to society. Let his execution be a warning to maligned minds around the country."

Joe Parker pondered and asked J. J., "When will the killing stop?"

"Crime is way down. The president is pulling troops back in all areas except Florida and California. Rehabilitation centers will help

254

shape future generations. Firing squads and sterilization programs have an immediate impact on our irresponsible members of our society. Castration has scared the hell out of violent domestic abusers."

Jan tried to see the bright side of life. "I appreciate the absences of street people and drug addicts from my neighborhood in Denver, but I wish we could return to a sane life without rehab centers, firing squads and gruesome sterilization."

The judge leaned back in his chair and gave a sigh. "Betsy and I are moving back to Deerpoint in a few months and soon I give up the reins to my job. It is ironic. Jim predicted bankruptcy of our country and forewarned us of a revolution. He died and we are still here in the aftermath of a chaos."

"It is bedtime for me. I need a ride home, J. J."

The judge arrived at eight in the morning. He was an early riser. Jan was dressed in her robe making coffee. The timing to clean out Jim's belongings was perfect for J. J. He was looking for items to place in the Smithsonian Institution. Ace arrived promptly at nine and they went to work.

"Guys, I will pile everything in the living room floor and you get rid of it."

Ace was going through the guns downstairs and let out a yell, "Holy mackerel! Look at the scope on this rifle. I have never seen anything like it. The scope flips down for a quick shot with open sights."

J. J. went downstairs. "He bought those for the revolution."

"He has enough ammunition to fight a war."

"That was the general idea. He had two bars of gold hidden in with the ammo. Later he moved them in here. See that loose piece of sheet rock; he hid the bars back there."

"I know about the two bars of gold. I flew them into Canada."

"That's right. I had forgotten. This is what I want."

"What is it supposed to be?"

"A rotary engine he invented but never developed."

"Judge, you knew him a long time, was he always different? You know what I mean?"

"When I met him he was a distraught man struggling with his life. He had returned from the front lines only a few weeks before

255

school started in Boulder. He was a hero in the Korean War. Did you know that?"

"I didn't know he had been in the service."

"There are a lot of things people don't know about the man. That is why I am picking up some of his things for a display at the Smithsonian Institution in Washington, D.C. We are going to call the display 'Revolution—USA 2000.' "

J. J. went upstairs and asked Jan for the Director and Terminator tokens.

"You mean those two buttons from the revolution?"

"Yes, those two buttons."

She opened the drawer of the night table and handed the tokens to him. "Here is that damn farewell pill. I will grind it up in the garbage disposal."

"Don't do that. I want that for my collection of items." It was an original white farewell pill in a black plastic case.

"What else do you want for your collection?"

"His half-moon glasses, one of his favorite smoking pipes, and other things that he used in his daily life."

"I have some pencils, a ruler, and some drawings of the rotary engine and other inventions he was working on."

"Great! That is exactly what I want for my display."

The judge fondled the tokens; he turned them over and reminisced at the date and the number one on the back.

Jan was pulling clothes out of the closets, "Here are two sweatshirts he liked."

"I recognize the sunflower; he wore it often. I never asked him what he liked about that sunflower."

"It had to do with his childhood on the ranch in eastern Colorado."

Jan tried one on but it was too big. She tossed it on the pile. "And here is the racket he held in his hand when he died in Mexico."

"I want that racket!"

"His fly rod and fly-tying gear are downstairs in the workshop."

"Let Ace have them."

"Pour me a cup of coffee, I need to talk to you about these tokens."

J. J. laid the tokens on the table facing up and then turned them over. "See this number one and the date?" She nodded. "He designed these tokens and had Fred Goldsmith make them at the Fine Jewelry store. These two were the very first tokens. They belonged to him. He gave number two through twenty-five to me. This is how instant capital punishment got started in Colorado and spread into the South and from there across the country. The revolution evolved in the midst of it all."

Jan was astounded at the story. She didn't want to believe it. J. J. told her how the Director and Terminator functioned within law-enforcement agencies and throughout the judicial systems in the hands of law-and-order people in America.

"Did Jim ever use the tokens?"

"I doubt it. I don't think he did. He quit hunting because he didn't like to kill for the sake of killing. He had done more than his share of killing in Korea, he told me."

"That sounds more like my Jim."

"He did flash the tokens to a patrolman. It was on the day the sports car broke down."

"Oh yes, that day. I thought he had lost his marbles. He wanted to set the car on fire. Those were trying times for both of us. He was selling his apartments, buying gold, and then we built the chalet. It was a miracle that we managed to get through those volatile times."

"I often wonder what got into me after my father's death. I must have reached a breaking point and the sickness of our society got to me. Jim came close to the cracking point and I went off the deep end. Jim and I were not alone in this state or in our country. We had lost patience with a liberal society. The inability to have control over one's destiny and the government destroying the core of society for the sake of saving a few losers got to many Americans. Jim presented his idea of instant capital punishment to me and I introduced it to the right people at the proper time and the revolution followed. Jan, I went out on a limb, I promised the president that you would accompany me to the capital."

"What for?"

"He would like to meet you. I think he expects you to present the tokens to him in person. We will display them at the Smithsonian Institution. He wanted to meet Jim, but that won't be possible."

"No harm in my going to Washington, D.C. When do we leave?"

"On Friday. The president will meet with you over the weekend. I appreciate you doing this for me on the spur of the moment."

Jan felt better after the house cleaning. Ace loaded the clothes, tools, fly-fishing gear, and a super collection of guns into his truck. He came back upstairs to thank Jan. "All these neat personal things that belonged to Jim make me feel like his nephew."

Jan gave him a hug and said, "I think our *Ensign* down at the dock wants you as its skipper."

"You are giving me that beautiful sailboat?"

"Why not? We hardly ever sailed without you. It's yours."

"Thanks, Jan. Anytime you want to go sailing, give me a jingle."

"I will, Ace. I thank you for coming to my rescue."

Jan had two days to prepare for her trip to Washington. Her life had taken so many quick turns she didn't have time to brood. J. J. took Jim's engine and other items he'd collected with him to Washington. Jan was introduced to another lifestyle when they arrived in Washington.

A limousine met them at the airport. "This is impressive," said Jan. "You must have inside connections."

"I do, right to the Oval Office in the White House."

"Where will I stay?"

"The driver will take you to your hotel. I will go to the apartment. Betsy is expecting me. We will pick you up at seven for dinner."

"I feel like a celebrity."

"Why not? You were married to a famous man."

"That I don't understand, and I never was married to him."

"Mere technicality. This is where I get off. See you later."

J. J. and Betsy took Jan to a fancy restaurant where they were welcomed like family. Jan noticed that nearly everyone knew the Crockers by their first name. When the check came she grabbed it and said, "You may have powerful connections, but I still have the bucks."

They returned to Jan's hotel and had a night cap. These were elegances Jan had never experienced. Jim used to take her to the Brown Palace in his old truck. That was fun, but nothing like this.

The next morning she had breakfast and waited for J. J. to pick her up. She became nervous over her appointment with the president. J. J. marched into the White House like he owned the place.

They reached the door of the president's office and J. J. told her, "I will wait for you in the other room."

A lady came out of nowhere and opened the door to the Oval Office. The president rose and asked her to take a chair by his desk. They shook hands and sat down.

"I have been waiting for this moment for some time, but I had hoped it would be Mr. Clark . . . and you. I am sorry that his heart attack was fatal."

"Mr. President, I think he wished it that way."

"Call me Max or General."

Jan fingered the tokens in her purse. The president reached over to a thick file and said, "Your late husband, ah, your late partner in life has quite a military record."

Jan glanced towards the file and looked back at the president. "He never talked about his military experience. I know he was disillusioned with the Korean War."

"We all were. He was up for the Congressional Medal of Honor and refused it. What a soldier." President Puckett ran his thumb across the side of the file and said, "It is all in here."

Jan glanced at the file again and saw that it was compiled by the FBI and had Jim's name on it, "File on James B. Clark." Perspiration formed on her brow. She tried to remain calm and collected.

"Did you bring the Terminator and Director tokens?"

"Yes." She jerked the tokens out of her purse and slid them across the desk towards the president. He picked them up and examined them admiringly.

"So these are the tokens that started the revolution."

"I don't think Jim Clark started a revolution."

"Well, that is according to Judge J. J. Crocker. He wants to place memorabilia that belonged to Mr. Clark in the Smithsonian Institution to commemorate the revolution. I think they are going to call it Revolution—USA 2000."

The president was more nervous than Jan but he tried not to show it. He had been hoping for a meeting with Jim Clark, but Jim had refused to sell out to the defense department or, more specifically, to the United States of America. Jim always told Dr. Klein that he would support the project financially until they discovered cold fusion. This was General Puckett's great moment and he didn't want

259

to bungle the deal. He had no idea how much Jan knew about the research project. Her son owned a small fraction of the company and was one of its employees, so President Puckett assumed that she knew something about Research, Inc. He continued the small talk until he concluded that Jan Bailey was in the dark about the secrecy of cold fusion.

"The reason I asked Judge Crocker to accompany you to Washington is to talk to you about Research, Inc. The tokens were only an excuse to bring you here."

Jan let out her breath, wiped her brow, and started to relax. This whole exercise reminded her of waiting in a dentist's office for a root canal.

"I want to talk to you about your stock in Research, Inc. Are you willing to sell your interest to us?"

"I will do whatever Dr. Klein suggests."

"Good. I feel better already. I don't know how much your son and Mr. Clark revealed to you about the project, so I have to second guess that."

"I own all that Jim owned, with the obligation of supporting the research until they discover whatever they are looking for or otherwise terminate their research."

"Mr. Clark refused to sell to the Department of Defense, that is why I am taking this opportunity to explain the government's position to you. We want to buy and support Research, Inc., with Defense money. Dr. Klein thinks they have discovered cold fusion, and I want the United States of America to own and control that new source of energy. Dr. Klein is willing to sell his interest to us and so is your son. I want your consent. Do discuss your decision with Dr. Klein but not with your son. Your son only knows that U.S. Industries, located in Virginia, is vying to buy out Research, Inc. U.S. Industries is a fictitious company we set up as a conduit for the government to own Research, Inc."

"Why all the secrecy?"

"This matter is top secret to prevent upheaval around the world and to protect the scientists working on cold fusion in Boulder. I don't trust the Arabs in the Middle East. Cold fusion is a clean, abundant supply of energy that will change the world. The new energy will cause a revolution around the globe. I want a peaceful

260

one. The balance of power among nations could be upset by cold fusion."

"I never attached such significance to Jim's investment or my son's work in Boulder."

"We know of other groups who are searching for cold fusion, but none are close to discovering it. We are prepared to issue government securities to the shareholders of Research, Inc."

"How much for my share?"

"Four hundred million dollars."

The amount did not faze Jan. She had yet to grasp what $50 million in bank stock meant to her.

"Then you agree to sell your share?"

"Yes, I do."

"My men will be in Denver next week to consummate the deal. We will handle it as a buyout by U.S. Industries at your attorney's office in the Bank of Colorado. We will issue a press release to that effect. We don't want to arouse the curiosity of the media. We want openness with secrecy. Do not discuss the details of our transaction with anyone and don't mention your total wealth to anyone for fear of creating suspicion, and that includes Judge Crocker out there."

"I understand."

"Let's have lunch." He pressed a button. "We are having lunch in here. Send in Judge Crocker." He got out of his chair, walked around to Jan, put his hand on her shoulder, and said, "Thank you, Jan Bailey. I feel relieved. Let me show you around this office."

They looked at pictures and presidential mementos. The view outside was dreary. Snow was forming on the lawns. J. J. entered the Oval Office.

President Puckett pointed to his chair. "That is the hottest seat I ever sat in. In a couple of years I shall walk out of here a free man." A light lunch was served. The president kept the conversation flowing with J. J. "So you are moving back to Colorado?"

"I am ready to leave as soon as you find a replacement for me."

They finished their lunch.

"So many have served beyond the call of duty. I appreciate what you have done for the senators, me, and our country. You served us proudly."

The president bid them farewell. On the ride back to Jan's hotel,

J. J. asked, "How about some sight-seeing while you are in the capital?"

"Not on this trip. The weather is deplorable. I am anxious to fly back."

J. J. waited while Jan packed her bags and then escorted her to the airport. "Thank you for making this trip. My job for the senators and the president is almost finished here. I will be looking forward to seeing you in Deerpoint, back in God's country."

"Bye, J. J."

Jan boarded the flight and gathered her thoughts of recent events. Unexpected things popped up all around her. She had no time to reflect on the past; she was busy living the present. She sat by the window watching the snow and drizzle outside. The plane lifted off. Jan's mind was on her family, Mark and Mary, little Jan, her other son and his wife, Judy, and a newcomer to the family, Charlie Buckner, and, of course, Ace. Jim's birthday had been last week and nobody had remembered. Jim oftentimes forgot his own birthday, but Jan never forgot. She fell asleep.

The flight arrived in Denver at midnight. It was cold and crisp. The sky was full of stars. She rode a cab to her townhouse, unpacked, and went to bed. She was home again. The next day she tossed some clothes into her car and drove to Mark and Mary's place. She was due for some selfish time with Mary and little Jan. Her next appointment was with U.S. Industries. She and Mark would make that trip downtown together.

Mark was always looking out for his brother. "Mom, we should set up a trust account for Bill? He is being left out of the family money."

"I will do that after we close the deal with U.S. Industries. I had five million in mind.'

"That sounds good to me." The sale of U.S. Industries went as smooth as silk; everything was prearranged. Jan, Dr. Klein, and Mark signed some papers and then left the office of Don Lawton, Attorney at Law.

Jan moved back to her townhouse and set up luncheon dates, made coffee dates, and put herself in a social whirlwind with her old friends. On a sunny day she itched for exercise. She drove to the Gates Tennis Center. It was a bright, sunny, winter afternoon. She hit tennis balls on the backboard. Doc and Helen arrived. Jan joined them in Canadian doubles, Helen and Jan against Doc. After some sun, exercise, and a bit of horsing around, they seated themselves on a bench that Jim and Doc had used many times to discuss world affairs and their theories on life. Doc was acutely aware of Jim's absences. He was having his soda pop alone.

A good-looking redhead was pushing a stroller up from the backboard area. She recognized Doc and asked him about Jim Clark. Doc answered, "He died while playing tennis with me in Guaymas, Mexico, over the holidays."

She put her hands to her cheeks and said, "Oh, no, my dear friend."

Doc got up and introduced Helen and Jan to her. He explained Jan Bailey's relationship to Jim Clark. They talked for about thirty minutes and then she left with her child, waving as they made their exit.

Helen said, "Cute little fellow."

Jan was not lost for words. "He looks happy and healthy, and he ought to. Did you see the breast he is feeding on?"

Doc laughed. "Jim made a bet with me that she would produce a light-colored Afro-American child within twelve months; and I'll be damned, he won the bet."

Helen broached the subject of the million-dollar bank stock gift that they received from Jim's estate.

Jan waved her off. "That million out of one hundred million dollars of bank stock didn't even dent his estate. I took the Research, Inc., stock and Vera, Jim's sister, wanted the Eagle Airways stock for her son. Vera and I split the bank stock."

"I didn't know we were in Jim's will."

"You weren't. We gave Jim's interest in a land-development project at Deerpoint to Judge Crocker and you received some bank stock. You two were Jim's best friends."

"That was very generous of you."

"Don't mention it. I did it for Jim."

Helen shivered and suggested, "How about a cup of coffee at Cherry Creek?"

They went for coffee.

"I read in the newspaper that a company bought out Research, Inc."

"They did. I no longer have to support the research project. U.S. Industries will support me in style for the rest of my life. I am not exactly poor."

Helen thanked Jan again for the retirement fund, as she called it.

"Doc, why didn't you forewarn Jim about his heart condition?"

"I did, many times. I told him to stay away from that greasy restaurant he ate at all the time after his divorce."

"He ate more than his share of steaks and butter. I increased my purchase of butter by one pound a week after he moved in with me. When did you first discover that he had a heart condition?"

"Many years ago. He feared a stroke would cripple him; that is why he was so hung up on the farewell pill."

"So that was the motivating factor behind the pill. Are you going to retire?"

"As soon as I finish my part on the identification chip. Have you been issued an IC?"

"I have been too busy; forgot all about it."

"Get one. You will need it to conduct business, vote, visit the dentist, doctor, get a driver's license, and many other things. It is an all-encompassing record of a person's life."

"I don't know if I have all of the information they will expect from me."

"Give them whatever you have. We have to start someplace. Children will have a near complete record as they grow up."

"Why do we need the chip?"

"It will serve health institutions, the government, and law enforcement with a complete history of a person, including blood type, diseases, vaccinations, military record, police record, voting record; you name it and the chip will have it on record."

"What if a person makes a fraudulent entry on his chip?"

"There is a master computer in Washington, D.C., that will carry duplicate information."

Helen questioned the chip. "Sounds good in theory, but will it work in practice?"

"It is better than what we have now."

Jan returned to her abode. The next day she returned to Deerpoint via Eagle Airways and she had a thrill. The plane dropped about five hundred feet after crossing the Continental Divide. When they landed at Deerpoint she saw that old black truck was gone. This pleased her. Out of sight, out of mind.

As spring emerged she skied on beautiful sunny days. She devoted most of her time to organizing the Music and Art Festival. One evening, while dining at the Buckskin Café, she saw two future executives of Eagle Airways, Charlie and Ace. They came to the café late with a couple of gals. It was apparent to Jan that they had spent considerable time at the Last Chance Bar. They greeted her and seated themselves with their dates at a table. Charlie sauntered over to her table and seated himself.

"How is Eagle Airways doing?" she asked.

"Getting there. How are you doing?"

"Learning to live life by myself. It was difficult at first but as every day passes, I find myself gradually adjusting to new life. Who are the chicks?"

"Some local gals Ace knows."

"Where are you staying tonight?"

"With Ace. We have a slight problem in our company. Don Dugan is getting nervous because somebody is playing games with our stock. It is very volatile at the present time. He fears a take-over of the company."

"Is he overreacting?"

"I don't know. I came up with an idea while loading baggage today in Steamboat Springs."

"You are loading baggage?"

"Yes. I am learning the business from the bottom up. The next item on my training program is to work in every ticket office of Eagle Airways. Ms. Dugan is a sharp gal. She has a plan to squelch the speculators."

"You not only look like Jim, you think like him."

"I take that as a compliment."

"The best I can give you."

"Why didn't your mother and Jim have a better relationship?"

"I guess they both were too much like their father."

"Good answer. When was the last time you saw Jim?"

"At Grandma's funeral?"

"When was that?"

"About twenty years ago."

"It is a shame that you never got to know your uncle."

"As I was saying, we need to put the speculators to rest. Word is out that these fellows have inside information and that is impossible. We are a tight-knit group at Eagle Airways. John Price and Don Lawton are above reproach; they were Jim's consultants. You once told me that we are family and if I needed help to call you."

"We are family and I am here to help. What is your plan?"

"Ms. Dugan suggested that you link up with a stockbroker, buy and sell on her signal, and I will do the same. Maybe we can shake out the manipulators."

"I met a gal playing tennis who is a stockbroker and loves to play hard ball. Charlie, just between you and me, I am loaded."

"I saw in the financial section of the Denver paper that U.S. Industries bought out Research, Inc."

"They did. Now I don't have to feed money into research and have mega-bucks for investments."

"I thought you got the short end of the stick when we divided Jim's estate."

"I ended up with a mighty long stick."

"I am glad to hear that. Jan, I didn't have the heart to ask my mother for additional money after she gave the airline stock to me."

"Don't sweat it. I will buy into Eagle Airways and enjoy doing it."

"I have to join the group. I am starved."

Jan stood up and extended her hand. "It's a deal. You can count on me."

"A deal."

Jan paid her check and went home. She watched the evening news, a habit she had acquired from Jim. They reported that the auto manufacturers were tooling up to build rotary engines within two years. The new engine would reduce noise by 50 percent and cut pollution by 80 percent. Jan smiled. If only Jim could have lived to see his dream become a reality.

The following morning she called Sally Mayfield and laid out her plan. Sally was ready to play hard ball. She then called Ms.

Dugan to confirm that she was prepared to do battle with local vultures. At the end of the skirmish, Jan owned a substantial amount of stock in Eagle Airways, and the family scored a success. Jan felt proud of herself. She had taken over from Jim in protecting the family from predators.

Jan was busy with the Music and Arts Festival. She visited Peggy Roberts at the architect's office and asked her to ride down to Joe Parker's property with her to pass judgment on her plan for a music and arts village. Peggy became ecstatic. She was overwhelmed. Jan left a deposit with her to commence on a sketch for the proposed complex. Creative Design went to work on the sketch immediately. They had done several scenarios for Joe Parker on the same piece of land. Joe had his dreams but lacked the capital to realize them. His property would be developed sooner or later because Deerpoint was a small town wedged into the mountains, with a ski area above and no place to expand except down onto Joe's property.

Jan became so engrossed with her project that she forgot about spreading Jim's ashes. They were in an urn in the living room. She had a larger hurdle that was haunting her at this time of the year, the villa in Guaymas. She wanted to stay at the villa for a spring vacation, but she feared making the trip alone.

Her morning began with a jog down to the airport and back, then she fixed coffee, took a shower, and had breakfast. She did her best thinking during these jogs; that is how she conjured up the idea for a music and arts village on Joe Parker's land.

On this particular morning the villa was on her mind. She called her stockbroker. "Sally, how would you like to go to Guaymas for a week?"

"When are we leaving?"

"That is up to you. I am free anytime."

"How about Friday afternoon?"

"You buy the tickets and I will furnish the villa with a sports car in the garage."

"I will get the tickets and call you back."

During the flight to Mexico, Jan learned that Sally Mayfield was an art major who had become a stockbroker. Sally knew more about art than Jan would learn in a lifetime.

They spent most of their time downtown at sidewalk cafés or walking around on the beach. They went sailing one time and played tennis every day. The pool was a nice place to lounge and discuss Jan's future complex.

"Jan, I am involved with the Denver art community and have a friend who has ties to the Denver Symphony. We can contribute talent to your program this summer."

"Anything we can put forth this summer will be better than nothing. Our first year will be difficult. Next year we will be better organized, and three years from now the complex should be built."

"This is a dream come true for me. As an art student I used to dream of what you are putting together. We used to talk into the night about holding art shows in the mountains."

"I expect you to ply a major role in my project. Come up to Deerpoint and review my plans. I need your input."

"I am so excited about your complex I want to open a brokerage house in Deerpoint."

"We are too small for that now, but in a couple of years your timing might be on target."

"Do you own the land for the village?"

"No, but I know the guys who do. Jim's friends."

"Do you anticipate a problem with them?"

"Hardly. They need my money to develop the land."

Sally laughed. She understood that kind of talk. It was hard ball and she enjoyed hard ball. They flew back, discussing their project all the way to Denver. Jan had made it across another hurdle, a visit to the villa without Jim.

Jan always spent a night or two with Mark and Mary on her trips in and out of Denver. Little Jan didn't take after her grandmother, she was unique unto herself. She was spoiled rotten. Mark invited his brother and Judy over for a family dinner. The boys missed Jim terribly but never mentioned him in the presence of their mother. They didn't want to upset her. She tried so hard to separate herself from the past.

Spring had flowed into summer. Jan could see the green meadows below and the mountains taking on a new look as the plane glided into the airport at Deerpoint.

She unpacked and called Peggy Roberts about the sketch plans for her proposed complex. Peggy and her associates dazzled Jan with their preliminary drawings. Jan picked up the drawings and started home when she decided to locate her two partners downtown rather than call them from the chalet. She found them at the Last Chance Bar.

"Hello, Jan. Join us for a beer."

"You guys were in here when I left for vacation and you are still here. I didn't come in to drink; I have the plans for my village. Can you meet me at the west meadow in about one hour?"

Joe answered, "We will be there." Joe finished his coffee, "J. J., she is all business today. We'd better get the hell down there. By the way, what village?"

J. J. took a puff on his cigar. "I am in the dark."

Jan put on her blue jeans, white blouse, cowboy boots, denim jacket, and climbed into her little white truck, drove down to the airport, then tailed back to the meadow in a large hay field. She parked between the judge's old jeep and Parker's large pickup truck, loaded with fuel tanks. Judge Crocker was standing behind Joe's truck, puffing on his cigar. He wore his crusty old cowboy hat and shiny boots. His boots never touched manure. Joe wore his Rockies baseball cap and reeked with oil and fuel. The guys were chewing the fat.

Jan took the drawing from the seat of the truck, opened the tailgate of the truck for a field table, and unfurled her plans. "I want to know what you guys think of my music and art village."

Joe was ready for this. "Let's see it, Jan."

"These buildings will be located right about here, and over there will be sixteen tennis courts, with a path leading to the club house and golf course. These paths are all connected throughout the complex, with irrigation water flowing along the side. This building in the back next to the assembly building I will call the Clark Institute or something like that."

"Boy, Jim would have liked this."

The judge was chewing on his cigar. "Yeah, too bad he isn't here to see it."

"I want lots of aspen trees along the irrigation ditches with daisies; he loved daisies . . . " She started to cry; the tears were flowing. She turned around and walked a few steps away, bent at the waist and knees, placed her elbows on her knees, held her face with her hands, and sobbed.

J. J. removed the cigar from his mouth and looked down at a clump of grass he was stubbing with his boot. Joe just looked to the west with a blank face; he was caught off guard. The two behaved like a couple of guys who'd erred and didn't know how to deal with it.

Jan stood up, blew her nose, wiped the tears from her face, turned around, and said, "I am sorry. I won't let that happen again."

Joe put his arms around her. "Ah shucks, Jan, we feel the same way about him, but we can't do what you just did because we are a couple of guys."

"Yes, you are a couple of guys. Well, what do you think of my plan?"

"I was tickled pink you offered to back my golf course with your money, but this is frosting on the cake."

J. J. looked at Joe and said, "I am speechless."

"Then you guys like my plan?"

"We sure do."

Joe was excited, "J. J., you'd better get on the ball and have this land annexed. We have to present a master plan to the town for the entire development. Jan, I think we need a full-time manager to move this project forward and keep it on track."

J. J. removed the cigar from his mouth. "I am available."

Jan squinted in the bright sunlight. "You are hired."

"We should form a corporation. Joe and I will take stock equal to our investment, and you, Jan, will receive stock in the corporation as you put money into it."

Jan was quick to reply, "Go for it, J. J."

Joe pointed to the east. "See that big tank? That is the town water intake from the river. We will have to move that upstream or it will be in the middle of my golf course." He pointed to the west across the entrance road into Deerpoint. "And that sewer plant needs to be moved downstream. Too close for comfort, if you get what I mean. Over there I have plans for an industrial park with employee housing and across the road a small shopping center with apartments and condos, and next to it a city park with tennis courts, softball fields,

270

and a large swimming pool. And below that we should build housing for locals."

Jan took a deep breath and said, "I see you have been doing some planning yourself."

"I have planned myself to death over the years and now I am ready for action. Hallelujah! Jan, I have to point out to you that the town will require us to expand the water plant, sewer plant, and do the infrastructure for the subdivision at our expense. I suggest we donate the park to the town, keep them folks happy, grease the wheels a bit."

"I have no problem with that, as long as I have free rein to build my village."

"J. J. and I will see to that. You have my word on it."

Jan offered her patented handshake. The project was going to be built and Jan Bailey was destined to become the matron of Deerpoint. Jan rolled up her drawings, and J. J. put the tailgate back up. She scraped the mud off her boots on the bumper and said, "And you two stay out of the Last Chance Bar."

Joe gave her a smile and winked. "Fat chance of that ever happening."

J. J. added, "Don't hold your breath, young lady."

She waved to them as she bounced her truck across irrigations ditches in the hay field.

Joe was not finished with J. J. "Can you start on this today?"

"I have to make a quick trip to visit five rehab centers around the state. Give me a week."

"OK. Put Silverman on the corporate papers before you leave and I will get Creative Design to prepare a master plan so I can run it by the town council. I have been waiting for this all my life. Let's hit it."

"First we have to go to the Last Chance Bar and have a drink on this. Jim and I used to do that all the time."

"I am going to have lunch and then it's go, go, go. J. J., you spend all of your life shuffling papers for the state of Colorado. I am going to make a businessman out of you if it kills me."

They drove back to town and parked in front of the Last Chance Bar. There were many greetings and wise cracks as they entered the bar. J. J. and Joe were regarded as big-time movers and shakers among the locals, with Jan Bailey's money.

"Do you think we will have a problem with the town council?"

"I don't think so, Joe."

"What if Molly Baker shows up and bitches like she usually does?'

"I doubt that will happen. Jan told me that she put up the money for the Buckskin Café. Besides, Molly has been working with Peggy and Jan on the summer Music and Art Festival."

"Well, I will be darned. I sure like the way our golden lady operates, as smooth as silk. And she has two things we need, money and her desire to invest it in our project."

Jan had lunch with Peggy at the Buckskin Café. They couldn't wait to reveal events of the day to Molly. She too was excited. Molly had a vested interest in Deerpoint, the Buckskin Café. Peggy worried that her husband would not survive the revolution with his real estate firm, Roberts Realty, intact. Shirley Parker was a part-time salesperson for him. It was a small operation at this point in time.

"Jan, my husband just listed this building with the surrounding land up to the stream yesterday. He said it is a good investment because Deerpoint now has a real future. Our summer business will complement the ski season and the town will become more viable. He thinks you ought to buy it."

"Thanks for the tip. I will buy it before it hits the market."

"Do you think he will get some listings out of the new subdivision? Joe's wife sells real estate part-time for him."

"Tell him not to worry; he will have the property to sell exclusively."

Peggy clasped her hands, ladylike, and said, "Oh, I am so happy. We are going to make it after all. The revolution was real tough on us. I supported the family and his business for the past three years."

"Peggy, he will make lots of money over the next ten years."

J. J. and Joe had their drink and finished lunch. "Joe, what are you going to do with the gravel and sand operation across the river by the airport?"

"Move it down to where the town park will be. I need lots of gravel for our development and we have to level out the land for the park. I am going to plant spruce and aspen trees along the river to shield the airport. I can't do much more, can't move the airport, it belongs to the county."

"That reminds me, we will have to deed your water rights to the town."

"That's your job. Don't tell me. You work for me and the golden lady, remember."

"I miss Jim. He was more fun to work with."

"Jim was a businessman just like I am. We take calculated risks, make decisions, and live by them. You, on the other hand, have been collecting a paycheck from the government all your life."

"Don't rub it in, Joe. I am trying."

The two guys bickered, teased, and baited each other. It was their way of communicating.

"Jan has been on my case to come forth with something original for her Clark Institute. I am lost on that."

"Turn Silverman over to Jan and that will solve your problem."

"Good thinking. Jim wasn't any better than I in coming up with a program. If Silverman had not become an attorney, I swear he would be a philosophy professor at a university."

"Is that so? I guess he is the right man for Jan."

"There isn't that much law to practice these days. Congress has dumped most of the laws into the trash bin."

"J. J., I'm going to Creative Design, and I take it you are on your way to see Silverman."

"Who will be the officers in the corporation?"

"I will be the president; you be the vice president and general manager. Shirley can be the secretary and treasurer."

"Joe, you are too direct. You would starve as a lawyer."

"Yeah, but I survived as a sand and gravel man without you." They parted for the afternoon.

J. J. had the thankless task of inspecting two juvenile boot camps, two rehab centers without walls, and the state prison. He left the toughest facility for the last on his agenda. J. J. was happy to return to Deerpoint and live a normal life again. Betsy was back to wait on him like an only child; he liked that. She too was content to live a simpler life, after a failed attempt of reliving the past in Maryland.

Sally Mayfield spent a weekend in Deerpoint with Jan to tour the music and arts village site. She took drawings of the village to her friend with the Denver newspaper. Deerpoint received a two-page spread in the Sunday edition. After the news story, Deerpoint was booked solid every weekend for the summer with people from Denver. Peggy suggested that they book in some Western and bluegrass groups for the locals and that put the finishing touches on a successful summer.

On a midsummer afternoon, Jan called Joe. "I need a favor."

"Shoot, what is it?"

"I still have Jim's ashes in an urn that I am supposed to spread on the eastern slope of the Continental Divide and on the western side. Could you fly me across the Divide to do this?"

"Sure. When do you want to go?"

"How about this afternoon at sunset?"

"Will do. Meet me at the airport about one-half hour before sunset."

Jan drove to the airport in her truck, parked alongside Joe's truck. She walked over to Joe; he was fiddling with the plane. He asked, "Have you ever had a ride in a plane like this?"

"I rode to Canada in a plane like this."

"No, no. The instrumentation on that plane cost more than this entire plane."

They got into the plane. Joe started it up and taxied to the end of the runway as if he were driving his truck around downtown. They approached the Continental Divide and Jan asked, "Have you ever done this before?"

"Once. Not much to it."

"You have to coach me."

Joe explained how he would slice up the side and then drop over the top. Joe tilted the plane and said, "Here we go now." She chucked out some ashes and Joe lifted the nose up, turned, tilted the plane again and said, "Now."

Jan spilled some ashes on the west side of the Divide and checked to see if she had any left. She did. She corked the urn and held it firmly in her hands. They flew along the Continental Divide at sunset. It was a beautiful sunset. She gave Joe a big smile, "Job well done."

"It is getting dark. I'd better take her in." They floated to the tarmac and parked the plane.

"You were right, Joe, there really wasn't much to this little ceremony."

She thanked him and he replied, "Anytime, young lady."

Jan drove back to the chalet, parked the truck, grabbed a spade, and dug a hole about twelve inches deep next to Jim's juniper, dumped the ashes with the gold from his teeth into the hole, and covered it up. She chucked the urn into a trash bucket, hung up the spade, and went upstairs to take a shower and dress for dinner.

J. J. and Joe met at their watering hole, the Last Chance Bar.

"I flew Jan over the Continental Divide at sunset. She spilled Jim's ashes on both sides. He had this thing about having been born on the east side and enjoying his last days on the west side, as Jan explained it to me."

"That sounds like Jim."

"She sure is a good-looking filly for her age. Her golden hair, shining hazel eyes, those freckles, that ever-pleasing smile, and I like the way she fills out her jeans."

"My old buddy Jim had good taste in women."

"For all the money she has, she paid a price for it."

"What do you mean by that?"

"I knew Jim as a tough businessman. He must have been hell to live with at times."

"Ah, Joe, you are misconceiving?"

"How would you know? You don't even know who you are."

They argued their way through two drinks and then went home without paying the check. They both ran a tab at the Last Chance Bar.

Jan put on her tan dress that Jim liked so much, slipped on her diamonds and a simple pair of earrings. With the top down on her Mercedes, she motored to the Buckskin Café. She was greeted by Molly with open arms. Molly always reserved a table for her by the fireplace. Local patrons knew that the table was reserved for Jan Bailey. Jan ordered her favorite dish, shrimp on rice, with white wine and cake for dessert.

"Oh my, you are all decked out this evening. What is the occasion?"

"Special. Tonight is for me and a man who shared his life with me."

"Oh, I see."

Molly sat at Jan's table to talk between greeting customers. Jan reached into her purse and pulled out the promissory note Molly had signed. It was for cash she needed to purchase the Buckskin Café.

"I will start to make payments on it this fall."

Jan took the note and tossed it into the fireplace and three seconds later it was smoke.

"Why did you do that?"

"That is my way of saying thank you for helping me get the Music and Arts Festival off the ground."

"You shouldn't have . . . "

"I signed a contract to purchase this building and the land surrounding it. I will be your landlord."

"I like that."

Molly seated more customers and returned to the table. "Now I can use the money I saved up to remodel the kitchen, repaint, and wallpaper the dining rooms. I hate this musty carpet in here." Jan was served and Molly returned again. "I am going to change the name of the café."

"What are you going to call it?"

"Molly's Place. I never liked Buckskin. They probably have not served deer meat here in a long time."

Jan laughed, "If ever."

"Next year I want to pave the parking lot, screen it off with bushes and trees, and out back I want to serve customers by the stream. Locals take the stream for granted; they only fish in it. What do you think, Jan?"

"Wonderful plan. I will pay for the outside improvements. Take your plan to Peggy for detailed drawings. I will hire the mayor to pave the parking lot and prepare the ground for the landscaper. Our locals need work. You and I will make this place the most charming restaurant in town."

"I am so excited about our plans for the future."

"I will need your help this fall when Joe Parker presents his master plan to the town council."

"You have it."

Jan finished her coffee and left a gratified person. She walked across the street to the town square where the festival was being staged. It was a dark evening. A floodlight illuminated Crocker's cabin at the south end of the square. She walked over to the cabin and looked at the brass plate on a post. The plaque read, "Miner's Cabin—John Jay Crocker, Sr.—Deerpoint Historical Society—Molly Baker, Pres.," and at the very bottom in the right-hand corner in small letters was, "Donor—Jim Clark." She walked past tents that had been set up for the festival and reached the parking lot where her car was parked. She drove back to the chalet.

It had been a full day and eventful week for her. After changing into her nightgown, she went out on the deck to take a peek at the juniper bush that was guarding Jim's ashes. She gave it a smile and went inside leaving the sliding-glass door ajar to let in the mountain breeze. She lay down in her bed and mused for a few moments, turned to her side, switched off the light, slapped her left fanny, buried her head in the pillow, and said, "Goodnight, Jim." She fell sound asleep.